The Red Paper

A Story of Resistance in WWII Japan

A Novel

by

Michiko Yoshikawa Johnson

ISBN 9780578439631

For my daughters, Maile and Sachiko

With gratitude to Kate Milligan,
for her collaboration to revive my story

Image of WWII era *akagami*, or red paper

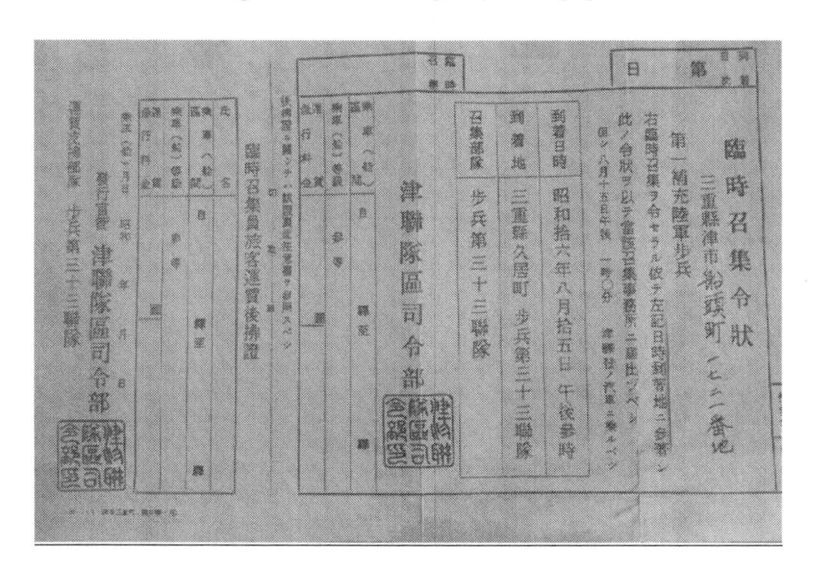

臨時召集令状

三重縣津市船頭町一七二一番地

第一補充陸軍歩兵

右臨時召集ヲ令セラル依テ左記日時到着地ニ参着シ

此ノ令状ヲ以テ當該召集事務所ニ届出ヅベシ

到着日時	昭和拾六年八月拾五日 午後参時
到着地	三重縣久居町 歩兵第三十三聯隊
召集部隊	歩兵第三十三聯隊

津聯隊區司令部

臨時召集員旅客運賃後拂證

發行官署 津聯隊區司令部

歩兵第三十三聯隊

PROLOGUE

Before she met Giichi, Kinuko had little interest in marriage. She dreamed of something larger in life, though she wasn't exactly certain what that might be. When it came to the future, her thoughts whispered like the wind through the pine trees outside her bedroom window in Kobe. Unlike most women of her generation, she couldn't imagine marriage being the ultimate happiness. At the age of eight, when her father died unexpectedly, she saw her mother's happiness evaporate before her eyes and along with it her sense of freedom. For ten years, Kinuko watched her mother, Etsu, fret about the arrival of monthly money orders from her parents and brother. As Kinuko grew into a teen, she cherished the memory of her father, a kind and gentle university assistant professor, but she wondered why her mother had been made so hollow by his death. Would her father have been affected the same way if her mother had died?

Each time the money orders failed to arrive in time to pay the bills, Etsu timidly approached the telephone, shrinking herself like a scolded child. Kinuko listened while Etsu offered seasonal greetings, inquired about the health of her parents or brother, and reported Kinuko's present affairs, before humbly asking if the money order had been mailed. The phone calls always ended with profuse thanks and endless bows.

Matters improved slightly when Kinuko was eighteen and her mother's father died. Etsu inherited a small piece of land enough to liberate them from worry about the monthly money orders, but Kinuko had already adopted the mindset that she must find a way to exist happily without relying on a husband. She studied art at Nara Women's University, initially thinking she might make a living as an artist, but soon recognized the immensity of that challenge, and after graduating, she went to work as an art teacher at a high school for girls.

Even then she felt uneasy. She ate little and seldom left the house on weekends or after a day of teaching. It wasn't that she lacked friends her age, she simply found that few of her friends shared her interests. Her mother assumed that what Kinuko needed was a husband, so she started arranging meetings with a matchmaker who incessantly brought photographs, wrapped in silk furoshiki, of eligible men.

"With her beauty and personality," the matchmaker would say to Etsu, peeling back the furoshiki, "she will have no problem finding a nice husband." Kinuko sat quietly while the matchmaker showered Etsu with a description of her daughter's beauty: "Her clear eyes, her exquisitely arched brows and smooth complexion, will surely attract any man she meets." Such words made Kinuko squirm with embarrassment and even disdain. She usually excused herself politely and retreated to her upstairs room, where she resumed her reading.

Only while reading could she forget about living in a society that treated unmarried women as if they were shiny trinkets for sale. Most evenings she confined herself to her room and read from her father's library: contemporary Japanese writers such as Shimazaki Toson, and Tsubouch Shoyo; Japanese classics like Seishou Nagon and Murasaki Shikibu; and Western classics such as Dostoevsky, Chekhov, Shakespeare, Dickens. She also read the German philosopher Kant and Dante. On her own she discovered the poetry of Yosano Akiko, a passionate female poet of the Meiji Era who defied convention and ended her loveless marriage by running off with her poet lover. Kinuko read Yosano's poems so thoroughly she could recite them all by heart.

Periodically her reading was interrupted by Etsu's pleas to meet the men arranged by the matchmaker. Sometimes Kinuko relented, but only to appease her mother. A few days after each meeting Etsu would come up to her room in the evening bearing a tray of tea. When Kinuko heard the quiet creaking of the wooden stairs, she quickly formed an excuse to decline the proposal. She watched Etsu pour tea into two cups and slide one across the tatami mat toward her. All the while her mother talked about the weather or some flowers beginning to bloom in the garden. At last, Etsu would lift her teacup, take a slow sip, and ask, "What do you think?" Then she would quietly await her daughter's reply, cradling the cup with anticipation.

Kinuko's answers became as predictable as her mother's question. "I don't think we are compatible," or "He seems to think that a wife is nothing more than a maid," or "He seems so nervous and high strung."

"Kinuko," Etsu would sigh, taking another quiet sip of tea before glancing at the books piled on her daughter's desk, "I think your head has grown too big. I wish you had been born a man."

"Mother, I think even for women there must be something more than getting married and having children."

"See, that's what I'm talking about, you think too much."

After Etsu left, Kinuko would lean against her desk and stare into the darkness beyond her bedroom window, listening to the sea wind sighing through the pine trees, as if softly whispering the answer she sought.

Besides teaching, Kinuko spent another year reading and, when in the mood, painting downstairs on the veranda. Then one day she found a photo of Giichi Sekihara on her mother's desk. She wondered how the photo could possibly have come to her from the son of the prominent novelist Ichiro Sekihara. Her heart began pounding the way it did when she read Ichiro's essays in *The Central Review*, essays that invariably criticized Japan's military aggression and emphasized the importance of diplomatic cooperation. She admired his courage, and she had recently gained even more appreciation for him after reading his novel, *Morning Glories,* the story of a clumsy old carpenter whose only son died in the Russo-Japanese War. Kinuko cried at the novel's ending, as the carpenter regained the ability to endure, when one morning his fatherless grandson came to his futon that stunk of sake and urged him to get up so he could see the season's first morning glories blooming in their small garden. Kinuko loved the novel's gentle prose and simple, emotionally compelling story. Kinuko had an image of Ichiro as a gentle yet brave man, and as she looked at his son's photo, she allowed herself to hope that Giichi might possess those same qualities. For the first time she surprised her mother by willingly agreeing to an arranged meeting. Overjoyed, Etsu contacted the matchmaker on the same day, and a week later Kinuko met Giichi at the house of the matchmaker.

When Kinuko was led to a gazebo in the garden, Giichi stood and bowed. "Pleased to meet you," he said amiably, without the overly silky smoothness she had found in men who worked for big corporations. He was tall, much taller than any man she had ever met. He had a smooth prominent forehead and the ridge of his nose formed a straight line through the middle of his angular face. His dark hair glistened naturally, free of the slick pomade so many men used. He dressed just as naturally, nothing ostentatious, just a simple dark blue suit. Everything about him suggested hidden depth.

As the matchmaker guided their conversation, Giichi smiled and spoke modestly unlike the others she had met, who prattled on and yet said nothing. He said he liked to read yet didn't mention his famous father. When Kinuko spoke, he leaned forward, tilted his head slightly and listened intently. Toward the end of the meeting, at the matchmaker's urging, they took a walk in her exquisitely landscaped garden. In the absence of the matchmaker, they turned silent, and Kinuko listened to the burble of water flowing into the pond where carp glided smoothly. The Japanese maples beside the bamboo fence were changing color, exuding hints of pale yellow and orange. She looked up to the sky and suddenly thought of blending colors on her palette, struck by the notion that the light blue of her kimono and the darker one of Giichi's suit, if carefully mixed, would perfectly match the color of the sky. In that moment, she forgot her misgivings about marriage.

While the autumn leaves glowed fire red Kinuko and Giichi courted. Every Sunday Giichi traveled to Kobe, where Kinuko waited for him at a quiet tea parlor off the lobby of the Oriental Hotel. Over a cup of tea or glass of fruit juice, they shared news of the previous week. Kinuko told Giichi about her most recent painting, and Giichi told Kinuko about his ideas about a book he had been reading. Then they headed off to visit museums or parks or the harbor, depending on the day. One Sunday they went hiking in the Rokko Mountains, where they paused to sit on smooth rocks beneath a cluster of trees and eat the lunch Kinuko had prepared. After lunch, sipping tea from a flask Giichi had brought from home, they enjoyed the scenery of the city and the sea that spread out below.

As fall deepened, Giichi proposed, and when Kinuko excitedly reported the news to her mother, Etsu wrote an elated letter to her brother, a general in the Japanese Imperial Army, seeking his approval. Kinuko anxiously awaited her uncle's return letter, thinking his approval a mere formality. Instead, Uncle Hirobumi arrived unexpectedly one morning after an all-night train ride from Tokyo.

Hirobumi sat with his back to the alcove, where Etsu had arranged nanten in a glazed black vase. Obeying her mother's command, Kinuko went to the kitchen to make tea. By the time she returned, they had moved beyond pleasant formalities. She sat rigidly beside Etsu and listened to her uncle's tirade.

"Have you lost your mind, thinking of marrying your daughter into such a risky family? Ichiro Sekihara is a leftist. He's been detained for investigation numerous times. Anyone in their right mind can guess what his son is like, just like his father, a man with dangerous thoughts."

"Listen, Etsu," he continued, towering over his sister's head. "Kinuko can do much better than this. I know some very ambitious young military men who would be excellent matches for her. The Sekiharas might be an old respectable family from Okayama, but their thinking is very dangerous to our country." Etsu kept her head bowed, reminding Kinuko of the long years of her mother's subservience to her brother. Suddenly, though, Etsu raised her head and spoke, startling Kinuko. "Kinuko thinks otherwise," she said. "Please don't take it personally, but she is not very fond of military men. All they think about is war. They love the country more than their wives. That's what she says, I'm very sorry."

"You have spoiled her," Hirobumi shot back. "Young women these days are dying to marry a dedicated military man willing to risk his life in the fight for his country, because they wish to dedicate themselves to their country by marrying such a man. You spoiled her by letting her have such lazy ideas. Those without rigorous military training lack a fundamental sense of duty. Their minds drift like feathers in the wind and come up with outlandish ideas, all useless to us. I'm absolutely against her marrying this man."

"I want my daughter to be happy," Etsu said. "That is all I wish." Her voice was low, yet Kinuko could detect its firmness.

"If you think her happiness will be secured by this man, do as you wish. You will only regret it later." Her uncle stood, his mouth pinched in a tight line beneath his thick mustache. Etsu followed him to the door, begging him to at least stay for lunch. While he put on his shoes, Etsu thanked him for making such a long trip to show his concern for her daughter, while Kinuko sat silently beside her. Together they bowed to Hirobumi as he stepped from the house and remained bowed until he was no longer in view.

After Etsu closed the door, Kinuko returned to the room where her uncle's untouched teacup sat on the table. She placed the tea service on the tray, deeply moved by her mother's stand against Hirobumi and yet certain her uncle's objection would ultimately keep her from marrying Giichi. In the family room, she saw Etsu sitting at the table, rubbing her temples.

"I'm sorry," Kinuko said.

"There is no reason for you to be sorry," Etsu replied, before taking the tray and carrying it into the kitchen.

Kinuko spent the afternoon in her room alone, her desire to marry Giichi growing even stronger in the face of this obstacle. Yet equally, she didn't want to ruin her mother's life. Her uncle had controlled Etsu for years, yet Kinuko realized that was his way of protecting his sister. Their old mother, Kinuko's grandmother, could die at any time, and when that happened, Hirobumi would be the only family left to Etsu. Kinuko knew her mother had borne enough sadness, and she didn't want to add any more.

That evening, Etsu came up to Kinuko's room, carrying the customary tray of tea. "Don't worry about what your uncle said," she began, "because I don't."

"Mother, he is your only brother."

"Yes, he is, but to me your happiness is more important than what he thinks. My real wish for you is to experience true happiness." Kinuko began crying as her mother continued. "I'd been worried...you are a little different from other women your age, and I kept wondering if there was a suitable young man for you...someone who makes you truly happy. That had kept me awake many nights until you met Giichi-san. I want you to be happy, Kinuko." Kinuko kept her tear-streaked face down, overwhelmed by her mother's love. It was the first time she heard her mother talk about happiness.

The next day, Etsu traveled to Kyoto to buy silk for Kinuko's wedding chest. To save money, she sewed the kimono herself, working into the night for weeks. Only days before the wedding, did she finally complete Kinuko's chest with the kimono.

At the end of February Kinuko and Giichi were married in the courtyard of a Shinto shrine in Osaka, where the full bloom of plum trees exuded a serene fragrance. All their friends and relatives gathered to celebrate their union. Except for Hirobumi.

CHAPTER 1

January 1945

When the air raid siren began shrieking for a third time, Kinuko was not particularly alarmed. There had been no bombing after the previous warnings, only the drone of B-29s in the distant sky. This time, she sensed something different; the siren wouldn't stop. She glanced toward Yuki's bedroom, where her three-year-old daughter had finally fallen asleep after the second warning lifted. As Kinuko stood to check on Yuki the floor vibrated beneath her. She hurried to the dining room and lifted the thick blackout curtain covering the window. The sound became more distinct—thudding in the distance. American bombs. Her heart started to beat faster. The long-dreaded nightmare had finally arrived. She strained to see where they were falling. Osaka or Amagasaki? Perhaps even closer. Where was Giichi? Antiaircraft guns started crackling through the darkness. Kinuko grabbed the candlestick from the table and hurried toward Yuki's room, the horror of Tokyo's suffering swirling in her mind. Five hundred kilometers away, the new and powerful B-29s had been incinerating people for weeks. The women. The children. Now this industrial region of Hanshin would face the same fate.

Somehow, Yuki remained asleep, and Kinuko hesitated next to her futon. Then a bomb exploded close enough that the windows rattled. In a panic, she set the candlestick on the floor, lifted Yuki into her arms and ran to the middle room. Her daughter's whimpers turned to howls as Kinuko lowered her into a corner and frantically pulled at the *tatamis* covering the shelter. The deep, terrifying growl of airplanes mingled with Yuki's wails. Kinuko kept tugging at the heavy mat but couldn't shift the *tatamis* enough to get at the floorboard. She broke out into a cold sweat. Then, through Yuki's cries and the growing roar of the planes, she heard the main door slide open.

"Giichi-san?" she called, her voice cracking with relief. Instead, the voice of her old neighbor, Mr. Chiba, called back, "Kinuko-san! They're coming!" He rushed into the room and pulled one mat aside and then another. Kinuko ran back to Yuki's room and grabbed her blanket. "Get in here, quickly!" Mr. Chiba said. "I'll put out the candle."

Kinuko cradled Yuki in her arms and felt her way down the steps into the dark hole. She pressed into a corner of the tiny concrete cubicle, trembling with terror. Soon, the faint candlelight died out above and Mr. Chiba squeezed beside her in complete darkness.

"What about Mrs. Chiba?"

"Don't worry. She's already in our shelter."

Then the sound turned deafening. Kinuko covered Yuki with her body. When bombers screamed directly overhead, her heart pounded wildly. She knew they would certainly die. In that moment of anguish, she felt a sharp sting of regret that she and Yuki must die apart from Giichi.

As bombers roared past and moved westward toward Kobe, Kinuko rocked Yuki in her arms and hushed her through chattering teeth.

"That was close." Mr. Chiba emitted a muffled sigh and leaned back from her.

For nearly an hour they clung together each time bombers approached and shivered in the cold January air that descended down from the open crawl space beneath the house. Eventually, there was a long silence. Yuki stopped whimpering and dozed against Kinuko's chest.

When the all-clear siren sounded, Mr. Chiba cleared his throat. "Finally," he whispered. "Poor child. I hope this is the last one tonight."

He lifted Yuki from Kinuko's arms and started up the narrow steps. Kinuko crawled up behind them, a numbing tingle in her legs. When she stood on the *tatami* floor, she wobbled for a moment and then shuffled toward Mr. Chiba's moving shadow, cradling the slight bulge of her womb in her hands.

Mr. Chiba lowered Yuki onto her futon, while Kinuko waved her hand overhead to find the light cord. A dull light spilled onto the bed from the single bulb covered by blackout cloth.

"Mama," Yuki moaned, pressing her tiny fists against her tightened eyes.

"Please, leave the *tatamis* for Giichi," Kinuko said to Mr. Chiba as she knelt next to Yuki. "It's late. Mrs. Chiba must be waiting for you."

"Oh, don't worry."

As she stroked her daughter's forehead, she heard the floorboard thud into place and then the tatamis sliding over it.

"Good night," Mr. Chiba whispered from the doorway. "The trams should be running now, so Giichi-san should be home soon. If not, I can come over any time."

Kinuko started to rise.

"No, no. Stay with Yuki-chan."

"Thank you, Mr. Chiba."

"Where is Papa?" Yuki whined.

"Don't worry," Kinuko said. "He'll be home soon."

Her daughter yawned, but Kinuko's worry intensified as she thanked Mr. Chiba again. At the sound of the front door sliding shut, she leaned against a cushion beside Yuki's futon and strained to hear a tram. There was no traffic on the Hanshin Highway. The neighborhood seemed to have settled for the night. Soon, Yuki's breathing was all she heard.

In the stillness, she felt alone. Since last September, about the time she told Giichi of her pregnancy, he had turned cold and distant and started coming home late, smelling of *sake*. Only when she asked did he mumble some excuse about extra work at Nippon Motors. Though she had eventually stopped asking, now she wished she hadn't. Anything, even listening to his feeble excuses, would be better than this painful waiting.

When the dining room clock struck midnight, she breathed deeply and tried to imagine Giichi safe, as if doing so would make it true. She closed her eyes and formed an image of him in a tram car, coming home from work, his body jostling with the tram's movement, his shoulders hunched against the cold. He sat alone and pressed his face to the window to peer into the darkness. His lips moved silently, but she could hear him. "Kinuko, Yuki, I'm almost home."

She tried to cling to that scene, but Yuki stirred and moaned, "Mama."

Kinuko quickly turned and gently patted her daughter's back. When Yuki quieted down, she closed her eyes again and forced her mind to escape to happier days with Giichi. She settled on a clear autumn day before the Pearl Harbor attack, before Yuki was born.

It was a Sunday, and lured by the blue sky Giichi and Kinuko boarded a train. They ended up at Lake Biwa. When they found a deserted shore, they sat on the pebbled beach and watched the afternoon sunlight sparkle on the surface of the water. Kinuko wondered how she might paint the scene, as she always did at the sight of something beautiful. "I'm not good at scenery," she admitted, "especially the reflection of light on water."

"You are good," Giichi insisted. "Look at the one you painted at Suma Beach near your mother's house. I love that."

"Thank you," she said, looking down modestly. "But what I'm saying is I can't feel the light moving and dancing by looking at that painting. To me it's kind of flat."

"Really? It looks very good to me. I feel as if I'm standing right on the beach, looking at the ocean."

Kinuko smiled. Whatever misgivings she had about her art, Giichi always made her feel proud of it, as if she were a great artist. Looking across the water, she realized for the first time that what Giichi thought of her was more important than what she thought of herself. With a sudden giddy urge, she stood and took off her white tabi socks, pulled up the hem of her silk kimono and waded into the lake. Giichi followed her, laughing, pulling up his pant legs.

"Don't get your kimono wet," he said. "If you do, we can't go home today."

"Let's not go home today."

"I have to work tomorrow," he said in a singsong tone.

"No, you don't *have* to," Kinuko said, mimicking his tone.

Giichi waded toward her and held his arms out, letting the cuffs of his pants fall into the water. They embraced, and the hem of her kimono dipped into the water and wavered beside his cuffs. Then they laughed hysterically until their stomachs hurt.

Kinuko felt liberated by the notion that her happiness would always be secure as long as she was with Giichi.

She yearned for the pure joy she had felt that day, but a distant rumble intruded at the fringe of her reverie. She lifted her head sharply and leaned toward the door. It was definitely a tram. She rose from the floor, feeling strength returning to her legs. It wouldn't matter what kind of mood Giichi was in. As long as he was safe and came home to her and Yuki, she would be happy.

At the sound of the tram screeching to a stop on the highway, Kinuko's heart pounded. She hurried to the north window and pulled the blackout curtain aside. Giichi's familiar silhouette stepped out of the faintly lit tram. His dark figure, tall and slender, moved to the top of the stairs leading to the road below. She let the curtain drop and nearly ran into the kitchen and started a fire. She wadded sheets of newspaper, placed them at the base of the hibachi and struck a match. When the paper flared up, she dropped wood chips into the flames.

She heard the main door slide open and rushed to the front room where Giichi was untying the laces of his shoes. "I'm glad you came home safely," she said. "I've been worried."

"At last," he said, meticulously turning his shoes so they pointed toward the door. The chill of his voice stabbed at her heart, and sadness eroded her excitement. Still, she forced cheerfulness into her voice. "Have you eaten?"

"No." He shook his head and pulled off his coat.

"That's what I thought. I just started a fire."

Kinuko took his coat. While she hung it on the stand in a corner of the front room, Giichi went into the dining room, sat at the table and picked up the morning paper from the table. Kinuko went back to the kitchen and dropped more chips of wood into the growing flame. The heaviness of the past few months returned, and for a moment she wanted to cry. She thought she understood his brooding. She knew he opposed the war, but so did she, and everyone felt the growing strain of the war pressing into their lives. Why could he no longer talk with her about it? Why did she no longer matter to him? Those questions often forced their way into her throat, but she always swallowed them, fearing his answer.

With a pan of miso soup heating over the coals, she put cold rice in a bowl and filled a kettle with water to make tea, then glanced into the dining room. Giichi was still in his office clothes—a white shirt and gray woolen trousers, with his tie loosened slightly. His suit jacket lay folded on a floor cushion beside him. He sat at the rim of a weak circle of light, cast by a single bulb in the overhanging lamp and muted by a lampshade swathed in black cloth. The bleak scene made the silence between them unbearable.

"How was your day?" she asked, again attempting to sound cheerful, yet realizing how foolish that must sound after the first night of heavy bombing.

"Fine," he replied, gazing at the newspaper.

"I've been worried," she continued. "The tram must have stopped many times."

He nodded without looking up.

"I was so frightened when the bombing began," she continued. "Mr. Chiba came over and helped me get Yuki into the shelter."

"I'm glad," he said, finally glancing up from the paper. "Please thank him for me."

"I will. Did you see any bombs from the tram?"

"No."

"Do you think the bombing will get worse?"

"I'm afraid so."

His jaw muscles loosened each time he spoke then knotted again. When steam rose from the soup, she removed the pan from the hibachi and put the kettle in its place. She glanced at the four pails of water in the corner. Above them, three padded black hoods hung from wall hooks—two large ones for her and Giichi, a small one for Yuki. She realized that in her hurry to get into the shelter she had completely forgotten about wearing the hoods.

As if they would help, she thought, such meager defense against bombs, and then she felt a strangling grip of fear. Tomorrow night the bombing could be even worse, and again they would be alone in the shelter, without Giichi. She recalled the searing moment of regret, the thought of dying apart from him. Now she knew what was at the heart of it—she wasn't certain if he still loved her. The realization that any of them could die in an instant shuddered deep inside her. She resolved that she could no longer choke back the words in her throat. She must ask him. Tonight.

Kinuko filled Giichi's bowls and sat across from him. Sitting in the bomb shelter with Mr. Chiba, she had felt more comfortable than now with her own husband. Giichi carefully sipped the soup, his throat pulsing with each swallow. She used to enjoy watching him eat, the simple movement of the prominent angles of his jaw and throat. Now something about his appearance disturbed her. She understood in that moment why the neighborhood chief, Mr. Hayashi, considered Giichi arrogant. The previously endearing sideways glance of his eyes and the forward tilt of his head, habits he had developed because of a childhood loss of hearing in one ear, now struck her as signs of evasion.

Kinuko sat quietly, waiting for him to finish, while the aroma of cooling miso rose from his bowl and wafted around her. She wondered if she would be able to face it—if he told her he no longer loved her, or even worse. She erased the worst from her mind; even if he was a son of Ichiro Sekihara, he would not do anything that extreme. He had a wife and a daughter and another child on the way.

As if reading her mind, Giichi put down his chopsticks. She poured tea into his cup with trembling hands, and after she set the pot on the table, she inhaled deeply and looked into his face.

"Please, tell me what has been bothering you. We used to talk about everything."

Giichi flinched; his shoulders drooped momentarily and then straightened. He appeared ready to respond but said nothing.

"I need to know what is wrong. You said the bombing will get worse. I must know what's bothering you before we die."

Giichi lifted his head and at last looked straight at her, with an unblinking gaze that made her even more uneasy.

"I'm sorry that I've been avoiding you," he finally said. "But I couldn't tell you—you are pregnant and—"

"Tell me what?" Kinuko's voice trembled.

"I've been wrong. I should have told you sooner, but I didn't want to hurt you. I'm sorry."

"Please, tell me now," she whispered.

"I have made a decision." Giichi's eyes glistened. "I have decided that when the red paper comes, I will refuse it."

Kinuko gasped so violently her body turned rigid. She had buried the possibility of this moment so deeply that she felt as if his words had actually reached inside her and ripped out a hidden piece of her flesh. Her mind swarmed with images of military policemen and Giichi's tortured body.

She looked up, pressing a high-pitched response through her tight throat. "No. You can't do that. They will kill you."

"I would rather be killed than go to war."

"But—," she desperately searched for words to oppose him.

"I-am-not-going-to-war."

His voice sounded so final that Kinuko stared at him blankly. "What about Yuki—and the baby? What will we do?" she whispered.

"I've already asked my father to take care of you and our children, if something happens to me. He is glad to help."

"I don't mean money. We need *you*." Sobs convulsed her shoulders, and she covered her face. She heard fragments of his voice drifting overhead—"...how sorry I would be....you are strong...." She covered her ears, unable to bear the cold realization that he didn't really care about them.

Suddenly, she pushed away from the table and shook her head hard. "No!" she cried and ran into Yuki's room, where she stood beside her sleeping daughter, muffling her sobs. Her uncle had been right. She slumped onto the cushion beside Yuki's futon, her uncle's words echoing in her ears, "The Sekiharas have dangerous ideas." She wanted to take Yuki in her arms and protect her from the knowledge that her father could so easily abandon her.

In the grim darkness, Kinuko heard Giichi approaching, his feet padding quietly against the *tatami* floor. Part of her hoped he would move past and go to their room, leave her alone, yet another part of her wished he would come in and tell her that he had changed his mind; he wouldn't refuse the red paper. The door slid open and he stepped inside. He stood quietly for a moment, and then spoke haltingly, "I'm very sorry. I don't expect you to forgive me for my decision or the way I've behaved. But I do love you and Yuki more than anything in the world. I want you to know that."

"Then please change your mind," Kinuko begged. "I don't want you to be killed."

Giichi didn't answer.

"Don't abandon us, please."

Giichi still did not answer.

For months she had yearned for him to say he loved her. Now it seemed impossible. No matter how many times he might say it, she couldn't believe that he loved her or anyone; he only loved his ideals.

After a while, she heard him backing from the room, and the door sliding shut, and the sound of him moving away from them.

CHAPTER 2

At six o'clock, Kinuko got up from the futon in the guest bedroom after the first night in eight years of marriage that she had avoided lying with Giichi. When the first tram rumbled past on the Hanshin Highway, her hair was already woven into a neat knot at the back of her neck. She sat in front of the mirror and traced the dark shadows along her lower eyelids with the tip of her finger. Her skin felt dry as autumn rice stalks.

Looking at her haggard face, Kinuko remembered how strongly her mother had stood against her uncle and hoped she could find her mother's strength somewhere within herself. She stood abruptly, pulled the silk drape over the mirror, and hurried into the kitchen, determined to go to Osaka and talk with Giichi's father, Ichiro. Surely, Ichiro would help her change Giichi's mind. No father, whatever his political leanings, would allow his son to throw away his life.

She groped for the blackout curtain at the kitchen window and pulled it aside. The faint dawn light revealed the soot-covered wall near the sink, where a day calendar hung from a nail. She saw the date on the top sheet—January 4, 1945, and realized she hadn't torn off a single page since B-29s started roaming above Hanshin. She leafed through the calendar with the ball of her thumb, until she found the present date, January 10.

Then Kinuko went about her morning chores with distracted resolve. She walked outside to get the morning paper, the loose cloth of her gray monpe pants flapping against her legs. As she reached into the wooden box for the newspaper, she noticed that the windows and doors of all the neighboring homes remained closed. Across the street, a line of houses stood behind the typhoon ditch that ran along the edge of the rugged pavement. All of the houses, one-story with identical black-tiled roofs, were separated by narrow, barely passable footpaths. In the deep morning silence, a heavy sense of isolation burrowed into her, a reminder of what she had felt when she and Giichi moved into this working class neighborhood in Ashiya. While their house looked like the others, it was the only one with garden on three sides. Though nothing extravagant, she knew many of the neighbors considered her garden a spacious luxury. Inside its low evergreen hedge stood a pine tree, a Japanese maple, and a plum tree. Coupled with Giichi's suit and office job, those distinctions kept most of the neighbors distant from Kinuko, yet that distance had never bothered her. There had been enough happiness in living here with Giichi and in her close relationship with the elderly Chibas across the street. But now that she carried the weight of Giichi's decision like a heavy stone in her heart, she realized there was no one here with whom she could share her burden. It wouldn't be fair to bother the Chibas with such an immense problem. They had their own family to worry about, a son now in Burma with the army.

As she lifted the newspaper from the box, Kinuko heard the Chibas' door open unexpectedly and turned to see Mr. Chiba step from the house, his neck swathed in the brown muffler Mrs. Chiba had knitted for him in the fall. Mrs. Chiba appeared in the doorway to see her husband off.

"Good morning, Kinuko-san," the couple said in chorus.

"Good morning. Mr. Chiba, you are leaving early this morning."

"A big shipment is coming in," he said, swinging his rickety bicycle from the wall beside the door. Mrs. Chiba smiled and waved to her, before stepping inside and sliding the door shut.

"Did Giichi-san come home all right last night?" Mr. Chiba called to her.

"Yes, by the last tram."

Mr. Chiba pushed his bicycle across the street. "You don't look well, Kinuko-san," he said as he approached.

"I'm fine." She forced a smile. "I didn't sleep very well last night, that's all."

"You should take Yuki-chan to my wife. There might be air raid warnings again tonight. You'd better sleep when you can."

"Thank you," she said. "I might do that."

He turned the bike and stepped onto the pedal, wobbling on the uneven pavement. Soon his bicycle disappeared into the dark shadow of the underpass beneath the highway. Kinuko continued to stare in that direction, then finally stepped back from the mailbox and returned to the house, thinking of the many evenings she and Giichi had sat with the Chibas, sipping tea and having easy conversation. She remembered the time only three months earlier when the Chibas came to congratulate her on her pregnancy.

"This is doubly exciting news for us," Mr. Chiba said, explaining that they had just received a letter from their daughter in Hiroshima and learned that she, too, was pregnant.

"Two new grandchildren at once," he had said with a glowing smile.

The memory of his smile filled her with sadness—her child might grow up without a father. But she pushed that thought away and placed the newspaper beside Giichi's cushion in the dining room, then started a charcoal fire in the kitchen.

The city's gas supply had burned off several months earlier, hissing away like the last breath of a dying dragon. Like everyone else, she had grown accustomed to cooking over charcoal, but this morning, as the charcoal began to burn with a blue flame in the earthenware hibachi, the smell wrenched Kinuko into a knot of nausea. She staggered to the sink and vomited dryly.

"Are you all right?"

Giichi's voice surprised her. She turned and saw him step into the kitchen in a blue house kimono with clumps of white lather on his chin. Then she leaned over the sink and retched again. She tensed as she felt his hand gently rubbing her back.

"I'll stay home, you need sleep."

Kinuko shook her head. "It's just morning sickness. I'm fine, you need to go to work."

After Giichi left the kitchen, Kinuko placed her forehead against the cool edge of the sink and breathed deeply. After a while, she stood up straight and lifted some of the red-hot coals with tongs and dropped them into the white porcelain brazier. She carried the brazier into the dining room, then made rice porridge, using rice left over from the evening before, and set it on the dining table next to a dish of pickled radishes. The rest of the rice she placed in Giichi's aluminum lunch box along with a pickled plum.

Giichi ate in a hurry and left earlier than usual. By eight-thirty Kinuko had already dressed and fed Yuki. While her daughter played with wooden blocks, she changed into a silk kimono and quickly examined her appearance in a mirror. Satisfied that the white collars crossed neatly at her throat, she hastily tucked a kerchief into a fold of the sleeve and called to Yuki, "We have to go."

Yuki scrambled into the front room. "Where are we going?"

"I'm going to see Grandpa; you will be staying with Mrs. Chiba." Kinuko immediately realized her mistake.

"I want to see Grandpa, too."

"No, you can't come with me today, but Mama will be right back." Kinuko took her hand and walked outside.

"I want to feed the carp with Grandpa," Yuki begged while Kinuko locked the door.

"Not today." Kinuko told her.

"But I want to. I want to go with you."

Kinuko took Yuki's hand and hurried across the street. When Mrs. Chiba slid the door open, Kinuko saw her eyes open wide at the sight of her going-out kimono. These days, with Hanshin under constant threat of air attack, the neighborhood women seldom ventured far from their homes.

"I want to feed the carp, Mama, let me go," Yuki pleaded, clinging to Kinuko's kimono.

"No, you can't," Kinuko said, pushing her toward the doorway and bowing to Mrs. Chiba at the same time.

"I'm sorry for the inconvenience," Kinuko said, "but if you could watch Yuki for just a few hours."

"I'm glad to do that," said Mrs. Chiba, pulling Yuki inside.

"Thank you," Kinuko said, bowing profusely.

"Please be careful," said Mrs. Chiba.

"Thank you, I will. I'll be back as soon as possible."

Kinuko trembled at the sound of Yuki's cries but did not look back. As she hurried toward the tram stop her thoughts shifted to Mrs. Chiba. Like Mr. Chiba, she never asked questions and was always ready to help. When Kinuko had been pregnant with Yuki, Mrs. Chiba ran errands for her, fetching anything from a bottle of soy sauce to a heavy sack of rice. After Yuki's birth Mrs. Chiba often slipped into Kinuko's garden at the first sight of rain, removed the laundry from the line and brought it into the house neatly folded.

The pleasant thoughts of Mrs. Chiba faded away, as Kinuko started up the concrete stairway to the tram stop. The strong wind sweeping up from Osaka Bay pushed her forward and lifted her kimono sleeves. Up on the highway she glanced at her watch and realized she could stay in Osaka no more than forty-five minutes if she hoped to be home in time to prepare Yuki's lunch.

Well past the morning commute, Kinuko easily found a seat in the tram. At each stop a few passengers got off and a few others stepped on, some carrying stained furoshiki bundles probably containing black market food. A government poster left over from the third anniversary of Pearl Harbor hung from the ceiling. "Remember the Glory of Pearl Harbor," its excited crimson letters proclaimed, in sharp contrast to the grim faces of the passengers. Kinuko glared at the poster. To her, the attack on Pearl Harbor did not represent a time of glory. Instead it marked the time when she began to sense the depth of Giichi's outrage against the government. She turned from the poster and looked vaguely out the window, thinking back to the evening of the Pearl Harbor attack...

Yuki, then six months old, fussed unusually before finally falling asleep. Kinuko had heard neighbors shouting about big news, but fearful of awakening Yuki, she didn't turn the radio on. Around six, she stepped into the kitchen to prepare supper and heard exultant military music blasting from the radio next door. The announcers sounded intoxicated, as if victory had already been achieved. Giichi strode in abruptly, his hair blown askew by the stiff December wind running down off the Rokkos.

"Why don't you have the radio on at such a crucial time?" he asked in an accusing tone. He yanked his shoes from his feet before leaping toward the radio on the china hutch in the dining room. A triumphant fanfare blasted through crackles of static; then came a proud male voice, proclaiming the news that had probably been announced throughout the day, "Before dawn this morning, the Empire of Japan opened hostilities with the United States of America as our Imperial Army and Navy attacked Pearl Harbor in the western Pacific—"

Giichi stood beside the radio, one hand planted on his hip, the other pressing his fedora against his stomach. Abruptly, he turned the radio off and began pacing around the dining room. "This is insanity! Total insanity!"

"Please, keep your voice down," Kinuko begged. Yuki was sleeping, but she worried even more that someone might hear him, especially the neighborhood chief, Mr. Hayashi, who would welcome any opportunity to turn Giichi in for speaking out against the Emperor or the military.

Giichi threw his hat onto the dining table and sat down. "This is the craziest thing I've ever heard." He pounded his fist on the table. "Attack, then what? They never think twice, those right-wing fanatics!"

A few weeks later the nation's fervor peaked amid New Year's celebrations. Newspapers announced the glorious progress of the war in huge, red type. Stirring renditions of "The Battleship March" blared from radios. Flags sprang forth like abundant flowers in winter—outside homes, schools, office buildings, shops, train cars, trams and streetcars. The triumphant rising red sun was everywhere.

On the first day of January, in keeping with tradition, Giichi, Kinuko, and Yuki dressed in their finest going-out clothes to visit Giichi's parents in Osaka for a family celebration. Yuki cooed and smiled at the sight of the bright red and white flags and beaming faces, and the sound of optimistic chatter, proclaiming the imminent rise of the Red Sun over all of Asia and perhaps beyond through this new year.

When they arrived at the elder Sekihara house, they found an equally festive atmosphere, though one inspired by tradition rather than war. Displays of fresh bamboo stalks and pine branches studded with tangerines outlined the gate. Inside the house, in the alcove of the reception room, a decorative, concentrically layered cone of rice cakes sat on a white wooden tray like a snow-laden pine tree. A single tangerine rested at the top of the rice cakes, and white paper streamers rippled down from the tangerine. The subtle aroma of New Year's Day zoni soup filled the formal reception room.

The family members sat around the rectangular dining table and exchanged traditional New Year's greetings. Ichiro, as the head of the household, solemnly poured sake into the small porcelain cups each held in their hands. Everyone took a small sip and then began taking food from the serving plates in front of them with lacquered chopsticks. Kinuko noticed that Giichi stared somberly and his plate remained empty.

"It's suicidal," Giichi said, looking to his father.

Ichiro placed his chopsticks on the table and glanced at the garden through the ornamental glass window that ran horizontally across the shouji doors. Kinuko followed his gaze to the pond, which rippled softly, reflecting a weak winter sun.

"Unfortunately, yes," Ichiro finally said with a small sigh.

"The end will be disastrous," said Giichi.

"How can you be so certain?" Kinuko asked.

Ichiro sat up straight, and Giichi let him answer.

"Unfortunately, you are right, my son. Japan seems to be doing all right, without considering the horrible waste of life and the drain on our economy. But now we have drawn America and the Allies into our Asian war. Japan cannot possibly match their resources and combined fleets..."

Giichi jumped in. "How can Japan depend only on 'Japanese Spirit' to win a war against the Allies? We will only send more and more men to war. This will end up just like the China War, an endless sacrifice of life."

Ichiro sighed again. "None of this should have happened. Japan should have withdrawn her troops from China long ago. That war alone has left such a mess, and now we have an even bigger one. I keep thinking about all the war widows and their children. How can they possibly survive with this inflation, with the government too busy fighting wars to help them?"

Kinuko shifted uncomfortably, knowing the Sekihara men would be arrested if someone reported their conversation, even though it was unlikely in this spacious neighborhood. She glanced at her mother-in-law. Sumiko kept her head down and continued eating with a blank expression, silently lifting her chopsticks to her small round mouth with the same elegance she taught her tea ceremony classes. Kinuko turned to watch Giichi anxiously lower the chopsticks into a bowl of black beans at the center of the spotless ebony table. Eating black beans on New Year's Day signified good fortune, but the beans eluded his grasp.

"In three years," said Giichi, "Japan will be finished."

Sumiko spoke for the first time, her voice calm but her face frowning slightly. "Giichi, please, today is New Year's Day. Let's talk about something auspicious, shall we?"

With the same calmness, Sumiko observed the dishes in front of Giichi. "You've hardly eaten anything. Please eat more." She then spoke to Kinuko. "Pour him some more *sake*."

Kinuko obediently picked up one of the sake bottles and tilted it toward Giichi's cup, but Giichi declined, raising his right palm to reject her offering.

Kinuko turned away from the tram window and wondered which she should have believed—the words of her military uncle, who seemed to have accurately predicted her future, or the words of Giichi and Ichiro, who seemed to have accurately predicted the fate of Japan. Just over three years had passed since that New Year's celebration, and it did indeed look like the country was almost finished. Still, refusing the red paper was no solution. She shivered, remembering Giichi's glistening eyes as he announced that he wouldn't go to war.

In Osaka, Kinuko stepped from the tram determined to gain her father-in-law's support. Together they would change Giichi's mind. But even before she reached the streetcar depot, her worry resurfaced. Ichiro might not look at the matter the same way she did. After all, he had taken many chances in his life without regard for their impact on his family.

Though Sumiko never talked with her at length about what she had endured, bits and pieces of conversation during the past eight years had revealed a clear picture of her mother-in-law's torment. The first time Ichiro was detained, for an essay criticizing Japan's brutal colonial policies in Korea, he returned home after two days with the flesh on his back shredded by blows from a bamboo stick. The detentions continued over the years, coming nearly as frequently as the publication of his essays, and Sumiko begged her husband to stop writing against the military. Eventually, Ichiro did stop, though not because of his wife's pleas. After Pearl Harbor, *The Central Review,* the nation's lone, strong anti-military publication, succumbed to the dictates of government officials and no longer accepted his essays.

As Kinuko neared the Sekihara house she attempted to find some hope in Ichiro's actions. He could have pursued other methods of publicly expressing his dissent. Perhaps he had recognized the futility of openly working against an absolute force, and if that were the case, he would surely recognize the futility of refusing the red paper, especially when it involved his son. By the time Kinuko tapped on the Sekihara door, she felt a renewed hope.

Ume, the Sekiharas' maid, opened the door. "Good morning, Young Mistress, what a surprise to see you," she said, then bowed.

"Good morning, Ume-san," Kinuko said. "I—I hope Big Master is home today. I would like to visit with him."

"Of course, please come in. Big Mistress is in Kyoto, though."

Kinuko felt relieved that her mother-in-law was gone. She could be spared the worry about her son's decision, at least for now.

Ume led her into an opulent reception room. Kinuko straightened and tucked the front of her kimono carefully and sat on the silk cushion Ume placed next to the shiny ebony table. When the maid left the room, Kinuko took her kerchief from her sleeve and pressed it with a shaky hand against her forehead and under her chin. She adjusted her posture, trying to sit in the dignified manner befitting a young mistress of the Sekiharas, a wealthy family of Okayama with large land holdings still farmed by peasant families. Everything in the room, old and priceless, had been passed down from generation to generation for centuries. In the alcove, a sixteenth century scroll hung on the wall. In front of it stood a tranquil oxidized silver crane. Across from the alcove, a black lacquered ornamental chest accommodated a white porcelain statue of Kannon, the Buddhist idealization of serenity and benevolence, her simple robe fluidly sweeping down to her heels, as if floating above all human suffering.

For eight years, Kinuko had been an obedient, agreeable young Sekihara wife, never talking harshly to her parents-in-law, never neglecting her duties. Now she felt uncertain about whether she could keep her composure in front of Ichiro. Her shoulders heaved with distress. She tried to calm herself as she heard his footsteps approaching. At the thought of his large physique appearing in the doorway, she quickly shifted on the cushion to sit even straighter. Like Giichi, Ichiro was tall but much more powerfully built, with large bones and prominent muscles—far from the pale, weak figure many perceived as the image of a man who made his living with a pen.

When the door rolled open, Kinuko nearly gasped at the sight of Ichiro. His hair had turned silver—more silver than black. His dark blue kimono fell loosely around him, especially in the front where the lapels crossed over his once broad chest.

"How are you, Kinuko?"

For a moment, Kinuko sat speechless as he lowered himself laboriously onto the cushion across the table.

"I'm well, thank you," Kinuko finally said and then coughed dryly under her kerchief. "And how are you, Father?"

"I'm well, thank you." Ichiro arched his back as if attempting to live up to his words.

"I hope Mother is well."

"She has come down with a slight cold but still went to Kyoto this morning because she didn't want to miss their last meeting."

"Last meeting?"

"Yes, they've decided to curtail their activities." Ichiro smoothed the hair along one temple. "The members have trouble getting there for one thing, and the government campaign of frugality has forced many of them to stop teaching the tea ceremony. It's very unfortunate."

"It is," Kinuko agreed. "I'm sorry to hear that."

"And Yuki? Is she doing well despite all this?"

"She's fine. I left her with Mrs. Chiba this morning."

"Oh, she is kind, isn't she? I'm glad you have such a nice neighbor, though I wish you could have brought her."

"So do I. I can't remember, when was the last time you saw Yuki?"

"In October. She came with Giichi one Sunday. He told me you were busy sewing blackout curtains."

"That is right. She wanted me to come with her that morning and feed the carp in the pond."

Kinuko tried to sound normal but heard a frightened edge in her voice. Still, Ichiro smiled, his eyes soft behind reading glasses. If he noticed, he hid it well.

"Yes, she loves the carp, doesn't she? It was nice and warm that day. She and I spent many hours in the garden, throwing fu into the pond until Grandma scolded us for over feeding the carp."

He clasped his hands, his left thumb gently rubbing a callus on his finger. His eyes, now turning sad, were on the pond, as if he were remembering the warm October afternoon he had spent with his granddaughter. Then, as if to sever himself from that memory, he abruptly turned to Kinuko. "Well, what has brought you here today? I don't mean to hurry you, but I suppose you must get home fairly quickly under these circumstances."

"Yes," said Kinuko, staring at the kerchief she squeezed in her lap. "This is about Giichi." She looked up to face Ichiro.

"Yes...?" Ichiro's thumb stopped moving.

Kinuko pushed the words out all at once. "Last night Giichi told me he is going to refuse the red paper." Tears gathered at the rims of her eyes. "I think it's foolish for him to just throw his life away no matter what he believes. He's only thirty-one, and—" Her voice trailed off, but she kept her eyes on Ichiro and blinked rapidly to stop her tears.

Ichiro dropped his gaze to his hands, drew in a breath and exhaled with a heavy sigh. "If he doesn't refuse the red paper, do you think he will survive the war and come home?" Ichiro asked. It sounded like a question to himself rather than to Kinuko. But Kinuko answered swiftly.

"I suppose his chances would be fifty-fifty if he goes to war, but he will never come back if he refuses to go. I can't bear the notion of Giichi being-"

The door slid open, and Ume entered with tea. Kinuko quickly dried her tears. She and Ichiro fell into an awkward silence as the maid gracefully slipped down to her knees to place a cup in front of each of them. She bowed deeply, first to Ichiro, then to Kinuko, before leaving the room soundlessly. Ichiro pushed the saucer aside and began rubbing his hands together.

"That is true, his chances are probably fifty-fifty if he goes to war," Ichiro said, again as if talking to himself.

"Would you please tell Giichi to change his mind? He is stubborn. Once he makes up his mind, he won't listen, no matter what I say. But if you and I talk to him together, he might hear us."

Kinuko held her breath. The shadow of Ichiro's hands moved slowly over the table, intensifying his silence.

"He is stubborn, like me," he whispered forlornly. "Yes."

"Would you, please?" Kinuko squeezed her kerchief even harder. "He might listen to both of us."

"When he came to tell me about this," Ichiro began slowly, "I asked him if that was what he really wanted to do, regardless of the consequences, and he said yes. I told him I would respect his decision."

Kinuko sat stunned for a moment. Respect his decision? She felt something hot flaring up inside her. Words formed at the back of her throat; does he think it's all right for his son to die? She began trembling and stammered, "I—I thought you believed life was more precious than anything else. If—if...." She gasped and couldn't continue.

Ichiro nodded and began softly, "Yes, I do believe that life is precious. That's why I'm against war, and the same goes with Giichi. I'm not saying I want him to die, no, of course not, never. But life is not only about our bodies—it's about our souls as well, Kinuko."

Now, against her will, tears streamed down her cheeks. Though she had feared he might not agree to help, she had not anticipated such heartlessness. She cried quietly, pressing her kerchief against her eyes.

"Listen, Kinuko," Ichiro said. "Unfortunately, we live in very, very difficult times. We are all tested in times like these. Each of us has to make decisions about how we will live. It's not easy. Some, like Giichi, were born to make the most difficult decision."

Kinuko kept dabbing her eyes, as if she hadn't heard him. Ichiro gazed at the middle of the table where the weak light reflected from the window, his right hand cupping his left elbow. He expelled a small, almost inaudible sigh before he spoke again.

"I understand how you feel, because I feel exactly as you do now."

"Oh, Father," Kinuko sobbed.

Ichiro frowned, his eyes on the table. "Kinuko, would you like to stay for lunch? I will tell Ume to fix something for us." He rose to his knees.

"Oh, no, please don't. I have to go home." Kinuko straightened herself; she wiped her eyes and touched her kimono collar. Ichiro sat again. Kinuko smoothed the wrinkles of her kerchief. "So, you are not even going to tell Giichi to think more about this. Is that what you are saying to me?"

"I know it sounds cruel, but it is his decision. I don't think he would change his mind just because I told him, anyway."

He turned his gaze through the glass panel to a pine tree which cast shadows on the surface of the pond. For a while Kinuko watched his gray temple, his pale profile. "I have to go, Father," she said abruptly. She stood, and immediately Ichiro stood too, lifting himself by pushing his hands against the table.

"I'm sorry, Kinuko, I'm so very sorry." Ichiro straightened the front of his kimono absent-mindedly and stepped around the table. "If something happens to Giichi,

Mother and I will take care of you and the children no matter what. I have promised that to Giichi."

At the corner of the table, he dropped his gaze for a while. Then he looked up. "Kinuko, he might—he might not receive the red paper, that is just a possibility. He hasn't been drafted so far, possibly because of his hearing or his job, and I'm hoping the war will end before that happens. But we must keep in mind that hope sometimes weakens the mind, maybe even poisons it, so don't hold your hopes high."

Not knowing what to say, Kinuko walked out of the room, and Ichiro followed her into the corridor. Neither of them spoke until they reached the gate, where Ichiro's bonsai sat on a wooden table.

"Take care, Kinuko," he said.

"You too, Father." She tried to hide her hostility. They stood facing each other for a few seconds without looking into each other's eyes. Then Kinuko walked through the gate. "Be careful now," he called to her. Kinuko turned and bowed without smiling, then hurried to the main street, where less than an hour ago she had stepped from the streetcar with a thread of hope tucked in her chest.

Kinuko boarded the tram for Kobe and sat amid the smells of stale wax, leather shoes, and wooden clogs. Fewer than twenty passengers were scattered throughout the car, all looking as if steeped in the knowledge that the peace of the morning might soon evaporate. They didn't know when the first air raid warning would come or where they would be when it came. Kinuko looked out the window toward the coast, where chimneys exhaled black smoke and the sea wind carried it inland, until it tapered off into the gray sky. The tram moved west toward a jumble of factories and poor homes: tin roofs, black tiles, cement, and wood, all weathered under the pale light of winter.

Kinuko placed an arm on the back of the seat in front of her and rested her forehead on it. The sickness from that morning had returned, only worse now as it mixed sourly with her anger toward Ichiro and the tight knot of loneliness around her heart. She began to think that deep down Giichi was probably just as heartless as his father. Yes, she had known their way of thinking, and most likely it was part of the attraction that had drawn her to marry Giichi. She felt as if she were being punished for her youthful rebellion. She decided she would never take a penny from Ichiro, even if she had to beg on the streets after Giichi was gone. Never!

An air-raid warning interrupted Kinuko's anger; its shriek smothered her like an invisible blanket—loud, furious, and urgent. The tram's brakes screeched. Some passengers were thrown against the seats in front of them. Those who had sprung up at the sound of the siren lost their balance and stumbled forward in the aisle. The tram settled to a stop with its front half on a bridge above the Muko River. All around them erupted a mad fury of black fumes from racing engines, auto horns, and bicycle bells. Drivers screamed at the cars ahead of them to keep moving. A few bicyclists pushed their way forward, ringing their bells shrilly, weaving between trucks and pedestrians.

Along the riverbank, a group of old men stumbled over white pebbles, heading for the safety of the bridge. They jerked their filthy kimonos up so they could move faster, revealing dingy long underwear. Some of them clutched handfuls of cigarette butts they'd collected along the river, holding them as carefully as if they were nuggets of gold.

Shafts of light poured through the openings in the clouds hovering over Osaka Bay to the south. Out of those clouds three bombers appeared suddenly and swept low toward the shore, advancing in a triangular formation. Kinuko saw tiny specks drop from the planes like black eggs. In an instant balls of fire mushroomed from the ground, then shot up in thick columns of black smoke. Kinuko watched as if viewing a movie. The shocking images came so quickly that they seemed unreal. She felt as if the world had stopped. Slowly, she realized that her house was in the same direction as the explosions. She thought of Yuki and pulled the kerchief out of her sleeve and pressed it to her mouth.

Several men lurched to the side of the carriage and craned their necks for a better view.

"Look!"

"Kobe, it must be near Kobe Harbor!"

"No, it's closer than that, maybe the Kawashima shipyard."

The shipyard—Mr. Chiba! Kinuko's stomach tightened. She coughed and spit a bitter yellow liquid into her kerchief. An image of Mr. Chiba pedaling away on his bicycle swam at the backs of her eyes.

The bombers flashed over the highway ahead and rushed toward the mountains, then turned and flew back over the bay, disappearing into the clouds. When sirens sounded the all-clear, the driver started the engine, and edged the tram cautiously forward. All around the world began to move again as if awakening from a violent sleep. Bicycles, carts, and trucks pushed forward on both sides, spilling onto the iron rails. They inched forward, then stopped to accommodate the bicyclists and pedestrians, then moved again, screeching and purring. Inside, the men chattered ceaselessly, peering out the windows, staring at the enormous black clouds of smoke drifting toward them.

"I'm almost sure it's the shipyard, see those chimneys there? It's hard to see because of the smoke, but—"

"You're right, it must be the shipyard."

By the time they approached her stop, the wind had pushed the smoke toward the mountains over Kobe. Kinuko held the soaked kerchief over her mouth as she shuffled toward the door. Her forehead felt clammy. She propelled herself home toward Yuki and Mrs. Chiba.

CHAPTER 3

Once more Giichi dipped his pen into the glass inkwell on his desk. Though he had arrived at his Osaka office earlier than usual, he had made little progress on the stack of documents piled on the wooden tray. Images of Kinuko constantly distracted him—her stunned words as she begged him to change his mind, the paleness of her profile over the kitchen sink, her refusal of his offer to stay home. With each new image, his guilt deepened. He had already called home several times with no answer. Where could she be? Or worse, perhaps she didn't want to talk to him. That would be understandable. He realized now how difficult the last three months must have been for her.

It seemed so stupid now—sitting in bars, drinking sake he didn't even want, delaying his departure for home, evading her efforts at conversation, sleeping with his back to her; all at a time when excitement for their second child should have drawn them closer together. He thought of her smile the day she announced her pregnancy—the radiant, cloudless smile he loved.

"I hope it will be a boy this time," she said. She wore an iris-patterned cotton yukata after her bath, a blue *obi* tied neatly around her narrow waist. She was so beautiful, so incredibly beautiful. Though the hardships of war had stolen the luster from her hair and the glow from her face, she radiated with the joy of another child. And yet, even then, he had to admit, something clouded the beauty he saw in her. He wondered how she could be so happy amidst a raging war.

A few weeks after her announcement, his friend Matsui received the red paper, and Giichi knew he couldn't wait any longer to decide. Matsui was the latest among his small circle of friends to be drafted. Like himself, Matsui had been classified B-1, backup reserves, for his physical problem—severe near-sightedness. Giichi had a hearing problem caused by a blow over his left ear during a military drill when in middle school. But by then, October 1944, all of the men on the active list had been drafted, as well as most of the B-1s.

The day Matsui left Giichi had gone to the Osaka train station to see him off. He stayed at the back of the crowd of Matsui's family and friends, watching them wave rising sun flags and hearing roars of banzai along the train. As the train moved from the station, his friend waved to him, terror showing through his weak smile, and Giichi looked away guiltily. He saw Matsui's little boy waving a tiny flag and thought of Matsui going to war to kill the fathers of other children. He wondered what Matsui would tell his son of his experiences, if he was fortunate enough to come home, and with that thought, Giichi knew that he would refuse the red paper. But the joyous image of Kinuko kept swirling in his head. "Hope it will be a boy...." How could he tell her without destroying her joy?

That day he began what would become his ritual of avoidance. Each evening after work he walked to the Osaka train terminal, bought the evening paper at a tiny stand, and then wandered into the labyrinth of alleys behind the terminal. He would step into the entry of bar after bar and peer into the murky red lantern light for an empty corner table. When he found one, he would slip into the thick smoke, the pungent smell of sake, and the noise of drunken chatter and rousing war songs. He always sat alone, ordered a bottle of sake, and opened his newspaper. For hours he would sip the bitter drink and stare at the newspaper, though he had difficulty focusing on any of the articles. News of the war reassured him that he had made the right decision but also reminded him of his high school friend Tanaka, whom he had visited at the Wakayama Sanitarium in the summer of 1938.

Tanaka had been drafted in 1936 and sent to China, where the Japanese army was about to advance south through Tientsin, Shanghai, Nanking, Hangchow and Canton. Two years later he was sent home to recover from tuberculosis.

During his visit, Giichi found his once light-hearted friend a changed man, dark and morose. Before leaving Giichi wished him a prompt recovery, but Tanaka blurted out that he would rather stay sick than get well and go back to war.

A few weeks later, Giichi received a long letter from Tanaka, secretly delivered by a mutual friend to avoid military censorship. Giichi destroyed the letter as Tanaka advised, but wiping the memory of it from his mind was not so easy. Following Yuki's birth in June 1941, the letter's images came back more strongly than ever. He couldn't look at his daughter or hold her in his arms without remembering the words on the final page: *"I hated with all my soul the captain who ordered me to commit these crimes, but I hate myself even more. One day while our unit was searching a house for soldiers of the Chinese Nationalist Army, our captain, irritated by a crying baby, told one of our soldiers to throw the baby up in the air. When the soldier refused his order, the captain shot him. Then he turned to me and gave me the same order. When I threw the baby into the air, he caught it on his bayonet."*

Though Giichi spent much of his time in the smoky Osaka bars trying to evade the memory of Tanaka's letter, his mind inevitably turned to the first real steps of his spiritual growth. He had grown up in the aura of his father's idealism. If not for the influence of his father, he knew that like much of his generation he would never have questioned Japan's aggression into China and willingly gone to war, believing that this war was to eradicate Western influence in Asia.

Though Giichi was born after the worst of his father's financial struggles, he learned at an early age how much Ichiro had sacrificed for his ideals. As the only son of a landlord, his father could have assumed management of the family's property and slipped into the comfort they had known for generations. Instead, after graduating from the Imperial University of Tokyo with a degree in literature, he went to work for a newspaper in Osaka where he hoped to develop his writing skills and gain financial independence from his family. His ultimate dream was to write novels revealing the depth of pain caused by social injustice. For seven years he chased news with a notepad and a pencil, seven days a week, twelve hours a day. He ate a meager bowl of udon twice a day to save money so he could quit the newspaper and start his first book.

After Ichiro married Sumiko, they moved into a tiny rented house in Tennoji, Osaka, where Giichi was later born. Ichiro started selling short stories here and there and shifted to part-time work at the newspaper. Sumiko helped out by teaching the tea ceremony in a rented room at a nearby temple. Four years later, around the time of Giichi's birth, Ichiro's debut novel, *North Wind*, was published and met with sufficient success for Sumiko to stay home and take care of Giichi.

Giichi remembered that his father always wrote in a modest room of four-and-a-half tatamis. His small, simple desk stood low to the floor, and the cushion he sat on retained permanent contours from the weight of his time spent writing. On his desk lay a thick frayed dictionary of *Kojien* next to a lamp covered by a cheap aluminum half-moon shade. When Giichi was five, his father's second novel was published, and the family moved to the house near Osaka Harbor, where his father kept a larger office and where his parents still lived.

The happiness of Giichi's childhood fractured when he was nine. By then, Ichiro had already received a death threat from a dangerous right wing group. His father's steady succession of novels had drawn increasing praise from reviewers, and amid growing popularity, his father had begun writing essays that more directly challenged social injustice and militarism. Black police cars showed up at their house, and officers stomped inside to search his father's office. The first time Giichi saw his father taken away for questioning his heart jumped with fear. He flailed at one of the policemen who led Ichiro away. "Don't take my father," he cried, tugging at the officer's sleeve. As his mother pulled him away, Ichiro said, "Son, I haven't done anything wrong. I'll be home soon. Just take care of your mother." Tears pooled in his eyes as he tried to wriggle out of his mother's grasp.

During the next several years, Giichi grew accustomed to the cold metallic glint of handcuffs, shiny black cars, and the rough hands of officers jerking on his father's arms. But what he never grew accustomed to was his mother's sorrow. When Ichiro was gone, Giichi and his mother slept in the same room to give each other comfort.

"Don't worry about your father and never be ashamed of him," his mother would say, her face sallow and her hands resting majestically on her lap. "He is a courageous man who writes what others are afraid to write. Someday everyone will realize that. So lay your head down in peace and go to sleep."

Despite her reassuring words, he saw that she huddled in a ball and her thin shoulders trembled after she assumed he had gone to sleep. One night, Giichi leaned toward her, not caring if she knew he was awake; he only wanted to comfort her. "When I grow up," he said, "I won't do anything to make you feel sad."

At the end of Giichi's long evenings in the bars behind Osaka Terminal, the memory of his promise to his mother would linger in his mind. He recalled that as he was growing up, despite his respect for his father, he wanted more than anything to spare his mother additional anguish. He wanted nothing more than a normal life: the smell of miso soup, clean sheets, and the warmth of a family after a day's work. Above all, when he married, he didn't want to inflict on his wife the same sorrow his father had inflicted upon his mother. So each night as the bar emptied and he knew that he must go home, he faced his greatest quandary.

He no longer doubted his decision. He was willing to die for his beliefs, but still the question remained—how could he tell Kinuko without making her feel what his mother had felt? Night after night when he returned home, he thought of their second child growing in Kinuko's womb, and yet he felt a distance growing between them as deep and silent as a mountain lake. He worried that if he didn't tell her soon, they might grow hopelessly distant from each other. Still, he couldn't decide how to tell her.

At noon Giichi put down his pen and took the aluminum lunch box from his brown leather bag. Then he distractedly rolled a set of chopsticks between his hands. Now that he had told Kinuko his decision, it seemed that all of those months of worry had been futile. Perhaps he had already forfeited her love. And worse, if the red paper came she and the children would suffer even more. He dipped the chopsticks into his lunch pail and pulled out a pickled plum. As its sharp sourness spread through his mouth the door squeaked open.

Giichi looked up and saw Mr. Kato pressing his stocky body between the door frame and the swinging door.

"They finally did it, didn't they?" his boss boomed.

Giichi lowered his chopsticks and stared at him.

"Haven't you heard?" asked Mr. Kato. "I thought everybody knew by now. It was the Kawashima shipyard, bombed. We could be next!"

"The shipyard?" Giichi pushed his chair back and stood. His stomach tightened at the thought of Mr. Chiba.

"Yes, it was bad this time; nothing like the small fires caused by B-25s. Looks like they'll be using B-29s from now on."

"You say it was bad?" Giichi asked timidly. "At the shipyard?"

"Yes, the worst bombing ever in Hanshin, they say," Mr. Kato replied, backing toward the doorway. "As I said, B-29s, just like in Tokyo."

Mr. Kato vanished into the hallway. As soon as the swinging door settled on its hinges, Giichi placed another call to Kinuko for any news of Mr. Chiba, but again there was no answer. He imagined Kinuko and Yuki in the bomb shelter. Or were they at the Chibas? But there was no telephone there. He closed his lunch box and pushed it back into his bag.

Shortly before one o'clock, the telephone rang. It was his father. "Have you heard about the Kawashima shipyard bombing?" Ichiro asked.

"Yes, I just did." Giichi's voice sounded hollow even to himself.

"I wonder—," said Ichiro. "I'm worried about Kinuko. She thinks the world of the Chibas. If something has happened, it would be a terrible shock to her."

"Yes, it would. I've been trying to call her all morning, but there has been no answer."

"Son—you might want to go home early to be with her, and to be of any help to Mrs. Chiba if—of course, it's your business, but—"

"I wish I could, but unfortunately, I have a meeting this afternoon."

"Oh, I see. If that's the case, I'll keep trying to reach her. By the time you come out of the meeting, I might be able to tell you how she is doing."

"Thank you, Father, I'll let you know, too, if I learn anything."

Giichi looked out the window and saw the white banner on the wall of the building across the street. "Remember the Glory of Pearl Harbor." Its huge red characters, the color of the rising sun, rippled in the January breeze.

"What glory?" he muttered.

He turned to the glass window of his office door and studied the gold imprint on it: Sales and Marketing, First Section Manager—reversed in his view. He had been promoted to that position eight days before Pearl Harbor, when the former manager, also a graduate of the Imperial University of Kyoto, was drafted. The new title never meant anything to him, especially after Pearl Harbor, when Nippon Motors, one of the nation's largest automobile manufacturers, evolved into a producer of military trucks, tanks, and jeeps. His main duty was to negotiate contracts with the military. There was little negotiation; the military basically defined its terms. By now, the survival of the company depended upon the military. In the dismal war economy, there wasn't enough money in the private sector for luxury items like cars.

Giichi turned back to the window and glowered at the Pearl Harbor banner. Though he was not in the army actually killing people, he was still part of the war machine, helping to build equipment that killed people. He shook his head, unable to sort it all out.

Later in the afternoon when he returned from the Nippon Motors managers' meeting, it was raining. He stared out his office window for a few minutes before placing another unanswered call to Kinuko. There were no messages from his father, so he assumed Kinuko must be at the Chibas. Giichi sat at his desk, pondering his meeting that afternoon with Kenji Nakayama, his best friend from university days. He had not seen Kenji in nearly two months.

A misty rain continued to settle on the street below, where a ragged paperboy screamed, "Extra, Extra!" as he carried a bundle of freshly printed newssheets over his scrawny shoulder. Giichi went to the hall and sent a female clerk down to the street with two one-sen coins. When she returned with the wet newspaper, Giichi glanced at the top headline, wadded the paper in his fist, and angrily tossed the ball into the wastebasket. The headline announced, "B-29 Attack Hits Kawashima Shipyard, Search for Survivors Continues."

At five o'clock, Giichi cleared his desk. He took a thick envelope filled with ten-yen bills from beneath a stack of papers in a bottom drawer and slipped it into the inside chest pocket of his suit coat. Then he pulled his winter coat and fedora from the stand in the corner and walked out. The building's only elevator was filled with clamorous conversation about the shipyard bombing.

"It's better to go straight home on a day like this."

"The radio said there might be more bombings."

"Even if it's raining?"

"Doesn't matter. They use radar."

"Exactly. Better not stop for sake."

Nervous laughter.

When Giichi reached the ground floor and stepped through the revolving door onto the street, he found the rain falling harder than it had appeared from his office window. He realized he didn't have his umbrella. Kinuko always reminded him of such details, but she hadn't this morning.

Normally, on evenings when he was to meet Kenji, he walked to the terminal and then to the designated bar; but without an umbrella, he decided to take a streetcar. He reached into his pants pocket to find the right change and waited under the eaves of the building. Gray dusk shifted into night. Lights went on here and there in buildings across the way and reflected on the wet asphalt of the street.

Soon the sidewalk was covered with a dense flow of office workers hurrying toward the terminal, their black umbrellas bobbing in the cold rain. The sight gave Giichi strange comfort. With these many men still around, why should he worry about being drafted? As a streetcar approached he pushed his fedora more firmly onto his head and rushed into the pressing mass of workers. The streetcar was already packed beyond capacity, and Giichi had to stand in the doorwell. He kept his hand pressed against the envelope inside his suit coat, holding it tightly to his chest. The streetcar stopped only twice before the Osaka terminal, and by five-fifteen, Giichi stepped onto the slick pavement. He started immediately toward the terminal building, taking the shortest route to the bar three blocks away where he was to meet Kenji Nakayama.

As he passed the entrance to the tram platform, Giichi saw a fresh notice pasted on the wall, announcing that tram service had been canceled for the evening due to the threat of Allied attacks. The last tram bound for Kobe would leave at 5:30, it said. He stopped amid the stream of passengers hurrying to the platform and looked at his watch—five-twenty. His mind raced: he could go to the bar and keep his commitment to Kenji Nakayama, then go by streetcar to his parents' home and sleep there for the night. But that wouldn't work; both Kinuko and his father would surely wonder why he hadn't gone home.

Along the platform, the last tram for Kobe swallowed a stream of passengers, its top glistening in the rain. Giichi stood motionless, torn by indecision. Once again, he pressed his hand against the envelope in his breast pocket. Well, he thought, I can always meet Kenji tomorrow. He moved onto the platform and hurried toward the tram. He edged through cracks in the human wall and found a standing spot near the front of the carriage, knowing this would be the first time he had ever failed to show up for a designated meeting with Kenji Nakayama. He hoped Kenji would understand and imagined his friend sitting alone in a corner of the bar in his ill-fitting suit.

When he arrived home, Giichi took his shoes off in the dark entryway and glanced into the faintly illuminated front room. Kinuko didn't come out to greet him, but soon, Yuki ran through the front room, announcing, "Papa, I was a good girl today."

"What did you do?" Giichi lifted her up in his arms and carried her into the dining room, where a sheet of paper and crayons lay on the candlelit table.

"I stayed with Mrs. Chiba, and I didn't cry when Mama went to see Grandpa."

Giichi winced, feeling an instant ache for Kinuko. He knew why she had gone to see his father, and knew, as well, that he had probably disappointed her. "That's good," Giichi said. "I'm glad you were a good girl."

Another candle burned on the kitchen counter, and Giichi saw Kinuko making rice balls in the dim light beneath it. He assumed the rice balls were for relatives gathered at the Chibas' and ached even more for her.

Kinuko looked up. "Welcome home," she said tersely, then quickly averted her eyes. With Yuki still in his arms, Giichi asked, "Have you heard anything about Mr. Chiba?"

Without looking up, Kinuko said, "No," and kept forming rice balls in her hands.

"I'm very sorry," Giichi mumbled. "I know how worried you must be."

He saw tears brimming from her eyes and watched her raise her arm and swipe her sleeve across them.

"How is Mrs. Chiba?"

"She's all right," replied Kinuko, her voice cracking a little.

"I'll go see her."

"You should."

Yuki slipped out of Giichi's arms and picked up a crayon from the dining table. "I can draw bombers, Papa," she said. "See? Boom, boom, boom."

For a while, Giichi stood in a daze and watched his daughter add finishing touches to her drawing of airplanes.

"Flowers would be better," he heard Kinuko say sharply from the kitchen. "Draw flowers, Yuki," she added.

"Yes, that would be better," Giichi agreed, realizing how much Kinuko must regret not having the time or materials to do her own painting. He looked into the kitchen. "Do you want me to take those rice balls to Mrs. Chiba?"

"No, I'll take them when I'm done." Her face was tight and pale.

Giichi left the house without the rice balls and made his way across the street. In the Chibas' entryway, an equally pale Mrs. Chiba greeted him. He repeated words of hopeful condolence in a muffled voice.

"Please come in," said Mrs. Chiba.

In her candlelit dining room, four men sat around the table, their faces creased in the nimbus of light—Mr. Chiba's cousin from Nara, another of his cousins from Akashi, Mrs. Chiba's cousin from west Kobe, and their old friend from Hirakata. After being introduced to each of them, Giichi again repeated halting condolences, then joined in the circle and exchanged a few words about how to find out Mr. Chiba's fate. Mrs. Chiba hung her head and fought back tears. Everyone fell silent.

The door opened quietly, and Kinuko came into the dining room with the tray of rice balls. Yuki followed her, clinging to Kinuko's monpe pants. Mrs. Chiba stood and thanked Kinuko over and over again.

"I'll get tea ready," Kinuko said to Mrs. Chiba.

"Oh no, I can do that, Kinuko-san. Please go home with Giichi-san. It's getting late for Yuki-chan. It has been a very long day."

Kinuko turned to Giichi. "Would you take Yuki home and feed her? I left our supper on the table. I would like to stay here with Mrs. Chiba for a while."

Her voice sounded startlingly unemotional. "Of—of course," he said. Giichi stood and stretched his hand to Yuki, but Yuki whined, "I want Mama to come home, too."

"Please," the Nara cousin said, "we'll be here all night, unless the trams begin moving, which is most unlikely. Please take her home, both of you."

Mrs. Chiba joined in, "Besides, an air raid warning might come soon. The neighborhood chief said he had ordered the whole neighborhood not to use electric light. So please go home together."

Everyone around the table nodded. Giichi glanced at Kinuko, hoping she would agree. Kinuko looked at Mrs. Chiba and they exchanged a sad gaze, their eyes blinking with tears.

"I'm all right, Kinuko-san," Mrs. Chiba said finally.

"Please, let me know if you need me," said Kinuko, and the two women held each other's hands for a moment.

Around eight o'clock, the radio announced bombings in Akashi, a city west of Kobe. At midnight came word that the Amagasaki plant of the Nishihama Steel and Heavy

Industry Company was hit and burning out of control. Yuki fell asleep in Kinuko's arms as the three sat quietly in the bomb shelter beneath their house.

After the all-clear sounded, Kinuko put Yuki to bed while Giichi shivered in the dark kitchen, gazing eastward at the red sky above Amagasaki. He wondered which would come first, the red paper or death in an air raid. As he pondered, he heard Kinuko come out of Yuki's room and then step into the guest bedroom, without speaking to him.

Across the street, no light shone from the Chiba house; but he felt certain Mrs. Chiba was still awake, sitting in the dark just like he was.

CHAPTER 4

The next morning, Kinuko got up early and hurried to the Chibas to help prepare breakfast for the visitors. After the men finished eating, she helped Mrs. Chiba wash dishes. Shortly afterward Giichi arrived with Yuki still in her pajamas.

"I decided to take the day off from work," he said to Kinuko and then delivered phone messages to Mrs. Chiba, including one from Katoko, the Chibas' daughter in Hiroshima. "I told her I would come and get you," he said, "but she heard Yuki crying and insisted that she call back in the afternoon."

"Thank you, Giichi-san. I'm sorry you had to take a day off from work because of this."

"Please don't worry. We all have to help find Mr. Chiba."

Kinuko took Yuki from Giichi, and he faced the men around the table. "I called the shipyard office in downtown Kobe several times, but the phone was always busy. Perhaps the radio will announce the names of the injured who were taken to hospitals."

They all nodded while Kinuko turned the radio on, but the news was about the evacuation of neighborhoods near military plants. Officials throughout Hanshin, expecting more bombings, ordered residents in those areas to seek shelter elsewhere. A combined task force of firemen, national guardsmen, vigilance corpsmen and local students would begin demolishing some of the homes in the abandoned areas to create fire lanes, making it easier to isolate bomb-related fires from the plants themselves. Affected families would be given cash compensation, a fivefold increase in food rations, and free canned goods. The announcer continued, "In most areas, this action will go into effect as early as this afternoon—"

"That is going to slow the rescue efforts," Giichi said. "Most men will be busy building the fire lane. I don't think we can depend on the officials to find Mr. Chiba. How about if we divide up and go to all the hospitals in Kobe? If each one of us visits three or four, we might be able to find him in several hours."

The visitors agreed, nodding and grunting.

Yuki, who had dozed off in Kinuko's arms, awoke and began to fuss. While the men discussed who would go to which hospitals, Mrs. Chiba urged Kinuko to go home.

"Poor Yuki-chan," she said. "How can she sleep with all this chatter?"

Kinuko agreed and carried her daughter back across the street. Once home, she knelt beside Yuki and patted her back, but when Yuki was just about to fall asleep, Kinuko heard the front door open, and then the shrill voice of Mrs. Hayashi, wife of the neighborhood chief. Frustrated, Kinuko hurried to the front room. When she saw the neatly folded khaki national uniform draped over Mrs. Hayashi's arm, her stomach knotted.

"As you might have noticed," Mrs. Hayashi began, "your husband is the only one who hasn't been wearing the national uniform in our neighborhood."

With Yuki's cries erupting from her room, Mrs. Hayashi continued, "My husband hopes Mr. Sekihara understands the necessity of keeping the neighborhood's spirits high, especially after what happened yesterday—"

"Let me go get some money."

Kinuko hurried to the kitchen where she kept her shopping basket and came back with her billfold. She quickly handed three ten-yen bills to Mrs. Hayashi, whose pursed lips and thin jutting face seemed to indicate an eagerness to pursue her lecture.

"My daughter hasn't been getting enough sleep lately," Kinuko said.

Mrs. Hayashi laid the uniform on the tatami floor of the front room, and Kinuko stepped down to the entryway to open the door for her. Kinuko forced a smile and bowed as Mrs. Hayashi stepped outside without another word. Kinuko left the uniform on the floor and returned to Yuki's room to coax her daughter back to sleep.

Sometime later, she heard Giichi return and go to the telephone. "Kawashima shipyard office," he shouted to the operator. A few seconds later, he slammed the receiver down. "Still busy!"

"Please," said Kinuko, "I just put Yuki to sleep."

"Sorry," said Giichi.

Kinuko picked up the uniform—a jacket, trousers and puttees, and held them out to him, hopeful that he would agree to wear them without argument. Giichi hesitated for a second. "Listen," he said. "I just spoke with Mr. Obata, the retired fireman. He said Mr. Chiba's name isn't on the list of injured who were taken to hospitals...or on the list of the dead."

"What does that mean?"

"Mr. Obata said it would be no use to visit the hospitals. He said the lists are pretty accurate."

"What does that mean?" Kinuko repeated. She began to tremble and staggered to the window.

"Please—let's not lose hope," she heard Giichi say.

She clutched the windowsill, feeling the last glimmer of hope vanishing, and stared at the Chibas' house across the street.

After a long moment, she said in a low voice, "So Mr. Chiba is dead."

"That's not necessarily true," Giichi insisted.

Sadness filled her chest and grew into a sorrow she didn't think she could bear. She turned mechanically and became oddly aware of the weight of the uniform on her arm. She lifted it toward Giichi. "Oh, this," she said.

"What about it?"

She thought for a moment, trying to recall what it was she meant to tell him, but she was too sad to talk about anything. She shuffled past him and went into Yuki's room where she sat and stared into space blankly, the uniform still draped over her arm.

Later, the phone rang again and Kinuko heard Giichi answer it.

"Oh, Katoko-san," he said helplessly to the Chibas' daughter. "No, the situation doesn't look good...yes...I'm sorry...I'll get your mother right away."

After Giichi left, Kinuko went to the phone.

"Katoko-san?" she said, and then didn't know what to say next.

Katoko's familiar voice came through the phone, clear and high, resembling Mrs. Chiba's. She apologized for calling so often and thanked Kinuko and Giichi for letting her mother use their telephone. "I wish I could be there," she continued, "but my midwife says I shouldn't travel. The baby might be only a few days away."

"I understand," Kinuko said. "Please don't worry about your mother. My husband and I will take care of her."

When Giichi returned with Mrs. Chiba, Kinuko handed the phone to her and sat in the dining room. As Mrs. Chiba began speaking, Kinuko could no longer hold her tears. She remembered how much Mr. Chiba looked forward to her and Katoko's babies, and now he might not be on this earth to see them.

In the kitchen, Mrs. Chiba clutched the receiver. "Yes, I'm all right. Giichi-san and Kinuko-san have been so kind. Don't worry about me. You just take care of yourself. I'll be praying for you and the baby."

After Mrs. Chiba left, Kinuko remained at the dining table, thinking about Mr. Chiba and how hard he had worked for his family since coming from Fukui. He had been only sixteen when he first came to Hanshin from a small fishing village on the Sea of Japan with five ten-sen coins in his pocket. After seven years of backbreaking labor, he finally gained a promotion.

"They gave me a position of pencils and books," was the way he said it, when he related the story to Kinuko. Once settled, he humbly asked his parents to arrange a bride for him. A year later, Sanae, the fourth daughter of a Buddhist priest, arrived in the city to join him in marriage.

Kinuko knew how frugally the Chibas lived—they purchased only the barest necessities and set aside every spare sen for the education of their son Takushi, who studied engineering at a nearby college. Mr. Chiba looked forward to the day of Takushi's graduation, when his son would achieve something he had not. Instead,

Takushi received the red paper a year before his graduation and went with the infantry to Burma. Still, the Chibas didn't utter a word of complaint. They never struggled unnecessarily against things they couldn't change. They were grateful for their blessings. Their attitude was in keeping with their belief that they were simply traveling through this life and would be reborn in the next.

Sitting at the dining table, Kinuko smiled sadly, remembering how she and Giichi laughed when Mr. Chiba joked that he might be an American in his next life.

By mid-afternoon, traffic on the Hanshin Highway was clogged with trucks and carts, all sagging under loads of household possessions, as families migrated from their homes near war-related factories. On her way to the Chibas, Kinuko stopped in the street and watched the procession—mounds of tables, desks, chests, futons, and kitchen utensils, representing whole lives, or even generations of family life in homes that would soon be destroyed. She sympathized with those whose lives were suddenly uprooted from the homes they loved. Still, she envied their closeness—husbands pulling carts with their wives and children walking alongside them. Though they didn't know what awaited them at their destinations, they were at least together.

When she walked into the entryway of the Chiba's house, she was greeted by silence. The shoes of the visitors were gone. Kinuko understood that they were eager to get home to their own families before the next bombings. Mrs. Chiba sat in her empty house rummaging through an old wicker trunk for a photo of Mr. Chiba. Stacks of old furoshiki, yukata, and Takushi's childhood clothes were heaped next to the trunk. She greeted Kinuko and then reached into the trunk for a brown envelope filled with photos. She gently pulled one of the photos from the envelope, gazed at it fondly for a while, and then handed it to Kinuko.

"This is the only photo of him I have," she said.

The photo was old and brittle, aged a sepia color. In it, Mr. Chiba wore a dark suit. He was young and handsome, yet he appeared slightly uncomfortable.

"It was taken twenty years ago," Mrs. Chiba said, "when he was awarded by the shipyard for having served for twenty years. That was the first time in his life he had a suit made."

Kinuko handed the photo back to her, and Mrs. Chiba smoothed it repeatedly against her lap.

"Would you like to come to my house?" Kinuko asked. "I came to help you with supper for your visitors, but they are gone. I don't want you to be alone."

"Thank you," Mrs. Chiba said, "but I should stay home. I want to be here when he comes home."

That evening, their neighbor Mr. Obata, the retired fireman, came to their house to inform them that Mr. Chiba's body had been recovered. The long wait was over. Kinuko felt as if a limb had been severed from her body. She wondered what had gone through Mr. Chiba's mind at the very moment of his death. Most likely, he didn't have time to think of anything. If he did, his only regret must have been that he had to leave his loved ones behind. She told herself that he had died in peace; he had lived a full life. He was kind and considerate. He worked hard and loved his family. A person like that wouldn't leave any regrets dangling between this earth and another world, if such a place existed.

She wondered if she would be able to accept death in the same way. Once more she hoped that if death must come, it would take all of them—her and Yuki and Giichi. Then she would have no regrets. Strangely, amid her sorrow, she remembered the national uniform and how much it meant to keeping her family together.

After supper, Kinuko put Yuki to bed and approached Giichi, who sat forlornly at the dining table staring at the day's newspaper. She began calmly but with determination. "Mrs. Hayashi brought the national uniform today. She said her husband expects..."

"Please," said Giichi, turning the paper roughly, "let's not talk about that now."

His response made her more determined to make him understand.

"Why not? You never know what Mr. Hayashi will do. He took a ration card from the Koyamas just because they didn't attend a fire drill. I have the feeling—"

"There was a case like that in Tokyo. The family sued and won. The Koyamas should do the same. That would help stop neighborhood chiefs from abusing their power. If each one of us had stood up against injustice, this damned war wouldn't have started in the first place."

"But you aren't talking about reality. Do you really think it's possible for anyone to stand up against—"

"I'm not going to wear a national uniform."

"All right," said Kinuko, "but please don't refuse the red paper. That is a matter of life or death. You shouldn't take it so lightly." She felt her voice cracking against his stubbornness.

"I've never taken it lightly—never."

For a moment she was frightened by the sharp glint in his eyes, but she couldn't remain silent. "I don't understand," she shot back. "Why can't you see it's so foolish? It's not going to change a thing in the world."

"I am not trying to change anything. I just don't want to go to war to kill another human being. They've killed Mr. Chiba. They went to war and killed him. That's what going to war does. I cannot do that."

Kinuko trembled at the unwavering conviction in his voice. "I just want us all to die together."

"Kinuko, you are the one who must face reality. Even if I went into the army, it would be unlikely that we would all die together."

When she started to cry, Giichi came around the table and sat next to her. "Listen," he said with a sigh as he put his hand on her knee. "The war could end before I get the red paper. And if not, it could end while I'm in jail. There is hope."

But Kinuko could feel none; she could only think of Giichi being tortured. Sorrow and fatigue drained her mind. Numbly she brushed the grains of rice Yuki had spilled into a bowl and gathered the other dirty bowls from the table. She carried them into the kitchen, placed them in the sink and shuffled into the guest room. The worst seemed inevitable. She had feared the bombing of Hanshin, and it had happened. She had feared that Mr. Chiba would not be found alive, and that had proved true. Now she feared that Hayashi would inform on Giichi for not wearing the uniform.

CHAPTER 5

Giichi buttoned his suit coat in the empty bedroom. He wished Kinuko were there to console him as he embarked on this dreadful mission to claim Mr. Chiba's body. Yet he couldn't blame her for having decided to sleep in the guest bedroom.

He slowly crossed the street and paced in the Chibas' entryway, where Mrs. Chiba soon appeared and bowed stoically. "Thank you, Giichi-san," she said. "I can never repay you in a lifetime for all of your kindness."

They set out into the blustery wind, Mrs. Chiba carrying a froshiki bundle containing her husband's only suit. They boarded a tram bound for Kobe and sat next to each other silently. Thirty minutes later, they climbed off the tram and approached the bomb site through streets littered with tangled hoses and haphazardly parked fire trucks. Mrs. Chiba staggered against the fierce winds sweeping up from the pier. Giichi slowed his pace so she could keep up with him.

When they reached the flat plain where the shipyard buildings once stood, Giichi lifted the thick strand of rope encircling the wreckage so Mrs. Chiba could duck under it, and then stepped under it himself. They stopped and looked across the barren landscape, dazed by the wide-open view of the sea beyond the pier. It might have been beautiful, Giichi thought, if not for the sprawl of charred rubble, strewn with blackened iron pipes, lumber, barrels, twisted metal, and other objects mangled beyond recognition. A bulldozer pushed and groaned through the debris; a crane lifted the blackened skeleton of a truck; the white helmets of masked relief workers bobbed like corks amid a sea of destruction. To the west, three green army tents ballooned and swayed in a wind thick with a raw smell that reminded Giichi of the dead animals he sometimes found while playing in the woods as a child.

Giichi quietly shuddered as he thought of the vanished shipyard, where Mr. Chiba had worked for forty years since coming from Fukui. Then he saw Mrs. Chiba lower herself to a seated position and tuck the furoshiki bundle against her stomach. He leaned down and held her quaking shoulders. She gasped softly with her eyes closed, as if she wanted to cry but too shocked and sad to make actual tears.

"Are you all right?" Giichi whispered, and immediately felt foolish for asking such a question. Of course she wasn't all right. But he found himself repeating the same question without knowing what else to say. This time she nodded, and in a few moments she rose. He put his arm around her shoulders, and they made their way toward a makeshift plywood building at one corner of the site. A crowd milled in front of the building. Some bent over cobbled desks, tracing their fingers over the lists of victims. Relief workers in black raincoats with black cloth armbands moved in and out of the building, faces windburned and eyes red.

Nearby, workers stood with a rice ball in one hand and a teacup in the other, eating in a hurry, while a group of women wearing arm patches from the local neighborhood association boiled water over hibachis just outside the snapping rag door.

Giichi pressed into the crowd and scanned the list tacked to the desk. His heart began to pound, fearing that he might miss Mr. Chiba's name yet hoping he wouldn't find it at all. Soon, his finger stopped over the name written in pencil: Saburo Chiba, tent 2, coffin 3. Giichi felt dizzy with the sudden realization that Mr. Chiba was now a number. He closed his eyes, then edged out of the crowd. He glanced toward the tents as he walked back to Mrs. Chiba. She stood with a kerchief pressed against her mouth.

"Tent 2, number 3," he mumbled.

Mrs. Chiba looked at him as if he had spoken a foreign language. Then she nodded, her face suddenly filled with fear. As they approached the tent the stench of death grew stronger. They stopped outside the tent, and he remembered what Mr. Obata had told him about Mr. Chiba's body. "It's a horrible sight," he had whispered low enough so Kinuko couldn't hear. Mrs. Chiba stopped beside him. They stood only three feet from the opening to the tent, staring across a distance that seemed impossible to cross.

"Do you want to stay here?" asked Giichi. "I can go in alone."

"Please, come with me," pleaded Mrs. Chiba, her eyes fixed on the entrance. They delayed a few more seconds, then went inside, where the fabric of the tent created a muffled darkness. Naked light bulbs hung from a center beam and swayed slowly above their heads. Murky incense smoke rose from metal urns placed every few yards. Just below simple pine coffins lay in two rows.

Giichi quickly removed his fedora and squinted at the numbers pinned to the tent above each coffin. Soon he found number 3. When he lifted the lid, he froze. Mrs. Chiba took a sharp breath through her kerchief, and he tightened his grip around her shoulders. Black stubs of arms and legs projected from the torso. Only the slightly gapped front teeth, oddly white against a blackened face, suggested Mr. Chiba's identity.

For a moment Giichi felt as if he had been tricked into this place by foul magic. Life was not meant to contain such visions. He thought someone might tap him on the shoulder and tell him this wasn't real. But he felt Mrs. Chiba's body trembling in his arms and knew he must accept that life could be this foul. He noticed her lips moving and understood that she was trying to chant a sutra even though no sound came from her mouth except for a clattering of teeth. In his entire life Giichi had never felt this helpless. He began whispering a sutra in a rapid stream, his eyes closed, legs numb, *"Namuamidabutsu, namuamidabutsu, namuamidabutsu,."* and they huddled together. Finally, Giichi opened his eyes and bowed respectfully to Mr. Chiba and guided Mrs. Chiba from the tent.

Outside, Mrs. Chiba collapsed against him and they slumped to the ground together. She emitted a sharp, thin wail that pierced Giichi's heart, and his sense of helplessness turned to rage. He imagined a blue-eyed pilot poised to pull the lever that would drop the fatal bomb on Mr. Chiba. If only-if only-his mind spun, if only this pilot's soul, some inner voice, had told him there were other human beings working beneath the roof of the shipyard; then Mr. Chiba and the others now in coffins would still be alive. He felt hatred. Yet, within that dark cloud, he knew that it was not hatred of the pilot, but hatred of war itself, the hopelessness of war—a cold mechanism that one mere pilot couldn't change. Still, Giichi knew that he could never be like that pilot, who, back at his air base in Saipan or Tinian, had probably been praised by his superior for carrying out his "patriotic" deed. "Well done," his commander must have said, smoke curling from the pipe in his hand. Giichi felt contempt for the human capacity to sanctify cruelty in the name of patriotism. Now he knew war firsthand; it ripped into the core of his soul, and he wondered why he had ever questioned his decision.

"Sorry," whispered Mrs. Chiba, drying her tears.

"Are you all right?"

She nodded weakly and they pulled themselves up together.

They stopped at the table inside the entry to the bombsite and Giichi told the man the number of Mr. Chiba's coffin and gave him the name of the funeral home that would later pick up his body. On the way home they stopped at the funeral home, where Giichi made arrangements for the delivery of the body and left the only suit Mr. Chiba had owned in his life, so he could travel in it to another world.

CHAPTER 6

Mrs. Chiba walked with gritted teeth in complete silence. Waves of nausea kept pushing into her throat and with each step she took, and she had to clench her teeth harder until she thought her jaw might break. Being brought up the daughter of a Buddhist monk didn't even remotely prepare her for this moment. When she'd seen her husband's charred body, her feelings couldn't be more opposed to Buddha's teachings. She felt a burning hatred, such that she had never experienced in her whole life. Still, she wanted to stay calm for Giichi, who walked slowly beside her. She knew how hard it had also been for Giichi to have seen the blackened body of her husband. She didn't want to cause Giichi greater burden or embarrassment She tried hard to contain her anger but couldn't. How could she? Then she realized it wasn't her body that was shaking. Instead, it was the darkest hatred in her heart that made her tremble. She felt a strange comfort from that. Still, she set her jaw even tighter and walked with awkward steps. It was the longest trip home she had ever taken.

As soon as she reached her house, she dropped her usual demeanor. She yanked the door shut, leaving a startled Giichi on the other side, kicked off her wooden clogs and ran into the room that she had shared with Mr. Chiba for thirty-three years. She threw herself on the cold tatami floor and sobbed uncontrollably. She realized she would never hear his voice.... "Sleep well Sanae, I'll see you in the morning." How she yearned to hear that voice again. How she yearned to be able to see him in the morning. She sobbed even louder when she realized she would never again feel his hand pat her shoulder when he said those words.

He had been her life ever since she left the snowy fishing village in Fukui to become his wife. She felt his absence like a physical force. Her guts knotted and ached. Her anger turned to grief and that felt even more unbearable. As scenes from the past began to drift through her mind, she writhed in agony, scratching the tatami.

The first time she met Mr. Chiba was at Kobe Station where she got off the train after the long trip from Fukui. She traveled alone because her mother couldn't leave her dying father. She hadn't known him or what he looked like. All she had known about him was his name, age, and what he did for a living. Yet, somehow, they found each other with no effort. Mr. Chiba approached her with a shy smile and a black umbrella in one hand. He stopped 4 meters away from her and bowed. He lowered his head even further and paying no heed to people passing between them, said, "Thank you so much for coming. I'm so glad you arrived safely." No words came out of Mrs. Chiba's mouth, but his smile was contagious and she found herself smiling, too. Much later, she laughed saying, "How careless I was! What if I had left the station with the wrong man!?" Mr. Chiba always smiled and said, "Oh, don't worry. That wouldn't have happened. I wouldn't have brought the wrong woman home. Never."

At each scene, she shed more tears. During those many hours, part of her wanted to at least push the hatred away, because her father had taught her that she should refrain from hating others at all costs. Now she wondered how. Every time she tried, her anger flared up again and again. She wished whoever killed him would face the same fate: charred black and unrecognizable. Then she quickly tried to wipe that thought in shame, but instead the thought repeated itself endlessly.

Eventually, the exhaustion from the last couple days overcame her, and she fell asleep, hoping she would never wake up. Sometime later, although a shrill siren woke her, she remained on the floor unmoving. She didn't even think of running down to her shelter. Nothing mattered to her without her husband. Then she vaguely wondered if she had remembered to thank Giichi properly. She didn't remember anything. She stood up slowly and dragged herself to the entryway. When she saw her clogs lying in disarray, she stooped and put them together and made a mental note to apologize to Giichi for her impolite behavior the next time she saw him. Above, bombers roared past, shaking her house.

CHAPTER 7

Shortly after Giichi left for Kawashima Shipyard with Mrs. Chiba, Kinuko bundled Yuki in a heavy coat and together they headed out for the ration center. As they approached the Hanshin Highway, Kinuko noticed debris strewn across the road below the highway, probably overflow from the jostling carts of the displaced families. She saw a crimson colored futon, a dented pot, and a broken doll. Yuki, too, saw the doll, and immediately let go of her mother's hand and reached down to pick it up.

"Look what happened to the doll, Mama," she said, her eyes serious. Below the doll's startled eyes its nose was chipped, a leg was missing and one sleeve was ripped at the shoulder, as if death had suddenly visited it.

"Leave it," Kinuko said sharply, suddenly forced to picture Mr. Chiba's agonizing death. She reached out to snatch the doll from her daughter's grasp.

"No," Yuki screamed, backing away and clutching it behind her. "She's wounded! A bomb dropped on her, Mama. We have to take her home and put a bandage on her!"

Kinuko dropped her arm and watched her daughter hug the doll. She felt herself awakening from a numbness she hoped would never end. Since the day Giichi confessed he wasn't going to war, she had tried to imagine that everything around her was a dream. But watching her three-year-old daughter, she knew she couldn't possibly hide from the reality of all that had happened, and tears ran down her cold cheeks.

"Don't cry, Mama," said Yuki, tugging at Kinuko's monpe pants, the doll securely wedged under her arm. "She'll be fine."

"Yes, she'll be fine," replied Kinuko, still thinking about Mr. Chiba. She remembered that for a time she had toyed with the notion of Mr. Chiba as her father-in-law. He would certainly have told Giichi to drop his nonsensical idea and go to war like everyone else. But Mr. Chiba wasn't her father-in-law and he was dead now. The pain began to throb again.

On the way back from the ration center, Kinuko carried a wicker basket filled with small sacks of flour and pressed barley, candles, incense, and a box of matches for Mr.

Chiba's visitation and funeral. Next to her, Yuki murmured soothing words to her injured doll. Their house came into view, with its wavy black tiled roof, the glass doors of the veranda that reflected the dull winter light, the low evergreen hedge. It was the house she had shared with Giichi for eight years, and she could picture its every detail with her eyes closed, even the shapes of the water stains on the eaves. Yet it looked empty now.

Across the street, the Chiba house seemed as empty as hers. In Mr. Chiba's small garden—she could hear Mr. Chiba describing it now, "as small as a cat's forehead"—his bonsai stood on the weathered wooden table as if unaware their master was gone. Seeing them tremble in the wind, Kinuko reached for Yuki's hand and held it tightly in her own.

At seven o'clock the next morning the radio announcer declared that snow was inevitable. By noon, four to five inches—an unusual amount for Hanshin—were possible. *"However,"* the announcer's voice hardened with a warning, *"the Central Military District has announced that in spite of the inclement weather sixteen B-29s were observed around six o'clock this morning and again at six-forty, three hundred miles off the coast of the Kii Peninsula. Residents of Kinki, especially those in Hanshin, are urged to take extreme caution."*

Kinuko glanced at the wall clock and told Yuki to hurry and finish her breakfast. Giichi could not ask for another day off work, and they had agreed that he would take Yuki with him and leave her with his parents in Osaka, so Kinuko could focus all her attention on helping Mrs. Chiba with the visitation and funeral. Kinuko impatiently thrust the spoon against Yuki's lips.

"Take it," she said, worrying that Yuki might not reach her grandparents' home before an air raid warning. But Yuki jerked her head away and said, "I'm going to give the carp lots of fu at Grandma and Grandpa's house."

"It'll snow today," Kinuko said, pressing the spoon to her mouth again. "You can't be out in the garden."

"Yes, I can," said Yuki, "because I like snow."

Kinuko warned, "If you aren't ready in a few minutes, your father will leave without you."

"I'm finished," announced Yuki, springing up from the table. "Thank you for breakfast!"

Kinuko exhaled heavily, placed the spoon in the bowl, and began dressing Yuki in a thick sweater and leggings.

"Is it going to snow?" asked Giichi, poking his head from the bedroom and fumbling with his tie.

"That's what they said," Kinuko replied.

"I like snow," Yuki repeated, before grabbing the injured doll from the table and taking off on a run around the dining table. Kinuko caught her by the waist midway through her second lap and slipped her arms into her wool jacket. "Stay still," she demanded, "while I button your jacket."

"No, I'll do it," Yuki protested, backing away from her. "I can button by myself." Yuki tackled the job with fumbling little hands. Giichi came out of the bedroom ready to leave, and Yuki ran to him with a shrill, "I'm ready, Papa."

"All bundled up?" said Giichi. "Let's go then."

He took Yuki's hand and headed toward the entryway where he squatted to lace his shoes with Yuki clutching his neck.

"I hope I can get home before the visitation," he said and picked up his daughter. "Why can't you come with us, Mama?" asked Yuki, her voice muffled against Giichi's shoulder, the injured doll dangling from her hand. The doll had rarely left her sight since she brought it home the day before. The bandage she asked Kinuko to put on its nose was still there.

"Because," Giichi explained, "your mother is busy today and tomorrow."

"Be a good girl," Kinuko said to Yuki, "listen to your Grandpa and Grandma."

Giichi opened the door and they started onto the street. A few flakes of snow were already floating from the sky.

As the radio announcer had predicted, three inches of snow fell by noon. In the midst of the falling snow, Mr. Chiba's body was about to arrive, and the radio announced an air raid warning in Osaka and a watch in the rest of Hanshin.

"The Central Military District announces..." Kinuko turned quickly to the radio, *"that the six B-29s are heading in the direction of the Japanese territorial sky and appear to approach the Hanshin area via Kii Peninsula. Their present location is approximately 30 degrees North Latitude and 140 degrees West Longitude..."*

Kinuko stood in front of radio for a moment, worried about Yuki in Osaka, wanting to call Giichi's parents. Yet she couldn't let Mrs. Chiba walk alone to the highway, where the funeral home would unload the casket. She hurried to the bedroom and slipped into her heavy winter coat and threw a black knit shawl over her head. The thought of the elder Sekihara's elaborate shelter, built the previous summer in a far corner of the garden, cement-fortified with electrical wiring, gave Kinuko some comfort. Yuki would be safe, she thought, and walked out the door. She waded across the snow-filled street to the Chibas' home, anxious to feel Mr. Chiba's presence one more time.

"They are bringing Mr. Chiba's casket soon," Kinuko told Mrs. Chiba. "We should hurry."

"How kind of you to let me know," said Mrs. Chiba, her eyes looking permanently red-rimmed. "But you shouldn't go, Kinuko-san. The cold air is bad for you when you are pregnant."

"I *want* to go, Mrs. Chiba," said Kinuko.

"All right," Mrs. Chiba said. "We will go together then. My husband will be happy to see us both."

Soon the two women clutched their shawls under their chins and slogged through the snow toward the highway. Halfway across the open field, Kinuko looked up and could faintly see traffic inching along the highway. A black hearse came into view, moving as slowly as a worm. It slowly settled to a stop at the top of the concrete steps. A thick layer of snow covered its roof. Three men stepped from the hearse and pulled the casket though the outswung door. Kinuko held her breath as they carried it down the steps. Snow fell over the white shroud that wrapped the casket, while the two women huddled together. Kinuko's teeth chattered as she envisioned Mr. Chiba atop his bicycle, his back straight, his strong legs pedaling, his brown knit muffler flowing from his neck. Now he was in a casket being carried down the steps in the snow. How was this possible? Suddenly, she remembered that it was Mr. Chiba himself who had once told her that nothing in this world is permanent.

Back at the Chibas' reception room, as she ran a towel over the casket Kinuko heard the sound of B-29s. Mrs. Chiba came into the reception room and sat beside it. Without regard for the bombers, she placed her hands on the tatami in front of her knees and bowed. "Welcome home," she said. Then she cried, pressing her forehead against the casket. Kinuko knelt beside her and stroked her trembling back. The sound of the planes grew nearer, and she found herself thinking of Mr. Chiba's words again.

Mrs. Chiba sat up and dried her tears with the frill of her white apron. Her eyes drifted toward the snow falling outside the window, where she gazed until the sound of the B-29s faded.

"I was only seventeen years old when we married," she began quietly. "And I hardly knew him. But my father was dying and my mother wanted me to marry before he passed on. The day I left my village in Fukui it was snowing like this. I sat beside my father's futon and thanked him for having raised me and said good-bye, though I didn't feel too happy about marrying a man I hardly knew."

Kinuko listened intently as Mrs. Chiba continued, her eyes gazing far away. "My father held out his hand like a brittle stick and held mine. By that time his speech was quite bad, but I carefully watched the movement of his lips. He said, 'Now Sanae, go and love your husband with all your heart, and he will love you in return." Mrs. Chiba stopped speaking and sat silently for a while as tears streamed down her cheeks again. "I still remember the tears in my father's eyes and how his hand felt when he said that. For thirty-three years I have honored his words and tried to love my husband with all my heart. Still, there are many things that I regret as I look back. Thirty-three years seems very long, yet it wasn't that long, after all."

She turned to Kinuko. "Kinuko-san, I know you are such a good wife, so I don't have to tell you this, but be as kind as you can to Giichi-san. Life is too short—too many regrets."

Kinuko resisted the urge to tell Mrs. Chiba about Giichi but wondered what Mrs. Chiba would do in her place. Would she have accepted such a decision by her husband no matter how much pain and sorrow it caused?

They sat silently and looked out the window, watching the snow diminish to a soft flurry. Envy began to fill Kinuko's heart—envy for Mrs. Chiba, a woman who had loved her husband and been loved by him for so many years. Again, she wanted to tell Mrs. Chiba about Giichi but felt that one sorrow was enough for Mrs. Chiba now.

By a quarter after four the snow had finally stopped falling, and their neighbors Mr. Obata and Mr. Tanaka brought cushions borrowed from a nearby temple. The arrival of the men and the cushions forced Mrs. Chiba and Kinuko to dry their tears and get busy with the final arrangements. Soon afterward, Mr. Hayashi, the neighborhood chief, who hadn't been to the Chibas' home since the shipyard bombing, suddenly showed up at the door and told Mrs. Chiba to draw her blackout curtains at five. It would get dark early this evening, he pointed out. He also told her that she shouldn't forget to turn off the lights in case of a watch or warning. "The enemy might be thinking," he added, "that we are not prepared because of the inclement weather."

After Mr. Hayashi left, Mrs. Chiba placed a tiny desk in front of the casket and covered it with a piece of white cloth. Kinuko put candles, incense, a brass bell, and a box of matches on it. Then they arranged cushions in small circles here and there throughout the room and started a kettle of water on the hibachi. Meanwhile telegrams arrived one after another from faraway relatives, informing Mrs. Chiba that they wouldn't be able to attend because of the snow. Kinuko realized that, except for her, Mrs. Chiba might be entirely alone hosting the visitation, so she hurried home to change her clothes.

When she returned to Mrs. Chiba's Kinuko went into the kitchen and prepared braziers for the guests. As she leaned down to put pieces of blazing charcoal into a brazier, she winced at a dull pain in her abdomen and remembered she had felt something similar when she went to the highway to meet Mr. Chiba's casket. But the warmth of the charcoal felt pleasant to her chilled body, and she soon forgot the pain. Kinuko put equal amounts of charcoal into the three other braziers, then carried one to the reception room and placed it in the middle of a circle of cushions. When she returned to the kitchen for the second brazier, another sharp pain ripped across her abdomen. She gasped and squatted on the floor. She held her hands over her abdomen and winced.

Mrs. Chiba stepped down to the kitchen floor in her white tabi socks. "What's wrong Kinuko-san?" she cried, squatting beside her. Kinuko gasped, and through clenched teeth, said, "It's nothing." She tried to smile but winced instead. Then the main door opened, and the first mourner called hesitantly, "Good evening." Mrs. Chiba stood, then sat down again.

"Please go to the door," Kinuko managed to say.

"I'll be right there," Mrs. Chiba called out, her voice thick with worry.

"Please go home and rest," Mrs. Chiba urged Kinuko. "I can handle this myself, really." She then pushed Kinuko gently toward the back door. "Be sure to call a doctor," she added before hurrying to the main door to receive the mourner.

Kinuko shuffled out of the house through the back door and sloshed through the snow in the dark. Just as she reached the door to her house another searing pain gripped her abdomen, this time so sharp it reminded her of the pain she had felt when Yuki was born. An unsought word filtered into her mind—miscarriage. She stumbled through the entryway, curled up on the cold tatami floor of the front room and moaned. A few minutes later the pain faded, and she stood and shuffled into the guest room. She slipped her coat off and crawled into the futon, ignoring Mrs. Chiba's demand that she call a doctor.

She closed her eyes, exhausted from pain and a day of crying. She pictured Mrs. Chiba scurrying to the door, leading guests to the casket, and fetching tea all alone. In the heatless house, her body remained cold for a long time, but when it finally warmed she fell asleep. She shifted between waking pain and sleep until she heard Giichi's voice close to her face. She opened her eyes and saw him peering at her with a candle in his hand, still in his coat.

"What's wrong?" he asked, "Mrs. Chiba told me you were having terrible pains."

Kinuko looked around as if she had awakened in a place she had never been before. "Are we under watch now?" she asked, looking at the candle Giichi held.

He nodded. She was surprised that she had slept through the siren.

"Are you all right?"

"I think so," she said in a raspy voice, before coughing and drawing her face from his. "What time is it?"

Giichi peered at his watch. "A little after eight."

Kinuko sat up, full of sorrow for having slept through the visitation. "I have to go back," she said. "Mrs. Chiba is alone."

"No, you sleep," said Giichi. "I'll go over there. I wanted to come home earlier, but there was an emergency meeting in the afternoon. It lasted until seven."

Giichi spread his cold hand across her forehead and left it there for a few seconds. His coat sleeve smelled of snow. "You don't seem to have a fever," he mumbled, before drawing his hand away. "Where was the pain?"

"Here," she answered, placing her hand over her womb, "but it's gone now."

"Good," he said and then stood quickly. "I must check on Mrs. Chiba. I'll be right back."

"Thank you," Kinuko whispered and closed her eyes again.

"Do you want me to leave the candle here or should I blow it out?"

Kinuko thought for a moment. "Would you leave it on the desk?"

Giichi cupped his hand around the candle and walked along the edge of the futon to the desk. He placed the candle there and tiptoed out. After she heard the main door close, she shifted her body and watched the candle flame. It flickered and then elongated into a perfectly still arrow in the quiet of the house. Unblinking, she stared at it, and eventually she knew what she felt. It made perfect sense. She would miscarry this child, doomed to be fatherless. She even felt growing hope that this sudden instinct would prove true as she recalled Mr. Chiba's words—nothing in this world is permanent. He was right. It made no sense to bring new life into such an uncertain world.

CHAPTER 8

Ichiro capped his fountain pen and placed it in the fold of his writing pad. It was only four o'clock, but already too dark to work, even with the window uncurtained above his oak desk. He leaned against the back of his chair, slid his fingers under his glasses to rub his eyes and gazed out the window.

The snowfall had diminished enough that he could discern outlines in the garden. Then he strained his eyes and gasped with alarm at the sight of his bonsais beneath a thick layer of snow. He had forgotten to cover them. Over the years he had developed a parental love for the plants. They responded to his care. He could detect the slightest blemish on their leaves, small changes others didn't notice. Yet on this day he had forgotten all about them, and now some of the less hardy ones might lose their leaves in the frigid weather.

It wasn't just the bonsai; in the last few months he seemed to have become generally absent-minded. He had difficulty focusing his attention, as if he were in his own cocoon while the world drifted around him. He hadn't been eating properly or sleeping well either, and his aging seemed to be progressing more rapidly. In the middle of the night, Sumiko often propped herself on one elbow and asked in a sleepy voice, "Should I bring you a glass of plum wine?" He always said no and tried to lie still so she would go back to sleep. When Sumiko asked him what was wrong, he simply shrugged and told her that he was just getting old, and that he had to accept it with grace. "It happens to everyone sooner or later," he told her. "That's life."

What he didn't tell his wife was that their son had decided to reject the red paper. He had already caused her enough of that kind of worry. Why should he frighten her now when nobody knew for sure if Giichi would ever receive it? The day Giichi revealed his decision, Sumiko was teaching a tea ceremony in her north wing tearoom. Later, after Giichi left, she asked, "What did Giichi have to tell you? Was it anything special?"

"No," replied Ichiro. "Nothing special. He just stopped before his lunch appointment in Minami."

That had been November 6, the day Giichi came, a little more than two months ago, the date now etched in Ichiro's mind as permanently as Pearl Harbor Day. The day had started gloriously, a crisp morning with the serene fragrance of chrysanthemums wafting in through an open window. The day seemed even more glorious because of his son's promised visit. When Giichi arrived, Ichiro was writing in his study, trying to finish the novel he had started a few years earlier. Lured by the crisp air, Ichiro suggested they go outside. He needed a break anyway, he told his son.

They walked together in the garden, the pond as smooth as a mirror, shaded only by a twisted pine. The moss looked as soft as velvet, absorbing the autumn sunlight. Despite the tranquility around them, Ichiro already sensed his son had something grave to tell him. As they walked along the stepping stones that led to the pond, Ichiro felt his heart beat faster.

He stopped at the edge of the pond and clapped his large hands. More than two dozen carp glided toward him with amazing speed, barely making ripples on the surface of the water. Their colors were as vivid as the kimonos worn by Heian court ladies—red, orange, yellow, white, black. Ichiro bent to take a dash of rice bran from a wooden container and sprinkled it over the water. He kept his eyes on the pond, feeling his son's silence. The carp surfaced, swallowed the bits, turned with immense grace, and swirled away as swiftly as they had come. Watching the carp settle deep in a corner of the pond, Ichiro remembered seeing the same grace in Kinuko when he had first met her. He knew even then that Giichi would fall in love with her.

Ichiro slowly turned to his son. "Let's sit on the bench, shall we?" Then, dusting the palms of his hands together, he walked ahead of Giichi to the stone bench across the pond. He sat there under the pine tree and made room for his son, but Giichi didn't sit. Instead, he paced behind the bench for a while and finally began to uncoil in words the long tormented process that had led to his decision not to go to war. Ichiro sat quietly the whole time, leaning forward with his elbows on his knees. Even after Giichi had stopped talking, Ichiro continued to stare silently at the pond. One question kept rolling through his mind, "Am I ready to accept my son's death?" He knew, of course that he could not tell Giichi to accept the red paper, when he himself had ignored his family's pain in order to follow his beliefs.

He knew how horrifying his detentions had been for Sumiko and Giichi, and yet he continued writing the kinds of essays that had led to his first interrogation. Staring across the pond, he remembered Giichi coming home from school just as he was being led to a police car. The image of Giichi flailing at the officers and screaming at them to release him had been etched forever in his mind, with a mixture of pride for his son's courage and guilt for having inspired the look of terror on his son's face. He knew those same contradictory feelings must be tearing at Giichi's soul now.

As Ichiro continued to stare into the darkness now overwhelming the sparkle of snow outside his study, his promise to Giichi weighed on his mind. He knew he could support

Kinuko and the children financially and felt certain he could protect them from harm, but what about their happiness? He couldn't buy that with money. In the receding twilight, he remembered how desperately Kinuko had asked him to convince Giichi to accept the red paper and how quickly she had turned and walked away from him, the hem of her kimono flapping angrily. That same day she had lost her dear neighbor. He could hear the sharp, accusing rustle of her kimono even now, as he sat at his desk, staring into the white silence of winter.

And by May he could imagine the circumstances in which she would be giving birth to a child. The bombings would certainly continue to escalate, and by then Giichi might not be with her. Ichiro began to shiver. The clumps of charcoal in the blue, glazed porcelain brazier at his feet had turned to mounds of ashes. Once more, he wiggled the big toe of his right foot, which had been numb since he had left the bomb shelter that afternoon, and again, no feeling returned. He crossed his arms wearily across his chest and blankly watched the straggling snowflakes floating outside the window.

Suddenly, he felt the urge to get away—from this dangerous city, the worsening war, everything. He stood and limped out of his study, crossed the dark corridor, past three equally dark rooms, and entered the family room. There, he felt immediate relief. The kitchen light filtered into the room along with the scent of cooking vegetables. He leaned into the kitchen, where Ume bent over a steaming pot, busily stirring its contents with long chopsticks.

"Oh, you must be cold, Big Master," she said, looking up from the pot. "I was going to bring some more charcoal to your study as soon as this was done. I'm sorry."

"No, it's not necessary," said Ichiro hastily. "I have to have a talk with Big Mistress. Where is she?"

"She took Yuki-ojohsan to the tearoom about half an hour ago," said Ume, squinting through the rising steam. "She wanted to keep Yuki-ojohsan in the warmest room."

"Oh, I was going to ask you to watch Yuki while I talked to her. Is that possible?"

"Yes, of course, this will be done in a second. Then all I have to do is to make the steamed eggs Yuki-ojohsan likes."

"Steamed eggs? What luxury! But can you handle both? Looking after Yuki and making them?"

"Oh yes," replied Ume, peering at the clock on the wall. "She can crack eggs for me. Besides, it's only five o'clock."

Ichiro laughed. "She'll probably just make a mess and create extra work for you."

Ume amazed him. Until a few months ago the Sekiharas had kept three maids, but as the war worsened the younger ones were advised to return to their villages to be with their parents. Sumiko tried to find local replacements, but most city girls had been conscripted to work at war-related factories. Yet Ume stayed on despite the increased workload, in part because she didn't have a family to go back to, but mainly because she was too loyal to leave.

"Thank you. I'm going to the tearoom now, would you fetch her when you are done cooking?"

"Yes, Big Master," said Ume, as she carefully lifted the steaming pot from the hibachi. "I'll be right there."

Walking through the long glass corridor that ran alongside the garden, Ichiro gazed at the snow, reflecting the light from the house, and felt as if he were walking in a vast winter field in the gray twilight. He stopped to breathe in the beauty of the snow-covered garden, noting the clean gentle contours blanketing evergreen shrubs, pines, the roof of the storage house at the far end, the plum tree next to it, and the two stone lanterns at the edge of the pond. The garden was the spirit of the house, he loved it immensely. The thought of leaving this house filled his chest with sadness. Still, he knew it was time as he turned to the soft glow on the shouji door of the tearoom where his granddaughter played. He ached, remembering the injured doll she carried protectively in her arms when Giichi brought her this morning, and then carried just as protectively into the bomb shelter a few hours later.

Sumiko and Yuki immediately turned to him as he slid the door open.

"Grandpa!" Yuki sprang to her feet and threw her arms around Ichiro's legs, looking up at him with sparkling eyes.

"Yuki, you haven't slept at all this afternoon, have you?" Ichiro scooped up her little body and held her against his chest as he moved to where Sumiko sat.

"I've tried to put her in bed a few times," Sumiko began, half laughing, half complaining, "but she just refused to sleep. I'm the one who's getting tired."

"Well, well," said Ichiro, peering into his granddaughter's eyes. "This little girl wants to play instead of sleep. Isn't that so, Yuki?

"However," he continued, putting her down, "Grandma and Grandpa need to have a talk now. So you stay with Ume for a while. She is coming to get you in a minute."

Even before Ichiro finished, Ume was at the door, wearing the broad smile that would coax Yuki into her care.

"No, I want to play with Grandpa!" Yuki clung to Ichiro's kimono.

"You can help me make steamed eggs," said Ume, with eyes twinkling. "Can you crack some eggs for me?"

"I wish I could do that," said Sumiko, feigning disappointment. "That sounds like fun."

"Crack eggs?" Yuki let go of Ichiro's kimono.

"Yes, crack four eggs!" said Ume, erecting four fingers. "That's what I want you to do for me."

Yuki's eyes widened with delight. "Four eggs?"

"Yes, four of them," said Ume, promptly lifting her into her arms. "We are going to be busy, aren't we?"

Sumiko gathered the scattered silk beanbags Yuki had been playing with and put them in a bright drawstring bag. Then she knelt at the side of the hearth, which was cut into the tatami floor, and rearranged the charcoal with iron rods, using them like long chopsticks. Ichiro settled slowly onto a cushion.

"What would you like to talk about so suddenly?" she asked quietly, still intent on the charcoal. "Is it something about your health?"

"No." Ichiro coughed dryly, covering his mouth with a fist. "I will wait until you sit."

Sumiko adjusted a cushion near the hearth and sat erect, her hands clasped softly over her lap, as if she were performing a tea ceremony. Ichiro listened for a while to the sound of the water steaming in the iron teakettle above the charcoal. He gazed down at the brocaded trim of the tatami in front of him.

"Getting in and out of the shelter is taking its toll on me," he sighed. "I'm already growing tired of it."

"Oh?" said Sumiko.

"I think it's time for us to move to Okayama."

Sumiko's eyebrows arched, but she was silent for a few seconds. "I thought you would never leave this house. What changed your mind so suddenly? May I ask?"

Ichiro sighed again. "The bombings will only get worse, I'm afraid. At the moment it seems like they are trying to destroy our war-related industries, but what will come next will be more indiscriminate, civilians and—"

Sumiko interrupted, leaning forward slightly and lowering her voice, "Don't you think the war will be over before it becomes that bad?"

Ichiro coughed out a humorless laugh. "Wishful thinking. Stubborn as they are, the military doesn't want to lose face. They are even preparing for a ground battle. They say they'll fight to the end."

Sumiko frowned again, looking as if she wanted to say something, but Ichiro continued, "Before it's too late, we should get out of Osaka. Let's take the whole family with us. And Ume, of course. Then Kinuko will be able to have the baby in peace, and Yuki will be safe."

Sumiko's eyes sparkled. "That's exactly what I've been thinking. But what about Giichi? Do you think he will quit his work and come with us?"

Ichiro tilted his head and stared at the trim of the tatami again. "I think it best he does, but he can come later, if that's what he wants to do," he said casually, and then looked up and spoke more confidently. "It's easy for a man to jump on a train at the last minute and flee. We'll see, he might quit his work right away and come with us."

Sumiko nodded and gazed at the charcoal glowing in the hearth. "Well, I hope your appetite and sleep problems will improve when we get to Okayama."

Her wish seemed a distinct possibility. The country house, several kilometers north of Okayama City, which Ichiro had inherited after his parents' deaths, had been their summer retreat. Ichiro loved to go there when Osaka sizzled with heat; his writing usually flowed amid the rural ease and cooler air. A long-time loyal family servant, Genkichi, tended the house while they were in Osaka and also farmed part of Ichiro's land, and just as meticulously and honestly, kept his books.

"What about trucks?" Sumiko asked suddenly. "Oh my, how many trucks will we need? Think about the things in the storage house. Trucks are hard to arrange, aren't they?"

"Freight train," said Ichiro. "Of course, we'll need trucks to take the furniture to the Osaka station, but from there, the furniture can go to Okayama by freight train. I will book both tomorrow morning before I go to Mr. Chiba's funeral. I'll have to let Genkichi know as well. We will be busy, Mother."

Ichiro stood and walked to the door. As he began to slide the door open, Sumiko asked, "When are you planning to tell Giichi and Kinuko?"

"Hmm," said Ichiro. "I'll probably wait until after the funeral. I'll have some time with Giichi then." He stepped from the room and turned back to her. "Now it's my turn to play with Yuki for a while."

"As you please," Sumiko said with a smile.

Ichiro stopped midway through the corridor as he had done before. The garden, dark now except for the white snow looming in the faint light coming from the tearoom, brought on memories of three decades in this house. They reeled slowly through his mind, like a revolving lantern. Then the garden blinked into darkness as the tearoom light went out. He saw Sumiko's black silhouette quietly approaching.

"I hope you have an appetite for the warm steamed eggs."

"Hmm, I will see. I hope Yuki didn't make too much of a mess."

"I hope so, too."

They stood facing the garden side by side. Ichiro felt cold air seeping from the glass onto his face and yet the warmth of his wife's body at his side. He sagged with heavy sadness, thinking of his son.

CHAPTER 9

Mr. Chiba's funeral ended with a hurried sutra reading precisely at eleven a.m., so mourners could reach their homes before the day's first air-raid warning. As the monks turned from the altar, Giichi stood and walked to the casket. He and three other neighbors lifted it from the floor and waited while Kinuko helped Mrs. Chiba to her feet. Then they proceeded slowly through the packed mourners amid a final tolling of bells and a swirling haze of blue smoke rising from incense sticks.

Outside the Chiba home the snow crumbled and shifted in the glow of the sun. Holding the weight of the casket, Giichi noticed water dripping from the eaves of the house gleaming in the sunlight. It occurred to him that perhaps yesterday's unusual snow was meant for Mr. Chiba, who had come from a snowy fishing village on the Sea of Japan and had often spoken fondly of snow falling on the beach in Fukui. "Good-bye Mr. Chiba," Giichi murmured as he helped slide the casket into the rear of the black hearse.

The hearse eased away, and Giichi stood next to Mrs. Chiba, while she thanked the crowd of mourners with silent bows. They returned her bows again and again and began to disperse with careful steps through slushy potholes, the women lifting the hems of their kimono. Giichi walked with Mrs. Chiba into the house, where the five remaining mourners were already restoring order, gathering cushions and placing sliding doors back in their tracks. Ichiro, wearing his family-crested mourning kimono, sadly lifted a cushion.

Giichi scanned the room for Kinuko—and then joined the others with the clean-up. When the flurry of activity settled, Giichi went into the side room where the monks had sipped tea before the sutra reading. There, he found Kinuko alone, gathering empty teacups and saucers. He noticed that she moved gracefully once again, seeming to have recovered almost miraculously from last night's severe pains. Still, her face bore a mixture of grief and weariness, and her black mourning silk added a tragic paleness to her skin.

"Are you feeling all right?" he asked.

"Yes."

"If not, Yuki can stay in Osaka one more night, and I can go to the crematorium with Mrs. Chiba so you can rest."

"I'll rest for awhile after this. We still have time before we go."

"All right," Giichi replied hesitantly. "Then I'll go to Osaka with my father."

He knew there was nothing he could do to change her mind. She rarely allowed physical discomfort to slow her, and given the current strain between them, she balked at any suggestion he made. As she stood up with the tray, he took it from her and carried it to the kitchen.

Ichiro sat in the front room offering further condolences to Mrs. Chiba. When they noticed Giichi, they made room for him to step down to the muddy concrete floor of the entryway.

"Are you coming with me then?" Ichiro asked Giichi.

"Yes. Kinuko says she is all right. I'll come with you to Osaka and get Yuki."

"As I said, Mother and I can keep Yuki as long as necessary. I can bring her home early in the morning when it's safer."

"We'll be fine. I have to go to Osaka anyway to pick up something from my office."

Twenty minutes later, Giichi and Ichiro entered a tram and stepped carefully through the aisle made slick by the melted snow tracked in by the morning's passengers. They settled into a seat with Ichiro next to the window. Ichiro smiled slightly, as if basking in the bright sunlight flooding through the window and grateful for the turn in the weather.

"It was a nice funeral," he said, "Simple yet dignified—very appropriate for Mr. Chiba."

"It was," answered Giichi.

"I'm very sorry you lost such a good friend."

Still haunted by the sight of Mr. Chiba's charred body, Giichi found it difficult to continue the conversation, and Ichiro fell silent, as if sensing his unwillingness to talk. They looked straight ahead and Ichiro eventually closed his eyes.

Later, as the tram curved along the bend of the Muko River, a shaft of sunlight fell over Ichiro's profile. He opened his eyes and blinked at the patches of snow shining brilliantly on the riverbank.

"Did I fall asleep?"

"For a while," said Giichi.

"Hmm," said Ichiro, peering at his watch. He adjusted his glasses, refolded his arms and straightened his back. "Mother and I decided yesterday that we should move to Okayama. I made arrangements with the railway this morning. Our furniture will be shipped there in a month. Then we'll leave."

Considering the increasing frequency of bombings, Giichi wasn't surprised. Still, he didn't know what to say. He knew his parents cherished their house in Osaka, their home of three decades, and their friends and all the memories. He did, too. He had grown up there rambling through the garden, stooping to splash his hands in the pond and distract the carp. It must have been a difficult decision for them, Giichi thought.

"You've made the right choice," he replied with an aching heart.

"I believe so," said Ichiro, "but what I really want to say is that you should come with us, all of you—I want Yuki to be in a safe place and Kinuko to have her baby without worries."

"I agree. Kinuko and Yuki should go with you."

"And you?"

"It's too sudden," Giichi said, thinking he sounded almost defensive.

"What do you mean by that? It might be too late rather than too sudden. Think about what happened to Mr. Chiba. It will only get worse."

"I know that," Giichi said, "but I can't resign from the company just like that—but, as you say, Kinuko and Yuki should get out of Hanshin."

"Definitely," Ichiro said. "It will be difficult for her to think about leaving Hanshin right after Mr. Chiba's funeral, but it's time to think about our safety."

"I'll talk to her," said Giichi. "I'll tell her tonight."

"Good. But I hope you can also come. Think about it."

"I'll see." He stared ahead for a moment. "The job is important," he said finally. Ichiro nodded grimly. "It seems so."

Giichi wished he could explain more about why he needed to stay in Hanshin, but some things he could not tell even to his father. Ichiro's eyes closed again, and beyond his father's still profile, Giichi watched the black and white banks of the Muko River snake past. Patience, he told himself, someday you can tell him. He dreamed of such a day after the war, when he would be able to talk with his father freely, and with Kinuko as well, about what he was doing now.

The tram rumbled on, nearing Osaka. Ichiro's head remained against the window, gentle snores puffing from his lips. Giichi tried to imagine living alone if Kinuko agreed to take Yuki and join his parents in Okayama. He pictured himself sitting in dim light with the blackout curtains closed, waking up alone in the cold house. Loneliness spread in his heart with more force than he expected. Still, he couldn't think of leaving the city and losing contact with his truest friend, Kenji Nakayama.

Giichi knew that Kenji was the only person who truly understood the anguish he had felt growing up as the son of Ichiro Sekihara and as a lonely boy in a military-oriented school world. In fact, Kenji not only understood the anguish he had carried throughout his childhood but explained it as part of what ailed Japan.

"Our leaders are demanding more and more conformity," Kenji told him, "and that will soon lead to our destruction."

Giichi met Kenji during their second year at the university, one of the nation's most prestigious, and one that had been a hotbed of liberalism, socialism, and Marxism until the beginning of the 1930s, when the authorities began to suppress academic freedom. A brilliant political science major, Kenji effortlessly received A's in every subject, while Giichi majored in economics and worked hard to achieve the same success. The son of a Gifu ceramics merchant, Kenji was short and skinny as a scarecrow but possessed insatiable intellectual curiosity, deep compassion for the underprivileged, and enormous passion for the betterment of society. His lush black hair and the bushy eyebrows above his wire-rimmed glasses looked odd atop his thin frame, but he never seemed self-conscious about his appearance. He was one of the shortest students at the university, and Giichi one of the tallest. When the two of them hurried to classes along the university's gingko-lined paths, the top of Kenji's head barely reached Giichi's shoulders. Other students joked about the peculiar sight of them together.

After a day of classes and study, they often spent the afternoons and evenings talking in Giichi's small room in a shabby boardinghouse. Whenever Kenji visited, Giichi shoved his dirty clothes into the closet, folded the layers of his futon together and pushed them against the wall to make room for his visitor. While Kenji sat with his back against Giichi's folded futon, Giichi usually sat with his back to his desk. When he had money, Kenji brought a cheap bottle of sake and poured it into chipped cups borrowed from the boardinghouse. In this fashion they talked into the night, sometimes imagining the delights of the women in the pleasure quarter along the Kamo River, but mostly discussing politics and how they wanted to live. They never worried about time or money or the cleanliness of their rooms or of themselves. But they worried seriously about the future of their country, which was moving increasingly toward military dictatorship. When the boardinghouse shut off the electricity at midnight, they lit an oil lamp, or if the moon was full, they sat and talked in the dreamy blue light that came in though the curtainless window.

Toward the end of their second year at the university, Kenji started talking about joining the Japanese Communist Party. It was the only viable way to fight the growing tide of fascism, he said. The mass arrests and torture in 1928 and 1929 had forced the party underground, but had at the same time made it stronger. As he spoke, Kenji would run his fingers wildly through his thick wiry hair and impatiently shake one of his crossed legs. Giichi would watch the dark shadows of maple leaves dance over Kenji's face in the moonlit room, amazed that everything his friend said made perfect sense.

"We should join the party together," Kenji said one afternoon in Giichi's apartment. "We need to be a part of an organization if we really want to change the direction our country is going." His eyes glowed with passion. "No one can achieve that goal by himself. Individuals are nothing by themselves, no matter how many."

Though persuaded by Kenji's words, Giichi decided he didn't want to join the party. To him, communism would simply result in another form of totalitarianism, not unlike Japan's military dictatorship. Still, he supported the party's anti-war goals and struggled to think of another way to stop the country's growing military expansion.

Then a few months into their third year, Kenji suddenly vanished from his life. Giichi assumed his friend had joined the communists and gone underground. He missed Kenji terribly and yearned for the passion of their late night conversations. He envied his friend's courage and the purity of his beliefs, but as much as he agreed with Kenji's burning idealism, Giichi's thoughts gradually turned to the stability of marriage and a job.

Nearly two years later, as suddenly as he had gone, Kenji reappeared, dressed in rags and unshaven, but with eyes that shone with remarkable clarity. They met in a cheap bar in the Minami district of Osaka, and once again Kenji urged Giichi to join the party, but by then Giichi was engaged to Kinuko and wanted no association whatsoever with the Communist Party. He told Kenji that he didn't want to inflict on his future wife the same sorrow his father had inflicted upon his mother.

Kenji said he understood. He wished Giichi nothing but happiness, then he pushed away from the table, slipped past the red lantern at the bar's entrance, and walked into a dark rainy night, leaving Giichi sick with shame.

Giichi looked over at his father, still dozing with his head against the tram window. He frowned sadly at the sight of his father's once-strong shoulders now drooping forward, the deepening wrinkles on his face, and his thinning hairline. The day before, when Giichi took Yuki to their home, his mother confided that Ichiro hadn't been eating or sleeping well the last two months. Giichi couldn't overcome the feeling that confiding in his father had added to his suffering, just as it had added to Kinuko's.

That evening, Giichi brought Yuki home and sat in the dining room, shuffling through the paperwork he had brought from the office. He waited for a chance to talk with Kinuko. Yuki had come down with a cold and a fever, and Kinuko took her to bed, where she had been reading to her for nearly an hour. When Kinuko finally came out of Yuki's room, Giichi put down his pen and rubbed his strained eyes. Looking up from the dining table, he announced, "My parents are moving to Okayama."

"Are they?" asked Kinuko, her eyebrows arching. "When?"

Giichi stood to turn off the radio he had kept on low volume—it had just reported an attack on a convoy transporting oil to Japan. Five of the twelve ships had been sunk in the Gulf of Tonkin. Giichi sat down again, expecting Kinuko to sit as well, but she didn't. Instead, she stepped down into the kitchen and began drying dishes.

"In a month or so," Giichi continued, "when a freight train is available." He waited a moment and then added, "I want you and Yuki to go with them."

"What about you?"

"I have to *work*," answered Giichi. "I don't want to depend on my father financially. Don't you want to get away from of all this?" He glanced wearily at the black curtains draped over the windows. "This isn't good for Yuki at all, for you either, especially when you are pregnant."

Without a word, Kinuko stepped into the room and rattled a stack of dishes into the hutch. Giichi understood her silence. Only hours earlier she had collected the ashes of Mr. Chiba, but he thought he must press forward, the situation was becoming too dangerous.

"Don't you think so?" he said.

"All of us should go," Kinuko replied, "though I don't want to leave Mrs. Chiba alone."

"I agree that Mrs. Chiba shouldn't be left alone. But if I stay for work, I can look out for her, she won't be alone. I just want you and Yuki to be safe."

Kinuko held the hutch door in one hand. "So do I," she said. "But I also want you to be safe. Our lives are nothing without you."

CHAPTER 10

Kinuko bundled Yuki in her heaviest hooded winter coat and lifted her into the buggy. As Yuki settled in with her injured doll, Kinuko pushed the buggy onto the street, beginning what had become an every-other-day trek to the lumberyard. It would have been easier for Kinuko to leave Yuki with Mrs. Chiba, but her daughter no longer liked to stay at the Chiba house. She told Kinuko that Mr. Chiba's new black altar frightened her. She often asked where Mr. Chiba had gone and was puzzled when told that he was now in paradise.

Unusually cold weather had settled over Hanshin and lingered as ominously as the daily threat of bombs. As the cold continued charcoal rations dropped to only four lumps per household and the price of firewood tripled. Kinuko did what she could, attempting to heat the house with charcoal and using rationed firewood for cooking, but the supplies always fell short, and in the evening they often hovered over dying charcoal fires, wearing several layers of clothing, eating cold rice.

When they reached the lumberyard, Kinuko found that even more families had become reliant on its supply of wood. Women, many with babies, waited their turn in the frigid cold. She stepped to the back of the line and shifted from foot to foot, while Yuki wandered off and showed her injured doll to anyone who would pay attention. On their way home, Yuki walked beside her, while Kinuko pushed the buggy filled with enough firewood for her house and Mrs. Chiba's. The buggy jerked over the rugged pavement and her breath jetted out in white clouds.

Now, three weeks after Mr. Chiba's death, grief rested constantly in her heart, and only gradually had she grown accustomed to his absence. She often awoke in the middle of the night, haunted by the image of bombs dropping over the shipyard and by thoughts of the horror Mr. Chiba must have felt that day. She would moan in grief during those wakeful moments, remembering how Mr. Chiba had looked forward to the birth of two new grandchildren, his daughter's baby and her own. Then she would moan again with guilt at the thought of betraying Mr. Chiba's memory. Although the sharp pains from the day of his visitation had abated, she still hoped for a miscarriage.

In addition to the treks for firewood, the cold weather provided Kinuko another strenuous task that offered the possibility of bringing on a miscarriage. Each night, the water in the four buckets outside the kitchen door froze over with a thick crust of ice. Each morning, she grunted while crushing the layers of ice with a hammer, before carrying the pails into the bathroom and dumping the slushy mixture into the bathtub for later use. Then, she would refill the buckets and set them outside the kitchen door, so the watchful neighborhood chief, Mr. Hayashi, could see them. She always waited until Giichi left for work before beginning the task, knowing he would insist on doing it for her.

One morning around six-thirty, Kinuko was startled from sleep by loud banging on a nearby door. She leaped from bed, slipped a coat over her sleeping robe, and hurried to the kitchen window. Lifting the blackout curtain, she peered out and saw Mr. Hayashi at Mrs. Chiba's door, pointing angrily at her water buckets, white vapor spewing from his flared nostrils. Through the narrow crack of her door, Mrs. Chiba nodded silently, clutching at the collar of her coat. Next door, Kinuko saw Mrs. Tanaka, the carpenter's wife, swing a hammer into one of her water buckets. Shards of ice sprayed from the bucket and settled in her uncombed hair.

Kinuko opened the back door a crack and waited, shivering in the frigid air. Mr. Hayashi marched toward her house, earmuffs dangling from his khaki cap and a clipboard under his arm.

"You too, Mrs. Sekihara," he bellowed, stopping in front of the empty flowerbed where her buckets sat. "You can't put out a fire with ice, can you?" He pointed to her buckets. "If I find ice in these one more time, I will reduce your food rations. Keep the water thawed at all times."

As Hayashi strode off to the Tanaka house, Kinuko took a bucket in each hand and carried them into the kitchen. Her cheeks burned with resentment for the power exerted by neighborhood chiefs. Though she had heard that many of them were fair and conscientious, others, like Hayashi, served as no more than authoritarian watchdogs, ready to pounce on the smallest infraction. It seemed a miracle to Kinuko that Mr. Hayashi had yet to do anything about Giichi's failure to wear a national uniform.

Giichi strode into the kitchen, tying a sash around his kimono robe, as Kinuko set the two pails in the corner.

"What was all that shouting about?"

"Nothing," Kinuko replied. "Mr. Hayashi said he will reduce our rations if our buckets aren't ready for putting out fires."

"Let me do it," he said, reaching for the hammer.

"Please get ready for work," she said. "I can do this."

But Giichi took the hammer from her hand, and while he crushed the ice, Kinuko pleaded, "Please, put on your national uniform before he does something about that."

"Don't worry," Giichi only mumbled. Then he went back to the bedroom, closing the door between the dining room and the middle room, a door they usually kept open. Despite her mood, Kinuko felt her heart plunge, as if his closing the door served to shut her out of his life even more.

Yuki awakened a short while later, and as soon as Kinuko dressed her, she ran to the bathroom where Giichi was shaving. Kinuko went back to the kitchen and, while preparing breakfast, listened to their conversation.

"Be careful not to cut your face, Papa," Yuki said.

"I will," Giichi replied.

"I want some soap on my face, too," Yuki squealed.

Kinuko pictured Giichi smearing a dollop of foam on Yuki's face as she heard her laugh.

She wished she could laugh with them. For months she had endured the barrier between her and Giichi, and now their roles were reversed—he was attempting to appease her. He came home early instead of late, he came home with the tangerines and rice crackers she liked instead of the smell of sake. But the kinder he acted, the sadder she felt; sooner or later he would be gone.

She wished she could accept his kindness instead of refusing it, and recalled that she had refused her mother's advice in just the same way when she was a rebellious school girl with long braided hair, a sailor jacket and pleated navy blue skirt.

"Acquire a tranquil mind," Etsu kept telling her. "Surrender yourself to a higher place in the universe."

But the prospect of Giichi's death made her realize how shallowly she grasped the lessons she thought she had learned. It was one thing to understand an ideal and another to actually live it. No matter how hard she tried, she couldn't calm her turbulent mind. She longed to break this cycle of anguish, and she wished she could smile one day and be nice to Giichi as Mrs. Chiba had suggested.

A week later, a black sedan stopped in front of her house and three men emerged from it, two black uniformed policemen and Hayashi in his khaki national uniform. Her heart fluttering wildly, Kinuko tried to put out the fire she had just started to prepare lunch. Through the smoke drifting across her vision, she saw Hayashi stride toward her. "May I help you?" she asked, feeling her knees weaken.

Hayashi took off his khaki cap and spoke curtly. "The Special Higher Police from Ashiya Police Headquarters have something they want to investigate." Then he put his cap back on, saluted the officers, and walked away in the direction of his home.

While the two officers examined the wooden name plaque on the main door, Kinuko pulled a piece of wood from the hibachi and beat it against the smoldering paper to make sure the fire was completely out. Then she walked across the empty flowerbed to the main door, anger flaring in her chest. Despite her repeated warnings,

Giichi still refused to wear the national uniform. The day she feared had finally arrived, she thought.

"I'm Toda," said the middle-aged officer, the shorter one, lifting a tattered identification card out of his breast pocket and dangling it in front of Kinuko, "and this is my subordinate, Konno. I'm afraid we have to come into your house."

Toda had bulging eyes and a black mole the size of a bean beside his left nostril. The younger one took off his cap and bowed, standing smooth-faced and nervous behind Toda.

"May I ask what this is about?" Kinuko asked.

"We'll talk inside," Toda said. "It's cold out here."

Kinuko, hiding her annoyance and fear, opened the main door and went into the house first. She heard the pounding of her heart while the two men stooped and removed their shoes in the entryway. Was it possible that this was about more than the national uniform? Did they already know that Giichi wasn't going to war? Had someone found out and informed the police? Giichi would never be so careless as to indiscreetly confide in someone. Perhaps Hayashi had hidden under their window at night and overheard their conversations?

Toda stepped up to the front room and casually placed his cap on the coat stand. Then, pushing his black-rimmed glasses more firmly against his face, he asked, "Where is your husband today?"

"He is at work," she said.

"At Nippon Motors in Osaka. Is that correct?"

"Yes."

"He's a section manager?"

"Yes."

Yuki, who must be hungry by now, came into the room and uncharacteristically said nothing. She walked up to Kinuko and clung to her monpe pants.

Toda nodded, moved past Kinuko and Yuki, and entered the dining room. Then turning to her, he said, "We received a complaint from Mr. Hayashi. He said your husband doesn't wear a national uniform despite his requests. What is the reason for that?"

"He—," Kinuko stammered, "he has trouble getting up early enough to put it on. He can't sleep very well at night. You see, those long puttees take him quite a while to wrap around his legs." She looked down.

"So, he does own one?" Toda asked.

"Yes, he certainly does," said Kinuko, glad she had bought it.

"Where is it?"

"In his clothes closet," answered Kinuko. "I'll fetch it right away, if you wish to see it."

"No, I'll get it myself," Toda said, heading toward the bedrooms. He stopped briefly in front of the open door to Yuki's room and then proceeded to the next room. He stepped into their bedroom and placed his hand over the knob of her tall paulownia chest.

"That chest is mine," she quickly told him. "It's not his." But it was too late; he had already pulled it open. A large cellophane bag of cotton tumbled out and landed at his feet.

"Hoh," he said, peering at Kinuko with a deliberate pause. "Mrs. Sekihara, I'm sure you know it's illegal to possess this much cotton." He picked up the bag and stepped toward her.

Yuki began to whimper, and Kinuko picked her up. She looked directly into Toda's eyes, "I was afraid miscarrying my baby in January. I needed cotton, so I bought it through the black market."

To her surprise, he dropped the bag, and it settled softly on the floor. Stepping over it, Toda advanced toward Giichi's closet across the room. He opened it and pawed through Giichi's clothes, then pulled out the new khaki uniform. He thrust it toward Kinuko. "Your husband should be wearing this instead of his unpatriotic Western suit. Otherwise, he will be taken into custody on the grounds of failing to comply with the regulations of the neighborhood association. Explain this to him."

"I surely will," Kinuko replied, enormously relieved to know that it was nothing more serious than the national uniform. Still, she felt anger toward Giichi for causing all this trouble. She took the uniform from Toda's hand and hung it on the red lacquered clothes stand in the corner. She would make sure Giichi wore it the next morning, and finally there would be one less thing for her to worry about.

When she turned back from the clothes stand, Toda was still in the middle of the room, scrutinizing every corner.

"Is there anything else I can help you with?" she asked.

"It's not necessary," replied Toda. "You just carry on with whatever you have to do. We'll have to go through things by ourselves."

She stood in silence, holding Yuki tightly in her arms. Toda walked toward the door and signaled to Konno. "Konno, start with the next room and work toward the front room. I have to concentrate on this room for a while."

"Yes, sir," the younger one said and immediately stepped into Yuki's room, as if relieved to finally have a task.

Toda returned to the bedroom and began rummaging through a stack of old newspapers, magazines, and books on the desk under the window. He first pulled the papers aside and picked up the books and magazines one by one, leafing slowly through each of them.

Panicked, Kinuko asked, "Excuse me, may I ask why you are doing this?"

A magazine open in his hand, Toda paused, glanced at her over his glasses and said deliberately, "Because we suspect that your husband might be a man with dangerous thoughts."

"Why do you suspect this?"

"We don't know. That's why we are investigating."

With that, he walked out of the room with an old issue of *The Central Review* and placed it on the dining table next to Konno's cap.

As he made his way back to the bedroom an air raid siren erupted. Yuki began crying, and Kinuko decided to take her to Mrs. Chiba. Toda ignored the siren. He opened a desk drawer. Kinuko waited for the siren to stop.

"I have to take my daughter to my neighbor's house. Please don't take anything out of our house while I'm gone."

She hurried to the kitchen, hearing Toda say behind her, "Madame, I'm a police officer. I don't steal from people's homes." She grabbed a tin box of crackers for Yuki and ran across the street.

Mrs. Chiba opened her door. "I was just about to come to your house to see what's going on."

"The Special Higher Police are at my house. Would you keep Yuki? I have to go back."

Mrs. Chiba's face turned pale. "What are they doing?" she whispered.

"They're looking for something."

"Don't worry, Kinuko-san," said Mrs. Chiba, retreating into the house with Yuki in her arms. "They can't find anything when there isn't anything to find."

The drone of B-29s approached, and Mrs. Chiba tightened her arms around Yuki. "We'll talk later," she said, as Kinuko handed her the tin box.

Kinuko hurried home, where she found Giichi's clothes strewn throughout their bedroom, and Toda kneeling among them, carefully going through each pocket and fold in the cloth. By now the B-29s were directly overhead, making a deafening roar that sounded as if they would rip the world into pieces. The house shook, windows rattled and the light bulb swayed above Toda's head, but he only looked up at the ceiling briefly and went back to the work of scrutinizing Giichi's possessions.

Seeing Toda's resolve, Kinuko realized she could do nothing to stop them. Let them do whatever they want, she decided, they certainly won't find anything. As far as she was concerned, there was nothing else in the house to suggest Giichi's "dangerous" thoughts; he had long ago burned Marx's *Das Kapital* at her urging, after she heard that a friend's cousin was arrested for owning a copy. Besides, this was her house. She would carry on with her own work while they wasted their time. She looked at the clock—twelve-thirty. She guessed they would soon leave for lunch.

But Toda and Konno did not stop. As the afternoon wore on, her tenuous optimism turned to despair. For the next three hours, the two men ransacked every inch of the house, while Kinuko sat in the dining room with a knot in her stomach, pretending to darn a sock. Their search was thorough and meticulous. They worked quietly, only speaking to each other when they needed to coordinate the moving of heavy furniture. They sifted through every conceivable space: a bookcase, drawers, clothes chests, and futon closets, inside the piano and gramophone, trunks and boxes, and underneath every piece of furniture. They leafed through every page of diaries, letters, books and magazines.

All the while, Kinuko attempted to maintain her composure. Outwardly she succeeded. When they looked at her, the two men saw her pressing a needle and yarn into one of Yuki's socks, apparently unaware of the humiliation and anger that roiled inside her. The thoroughness of their search not only humiliated her, it also began to raise a cloud of doubt about Giichi. She began to wonder what he had done to deserve this. She couldn't believe that the mere matter of a national uniform required a search this thorough. It seemed to her the men wanted to prove something definite—something even more serious than the vague notion of Giichi's "dangerous thoughts."

She began to think about all the late nights the previous fall when she waited for Giichi to come home while his supper sat cold on the table. Perhaps he had gotten involved in some kind of antiwar activities. Only when confronted had he confessed to her that he would refuse the red paper. He had said he didn't want to tell her his decision for fear of her anger and sorrow. What else had he been afraid to tell her?

As her thoughts mushroomed, her fear grew until she felt she could no longer bear it. Finally, she heard Toda's weary voice, "It's time for lunch, I suppose." Relief washed over her, but the fear remained. Soon the two men appeared in the dining room with nothing in their hands, but even that did not eliminate her fear.

"We're finished," Toda proclaimed. "Our apologies for the inconvenience."

Without responding, Kinuko rested the sock on her lap.

"Before we leave, however," Toda said, taking a small notebook out of his pocket, "I have to ask you a few questions."

"Please, go ahead," said Kinuko, coiling the yarn around the needles.

"Your husband's father is Ichiro Sekihara, is that correct?"

"Yes," she replied, seeing no point in denying the fact, yet feeling her mouth go dry.

"Fine," Toda stopped and peered down at her as if to make sure he would not miss any change in her expression. "Do you know anything about a man named Kenji Nakayama?"

"No."

"You don't, all right, that's fine. But have you ever heard your husband mention the name? That he used to be his friend in Kyoto or that he sees this Kenji Nakayama from time to time?"

"No, I haven't at all—I've never heard of Kenji Nakayama. Who is he?"

"Well, I hate to be the one to tell you this, but since you've asked, the man is a Communist."

"Communist?" said Kinuko, feeling her heart constrict. She knew how severely communists were brutalized. "My husband is not a communist," she declared. "He has nothing to do with them. Actually, he is against communism."

"Madam, don't get so excited. The issue here isn't whether your husband is a communist."

"What does this man have to do with my husband then?"

"You don't have to know these things. No need. Now, this is a personal question, but how much money does your husband make?"

"I don't know," she replied flatly. Her instincts told her not to give a definite answer.

"How much money does he give you each month?"

"I don't know. I just ask him for some whenever I need it, and I don't keep track of it. Why are you asking me these questions?"

"This is just a routine thing. We ask these questions when we suspect someone might have dangerous thoughts. Anyway, where were we? Oh, yes, what does he do with the rest of the money he earns?"

"Well of course, he spends some on his own for commuting and such, and the rest should be in the bank."

"I see, in the bank. Do you know how much money he has in the bank?"

"No, I don't."

"Hmm, does he gamble?"

"No."

"All right, another personal question, this will be the last one. Does he have a mistress? A geisha or something?"

Konno, who had been listening to their conversation, dropped his gaze to the cap he held at his waist and began fumbling with it. For a flicker of an instant, Kinuko almost laughed as she imagined a bleary-eyed Giichi sitting next to a painted woman with a sake cup in his hand. She had heard that geisha had disappeared long ago because of the government campaign for frugality.

"No, he doesn't," she said. Then suddenly, she wished he did have a geisha, that he frolicked into Kyoto every now and then and indulged himself with sake and the perfume of women in silk kimono. Then, at least, he would be an ordinary man who would never dream of such a thing as refusing the red paper. Then he would be on this same earth with her, even though his mind might occasionally drift off to his mistress.

Toda opened his notebook for the first time and flipped a few pages back and forth. Then he scratched his mole for a moment and suddenly closed the notebook. "Well," he said, pushing it into his pocket, "That's all I wanted to ask you. I appreciate your cooperation."

As Konno picked up the issue of *The Central Review* Toda had taken from Giichi's room, his stomach grumbled. Embarrassed, he blushed. "Konno," Toda teased him. "No manners." Then the two men headed toward the door, Toda laughing and Konno scratching his head.

The calmness Kinuko had exuded during the search evaporated as soon as they left. She dropped to the cold floor of the front room and felt incapable of getting up. Despite her desire to call Giichi, her legs wouldn't move. Her head swirled with Toda's questions—Did Giichi know the communist? How much money did he make? How much did he give her? What did he do with the rest of his money? Gambling, a mistress? She was filled with confusion and fear, and the questions made no sense to her.

Eventually though, as the initial shock faded and she was able to focus her mind, she thought about all of the questions. Toda wanted to know if Giichi knew the communist, and where the rest of Giichi's money went after he gave her what she needed for running the household. Why? Because they suspected Giichi might have been contributing to this man. The frightful scenario began to make sense to her. She felt a fog of deception lifting, revealing a clear picture. It seemed to her now that rejecting the red paper was only one of the secrets Giichi had concealed from her. He probably had others—just as Toda surmised.

This new notion reminded her of the gray shadow that Giichi always seemed to carry around him, as if he were concealing something from her and the rest of the world. At times, this gray shadow made her feel lonely, as if she were living with only part of him. Yet it wasn't something clear enough for her to confront him with or even to articulate. She knew he was a deep thinker—a quality that had attracted her in the first place. And she also knew that he didn't always reveal his thoughts as ardently as his father did. When she felt lonely, she told herself that was the way he was, and over time she had come to accept the part of him she couldn't get to. But now, it was becoming clear to her that the shadow he carried was a reflection of his inner secrets. It made perfect sense to her why Giichi had chosen to live in this working class neighborhood.

She remembered the puzzled, even embarrassed, looks from her friends when she told them where she and Giichi were going to live. They were polite, and their expressions lasted only a fleeting moment, but that was enough to let her know they were wondering why she had chosen a husband who rented a house in the working class neighborhood of southern Ashiya instead of Nishinomiya. After all these years, she realized she had been the only one who hadn't wondered.

In fact, when she came to this neighborhood for the first time, a few days before her bridal furniture was delivered, she thought she would love Giichi more for his modesty. She had known sons of well-to-do families among her relatives and friends' husbands who wished to live away from their parents after marriage, and yet wanted to maintain a standard of living equaling that of their parents, even though they couldn't afford it. Their parents bought or rented a house for them, and they lived in it as if they were entitled because they were the sons of wealthy families. She greatly disliked those men. Besides, she didn't see anything wrong with the house Giichi had rented. Though it was quite old, it was well kept, and it had everything they needed. She knew Giichi could easily afford a better home if either of them wanted it, but she didn't feel it necessary. She had grown up believing that grasping for materialistic pleasure was vulgar, something she had learned from the samurai values of her mother.

Kinuko continued to sit in the front room until Mrs. Chiba brought Yuki back. When Mrs. Chiba saw her sitting pale and expressionless, she quickly turned and hurried home to fetch some dried herb. She returned to boil the herb in Kinuko's kitchen, telling her that it might help calm her nerves. While waiting for it to boil, Mrs. Chiba tried to comfort Kinuko, who now sat at the edge of the dining room, facing the kitchen and hugging her empty stomach. "It must be a mistake," Mrs. Chiba said, watching the kettle. "Giichi-san hasn't done anything wrong. That's why they couldn't find anything. When he comes home, you'll find this is some sort of mistake."

But Kinuko wasn't listening. Instead, she was silently preparing to confront Giichi. She didn't care about the money, and she didn't worry that he had spent their money on a woman or gambling. She simply wanted to know the truth, and if she could, help save him from the danger he faced, whatever it was. Soon a strong medicinal aroma filled the kitchen, and Mrs. Chiba poured the steaming herbal liquid into a cup. Kinuko took a slow, careful sip. As its bitter taste settled on her tongue, she decided that knowing the truth, no matter how bad it might be, was better than not knowing.

CHAPTER 11

Giichi shuffled through the dimly lit fourth-floor corridor of his office building, his hands deep in his pockets. As he came to the swinging door of his office, he pushed it open with his elbow. For a moment, he stood inside the door and gazed down at the floor in a vain attempt to sort through the thoughts cluttering his mind. As the door swung back into place with a squeak, Giichi went to his desk and sat down, trying to go over one thought at a time: his parents' upcoming departure from Osaka; Kinuko's refusal to move to Okayama without him; then Kenji Nakayama who he had not seen for more than two months, and on top of all that, the matter that had just been decided at this afternoon's company meeting.

Starting tomorrow, the company would transport excess parts to military-appointed buildings in various suburbs to keep them from being bombed. As usual, the military didn't give many specifics, but managers at the meeting guessed grimly that the enemy had learned the location of the company's plants, and that they would soon be bombed. Eventually, new assembly lines were to be established in the suburbs. Meanwhile, parts would be transferred back and forth to the various plants in the city in order to keep production afloat. Any employee who could drive, managers included, would be shifted into the transportation project. Giichi was among those assigned to drive a truck. Though no one mentioned the risks involved, it would obviously be dangerous. Giichi knew Kinuko would again tell him to quit his job and move to Okayama with her and Yuki.

He leaned back in his chair and stared at the dark window. He saw his reflection sitting at his neatly arranged desk—the tray that held office documents, the morning paper next to it, and the crystal inkwell given to him by Kinuko. Although in his youth he had allowed himself some time to be disorderly, he was by nature a meticulous man, organized, prompt and efficient, both at work and in his private life.

Yet here he was, mired in frustration, unable to deal with the most important matter. His parents would be moving in nine days; time was running out. He knew he was responsible for Kinuko's refusal to go with them. She had told him clearly that she would move only if he went with her, though he didn't quite understand why she wanted him with her when she acted as if she didn't need him at all. But that was beside the point. He couldn't go because of his arrangement with Kenji Nakayama. It wasn't simply a matter of handing part of his monthly earnings to an old friend; it was an act that helped define who he was. He had to keep doing his part in fighting against the military dictatorship, however small that role might be. In fact, he now realized that this aspect of his life was as important to him as his family, though it was impossible to compare the two matters as if they were at the same level. If only he could explain all of this to Kinuko.

Giichi picked up the morning paper and once again examined the article that outlined another of the problems that troubled him. "*Thirteen communists arrested in Kyoto.*" The article mentioned no names but boasted about the most comprehensive communist arrest in recent years. Giichi didn't like the fact that it happened in Kyoto, though he wasn't sure that was where Kenji's cell operated. He had never asked, and Kenji would have been unable to tell him. Giichi simply brought cash and Kenji took it with whispered thanks. Afterward, they embarked on a harmless conversation that could be heard by anyone—the weather, mutual friends, and how the war was going.

He folded the paper and glanced at his watch—five-twenty. He and Kenji were to meet at six. It was still a little too early to go to the bar arranged as the site of this month's meeting, but he decided to leave, anyway. He glanced at the door to his office, unlocked the bottom drawer of his desk, and took out the envelope he had put there in the morning. It now contained three months' worth of donations, the equivalent of his monthly salary. He quickly pushed the bulging envelope into the inside pocket of his suit jacket, stood up from his desk, put on his coat, and walked out of the office.

When he stepped from the building, he stood alone on the sidewalk. Radio reports predicting air raids had nearly cleared the street. In the distance, a few office workers hurried toward the terminal and a few others waited for a streetcar with collars turned up and hands in pockets. Although it had been a little warmer the last two days, the air still turned icy as soon as the sun went down. Light shone from two windows in buildings across the street. Between the dark silhouettes of buildings, the last orange light lingered at the bottom of the skyline. A streetcar stopped, but Giichi decided to walk; he had plenty of time. He walked slowly, pushing his fedora firmly onto his head and pulling up the collar of his coat against the stinging air.

For an instant, the bark on the naked ginkgo trees along the street glowed in the light from a streetcar. After the streetcar rumbled past, the trees receded into darkness. In the spring they bore profuse fan-shaped leaves, canopied above the sidewalk. In autumn the leaves turned bright yellow and eventually covered the street like a lush mat. Giichi remembered how before Yuki's birth, Kinuko used to meet him at the revolving door as he emerged from the building at five. They would walk side by side under these ginkgo trees to a restaurant or play or concert, as the yellow leaves crunched softly beneath their feet. She often leaned down to pick up a leaf and admired its perfect shape, twirling the stem between her fingers. In her fuchsia and tea-green kimono, she was so beautiful that people stopped to look at her.

Giichi kicked a cigarette butt that lay on the sidewalk. "Damn!" he cursed quietly, suddenly feeling how relentlessly the war had torn them apart. The last several weeks she seemed to have abandoned him with an icy coldness that stabbed his heart. She slept in the guest room and placed meals on the table with few words. When he spoke to her, she answered tersely and didn't leave any opening for him to continue talking. He wondered why she couldn't understand him. Yet he couldn't blame her, he had treated her the same way all through the fall. What kind of wife would smile when her husband told her he would refuse the red paper? And then refused to move to a safe place with his family?

By the time Giichi reached the Osaka terminal, the orange hue in the sky had vanished into darkness, and the whole metropolis lay deep in the cold winter night. He walked into the station building and approached the newsstand at the corner of the littered concourse. He picked up the freshly printed evening paper and dropped coins into the shriveled palm of the old man who sat among the stacks of papers and magazines. The man looked at the coins with his good eye and reached into his filthy pouch for change. Giichi waved his hand to dismiss the change. The old man smiled, his milky eye swimming in its socket. Giichi nodded, almost relieved to see someone smile. He tucked the newspaper under his arm and headed toward the back of the station. It was still only five-forty, but he could sit in the warmth of the bar and wait for Kenji. Tonight he would tell his friend that he was moving to Okayama, and that he would no longer contribute money to their mutual cause.

He walked into Mikiya, three blocks north of the station. As usual, Giichi sat at a corner table and ordered a bottle of sake. Out of habit, he carefully scanned the crowd. Though he knew no sure way of recognizing a plainclothes policeman, he would leave if he saw anyone who looked suspicious. Tonight, the crowd gathered in groups of three to eight. Hands busily poured sake and conversation resounded in bellows. No one seemed interested in anything outside his own group. Giichi leaned back in his chair and vaguely watched the madam weave through the crowd. Middle-aged and stout, she edged past hand-waving customers, carrying a tray of steaming bottles of sake.

Giichi spread the paper on the table and curled his hand around the newly served warm bottle. He wasn't in the mood for sake but drank it anyway to warm his frigid body. The taste of third-rate sake made him wince; it stung his tongue and burned his throat. Nevertheless, with his eyes on the paper, he drained the cup slowly until his tongue grew accustomed to the pungent taste.
He practiced how he would tell Kenji, silently searching for the proper words, "*I'm sorry but I have a pregnant wife and a child to think about and I hope you understand...*" Suddenly, it occurred to him how much the words sounded like those of a man trying to end an affair, and he realized that this act of giving money to Kenji Nakayama was entirely like an affair.

He hid it from Kinuko as carefully as an unfaithful husband would hide liaisons with a mistress. He never fully committed himself to Kenji or their cause, not in the same way Kenji did. He could always return to his family, while Kenji struggled alone in the dark folds of Japan's anti-war subculture. Like an unfaithful husband, he could back out of their arrangement at his convenience. The thought disgusted him. But what else could he do? He knew he couldn't live like Kenji, even though he passionately admired Kenji's burning desire to stop this war, he had a family to care for. Still, a sense of shame gripped him, and his mind grew more unsettled. He recalled the night this arrangement had started, the night when Kenji reappeared, and Giichi told his friend that he was to be married and that he would not join the communists. Kenji had accepted his decision and left him alone in the bar, feeling as he now felt, alone and ashamed.

But that night, Giichi had finally chased after Kenji, forgetting his vow to be blind to the world in exchange for personal happiness and a normal life. "Wait," he called to his friend, already far away in the rain-soaked street. He ran to Kenji's side, and they walked together in silence through dark alleys, turning here and there until they reached a deserted shrine awash with a strong scent of Japanese cedars. "Look," said Giichi. "I have a job. I've started earning money. Let me help you with money. I want to help the cause through you. However you spend it, that's your business—on yourself or share it with your comrades, I don't care. It'll be for our mutual cause, either way."

Giichi awaited Kenji's answer, as raindrops splashed on his friend's glasses and sent back a reflection of the light filtering through the trees. The thick smell of Kenji's unwashed clothes mixed with the fresh fragrance of rain, a hint of the dust on the outer corridor of the shrine, and the wet pebbles in the courtyard.

"We certainly need money," Kenji said at last. "Many of our members have families they can't support since they have gone underground or are in prison."

"Then let me help."

"Do you really know what you are getting yourself into?" Kenji turned his gaze to the darkness of the courtyard. "If you are caught, you will be labeled a communist sympathizer, which is the same as being labeled a communist. You could be killed. Or through you, they will try to get me. I'm not saying I don't trust you completely, but you never know. We are all human, after all."

Giichi knew immediately that Kenji feared he might confess under torture. To prove his trustworthiness, he insisted more strongly that Kenji allow him to make donations. "Listen, I will soon be married," he said, "I can't live like you, but I have to do something to help. Otherwise, I won't be able to live with myself."

Only weeks later did Kenji agree, and their secret arrangement began. That was more than eight years ago. Every month he met with Kenji in a different bar in a different district and donated one-third of his salary to help the families of the brave men who infiltrated the military, or painted anti-war signs on the sides of buildings in the dead of night, or died in prisons for whatever desperate acts they had carried out for the good of the country.

During the years of their arrangement, Kenji sometimes failed to show up for their meetings, and Giichi would worry that something had happened to his friend. Today's news of arrests in Kyoto made Giichi's stomach churn. He looked at his watch. It was six-fifteen and still no sign of Kenji, no customer wearing an ill-fitting suit, no shining eyes. For the first time, Giichi realized that the concern Kenji had voiced years ago was now his own concern. What if Kenji had been arrested and divulged *his* name? He picked up the bottle now lukewarm and half full, but he had no interest in finishing it. He folded the paper and stood, then groped in his pocket for cash and handed three wrinkled one-yen bills to the madam, who thanked him with a smile that flashed gold teeth.

Giichi reached the tram bound for Kobe just in time to jump inside before the door closed and the departure bell stopped clanging. Immediately, the tram began to move. With his heart pounding, Giichi settled on a seat close to the rear door and placed his bag on the empty seat next to him. He looked through the car and observed two dozen or so other passengers. Except for a few women, they were mostly tired-looking office workers eager to get home before being stranded by an air raid warning. The majority wore national uniforms, looking like soldiers with black or brown leather bags instead of guns.

This evening, he was glad no one sat next to him as he continued to brood over his numerous problems. Fifteen minutes later, the wail of a siren interrupted his thoughts. The lights flickered off, the tram screeched to a stop, and Giichi was thrown forward, his chest thumping against the seat in front of him. He heard the thud of his bag on the floor. Cursing silently, he clawed for it and then wiggled back onto the seat in the dark. He adjusted his coat and automatically pressed his hand against his breast pocket. When he felt the envelope, he relaxed. This wasn't the first time he had been stranded on a tram. By now, he had learned to stay calm. While some passengers wailed, he closed his eyes. There was no point in getting upset with circumstances that were beyond anyone's control. Usually, after several minutes, the siren sounded the all clear, the lights came on, and the tram moved again, though the process sometimes repeated itself over and over during the long ride home.

Tonight, it was different. Within a minute, the loud drone of B-29s replaced the shrill scream of the siren. Anti-aircraft guns began firing, *bun-bun-bun-bun-bun,* and threads of light crisscrossed the vast expanse of dark sky. Giichi clutched the metal bar of the headrest in front of him and held his breath, his eyes chasing the orange lights and his heart drumming in his ears. The B-29s tore the air directly above and Giichi pressed his head against the back of the seat. There was a jolt and before he knew it, he was crawling on the floor. Flashes of light illuminated the inside of the car. Bombs slammed nearby, and his forehead banged against the hard floor.

In a few minutes, the noise of the B-29s faded and the tram steadied. Giichi inhaled stale floor wax, a smell that seemed oddly pleasant as he realized he was alive. Then he smelled something burning. He propped himself on his hands and knees, craning his neck like a turtle. The smell intensified, and the windows on both sides glowed red. He crawled to a window and peeked out. He gaped and jerked away from the window. Less than fifty meters away, flames engulfed the poorest section of Amagasaki, where in daylight he often saw children playing in the alleys and women chatting beneath laundry poles. Screams erupted behind him. He turned to see torches of fire shooting up from a cluster of ammunition factories. Red shards rained down and drifted toward them.

"Move!" "Start the engine!" "Hurry!" passengers screamed. The carriage trembled and began edging forward without lights then came to a stop about three kilometers down the tracks. Behind him, fires raged in the dark sky and fire bells rang furiously. He shivered. Children and housewives were probably burning in that fire at this moment, just like Mr. Chiba. Thoughts of Kinuko and Yuki entered his mind like a hot needle, and he closed his eyes, murmuring, "They have to leave. They must."

When he finally reached home two hours later, Giichi found Kinuko just inside the door. "You must get out of Hanshin!" he hissed, and then seized her shoulders and shook her. "Amagasaki was hit again. People's homes are burning. It's not just plants and factories anymore! Do you hear me? You and Yuki have to get out."

"I know, but I have to tell you something!" she shouted back at him.

"Don't tell me anything. You have to go to Okayama!"

Kinuko pulled away from his grip, and he felt her breath thicken in the darkness.

"Listen!" she rasped. "The Special Higher Police came today!"

Giichi suddenly slumped onto the edge of the front room. They have captured Kenji, he thought, holding his head. Then just as quickly, he stood again. Now more than ever, he knew that she and Yuki must leave. If he was going to be arrested, he didn't want them to see it happen. "You should be worrying about Yuki's safety instead of the police! You'd better-"

"I'm scared to death!"

Giichi slumped down further and pulled off his shoes. Then he stomped into the dining room and threw his bag on the floor. He heard Kinuko sobbing in the entryway while she locked the door. When she came into the dining room, she moved into the arc of the candlelight and set her glittering eyes on him.

"It's not just the national uniform."

"What nonsense," Giichi blurted out, yanking off his coat.

The candle flickered, and Kinuko shot back, "Don't be so ridiculously stubborn!" She shook her hands in exasperation. "It's just something to wear. What does it really matter?"

Giichi slumped down cross-legged next to the dining table.

"I will wear it," he spat, "if you want me to so badly. But you must take Yuki to-"

"That's not all I have to say. Who is this communist, Kenji Nakayama?"

Giichi felt his heart jump. "I don't know," he said. "I have no idea."

"You have to tell me the truth," Kinuko said, already softening her tone. "Two policemen rummaged through every part of this house for three hours."

"Listen," he said, trying to gather his thoughts as he stood. "I'll change first, then you tell me all about it."

His skull throbbed; the scene in Amagasaki still raged at the backs of his eyes. There was too much to absorb. He picked up his bag and coat, walked into the bedroom and closed the door behind him. He stood in the darkness for a few moments to listen for Kinuko. When he felt certain she was not near, he groped for the top of the desk and lit a candle. Then he took the envelope out of his pocket and wrote his father's name on it. If the police came back before tomorrow morning and found it, he would say it was a payment on a debt to his father, who was soon leaving for Okayama. Otherwise, the first thing in the morning, he would place the money in a bank account in the suburbs where they wouldn't consider looking for it. He would have the chance when he drove the truck tomorrow. He opened the futon closet and tentatively placed the envelope under the bottom layer.

He began to undress, hanging each item carefully, taking his time, while his mind raced crazily. Kenji must have been one of the communists arrested. He must have confessed under torture. No, he thought, that couldn't be. Kenji would never confess! He would die rather than sell out a friend. He was a disciplined man, like steel. How else could he have given up everything for his cause? But he was also human.

Giichi felt the dryness in his mouth. He threw his robe over his shoulders and tied a sash around his waist, preparing himself to face Kinuko. She seemed determined to probe his secret life, but his determination was as strong as hers. He couldn't possibly tell her the truth. Aiding a communist was a crime. And knowing that someone aided a communist was also a crime. He had to keep her completely out of this affair. The less she knew, the safer she was.

He returned to the dining room, his back straight. Kinuko was in the kitchen, pouring hot water into a teapot, her profile hard in the nimbus of candlelight, her shadow and the steam from the pot moving on the wall. Giichi sat down with studied calmness and lifted the cloth that covered his supper.

"I'm ready," he said, picking up his chopsticks, "Tell me what happened."

"Mr. Hayashi brought them at lunch time," she replied, putting a lid on the teapot. "There were two of them; they were here for three hours."

She was calmer now, as she carried the tray of tea to the table.

"That Hayashi is a spy," Giichi said evenly. "I knew it."

Kinuko placed the tray on the table and sat across from him. "Then why didn't you wear the national uniform if you knew that?"

"Let's not go back to that. I've already said I will wear it. What did they find after three hours?"

"*The Central Review*," answered Kinuko, pouring tea into his cup.

"See. What else could they find?"

"But it gives them a hint of what kind of person you are."

"It does, but reading doesn't constitute a crime."

"That's not what really scares me. They asked me so many questions about you."

"All right." Giichi put his chopsticks down. "Tell me from the very beginning—from the time they came into the house."

Kinuko slid a cup of tea toward him and paused for a moment before she spoke. Then she sat erect and recounted in detail the whole episode, the names of the policemen, what they looked like, what they did, what they knew about Giichi, what Toda asked her, carefully following the chronological order. She maintained her calmness, but her eyes occasionally glistened. Giichi listened quietly, chewing his food slowly, occasionally interrupting her with questions to get every detail.

When Kinuko finished, she shifted her body, sat even straighter, and said with calm determination, "Now, please tell me the truth. It's obvious that they suspect you have a connection with the communist. If you've given him money, I don't care, but I want to know the truth because I am your wife. I've always felt you were hiding something. Is that why you want so badly to send me and Yuki to Okayama?"

"No!" He shook his head. "Don't you understand, I'm truly worried about you and Yuki's safety. You should have seen the bombing in Amagasaki!"

"Then we all should go to Okayama. But before we talk about that, tell me the truth, please."

Giichi put down his chopsticks, coughed a little, and took a sip of tea. "Believe me, I don't hide anything from you, and I'm very sorry this happened. Maybe it's my fault. I should have worn the national uniform, as you insisted. Then this wouldn't have happened."

"You really don't know the man? You haven't given him money?"

"I was just trying to recall who he was while I was changing. The name sounded familiar."

"And?"

"When I was at the university, I think there was a student by that name. For a very short time, I used to sit next to him in some classes, or chat between classes. But I've never seen him since."

"Was he a communist back then?"

"I don't know," replied Giichi. "I didn't know him that well. Anyway, don't worry, nothing will happen, as long as I wear the national uniform. Tomorrow I will wear it, so you can stop worrying."

Kinuko stared at him. She didn't appear totally convinced; a slight frown creased her forehead. He kept eating, trying to chew nonchalantly.

"Are you sure you are telling me the truth? Are you sure you haven't had any contact with the man? I'm not trying to accuse you. I just want—"

"Why do you repeat the same questions?" Giichi demanded. "I already said I don't know him."

"Then why did they search the house all afternoon and ask me those questions?"

"I don't know—I wish I did. But this is what I've figured from what you've told me. Hayashi is a spy. Remember when he made himself the neighborhood chief? He wasn't voted in and no one from the city appointed him. He retired from the Ashiya Police one day and was suddenly a neighborhood chief the next. Anyway, he must have gone to the station where he used to work and told them, 'There is a man in my neighborhood who doesn't wear a national uniform. He seldom attends the neighborhood meetings. His father is Ichiro Sekihara. You should check him out. Something might turn up.' After all, that is what Hayashi has always wanted to do—humiliate me."

"But what about this communist?"

"Maybe they are looking for the man, and maybe someone told them I knew him a long time ago in Kyoto."

Kinuko sighed and looked down. She still didn't appear convinced. The dying nub of the candle flickered on the table.

"I should have told them you have a mistress, then they might have believed that was how you spend your money instead of giving it to a communist," she said.

Giichi suddenly felt tired, physically and mentally. He put down his chopsticks and rice bowl, took a sip of tea and stood up. "I'll go see Yuki," he announced.

He tiptoed into Yuki's room. The blackout was still in force, and he lit a candle. When the sudden light spilled over her face, Yuki stirred and shifted her body with a soft murmur, but she didn't awaken. Soon her breathing returned deep in her pillow. She slept in patched flannel pajamas with her injured doll beside her. A surge of pity filled him—this child had only known a world of war, and her father might soon be arrested and taken from her. He sat quietly beside her futon and gently touched her hand. It felt cold. He lifted the cover and slowly put her hand beneath it. Then he gazed at her—her soft cheeks, black eyelashes, delicate brows like her mother's, and shiny bangs that parted slightly in the middle.

As he sat next to her, his plans came as naturally as the steady flow of her breath. Tomorrow, first thing in the morning, he would submit his resignation, then call his parents to tell them that Kinuko and Yuki would go to Okayama with them. He would follow them as soon as the company agreed to let him go. Then everyone would be happy. Yuki would be safe, and Kinuko, who had an inkling of his secret, would have to admit she had been wrong. Everything would be fine, except for the gulf that would continue to separate his facade from who he really was. He had lived in two worlds for eight years, carrying his burden of secrecy, and he had succeeded thus far, even during these confrontations with Kinuko when she seemed perilously close to learning the truth. As long as the war continued, he had no choice but to live in spiritual turmoil. If Kenji had actually been arrested, he couldn't be contacted anyway. Forget about contributing to his cause, Giichi told himself, escape to Okayama where the sky is blue and trout swim in the cool creek. Let Yuki run about in a meadow this spring.

Giichi began to feel as if the weight of a stone had dropped from his stomach. Though he worried about Kenji's fate and his own, he hoped his friend still slipped through the streets late at night, hanging posters with antiwar slogans or pasting them on buildings, poles, and the sides of bridges. The police certainly suspected his money arrangement with Kenji and possibly knew about their past friendship, but they must not have definite proof or they would have arrested him instead of searching the house. Still, he knew he should be careful from now on. Tomorrow, he would wear the national uniform and hide the money.

He touched Yuki's hair softly, then stood quietly and blew off the candle. When he left the room, the smell of melted wax permeated the darkness. "Kinuko?" he called in a low voice outside the guest bedroom.

"Yes," her muffled voice replied.

"May I come in?"

"Yes."

He opened the door and found her sitting on the futon combing her hair. Her long straight hair cascaded over one shoulder, and shadows moved across her face as a candle wavered beside her. She rested the comb and mirror on her lap and observed him in silence. He took a few steps toward her. "Tomorrow," he said, "I'll tell the company that I'm going to resign."

A faint sigh spilled from her lips and her face softened. She looked up at him serenely. "Will you sit down?" she asked quietly, placing her comb and mirror beside her.

Giichi sat next to her and took her hand. He hadn't touched her for so long. Her hand was cold and limp yet soft as a feather. The feel of it brought a sudden tightness to his throat. "We'll go to Okayama together," he whispered, "all of us."

"I'm glad," she said evenly. Then she looked down for a second and added, "I'm sorry about what I said."

"What do you mean?"

"That I should have told the police you have—a mistress."

"That's all right—I'm sorry you had to go through all that. It must have been terrifying."

"I hate this war," she said, drawing her hand from his to cover her face. "I hate it—I hate everything about it. It killed Mr. Chiba. We can't get enough good food for Yuki, we always have to be afraid of Hayashi or the police." She drew in a long wet sigh.

"It will end," said Giichi. "It will end someday—soon."

Nodding with a weak smile, she leaned softly against him, her hair flowing over her shoulders, glowing in the soft candlelight.

"Everything will be fine," Giichi told her, gathering her hair to one shoulder. "We'll be safe in Okayama and after the war we'll come back to Hanshin and live in a bigger house, because we'll be coming back with another baby."

Kinuko's shoulders trembled.

"The war will end soon," Giichi repeated. "It must," he added with desperate hope. Gently, he guided her onto the futon so he could lie beside her.

CHAPTER 12

Kinuko poured whipped eggs over sizzling onions and quickly formed an omelet over the hibachi. She hadn't made anything this special for a long time. It was rare to be able to have eggs these day, but she was able to buy two from Mrs. Tanaka who had gone to the countryside previous day to buy them on the black market. She felt blessed as the sweet aroma of eggs and onions filled the kitchen. During the three days since Giichi began wearing the national uniform, Kinuko felt their home had returned to something resembling normalcy, and the wafting aroma of a prewar meal added to the illusion that everything would be fine.

Sitting at the table, awaiting the special breakfast, Giichi still didn't look entirely comfortable in his uniform, but at least he appeared more comfortable than on the first morning he wore it, when he had stepped into the dining room with slumped, defeated shoulders. She had to admit she didn't like the way he looked in the uniform either, but his willingness to do whatever was necessary to maintain peace within the family made her feel as buoyant as a dandelion seed drifting in the wind. It also rekindled her hope that he might reconsider his decision to refuse the red paper. Though she and Yuki would move to Okayama with Ichiro and Sumiko in one week, she knew now that Giichi would join them a few weeks later when his resignation became official.

For the past two evenings Giichi had regaled Yuki with stories of his childhood vacation in Okayama—her Grandma cooling a huge watermelon in a well in the morning and cutting it in the afternoon for everyone to eat, Grandpa fishing in the river and coming back with a bucketful of fish. "The sky is so big and blue there," Giichi told her, spreading his arms wide. "And chickens run around in the back yard."

"Chickens and watermelons and fish?" Yuki uttered with wide glowing eyes.

Watching her excitement, Kinuko realized that her daughter had only seen those things in books.

Giichi ate his omelet, telling Yuki they would be able to eat eggs every morning in Okayama.

"Eggs every morning?" Yuki shouted.

"Yes, every morning," Giichi replied as he stood to leave.

Yuki dropped her spoon and wrapped her arms around his legs. Giichi lifted her up and nuzzled his face against hers.

"Papa has to go now," he said.

"Are you driving a big truck today, too, Papa?"

"Yes, I am. Be a good girl while I'm gone, all right?"

Giichi lowered her to the floor and bent over in the entryway to fasten the clasps of the new jikatabi shoes Kinuko had bought for him, thinking they would be more suitable for truck driving than his dress shoes.

"Bye, Papa," said Yuki, waving her little arm vigorously.

"Bye," said Giichi, waving back, as he walked out the door. "Be a good girl for Mama. I'll come home early."

With Yuki in her arms, Kinuko stood in the doorway, watching him walk toward the tram stop. The air was still chilly, but the crisp morning light suggested a warmer day than the one before. The mist in the cleft of the mountains began evaporating under the sharp light from the east, and the sky above was clear blue. She felt a little nostalgic, thinking she might never see Giichi off like this once they moved to Okayama. Now Giichi started up the concrete steps leading to the Hanshin Highway. Momentarily, the image of Mr. Chiba disappearing into the underpass that last day flashed through her mind and sent a shiver of apprehension through her. Nothing could be taken for granted. She shook off the feeling and thought of the preparation for their move to Okayama, where they would all be together in safety. The worst part would be her separation from Mrs. Chiba.

Kinuko closed the door and began sorting clothes for their departure. She started a pile for each of them. It was difficult to know what to take. She didn't want to pack too much, but they might be in Okayama for a long time.

An hour later, the phone rang and she hurried to answer it, thinking it was Sumiko, suggesting additional items to pack.

"Sekiharas," she said pleasantly. "May I—"

"Mrs. Sekihara?" It was a man's urgent voice.

"Yes?"

"This is Kato, from Nippon Motors."

"Oh, yes, Mr. Kato," she said, bowing slightly and wondering why he would call. Giichi should already be at work.

"We've just gotten a phone call. I'm sure it's nothing...but we've gotten this call from the Ashiya Police."

Kinuko felt her heart tighten.

"Ashiya Police?" she finally managed to say. "About, about my husband?"

"Yes. I'm afraid they took him in. I asked them why, but they wouldn't answer. I'm sorry...."

Kinuko felt as if she had descended into a horrible dream and remained speechless as he continued, "All they said is your husband wasn't coming in to work today...are you all right, Mrs. Sekihara? Are you still there?"

"Yes."

"I'm sure it's nothing serious, but if he doesn't come home today, please call me. If there is anything I can do, please don't hesitate to call. My home number is—are you ready to write it down?"

"No..."

"Can you get a pencil and paper?"

"Y-yes."

Kinuko put down the receiver. When she finally came back to the phone, her hands shook and it took her a while to write down the number.

After she hung up the phone, she paced around the dining table clutching the number in her shaking hand. Then she suddenly strode to the veranda, where Yuki was playing with blocks, and lifted her from the floor without warning. Yuki screamed for her injured doll. Kinuko picked up the doll and carried Yuki across the street.

"What is it?" Mrs. Chiba asked, taking Yuki from her.

"Nippon Motors called. Giichi is at the Ashiya Police Station."

Mrs. Chiba grew pale but said calmly, "I will watch Yuki-chan. Don't worry. If there is anything else I can do, let me know. I'll be here with Yuki-chan."

Kinuko went back to her house and approached the phone, suddenly yearning to hear Ichiro's voice. Earlier, in spite of her anticipation of moving to a safe place, she remembered that she had dreaded living under the same roof with Ichiro because he failed to support her regarding Giichi's red paper decision. Now, she couldn't think of anyone else to talk to. Her hands shook, as she waited for someone to answer. The telephone kept ringing, and finally, she heard Ichiro's voice.

"Sekiharas. May I help—"

"Father! Giichi—Giichi was taken to the Ashiya Police Headquarters. His office just called!"

"Calm down, Kinuko, just calm down now," his voice wheezed. "Why? Did they tell you why? Never mind, I'll be right there. Or should I go straight to the police station? Yes, I'll leave right now."

"I'll meet you there, Father."

"No, don't. It's not a pleasant place for—"

"I'll meet you there."

"All right. But be careful on the way. Be careful."

The double doors of the Ashiya Police Headquarters stood wide open, though not in a way that felt inviting. In her whole life, Kinuko had never stepped into a police station, and the sight of the lobby frightened her—two black-uniformed officers whispered conspiratorially with wooden batons dangling from their belts. Other officers hurried in and out, their leather boots echoing against the concrete floor. When she saw one of them drag an emaciated old man in handcuffs across the floor and slide him into a dark corridor, her knees locked. Feeling as if someone else's legs moved her, she finally entered the lobby, where a light fixture hung from the tall ceiling, the bottoms of its four globes dark with accumulated dust. Only one of the four bulbs glowed with light, the other three had either burned out or were unscrewed from their sockets to save electricity.

Kinuko looked around, searching for a reception desk or window. But the window, above which two Chinese characters indicated reception, was closed. She shuffled to the wooden bench in the corner of the lobby and sat with her eyes fixed intently on the entrance.

When Ichiro strode into the lobby, she sprang from the bench and rushed toward him, shouting, "Father!"

"I'm glad you called," said Ichiro, breathing heavily. "Don't worry, everything will be fine. I'll talk to someone. Stay here and wait for me."

He led her back to the bench, where she sat as obediently as a child and looked up at him. "The other day," she panted. Ichiro bent over to listen, placing his ear close to her mouth. "Two Special Higher Policemen came and searched our house. Did Giichi tell you?"

"No," Ichiro said, shaking his head as he sat beside her. "I didn't know that. What did they want?"

"They seemed to suspect Giichi had a connection with a communist named Kenji Nakayama. Has Giichi ever mentioned anything about this man?"

"No, he hasn't. Does Giichi know him?"

"He said he knew him a little when he was a student in Kyoto."

"Did they find anything during the search?"

"Just a back issue of *The Central Review.*"

"Is that all? I think they are after the poor communist, not Giichi. But they have him here now and we have to deal with that."

"What can we do?"

"I'll find an officer," he said. "There has to be a simple explanation for this."

Kinuko watched Ichiro walk toward the closed reception window. His mere presence in the huge concrete tomb of the lobby gave her a hint of the long-forgotten feeling of security that had surrounded her as a child, when she snuggled against her father and listened to him read stories that made her laugh. While Ichiro knocked on the reception window and waited for it to open, she felt optimistic.

But her optimism evaporated with every passing moment. An hour later, they still sat on the bench; the window never opened again. Ichiro tapped the window a few more times, but no one came to open it. He paced impatiently and sat and paced again and finally settled next to Kinuko, exhausted. It was almost noon when Kinuko finally spotted the young officer stepping into the lobby through the swinging door.

"Mr. Konno," she uttered, struggling to stand from the bench.

Ichiro jumped up. "I am Giichi Sekihara's father. And you are?"

"I'm Konno from the Special Higher Police."

"May I ask you why my son was brought here?"

"Officer Toda directed me to tell you that he thinks your son might have a very important piece of information regarding one particular communist. So he is being questioned."

"My husband doesn't know Kenji Nakayama," Kinuko protested. "He vaguely remembers there was a student by that name. That's all he can tell Mr. Toda."

"That means my son doesn't have to be here long, doesn't it?" Ichiro interjected.

"I can't tell you how long we'll need him."

"But can't you give us an approximation?" Ichiro pressed.

"No, I can't," Konno said, irritation spreading across his face, "because it depends on how cooperative your son is. Could be just a day or two, could be a week. It will be up to him."

"A week? That's ridiculous!" Ichiro blurted, and Kinuko nervously tugged at his sleeve.

"Officer Toda doesn't know how long he'll be here," Konno raised his voice slightly. "If he doesn't know, I don't know either."

With that Konno turned on his heels and started to walk away.

"Please, my husband has nothing to do with this communist," Kinuko cried, but he quickly disappeared through the swinging door. Kinuko's vision went black and she dizzily sat back on the bench. She lowered her head and covered her face.

"Let's—let's sit here for a while," she heard Ichiro say. "Then we will go home by taxi. Don't worry. He'll be fine. He might come home this afternoon and tell us we were silly to have worried for nothing."

Back at Kinuko's, Ichiro hurriedly laid out her futon and urged her to sleep. She figured he was right; sleep seemed the only way to forget her agony. But when she awoke several hours later, she felt even worse. She had slept, not only while Giichi suffered in jail, but also while someone else took care of her child.

The light in the room was fading. She should be cooking supper instead of lying in bed. She wondered where Yuki was, if Father had gone home. She quickly straightened her clothes, though her pregnant body wouldn't move as fast as she wanted it to.

Gathering her hair together at the back of her neck, she shuffled toward the dining room and heard Ichiro's voice through the closed door. So, he had stayed there all afternoon. She searched for an excuse for having slept so long, but his voice sounded so dejected it frightened her. She had never heard him talk that way. H was the man she always found full of confidence. Holding her breath, she listened.

"I'm sorry, I've lied to you," she heard him say. He seemed to be talking to his wife. Kinuko wondered what Sumiko had done when the police took Ichiro away. Sumiko was not a native of Hanshin; she would have had no family to call for help, no parents or in-laws. Yet Kinuko felt certain Sumiko would never have slept in broad daylight, no matter how difficult her struggles. The guilt overwhelmed her.

"Don't be discouraged," Ichiro's subdued voice continued. "He will get through this, believe me. Yes, I will tell her that when she wakes up. Don't worry about her, she'll be all right. Yes, I'll see to that. Anyway, I will call you tomorrow. All right then. Take care."

There was a click of the receiver, then silence. Now her mother-in-law, too, knew that she had slept the whole afternoon. After a moment of hesitation, she slid the door open.

"Kinuko," said Ichiro. "How you are feeling?"

"I'm fine, thank you."

"That's good. I'm glad."

"I didn't mean to listen, but you should go home. Mother needs you."

"She has Ume. I don't want you to be alone tonight."

"I'm fine—and Giichi still might come home."

"Kinuko," Ichiro said, then paused for a moment. "I—I hate to tell you, but Giichi is not coming home tonight—I called."

Kinuko sat down and stared numbly into space. Ichiro stepped up to the dining room. "Go back to bed." he said gently. "Mrs. Chiba has been most kind. She already offered to keep Yuki overnight. You are still pale."

Kinuko shook her head and mumbled, "I have to cook."

"I can cook, Kinuko."

Startled, she looked at her father-in-law. Ichiro and cooking had never gone together in her mind—a man who always held a pen, a man who lived with a wife and maids wasn't likely to know much about a kitchen.

"You can cook, Father?"

"Of course, I can."

Kinuko laughed a little, but Ichiro was serious.

"I used to cook when I was single."

"That's a long time ago, Father."

"It is, as a matter of fact, but—"

They began laughing. It was a quiet laugh filled with grief. Even then Kinuko felt guilty, imagining Giichi alone in a dark cell with no one to talk to, let alone laugh with. Before tears could begin falling, she abruptly stood and stepped down to the kitchen. "I'll cook now, Father," she said.

"Then I'll help," said Ichiro.

Kinuko felt uncomfortable, but he was already in the kitchen, tucking up his sleeves. So she asked him to start a fire, while she rinsed the rice. Ichiro took the hibachi outside the kitchen door. It was getting dark, but through the window, Kinuko could see the dark figure of her father-in-law bustling over his task. He coughed, rubbed his eyes, and squatted down in front of the hibachi with the awkwardness of a person unaccustomed to domestic chores. But he appeared earnest, and soon he had the fire ready. He brought the cooker in and mumbled modestly, "Hope this will work."

Kinuko placed a pot over the heat, and Ichiro went through the house, closing the wooden shutters and curtains. Kinuko remained in the kitchen and prepared miso soup, finding comfort in the sound of the rattling shutters and the swish of the curtains. At the same time it reminded her of the immense sorrow of the evening ahead without Giichi. Nevertheless, she regretted she didn't have better food for her father-in-law's rare visit. While Ichiro went to Mrs. Chiba's to get Yuki, she set the table.

An hour later, they were all seated around the table, and Kinuko began ladling soup into the bowls.

"Where is Papa?" Yuki suddenly whined, her chin on the edge of the table.

Startled by her question, Kinuko held the ladle over the bowl and glanced at Ichiro. Without hesitation, he replied, "Your father is still out working, driving a truck to a faraway place. He can't come home tonight, but Grandpa is here instead."

His voice sounded matter-of-fact, he didn't flounder at all, as Kinuko felt certain she would have. She was relieved, but Yuki continued, "Is he coming home tomorrow?"

"He might, he might not. But I'll be here until he comes home. Don't you like Grandpa to be here?"

"Yes!" Yuki cried, sitting up straight.

"Good, let's eat, shall we?"

Ichiro moved closer to Yuki and helped her with her spoon. She seemed satisfied now. Kinuko struggled with her food in silence. She absent-mindedly listened to their banter, but her mind drifted off to a dark corner of the Ashiya Police Headquarters, tormented by thoughts of Giichi suffering alone. If he was cold, she wanted to be cold with him. If he was eating rotten food, she wanted to eat it with him. If he was being beaten, she wanted to be beaten instead of him.

The rest of the evening revolved around Yuki. Ichiro played blocks with her, while Kinuko washed the dishes in silence. When an air raid warning came, Ichiro pried up the tatami mats and baseboard. The three hid in the cold, musty hole with blankets wrapped around them and a candle illuminating their faces. Ichiro held Yuki and told her stories while Kinuko listened quietly. Between warnings, Kinuko helped Yuki brush her teeth, and Ichiro played horse with Yuki in her pajamas. Overly excited by his presence, she demanded that he go faster, shrieking and giggling until they both fell to the floor and gasped.

It was almost eleven when Yuki finally collapsed on the floor, her thumb in her mouth and the doll wedged between her arm and her chest. Ichiro carried her to bed and gently removed the doll. "Well," he sighed weakly and swept his hand across his forehead, as he stood up from Yuki's futon.

The weight of Giichi's absence descended on the house now that it had gone silent. A chill settled in. Though they were both exhausted, sleep didn't seem possible. They stood awkwardly in the dining room and listened to the radio, not knowing what else to do in the thick silence. But the news only added more weight to their weariness. Through persistent electronic crackles, they heard that earlier in the evening the Allies had destroyed bridges over the Yodo River in Osaka, killing citizens who had evacuated their homes and gone under the bridge for protection.

Ichiro sat down, muttering incomprehensibly. Suddenly, he appeared old and weary and inconsolable as he rubbed his face.

"Father, you must go to bed," Kinuko said. "I'll prepare a futon for you."

"Oh, don't worry," Ichiro mumbled, adjusting his glasses and blinking weakly. "I can do that later. You should go to bed." With that, he picked up the morning paper beside the table. The light bulb above dropped a dull circle over the paper as he unfolded it. He stared at it with his mouth shut tight.

Leaving him alone, Kinuko laid a futon for him in the guest bedroom. As she smoothed a clean sheet over it, she thought about how intensely she had ignored Ichiro since their meeting in January. She felt certain he had been aware of her anger toward him, and yet, without a trace of reproach, he had come immediately when she called. If not for him, she didn't know how she would have gotten through the day.

Now feeling more guilty than resentful, Kinuko crept back into the dining room. When Ichiro noticed her, he uttered, "Oh, Kinuko," then began fumbling at the fold of his kimono. "I'm sorry, I forgot all about the letter from your mother. While you were resting, a postman came, so I took your mail."

Out of the fold, he produced the letter and handed it to her. "I've been getting so forgetful lately. I'm sorry."

"That's all right, Father," Kinuko said. The letter felt warm in her hand and slightly curved in the way it had lain across his chest. The warmth of it made her feel even guiltier. "You had other things to worry about," she added.

"That's true, but you needed to hear from your mother on a day like this."

Ichiro should have been right, but these days, her mother's letters had become a burden. Ever since Giichi revealed his decision to reject the red paper, Kinuko felt as if she no longer had anything to tell her mother. Without mentioning Giichi's decision and the turmoil in her life, what else was there? With every letter she received, Kinuko grew more despondent about her inability to be truthful, and more recently, the letters made her feel weary, filled as they were with the worry of not hearing from her daughter. Especially tonight, her mother's letter seemed even more of an intrusion. She already knew what it would say but opened it because Ichiro seemed anxious for her to read it.

Last fall, predicting Allied bombing in big cities, Etsu had locked up her house in Kobe and moved to her hometown of Sasayama, sixty kilometers north of Hanshin. Since moving, she constantly urged Kinuko, Giichi and Yuki to come and live with her. In an apparent effort to entice her daughter to join her, she usually mentioned the peacefulness and beauty of the countryside—the blue sky and the sweet air. She ended each letter by reiterating that they were welcome anytime. The old samurai house, she emphasized, was too big for her, and she would love to see Yuki running freely in the garden.

In this letter, as Kinuko expected, she sounded more desperate than ever. "*As you well know, the matter is becoming life or death.*"

She vacantly stared at her mother's flawless handwriting. As always, she had written with a brush and traditional black ink. Etsu rigorously avoided a pen, claiming that a letter written with a pen would give the recipient the impression that the sender was being hasty, thus showing less respect, and accordingly, the recipient would take the contents of the letter less seriously. So she wrote with ink in the old-fashioned manner, painstakingly rubbing an ink-stick against the wet surface of an inkwell. Etsu was thoroughly the daughter of a samurai. Even though nearly eight decades had passed since the end of the Shogun Era, she stubbornly rejected the new trends of convenience. Kinuko pictured her mother writing this letter, her brush flowing on the stationery, her wrist moving swiftly yet with elegance. What would her mother think if she told her that everything Uncle Hirobumi had predicted was happening now—Giichi was in jail, and she sat with Ichiro Sekihara in the absence of his son—both men with "dangerous thoughts."

"How is your mother faring in Sasayama?" asked Ichiro, as she wearily put the letter back in the envelope.

"She is doing fine. She seems to love country life."

"I'm very glad to hear that. She's very wise to have moved way in advance. I'm sure she must be worrying about you."

"Yes. I wrote to her the day before yesterday to tell her we're moving, but she obviously hasn't received it yet, and now—"

"Kinuko, you and Yuki should leave for Okayama with Mother as scheduled, even if Giichi doesn't come home for a while."

That sounded impossible to Kinuko. How could she leave while he was in jail? "I understand how you feel," he continued. "But things are getting worse. If—if Giichi doesn't come home in the next several days, I'll stay here alone and as soon as he's released, he and I will lock up the house and join the rest of you in Okayama. What do you think?"

"Do you think it will—it will be that long?"

"Let's hope not. I'm just talking about 'if.'"

After that, they turned silent, Ichiro staring at the newspaper and Kinuko fumbling with the letter.

"Well," said Ichiro finally. "I think it's time for both of us to have some rest. Tomorrow morning I'll go there again. I'll go every day until they release him."

Ichiro folded the newspaper and rose from his cushion laboriously. He patted Kinuko's shoulder as he walked past her. "Good night," he said. "You are going to bed soon, I hope."

Kinuko felt a sudden rush of tears in the back of her eyes. "Father," her voice cracked. "Thank you for being with me tonight."

"I wanted to, Kinuko—try to sleep as best as you can."

His voice was so soft that Kinuko could no longer hold her tears and allowed them to flow freely. Ichiro lowered himself beside her. "Have faith in him," Ichiro told her. "That's all we can do."

Kinuko nodded with tears flowing down her cheeks. Then she blurted, "I'm—I'm sorry I was so angry at you. I'm sure you—you felt that."

Ichiro held her shoulders gently and said, "That's all right, Kinuko. I don't blame you. I don't blame you for that at all."

Kinuko could no longer control her sobs. All of the emotion she'd suppressed for weeks began flooding out of her.

Ichiro hushed her gently, "All right, all right, everything will be fine. Now you need some sleep. We have to go through this together."

Kinuko nodded. After a while, as if all of the sorrow had drained out of her, she said quietly, "Please go to bed, Father."

"Are you sure you are all right now?"

Kinuko nodded again.

"All right then," said Ichiro. "Don't stay up too late."

He shuffled out of the dining room, and Kinuko sat and watched him disappear into the darkness. On the wall the pendulum clock ticked diligently. It was the only sound in the house at the end of their agonizing day. She listened to it for a while, thinking of Giichi. Then she remembered the day she had found his photo on her mother's desk—the day that had marked her destiny; and the images of Ichiro Sekihara and his son she had formed during the time leading up to the first meeting with Giichi—courageous yet gentle, the type of man she yearned for. It was true that she had been drawn to Ichiro's fame. But eight years later, he was an aging man who grieved his son's fate, who worried about his family, and who still tried to live with grace.

It was strange to her now that this day, however agonizing, had erased her grudge against Ichiro and brought her even closer to him. Kinuko cried a little more, hoping that Ichiro, despite his worry, would be able to get some sleep before the unknown events of tomorrow. As for Giichi, she now believed more firmly than ever that he was his father's son, and for the first time in many months, that thought comforted her.

CHAPTER 13

Ichiro stood outside the Ashiya Police Headquarters clutching a bundle containing toiletries, clean clothes and a blanket. He remembered how cold it grew inside those concrete cells, especially now, just before dawn, when an icy chill emanated from the walls and settled in the bones only to recede later in the day. He wished he could walk right into Giichi's cell and cover him with the blanket himself.

The cold seeping through his kimono, he began to pace slowly back and forth along the street, always keeping the door of headquarters in view. He had no idea when the morning shift began or if Konno would even arrive with that shift; but if he could just have a word with him, he thought, he might possibly arrange a meeting with his son. Failing that, perhaps Konno would at least allow him to take the bundle to Giichi's cell. And failing that, he would sit again in the forbidding lobby. Even if thick walls separated them, Ichiro felt Giichi would know he was there.

Ichiro realized that entering the building would likely conjure images of his own brutal treatment decades earlier, but even that would not matter if he could be near his son. In fact, shivering now in the winter cold, those memories already invaded him as if he again stood in buckets of icy water with numb feet and with Buddhist meditation the only thing keeping him from screaming for mercy. Then the image of Giichi superimposed itself over the images in his memory, and Ichiro shook his head. No, not my son, he murmured. Ichiro believed in Giichi's strength, but knew he must do what he could to make the ordeal easier for him.

Occasionally, an officer or a guard approached the side door and slipped inside. Otherwise, the gray concrete building gave no hint of the activity that Ichiro imagined inside. He kept pacing the deserted street, pretending to be an old man out on an errand, hoping his son knew he was near.

A half-hour later, the sun rose and Ichiro saw a man appear at the street corner—short, middle-aged, with a black mole on his face, matching Kinuko's description of Toda. Instantly, Ichiro felt a surge of anger and started across the street in big, fast strides. Just as quickly he stopped himself, realizing that confronting Toda would do more harm than good. An officer of the Special Higher Police would simply absorb his anger and make Giichi pay for it. He watched Toda disappear into the building, swallowed hard, and began pacing again.

A few minutes later, he saw Konno approach, his face red from the morning chill. Ichiro started across the street and their eyes met. Konno slowed his pace, appearing surprised to see him.

"Good morning," Ichiro said. "May I trouble you for just a few moments?"

Konno stopped with an expression that blended sympathy and annoyance. "What can I do for you?" he asked cautiously.

"I wonder if you could arrange a meeting with my son. I would appreciate it greatly."

"Anyone under investigation is not allowed visitors."

"Please, even for a few minutes."

"No, Officer Toda wouldn't allow it."

Ichiro's spirits sank, but he continued, holding the bundle out to Konno. "Then would you at least give this to him?"

Konno took the package. "I'll take it inside and ask Officer Toda if I can." He started toward the door.

"Excuse me," Ichiro said.

Konno stopped and turned to him.

"May I see Officer Toda? I would appreciate it if Officer Toda could explain this matter."

"The matter is your son's possible involvement with the communist, as I explained to you yesterday."

"Yes, I understand, but this is a total surprise to me. He has never mentioned any involvement with communists—ever. So I would like to know what actually happened—or how long he is going to keep him. Please, I will wait as long as is necessary."

Konno appeared to sense Ichiro's desperation. "I'll try," he said.

"Thank you. That's very kind of you."

"The door doesn't open for the public until nine, but you can come in and sit inside. Though I can't promise you anything."

Ichiro thanked Konno again and followed him into the gloomy lobby. After Konno disappeared behind the swinging door, the lobby was deserted. Still, Ichiro could think of no place he would rather be. He was now in the same building as his son.

For the first hour he sat on the same bench where he had sat with Kinuko the day before, his spine erect and unwavering. After the receptionist opened the main door, a little traffic flowed in and out, but neither Konno nor Toda appeared in the lobby. By mid-morning Ichiro began to pace, and then alternated between pacing and reading an old newspaper someone had left on the bench. Eventually, he shifted to prayer and an internal heartfelt conversation with Giichi—I'm here with you, son. Be strong, I'm here. He repeated the same words over and over again.

As the morning wore on, his energy began to fade. Whenever he glanced at the clock above the reception window, the hands never seemed to move. At noon he realized the minute hand had made five revolutions and there was still no sign of Toda or Konno. Ichiro leaned forward and clutched his head in his hands. His thoughts drifted to his wife as they usually did when his spirits were down. He wondered how she was faring by herself in a house growing increasingly empty, undoubtedly worrying about Giichi. She wasn't a woman who cried easily; as far as he knew, she had endured the suffering he had put upon her without a single tear.

He imagined her cleaning a lacquered box, her arms extended and her head drawn back to avoid the dust. Her dark eyes shone in her tight face as she focused on her busy hands. That was how she dealt with hardship and sorrow, by keeping constantly busy. Ichiro wished he were with her now. Still, he did not move from the bench.

Once again he glanced at the clock—a few minutes before one. He felt his stomach grumbling and finally stood and shuffled toward the door. At the entrance, he turned and spoke to the empty chasm of the lobby, "I'll be back, son. Hold on. I just need to see Mother for a while. I'll be back."

At the Osaka railway station he stopped to call Kinuko. Above the main concourse, a train rumbled like thunder and the telephone booth rattled. Sticking a finger into his ear, he yelled into the phone, "Don't be discouraged. I'll be back this evening."

The noise temporarily erased Kinuko's voice, but when he heard her again, she sounded calm. "...worry about me. Mother needs you at home. I will go to the police tomorrow myself, if he doesn't come home today."

"Mother is all right," he said. "I'll be back later."

He stepped from the phone booth, slipped into the thick crowd, and began moving like a sleepwalker, buffeted from side to side. Eventually, he emerged from the station and followed a stream of pedestrians moving toward the streetcar depot. Wrapped in a painful muddle of thoughts about Giichi, Kinuko, Yuki and his wife, he barely noticed where he was going.

Sometime later, a warning siren stirred him back to the harsh reality. When he heard a siren, he realized he was sitting in a streetcar with fearful passengers squinting out the windows. Several moments later B-29s began to release their bombs. The streetcar rattled and shook but kept moving. Eventually they left the war behind, as if nothing had happened.

Ichiro did not fully slip from his dreamlike state until he entered the gate of his house. As he stepped into the entryway, he saw Ume stuffing guest cushions into a big sack in the front room.

When she saw him, she let the sack fall to the floor. "Big Master!" she cried, "I'll go fetch Big Mistress right away."

"Tell her I'll be in the reception room," Ichiro said.

From the entryway he slowly studied the empty front room. An old linen sheet was wrapped around his favorite antique screen with strands of twine holding it in place. The walls were completely bare, all of the paintings removed, including the lacquer-framed watercolor of green chestnuts done for him by Kinuko on his sixtieth birthday. Among the many paintings he had collected, he had cherished that painting in particular. Kinuko's gentle, poetic use of green shading had often comforted him when he was tired or depressed. He had rarely found painters that matched her ability to reveal the very essence of an object with such love and care. Now, when he needed to see it most, it was gone.

He slipped out of his paulownia clogs and stepped up to the front room and walked through the box-cluttered corridor and into the reception room, where he stopped for a moment to study its emptiness. He settled into a meditative position on the floor and gazed through the windows out into the garden, the only place that remained unchanged.

For a moment he felt calm, gazing at the serene pond reflecting the sunlight, and then he heard rustle of Sumiko's kimono. Ichiro turned to see her rush into the room, her kimono sleeves tucked by cords to keep them from flapping while she worked.

"Where is Giichi?" she whispered, her sunken eyes glistening.

Ichiro shook his head weakly. "He is still there. They won't let me see him."

Sumiko stood unmoving.

"Sit down," Ichiro said.

She stepped toward him, removing the cords from her sleeves, and knelt before him with her knees nearly touching his. "Won't they even tell you how long they will keep him?"

Ichiro shook his head again.

Sumiko began to tremble. She wedged her hands tightly between her knees to stop their trembling. Ichiro thought she might be having visions from the past—a bloody bamboo stick ripping their son's flesh. He spoke quickly, before his breathing could become difficult.

"Don't ever doubt his strength," Ichiro blurted out furiously. "He is tough. Don't ever forget that."

Sumiko looked up and their eyes met. She nodded.

Ichiro placed his hand over hers and squeezed it. "It could be a few days, but he will come back. He will, like I always did."

"Please, let's postpone our moving. We shouldn't leave Osaka until Giichi comes home."

"No. Last night they bombed bridges. Today they bombed who knows what. It will not end. The women must go. I will stay behind." He stood. "I'll do some packing, then I need to go back to Ashiya."

She spoke before he reached the door. "What about this communist?" She looked up at him as he turned back to her. "On the phone, you mentioned a communist."

"I'm sure it's nothing. We know Giichi is not a communist."

Her shoulders began to heave, and he walked back to her and patted her tenderly. She sat up erect, sniffling back tears. "It's my fault," she said. "I should have done something then."

Ichiro knelt beside her. "What do you mean?"

"Surely you remember. When Giichi was at the university. I told you about it then, about the communist in his room."

"That was nothing," he said. "He was just a student then, exploring different ideas." He realized how much those words echoed what he had told her years earlier, when she returned from her monthly meeting with the Tea Ceremony Teachers association in Kyoto. She always took advantage of those meetings to visit Giichi at the Imperial University of Kyoto and take him a bundle of his favorite foods.

Ichiro clearly remembered the day that now haunted Sumiko. She had gone to Giichi's room as usual, but did not knock at his door because she heard the voice of a young man urging her son to join the Communist Party.

Ichiro laughed when she first told him of the incident, nearly making light of her concern.

"They are students, Mother," he had said. "They talk about politics, just as housewives talk about their children or the price of food. It's natural for students to seek truth in order to decide how they want to live. At that age they tend to be idealistic, and then they change later in life. That's what being a young scholar means."

"You never changed," Sumiko snapped. "I don't want him to go through what happened to you. That alone was enough for me to endure. You must speak with him."

Ichiro shifted uncomfortably. "What did Giichi say to this student, anyway?" he finally asked, without looking at her.

"He didn't seem to agree with what his friend was saying, but I couldn't hear him very well. Will you please warn him about what he is getting himself into? You very well know that communists are the ones who are most severely treated. I don't want our son to be a communist or to be associated with them."

"I will do that," Ichiro agreed, and in truth, he had spoken with Giichi about communism in the past, but only because it had come up in one of their many conversations about politics.

Now, while she continued to lament, he wondered if his wife might have been right. "I should have done something then," she repeated. "I should have gone into the room and asked that student to leave my son alone."

"Don't blame yourself," Ichiro told her. "I'm sure this has nothing to do with political ideas. It sounds as though it has more to do with a mean-spirited neighborhood chief. Someone who just doesn't like Giichi."

When Ichiro entered his study, his heart ached at the thought of his wife blaming herself. She, of all people, had made every effort to steer Giichi away from controversial political ideas. If anyone was to blame, it was he himself. Giichi certainly shared his political views. Still, that shouldn't have gotten him into trouble. As far as he knew, his son always kept his ideologies to himself. Still, Ichiro knew how the system worked. Under the present Fascist government, spies were everywhere, listening for utterances as innocent as a wish for the war's end. The authorities were probably even more paranoid with almost certain defeat looming ahead. Though none of the major newspapers reported it, Ichiro had recently heard from a journalist friend that at the Yalta Conference, Stalin had agreed to join the United States to finish off Japan. Under those circumstances, the war zealots might be hoping to silence as many dissidents as possible in the time left, and simply being the son of Ichiro Sekihara would be enough to invite investigation.

Ichiro attempted to distract himself with packing. He saw that his study remained exactly as he had left it the previous morning—old tangerine crates, stacks of books and magazines, boxes of index cards, cases of writing pads, notebooks, all piled like uneven mountains. Throughout their marriage, Sumiko had never touched anything in his study out of respect for his work. This was his domain, as the tearoom was hers.

Originally, he had planned to pack his books according to category—Oriental literature, Western literature, history, philosophy, dictionaries, magazines, etc. Now he looked at the labeled crates wearily, grabbed a handful of books, and dropped them into the nearest crate. When it was full he began to fill the next one.

For the next three hours he busied himself without a break, hoping to exhaust his anguish. By five o'clock, all the books and magazines were in crates, the shelves and desk drawers were empty, and the desktop was nearly cleared. He sat on the edge of the faded black leather sofa with a groan, then leaned forward and took off his glasses to rub his eyes. For a while he looked around his dismantled study, his glasses dangling from his hand. Through blurred vision, he noticed the antique Chinese lamp on his desk given to him fifteen years earlier by an editor in honor of his award-winning novel, *A Song of Villagers*. It was the story of a peasant woman who could not bear children, and who, for that reason, was pressured by her in-laws to leave their village. But she stubbornly stayed with her husband, adopted a baby boy, and raised him with love. Ultimately, her adopted son died in 1894, while fighting in the Sino-Japanese War.

Ichiro thought about the poor village woman and about the old carpenter in his earlier novel, *Morning Glories*, both of whom had lost sons to war. In fact, it was because of those novels' depictions of grief for sons lost in war that Japanese authorities had banned them in 1943. He recalled how he felt when copies of those books, along with other "undesirable" ones, were removed from the shelves of bookstores and libraries. In Tokyo, officials ordered a library to burn the books on the street in front of the building, then notified major newspapers to make sure the story appeared in the next editions. That day,

Ichiro felt as if his children had been burned. And that evening, he drank sake until he could barely stand. In this war, too, it seemed, those in power not only killed people, they attempted to kill all emotion and hope.

He put his glasses back on and stood slowly, looking for a suitable box for the lamp. Two glass jars on the windowsill caught his attention. They had been sitting there for so many years he had forgotten about them. Seeing them, tears filled his eyes. He squeezed between the crates and boxes and leaned across his desk to retrieve them from the windowsill. One contained a monarch butterfly and the other a dragonfly, both brittle and faded, as though they would crumble into motes of dust at the slightest disturbance. Ichiro carefully lifted the jars, one in each hand, and held them close to his ears. He shook them gently and heard his son's voice—still sweet with youth.

"Father!" Giichi used to call, bursting into the study with the insects he had caught, sweaty bangs pasted to his forehead. His catch could be dragonflies or butterflies like those before him, or crickets and grasshoppers kept in a bamboo cage.

When Giichi entered the study, Ichiro might have been writing or contemplating or taking a nap on the sofa with a soft breeze brushing his face, the scent of early chrysanthemums pleasant in his nostrils. No matter what he'd been doing, as soon as Giichi came into the room, they would put their heads together to admire the colors and patterns of the butterfly or to talk about the enormity of the dragonfly's eyes or the scariness of the centipede. Then, eventually, Ichiro would pick up his pen again, and Giichi would take a science book from Ichiro's bookshelf and read on the couch, lying on his stomach, his legs crossed in the air.

Ichiro had sometimes asked Giichi to stand straight against the doorframe so he could measure his height. He'd hoped his son would grow strong and healthy, but more importantly, he hoped he would have happiness.

Now, as he stared at the two dusty jars, he wondered if he had made a mistake in the way he directed Giichi as a boy. He wondered whether he should have led his only son toward a more earthy way of thinking instead of instill him with idealism. Should he have told him to accept the world as it was and to concentrate on his personal happiness? Suddenly, idealism seemed like nothing more than words on paper that would simply dry only to be blown away by a gust of wind.

He sat on the sofa again, holding the two glass treasures, his head saturated with sadness and confusion. For a while he contemplated the emptiness of his bookshelves, and his questions repeating themselves in his brain. Finally, he stood up, wrapped the jars in newspaper and placed them securely in one of the crates.

When he prepared to leave, Sumiko met him in the front room with yokan wrapped in furoshiki. Because of the severe shortage of sugar, yokan was a rare treat she kept for visitors only. "Please give this to Giichi," she said. "He likes these." Ichiro took the bundle and left without looking back at her.

CHAPTER 14

Giichi awoke on a squeaky cot and noticed gray light already filling his basement cell. He glared at the barred window and cursed. After four days and nights of constant filth and fear of torture, morning brought only despair. He pulled the greasy blanket up to his nose and curled into a ball. He rolled from side to side on the stained futon for several moments, then cursed again and kicked the blanket aside. In a corner of the cell, the stream of his urine splashed inside a rusty pail, and the fetid odor of his waste from the previous day rose to his nostrils. He jerked backward and winced. Even after four days, he couldn't believe the filth of life in jail. He hadn't been allowed to bathe or brush his teeth since the day he arrived, and the stench of his waste hovered in the cell long after the janitor removed the bucket and dumped it each morning.

Still, he made efforts at cleanliness. When he finished urinating, he twisted the rusty handle of the faucet protruding from the wall. He leaned down and cupped icy water in his hands from the cracked rubber hose that hung from the faucet. He splashed water on his face and shivered. Then he unbuttoned the shirt of his national uniform and used a portion of it to dry his face. After that, he used a corner of the blanket to dry the water that had splashed onto his feet. That was as much grooming as he could manage; there was no soap, towel, toothpaste, brush, or comb, nothing. He was glad he didn't have a mirror; he could only imagine how awful he looked.

He sat back on the cot and rubbed his hand against the stubble growing like wire on his chin. Staring vacantly at the gray window, he wondered if he could stand another day—the disgusting meals, morning-long interrogations, afternoons of endless regret and doubt, and long dark evenings, when his anguish plunged to its greatest depth. Again, he wondered if he would have his father's strength, enough to endure this ordeal without breaking. He might weaken and tell Toda about Kenji. Then he could walk out of this stinking cell once and for all. Kinuko would be happy, his parents would be happy, and of course, Yuki. He imagined her running to the door, smiling and squealing with joy. He could hear her sweet voice and feel her soft cheeks.

Giichi threw himself onto the cot and writhed in agony. Then, he forced himself to lie still. As he tried to steady his rough breathing, he thought of a dying goat he had seen in a farmer's yard in Okayama when he was a child. He remembered its sad watery eyes vividly, and how quietly it accepted death as it breathed its last breath. Now he understood how the goat felt.

Slowly, he sat up on the cot to meditate. He was not a practiced meditator, and often his efforts failed, leaving him with even more self-pity and remorse than when he began. But sometimes they calmed him and enabled him to believe he would survive. He arranged himself cross-legged in the middle of the wobbly cot and placed his hands lightly on his knees. As he began breathing steadily, he remembered how easily his father slipped into meditation—early in the morning or in the evening or even right in the middle of his writing, sometimes in the room next to his mother's tearoom, other times in his own study. At first, it seemed strange to watch his father sitting so long in the stillness of meditation.

One day, when he was seven or eight, Giichi asked his father why he meditated.

"To cleanse my mind," Ichiro replied. "Just as our bodies need to be cleaned, our minds need cleaning as well."

"But how do you clean your mind sitting like that?"

"I try to empty my mind, which means I try not to think of anything."

"Why do you do that?"

"Well, I feel better after doing it, stronger in knowing what is right."

Giichi wondered how anyone could feel better simply by sitting and not thinking of anything.

When he was thirteen, his father prepared to go to a temple in Kyoto.

"I'm going there to do zazen. Would you like to come along?"

This was only days after his father had come home from jail, and he was still weak and every movement brought back the pain of torture. Since coming home, he had left the house only once, struggling with a cane to the neighborhood doctor's office.

Giichi's mother opposed this trip because of Ichiro's health, but Giichi immediately said yes, sensing his father's need to go and feeling obliged to be with him.

"A monk might hit you," his father warned, "if your posture is bad."

"I will come with you and sit like you do. I won't move a bit."

"All right then," said his father, smiling, while his mother looked at both of them with a sigh of resignation.

For three days, they ate and slept side-by-side in a huge temple hall. Twice a day they sat in meditation sessions; in between they took walks or read. Giichi tried to help his father with his meal tray and futon, but his father declined his offers and insisted on doing everything for himself with a slowness that was painful for Giichi to watch. Limping through the long corridor with his meal tray, his father said, "I didn't bring you here for my convenience, son. Besides, I need to feel I can do this."

By the time they left Kyoto, Giichi had discovered that strength had more to do with mind than body. Until then, he had thought strength was something that belonged to a sumo wrestler or a boy who could run fast or lift heavy loads. Now, he saw his father as a person of true strength. Though his father might appear physically weak to outsiders, sitting on a train with a cane between his knees, Giichi felt fortunate to have him as a father.

"How did you like it, son?" his father asked on their way home, turning to him with his hands capping the top of his cane. "I feel better," Giichi replied. And they laughed together, with the early summer breeze blowing through the open windows as the train sped toward Osaka.

Now, in his cell, Giichi sat still, his eyes closed, remembering that distant time and the drone of the cicadas as he sat next to his father in the quiet Zen hall in Kyoto. Then he cleared his mind and meditated the longest he had since coming to jail. When he finally opened his eyes, he indeed felt ready to endure the day. He looked forward to breakfast and especially the old jailer who brought it. Though he would bring the usual—a tasteless mixture of oat and rice gruel or cold chunks of boiled sweet potatoes, he would also bring the warmth of his concern. With every meal, the jailer advised that he eat everything. When he returned half an hour later, he would inspect Giichi's tray. If the tray was empty, the jailer nodded and smiled; if some food remained, he shook his head sadly. Giichi once asked why he cared. "You can't keep your spirits high when your stomach is empty," the jailer replied.

The jailer's kindness reminded him of something Kenji Nakayama once told him—that there are communists in the military and even on the police force. Giichi wondered if the old jailer might be a communist but thought it more likely he was just a decent human being working in a harsh place. At any rate, Giichi did his best to eat the awful food, both to please the jailer and because he believed the maxim about keeping his spirits up.

Giichi jumped from the cot when he heard the jailer's footsteps approaching.

"It was bad last night," said the jailer, sliding the tray through the door.

"I could hear it. Where exactly did they bomb?" Giichi asked.

"Amagasaki and Kobe. Osaka, too, it seems."

Then the jailer's small eyes turned hard, and his index finger tapped the wooden tray as he edged it closer to Giichi. As soon as the old man closed the grate and walked away, Giichi quickly placed the tray on the cot and reached up for the light cord, his heart racing. He carefully searched the tray, and beneath the bowl found a piece of paper that seemed to be cut from a used envelope, neatly folded and slightly warm from the bowl. Hiding it against his body, he unfolded it with his back to the door.

Your father is upstairs every day, negotiating your release. Also, there are packages from your family. Officer Toda has been keeping them. I will try to get them for you. Keep up your strength.

Though in unpracticed handwriting, the note appeared to be written patiently and diligently, character by character, with a crude pencil. Giichi imagined the old jailer writing at home in the evening, licking the lead tip between each character. Tears blurred his vision, as the jailer's kindness and his father's love seeped into his heart. He quickly swiped his arms over his eyes and tore the note into bits as tiny as grains of rice. Then he pushed them deep into the mattress through the torn seam.

When the jailer returned to fetch him for interrogation, Giichi asked, "When did you see my father? How is he?"

"I didn't see him," the jailer whispered. "The receptionist told me. He said your father is staying at your house."

When Giichi arrived at the interrogation room on the second floor, cigarette smoke had already dimmed the light of the naked bulb. Amid a swirl of smoke, Toda stood with a cigarette dangling from the corner of his mouth. As Konno escorted Giichi to the chair, Toda stubbed it out in the ashtray and leaned over the desk. "Let me see," he growled, unfolding his nicotine-stained fingers one by one. "It's been four days, and you get more handsome each day, don't you?"

Cold anger flashed through Giichi, but he knew by now that it was not safe to lash out at Toda, nor was it safe to ignore him. Toda scrutinized him from head to toe with a thin, sarcastic smile, awaiting a response. Emboldened by the knowledge of his father's presence in the building, he looked directly at Toda, forced a smiled and finally replied, "I suppose so."

Toda frowned. "Don't you want to go home and wash yourself and shave?"

"Of course, I do."

"Then it's time for you to cooperate. I'm getting sick of all this. I'll tell you one last time. Cooperate—for your own sake."

"I wish I could," Giichi said, letting his shoulders sag to show remorse. He felt confident now that he could never betray his friend to this yellow-fingered torturer. Betrayal would only set off a chain of more violence and death. Kenji had once told Giichi that the Special Higher Police considered communists less than human and that killing them meant nothing. The more communists and dissidents they successfully tortured, the higher the status the officers achieved.

Toda paced around Giichi's chair, now tapping the bamboo stick on the floor. Giichi sat up stiffly, his eyes downcast and stomach muscles tightened. Toda's short legs passed through his vision several times.

"All right," Toda said, finally coming to a halt behind his desk. He placed his bamboo stick on the desk, sat down, and clasped his hands. "We've been talking about this for days, but this time I want you to listen. Aiding a communist in any way is a crime. You could spend at least another five years in that stinking cell if you want to. We know Kenji Nakayama has been living off the contributions of communist sympathizers like you. So, which do you prefer, rotting away in that smelly cell or telling me everything you know about him and going home today? It's your choice."

Despite the fear inspired by Toda's methods, by now Giichi felt absolutely certain they didn't have the slightest evidence of his arrangement with Kenji. All of the previous interrogations seemed to be based on nothing more than speculation—he used to know Kenji, he lived in a rented house in a working-class neighborhood, and he was the son of Ichiro Sekihara.

"I am not a communist sympathizer, Mr. Toda." Giichi looked up at Toda. "I don't believe in communism."

"Listen!" said Toda, suddenly slamming the bamboo stick across the desk. "I don't care if you believe in communism or not. I'm talking about the fact that you've been giving him money. Admit it, tell me where you met Kenji Nakayama to give him money."

"I've never given money to anyone."

"Then why do you live in that working-class neighborhood like a welder or carpenter? We both know you could afford to live somewhere else."

"I don't need to live in a fancy neighborhood. My parents own a comfortable home which will eventually be mine."

"It doesn't matter what kind of house your parents have. With your education, soon you'll be a big shot in that fancy company. A person like you doesn't live in a shabby neighborhood like that unless you have something to hide."

"With the war going on, I've given up on that kind of future," he said. "I've told you that I am resigning from the company, haven't I?"

"To move to Okayama for safety, you said, but you thought you would be able to hide in Okayama, didn't you? Too bad we caught you in time."

"Everything I've been telling you is—"

"A lie! No matter what you say, I've compared how much you make at Nippon Motors with how much money you've saved, and it amounts to nothing after what you've funneled to the communists!"

"You can compare my salary to my bank account," he said, "but that only proves that I don't handle money wisely." Today, he decided to add touches he thought would sound reasonable from Toda's perspective. "Perhaps it's because I grew up in a comfortable family; I never learned how to handle money properly; I always thought it would be there, and, as I said before, I probably spend too much money on *sake*."

Toda propped the stick against the desk and lit another cigarette, as if he hadn't heard what Giichi said. Then he held the cigarette at eye level and grimacing, examined it for a while. "We have even stronger evidence," he finally said, still looking at his cigarette.

"What evidence?" Giichi asked, and immediately knew he should not have spoken.

Toda put down his cigarette, picked up the stick, and held it upright only a few inches from Giichi's eyes.

"Look," he sneered. "This ordinary bamboo stick has tremendous power. I don't have to tell you the evidence I have. This will make you tell me. Like this!"

Suddenly, Toda raised the stick high and Giichi ducked. The stick whacked against a leg of the chair with a cracking sound and Giichi toppled to the floor as the chair collapsed beneath him. Covering his head, he heard Toda shout, "You should be thankful it wasn't your own leg! Get up, you fool!"

Giichi scrambled up, picked up the chair, and sat on it quickly. The chair wobbled on its broken leg. Toda began screaming, his face flushed red. He slammed the stick against the desk, froth oozing from the corners of his lips. "I've been very patient, but you are pushing me beyond my limits! I have treated you well because you work for Nippon Motors, because I thought a little discomfort would convince you, but that will change. You should be thankful I've been in charge! If it were someone else, you would be dead by now! Dead, do you understand? You don't think I will do it, but you will see I can!"

For the first time, Giichi felt real fear. He knew he had underestimated the brute power Toda held over him. Teetering on the wobbly chair, he felt his heart jump with every shout. Abruptly, Toda tossed the stick aside, grabbed Giichi's shoulders, and shook them so hard that Giichi's neck snapped back and forth and the chair collapsed beneath him. Giichi fell backward and landed on the floor with a jolt. Struggling to stand, he heard Toda stomp to the door and scream, "Konno, Konno!"

Konno hurried in and lifted Giichi from the floor by the arm. "Lock him up!" Toda shouted, as he kicked Giichi in the leg. "Get him out of my sight! Tomorrow I will kill him!"

As Konno pulled Giichi from the room, Toda wagged a finger close to Giichi's face. "Tomorrow we will get this over with. Then you won't even have time for regrets. Remember that!" A spray of Toda's spit landed on Giichi's cheek. Wiping it away with his sleeve, Giichi limped out of the room. He had never seen such hatred, and while he tried to reconcile the reasons for that hatred, now he knew it didn't matter. The world was not reasonable, his luck had run out. Toda, his tormentor, was actually right. He had been patient, and tomorrow he would surely use that stick. After five days of Toda's toying with him, Giichi knew he meant it this time. Toda's colleagues were probably laughing at him. After five days with the son of Ichiro Sekihara, he had nothing to show for it but his anger.

Back in his cell, Giichi slumped on the cot and closed his eyes. Listening to his thudding heartbeat, he asked himself once again, "Will I be able to keep my mouth shut no matter what?" Images of Kenji in a torture room flashed into his mind. He heard the cracking and thumping of bamboo sticks, pictured Kenji's body twitching in a pool of blood, his glasses shattered. Giichi sat up from the cot and gasped for air.

His mind was set. Certainly, he had allowed himself to toy with thoughts of betrayal when his spirits were low. But betraying Kenji would be betraying his own soul. He would rather die than betray a friend who had long ago given up all personal desire in order to fight the fascist government. Kenji never spent the money he gave him except for cheap meals from street hawkers or for tram fare. The rest went to anti-war activities carried out at great risk.

On the way to work, Giichi would sometimes feel his spirits rise with pride when he saw bright red anti-war slogans pasted on power poles or walls or bridges. He wondered in awe how those feats had been accomplished amid tight patrols.

And perhaps even more impressive was the fact that while Kenji lived outside the ordinary life others desired, he understood and respected their pursuit of personal happiness. He was happy for Giichi that he had a wife and a daughter to love. For eight years he had worried more about Giichi's safety than about receiving money from him. He never stepped into a designated bar when he suspected he was being followed, and he stayed totally clear from Giichi's private life.

Shortly after Giichi and Kinuko married, he had invited Kenji to his home for a hearty meal. "Just once couldn't do any harm, could it?" Giichi asked, pained by Kenji's sallow cheeks. But Kenji shook his head firmly, stressing that it would be a grave mistake for him to invite a communist to his new home. "I would love to meet your wife," Kenji said. "But it's not a good idea."

Kenji asked to see a photo of Kinuko instead. With one glance at the photo, he beamed, "What a beautiful woman."

He continued to gaze at the photo, his eyes turning dreamy.

"What a lucky man you are," he finally sighed. While Giichi scratched his head, Kenji continued, "I envy you, but I think I'll have to wait until the next life to have a wife. I hope there will be no more war by that time."

"You don't have to wait until the next life," Giichi objected. "You might want to marry after the war is over. Isn't that why you are doing what you are doing, so everyone can live happily?"

Kenji only laughed and shook his head. "Anyway, I wish you the best. I really do." Until then, Giichi had never given a thought to the "next life," nor did he think that Kenji really believed in it. But now, curled up on the cot in his jail cell, he suddenly wished for such a thing as a next life for those who were denied a chance in this one. Perhaps even he would need another lifetime to fulfill the wish for a happy life with Kinuko that Kenji had wished for him many years ago.

When the jailer brought his lunch, Giichi whispered to him, "I know it is a lot to ask..." He stared into the man's kind eyes and decided to continue; after all, he had nothing to lose, tomorrow he was to die. "Could you pass a note to my father?"

The jailer glanced quickly to his left and his right. "It would be too dangerous to give it to him in the lobby..." Giichi sagged. "But I could take it to your home."

"Are you sure?"

"Shh...not so loud." He glanced again toward the hall entry. Then he nodded slightly, with his eyes hard and penetrating.

Giichi awaited the jailer's return, thinking of what he would convey in his final message to his family. After what felt as forever, the old man came back and slipped a folded piece of paper and a pencil into Giichi's hand as he retrieved the food tray. Looking at Giichi's unfinished meal, he groaned, "You hardly ate."

Giichi sat on the cot and unfolded the tiny piece of yellowed rice paper smaller than his hand.

"Will be back at five. Write directions to your house on the back."

Giichi smoothed the sheet of paper against his thigh, then sank to his knees and held the paper against the door with one hand and wrote with the other. Though his hands shook, he managed to draw directions to his house. By the time he turned the paper over to write his message, he could no longer control his hands. He licked the end of the pencil and breathed deeply, but as soon as his pencil touched the paper, his hand shook wildly. After several attempts, he pushed the paper and pencil deep into the torn seam of the mattress, lay back on the cot, and closed his eyes. Eventually, his mind calmed and he retreated into his usual afternoon reverie. As always, one memory brought another, and then another, until he was living inside a lushly textured dream.

The first memory took him back to an ordinary Sunday afternoon during the summer after he and Kinuko were married. That morning, Kinuko returned from a farmer's market with a basket full of fresh vegetables in one hand and a bunch of summer lilies in the other. She wore a butterfly-patterned cotton yukata and a deep blue obi. Her bare feet moved like silver fish, and the fragrance of vegetables and flowers surrounded her like perfume.

In the afternoon, she arranged some of the vegetables on the rattan table in the open veranda—cucumbers, tomatoes, eggplants, and squash; and then she prepared a canvas and proceeded to paint the scene with watercolors. Giichi, in his cotton yukata, lay on a nearby tatami with a book in his hand, facing her canvas and the sky above. Everything seemed idle under the blue sky and its gigantic clouds, morning glories wilted and sunflowers were still. Trams only passed twice each hour. In between, no noise came from the Hanshin Highway. The only sound to break the silence was the gentle scratch of Kinuko's brush mixing colors on her palette and the sleepy voice of a tofu vendor coasting slowly past the low hedge around their garden.

Giichi eventually fell asleep with the book on his chest and awoke later to see the finished painting and her colorful palette at the bottom of the easel. He arose from the floor and approached the canvas, his eyes and mouth wide in amazement. The vegetables in the painting seemed more real than the real ones, the colors translucent, succulent and delicate. She had used colors he wouldn't even dream of using—a white tint on a tomato and eggplant, subtle blue and yellow streaks on cucumbers.

Soon Kinuko appeared with cups of chilled green tea on a delicate glass tray. She sat on the floor and moved a pale blue fan through the air, wafting away the moist air.

"Kinuko, this is so beautiful," Giichi uttered, still gazing at the canvas. "It's...it's like a poem on canvas."

"Do you really think so?" Kinuko said happily. "I've always thought painting was like forming a poem. A painter arranges shapes, colors and light just as a poet arranges words."

"But how do you come up with these colors—ones I can't see on the real vegetables, and yet once I see them I know they are there?"

"I don't know," Kinuko replied, smiling, "but I usually talk to the things I'm painting and listen to them carefully."

Giichi's eyes opened even wider.

"You think I'm strange, don't you?" asked Kinuko, laughing.

"No, no, I don't."

Giichi sat and sipped his tea, smiling and shaking his head. Soon Kinuko put her fan aside and picked up the book Giichi had been reading. The afternoon passed slowly, Giichi lying idly, Kinuko reading and sipping tea—one of those afternoons during which they did nothing in particular, made no plans.

Often those summer afternoons produced huge clouds and stuffy air. At such times, Kinuko predicted an approaching rain shower, then sure enough, the sky would turn soft gray and the wind chimes would start making incessant, silvery sounds under the eaves.

Even now, lying on the cot with his eyes closed, Giichi could smell the approaching rain and vividly see Kinuko running out and back into the house with arms full of fresh laundry. He was so happy during that time, just spending those days with her, a woman with gifts and elegance unlike any he had ever known. She had an aura that made him feel as if he were at the center of the universe, in a warm cocoon, forgetful of everything that bothered him—dark clouds in China, the possibility of being drafted.

Eventually, his memory drifted from those afternoons with Kinuko to a more recent time, in 1943, when they visited Hanshin Park. By then, only sixteen months into the war against America, the country had lost much ground in the Pacific. And though the government never admitted the unfavorable turn of the war, it decreed that everyone must curtail leisure activities when the nation's soldiers were fighting so hard. As a result, the region's favorite zoological park grew empty in a matter of months and was eventually closed. Giichi had spent many Saturday afternoons in that park, reading on a bench, while Yuki excitedly toddled from one birdcage to another, pointing her small finger at the fluttering activity inside. She loved birds so much that her first spoken word, after Mama and Papa, was bird. The day before the park was closed, Giichi and Kinuko took Yuki there to say good bye to the birds, but that day Yuki stayed in the sandbox, squatting and digging in the sand. It was an early spring day, sunny but windy, and with each gust of wind, the hood of Yuki's coat ballooned behind her head and the next minute deflated, as grains of sand settled in her hair.

"Yuki, let's go see the birds," Giichi suggested again, dusting the sand from her shiny black hair. "It's too windy to play in the sand." Still, Yuki wouldn't move, and Giichi finally scooped her up in his arms and walked to a birdcage, cajoling her to keep her from protesting. Near the birdcage, he was elated to see a photographer wandering in search of customers. Giichi posed in front of the camera, with Yuki in his arms, Kinuko beside him and a bright tropical bird perched behind them. By the time the photographer had set up his tripod, stuck his head inside the black box, and finally said, "Smile," the bird had flown to a corner of the cage, out of the picture.

Later, when Ichiro saw the photo and heard the story behind it, he burst into laughter. "Funny," he said, his belly shaking. "When you got the photo, you found no bird." Sumiko laughed too, covering her mouth. "But," she said, "This *is* a very nice photo of the three of you, really."

"It is," Ichiro agreed. "It is a nice photo."

Sumiko gazed at the photo for several more seconds, her eyes turning sad. "When Yuki is old enough to understand," she said, "you should tell her the story. I hope by that time the war will be over and Hanshin Park reopened."

"Indeed," Ichiro nodded, and there was a moment of silence. Then as if to shrug it off, Ichiro turned to Giichi, "How about a little sake tonight after dinner, just the two of us. We haven't had a chat for a while."

"Giichi has work tomorrow," Sumiko interjected, glancing at Kinuko.

"It's up to him," Kinuko said. "I can go home with Yuki, and Giichi can go to work from here tomorrow morning."

"Oh no," Ichiro said to Kinuko, "I don't want you to go home with a little one at night. Why don't you and Yuki stay here, too, and go home tomorrow?"

After dinner, the women left, Kinuko to prepare Yuki for bed and Sumiko to prepare for the next day's tea ceremony lessons. Soon a maid arrived with a tray of steaming sake bottles and cups. As soon as she placed them on the table, Ichiro picked up one of the bottles and reached toward Giichi, who held out his cup to accept the wine.

"This is to you, son," said Ichiro, pouring *sake* into his cup. Then it was Giichi's turn. "This is to you, Father." The sweet, pungent aroma rose from their cups, as they raised them to each other.

Giichi had never really enjoyed drinking sake, except with his father. Before Pearl Harbor, he was sometimes obliged to attend parties entertained by geisha. But the wine poured by women who offered superficial compliments for money and the advancement of their careers never tasted as good as that poured by his father.

That night, he and his father relaxed cross-legged on cushions and talked with each other like best friends, straight from their hearts—about Giichi's job, Ichiro's writing, Yuki, Japanese chess, and eventually, politics. They remained cheerful, even when the discussion drifted to the war, and the more they drank, the more they agreed on their country's disastrous course. Giichi wished they could talk like this forever, as they never could in public. He cherished this time with his father like no other, but he detected fatigue in his father's face.

Across the table, Ichiro lifted his glasses, rubbed his eyes and blinked weakly. Giichi suggested they both go to bed. Ichiro shrugged it off and announced jokingly that he was still too young to go to bed that early. But when the clock struck the hour, Ichiro looked at the watch under his kimono sleeve and groaned, "Already eleven." Once again, he rubbed his eyes and turned toward the dark garden beyond the screen door. "No more Hanshin Park," he mumbled, his fingers lightly tapping the edge of the table. Then he suddenly turned to Giichi, the rims of his eyes slightly red from the *sake.*

"Anyway," Ichiro began, stretching his back, "let's not give up our personal hopes. War or not, life goes on. Yuki is growing, and time won't wait for us. She will be grown up before you know it. It was just yesterday when you were her age, my son, yet you already have a child of your own."

Now, two years later, Giichi still remembered his father's sad and tired face as he stood to go to bed. Sitting up on the cot in the confinement of his dark cell, Giichi once again pondered his father's words from that evening. Even then, his father had foretold his current dilemma—how was it possible to assure the life and happiness of his family and still maintain his integrity? Must he sacrifice himself?

The light from the high window faded and urged him to write the note. Giichi put aside his reverie, retrieved the piece of paper and pencil from the torn mattress, and wrote in tiny characters:

> *Father, I'm sorry that I've caused you heartache and inconvenience when you are about to leave Osaka. I truly appreciate that you are here every day to be near me. However, I urge you and Mother to get out of Hanshin before it's too late. And please take Kinuko and Yuki with you and tell them I love them with all my heart. No matter what happens to me, I want them to live on. I'm doing fine and will be fine, I know that you have gone through the same and survived. Please pray that I have a fraction of your strength.*
>
> *Your beloved son, Giichi*
>
> *P. S. I've been doing zazen and have learned that it gives me strength as you taught me.*

Giichi passed the letter to the jailer after supper. That night he slept peacefully for the first time since coming to jail.

The next morning he was startled awake by the key clanking against the cell door. Gray light already spread across the cell. He heard the old man's voice, "Wake up now. It's time to get cleaned up."

Giichi crawled out of the cot in his wrinkled national uniform and turned on the light. As he blinked under the naked light bulb, the jailer tottered in with a furoshiki bundle, followed by a janitor carrying a bucket of hot water and a white enamel basin.

"Here are your toiletries," said the jailer. "Let me know when you are done. I'll be outside."

Giichi unwrapped the bundle and discovered a blanket. As he unfolded the blanket, he found his toothbrush, a can of tooth-cleaning powder, his shaving set, a celluloid soap case, a small hand mirror, a towel, and a tin box of crackers and a block of yokan. He lifted each of the items, one by one, inhaling the smell of home, wanting to know what Kinuko and Yuki were doing at that exact moment. As he cleaned himself, he remembered the old ritual of the samurai who cleansed body and soul before committing suicide.

When he finished, the jailer stepped in and slipped a tiny ball of paper into Giichi's hand. "Read it quickly," he whispered, "while I wrap up your belongings."

Giichi felt his heart pounding. He took the wad of paper to a corner of the cell and quickly unfolded it. Two different styles of handwriting jumped before his eyes—Kinuko's, neat and delicate, and Ichiro's, flamboyant and flowing outside the lines.

> *Dear Giichi-san, Father and I are elated that you are well. But my heart aches thinking how hard your life in jail must be. Yuki misses you but she is fine. Your father has been very kind and stays with us every day, which leaves the responsibility of packing and moving solely to Mother. Yes, I will send Yuki with Mother and Ume to Okayama. I understand that you want me to go as well, but I can't. I'll wait here until you come home. I've been praying hard that it'll be soon.*
>
> *Kinuko*

> *My Dear Son, the jailer is kindly waiting, and I must hurry. Your mother is leaving for Okayama the day after tomorrow with Yuki and Ume. They bombed more bridges on the Yodo River last night. Don't worry, Kinuko and I will be fine. Until then I will continue to wait for you in the lobby. I am very proud of you, son, and convinced that you will get through this difficult time. Both Kinuko and I have faith in you*
>
> *Your Father*

Giichi gripped the note and silently wept. The old jailer approached him and patted his shoulder. "Sorry," he whispered. "I have to destroy that."

Clutching the note, Giichi slipped down to the floor, his back scraping the cement wall. Squatting on the floor, he thrust his hand up and held the note out to the jailer without looking up, like a child relinquishing his favorite toy. By the time he knew what had happened, the jailer had taken all of his toiletries and left the blanket and food. He knew the yokan was from his mother and the crackers from Kinuko. He held them in his hands for a while, debating which to eat first. Finally, he decided on *yokan* and peeled the wrapper from it, broke it into halves and began chewing one half. As the taste of sweet bean spread in his mouth, he thought of his mother wrapping the treat. As a young boy, he had promised her he would never burden her with worries as his father had done. Yet here he was in jail, eating food wrapped by her sorrowful hands. Feeling the grip of her anguish, he became aware of a suffocating lump pushing up to his throat, but he kept chewing, needing to feel her unchanging love.

As he swallowed the yokan, he felt his spirit growing from his mother's love, from the love and strength of his father, his eternal hero, from the love of Kinuko and Yuki. He knew that he would not betray Kenji. If Toda thought allowing him these luxuries would weaken his spirit, he was wrong.

CHAPTER 15

On the morning of Sumiko's departure for Okayama, Kinuko unlocked the suitcase she had packed for Yuki and pulled out her woolen jacket. Despite a recent warming trend, the weather had turned wintry again. As she slipped Yuki's arms into the jacket, she told herself once again that she was doing the right thing and forced to the back of her mind the fact that soon Yuki would be separated from her. The previous night, Ichiro had suggested that she stay home while he took Yuki to the station, implying that the crowded station was no place for a pregnant woman. But how could she stay back when her three-year-old daughter was leaving without her parents? Kinuko had insisted on going with them.

"We should get there well before the train leaves," Ichiro called from the guest room. "I'm sure it will be chaotic there." There had been rumors that rail travel would soon be limited only to military personnel because of fuel shortages.

A little after eight, Mrs. Chiba came over to see Yuki one last time. She hugged Yuki and said, "How nice that you are going to Okayama with your Grandma! That will be fun!" After she left with tears in her eyes, the three set out against a north wind. Ichiro held Yuki in one arm and the suitcase in the other. Kinuko carried a smaller suitcase. On the Hanshin Highway the wind blew up yellow shreds of dried horse manure, a new sight on the highway and another result of the fuel shortage. Kinuko walked silently beside Ichiro with her back to the wind, covering her nose with her shawl.

"Dirty, dirty," Yuki said, pointing at the piles of animal waste. She didn't yet understand the purpose of the trip, let alone that it was at the request of her jailed father. In fact, she was excited about traveling with her grandmother. When the tram arrived, she merrily sang a choo-choo train song, which made Kinuko grow even more silent.

As Ichiro had predicted, the Osaka railway station was absolute chaos, teeming with people eager to flee the city. They pressed against each other in a mass of bodies and milled about pieces of luggage on the floor of the concourse. Here and there arose cries of banzai, and flags of the rising sun were waved for newly recruited soldiers. Kinuko followed Ichiro as closely as possible but lost sight of him halfway up the steep steps.

"Mama!" she heard Yuki cry, and then saw her daughter clinging to Ichiro's neck in the furl of the crowd at the top of the stairs.

With her last ounce of strength, Kinuko kept climbing. Her heavy stomach bumped against an old man in front of her and the suitcase thudded against passengers swarming past her.

"Mama!" Yuki called again in a teary voice from the top of the steps. Ichiro waited, struggling to keep his footing.

As soon as Kinuko reached the platform, Ichiro began running alongside the train, weaving through the crowd. Again Kinuko fell behind, struggling along, keeping her gaze on Yuki's head bobbing above the crowd.

Two-thirds of the way across the long platform, Kinuko stopped and gasped for air; in the distance she recognized the faint sound of Ume's voice. "Big Master! We are here! Big Master!" Kinuko hurried toward the voice until she saw Sumiko and Ume sitting inside the train in window seats. The car was packed, its center aisle jammed with standing passengers, and the overhead shelves full of luggage. Still, some people kept pushing inside, while others stood at the edge of the door and held grimly to the doorposts.

Fighting back tears, Kinuko hugged Yuki. Then Ichiro handed her through the window to Sumiko. Yuki grabbed the window frame with sudden fear washing over her face. Sumiko and Ume stood and pulled her into the train.

"Mama, come with me, Mama!" Yuki screamed, arching her body in Sumiko's arms.

"We'll have fun in Okayama, Yuki. We'll go see some chickens," Sumiko desperately cajoled, struggling to keep her screaming granddaughter in her arms.

"No, I don't want chickens, I want Mama! Come with me!"

Ume quickly pulled a cracker from her pouch, but Yuki pushed it away. Kinuko tried to smile and say something motherly, but a thick lump of pain seized her throat and she stood speechless. Meanwhile, Ichiro pushed the two suitcases through the window.

The departure bell shrieked, and the gasps and screams of last good-byes rose all around. "Yuki, be a good girl!" Kinuko finally yelled. Yuki leaned forward and stretched her arms out of the train. Tears streamed down her cheeks. The train lurched and emitted steamy hisses as it began to move. "I will come soon!" said Kinuko, running alongside the train, no longer able to hold back her tears. Sumiko pressed a handkerchief to her eyes and then waved it out the window.

"Send us a telegram when you get to Okayama," yelled Ichiro.

The train gathered speed as it moved through the station. Dazed, Kinuko watched it rumbling away. Arms holding handkerchiefs waved out of the windows like the many legs of a centipede, but they were soon so far away that it was impossible to tell which was Sumiko's.

With Yuki gone, the house fell into a solemn silence. While Ichiro trudged off each morning to maintain his vigil at the Ashiya Police Station, Kinuko seldom left the house. Only Mrs. Chiba visited her. The day after Giichi's detention began, Hayashi dishonored them by removing the Sekihara nameplate from their door, and then heaped on additional insults by confiscating the family's ration card and encouraging neighbors to disassociate themselves from such an unpatriotic family. After that, the neighbors avoided Kinuko. When they met her in the street, they looked down and pretended they didn't see her.

The neighborhood shunning had little effect on Kinuko, occupied as she was by the sorrow of her separation from Yuki and thoughts of Giichi in jail. She quickly learned that keeping herself busy was the best way to fill the void left by their absence. Although she had longed for more time to read since Yuki's birth, now that Yuki was gone, reading seemed meaningless. Instead, she focused on other long neglected tasks—mending old clothes, resizing her old clothes to fit Yuki, and writing to the friends and relatives she had long ignored. Occasionally, she went out to buy food for which she paid five times the ration price without the card Hayashi had taken from her.

In the evenings, Kinuko cooked and waited for Ichiro to come home. After supper she continued the tasks that now consumed her, while Ichiro read the newspaper or books from their bookshelves, though he too seemed incapable of enjoying reading. Since the day the jailer brought the note from Giichi, they had heard nothing, and Ichiro soon stopped talking about his daily visits to the police station.

A warning siren often broke the evening silence, but she and Ichiro no longer hurried to the shelter. They continued to sit wherever they were and pretended they didn't hear the bombs exploding in the distance. Throughout the distant perilous sounds, Kinuko's hands moved faster and Ichiro's lips pursed tighter. The knowledge that someone was dying at that very moment drove them to deeper silence.

They seldom listened to the radio either, as news from the Supreme War Headquarters only added to their frustration. The radio accounts exaggerated minor triumphs to make them sound like huge victories and downplayed Allied advances to make them seem insignificant. Kinuko couldn't imagine that anyone in the country still believed the reports. They must know the truth. The war was a lost cause.

One night, they happened to listen to the news and learned that the island of Iwo Jima, about fourteen hundred kilometers southeast of Tokyo, had been hit with a fierce assault by American troops. This represented the first time in the nation's long history that a foreign enemy had ever set foot on Japanese soil. The radio report indicated that Japanese troops were fighting against immense odds but would never succumb to the enemy offensive.

Ichiro sighed. "The Allies are getting closer and closer to the mainland. If they take Iwo Jima...." He paused and sighed again.

"It will mean more bombings, won't it?" Kinuko said without looking up from the frayed sweater she worked on.

"I'm afraid so," Ichiro replied somberly. "Until now, the Japanese air base on Iwo Jima prevented some B-29s from reaching us. But the situation is changing. I'm glad at least that Mother and Yuki are in Okayama."

A sudden jolt of fear seized Kinuko as she realized that she might never see Yuki again. Recently, she had begun to think that it might be some time before she could join her daughter; but she had never considered the possibility of permanent separation. She reached into the shirt pocket where she kept the telegram that had come the day her mother-in-law and Yuki arrived in Okayama. She unfolded the fragile sheet, taking care not to rip its thin creases. She gazed at the katakana letters as she had done a thousand times before. "ARRIVED IN OKAYAMA SAFELY. YUKI FINE. SUMIKO." She continued to gaze at her daughter's name. Now those written symbols were all that she had of Yuki. She glanced at the clock and wondered if her daughter was already in bed, if she was crying from missing her, if she was angry at her mother for sending her away.

"Well," Ichiro's voice interrupted Kinuko's sad thoughts. "It won't be too long before we can join them; Giichi, you, and me. Don't worry. Everything will be fine."

Kinuko folded the telegram and smiled at Ichiro weakly.

On March 1, the tenth day of Giichi's incarceration, the government announced the start of an invigorated defense program, "A day for all citizens to prepare for the ground battle on the mainland." "Fight to the last Japanese," became the new national motto. In Hanshin, as throughout the nation, government officials filled the airwaves with calls for expanded bamboo spear training. Kinuko cringed at the news. The drills were nothing new, they had been conducted throughout the war, and in fact she had participated in them until the end of the previous year when she was excused because of her pregnancy. Now she feared she would be drawn back into them, and within minutes an announcement came over the radio that every unemployed citizen between sixteen and sixty would be expected to attend.

The next morning, as Kinuko sat on the veranda unraveling yarn from old sweaters, she heard engines roaring outside. Three army trucks plowed into the open field between her house and the Hanshin Highway. Vigilance corpsmen, dressed in identical blue national uniforms, jumped out of the vehicles. Kinuko spotted her neighbor Mr. Obata, the retired fire fighter who had told them of Mr. Chiba's death so long ago; it seemed so long ago, as if years had passed. Schoolboys leaped from another vehicle. Throughout Japan, schools had been closed in preparation for the possibility of a ground battle. Altogether, it looked like there were about a hundred men and boys, each carrying a gardening hoe. Without delay, they began hacking down the brown spikes of dead weeds and churning the soil. Soon another truck arrived, loaded with sharp bamboo spears. Some of the men began unloading the spears as seriously as if they were actually handling effective weapons.

For a fleeting moment Kinuko felt like laughing, then a shiver rushed through her. For the first time she felt real fear at the thought of approaching Allied troops. What would the American soldiers actually do once they landed on the mainland?

According to the Japanese government, everyone would be killed without mercy. Brutal invaders would rape the women to satisfy their desire for flesh. They were crude and shameless, unlike the Japanese soldiers who never raped or killed innocent civilians.

Yes, she thought, the Allies were killing innocent Japanese civilians every day; she had lost Mr. Chiba to their bombing. But Kinuko knew she couldn't believe everything the government said. Before all publications about America were banned, she had read that America was a land of freedom, where the citizens could voice their opinions without being arrested like Giichi. Women voted just as men did, and people went to church each Sunday to hear words of love and forgiveness. Were the people of such a country really as bad as the Japanese government portrayed them? But this is war, she thought, and killing is the very nature of war, regardless of which side you are on. For the sake of their country, decent people killed each other. Why? Why did anyone have to be killed? Why would she have to be killed? Her heart began screaming, "No, no one can kill me. I am Yuki's mother. No one can take me away from her!"

Suddenly, she felt as if someone had struck her head. This was.... her head began to spin as the thought formed, this was what Giichi had been talking about all along. Giichi was right. If you didn't want to be killed, then you should refuse to kill anyone else. It was as simple as that. Yet too few humans took that simple, honest logic as seriously as Giichi. Everyone knew killing was wrong, yet when called to war, everyone went, except those like her beloved Giichi. At the core of their hearts, how could they justify the act of killing? Surely, they didn't *want* to be killed or to kill. Wherever they were fighting, Japanese or Americans, they wanted nothing more than to be at home with their loved ones, just as she yearned to be living with Yuki and Giichi again. Still, nations fought ceaselessly against each other, using stupid excuses. Kinuko pulled the yarn harder. Her face swelled red and hot with anger at the foolishness of humanity and especially at its governments.

Outside, the activity continued—weeds were removed, huge stonerollers flattened the churned soil, pieces of planks were formed into a podium and a flagpole was raised. By mid-afternoon the field looked like a makeshift school playground, except for the bamboo spears piled beside the podium. When patriotic shouts of banzai roared into the house, Kinuko looked outside again. She saw most of the neighbors, including Mr. and Mrs. Hayashi, standing at the edge of the field with rising sun headbands tied across their foreheads, fervently shouting and waving their arms. Traffic slowed and stopped along the Hanshin Highway, while drivers and passengers observed the spectacle in the field below. At each shout of banzai, Kinuko wondered what was going through the minds of those in the crowd. Did they truly believe in what they were doing? Did they believe there was hope in such a primitive weapon as a bamboo spear? She felt a pang of pity and disgust. Soon the men dispersed, and the traffic on the highway began moving while the neighbors headed home. Shortly after, Mrs. Hayashi visited.

"I didn't see you out there," she began as soon as Kinuko opened the door, "but I hope I'm going to see you tomorrow. It'll be eight o'clock. My husband thinks you are still capable of the spear drills. Please be sure to wear this." She handed Kinuko a headband just like the one she was wearing. "A newspaper man is coming. We should all look patriotic." Kinuko only smiled and took the headband with a bow.

The next day, Kinuko, only visibly pregnant woman, was one of the sixty-seven citizens—mostly housewives—from ten local neighborhoods assembled under thick clouds for the first defense drills, each wearing a rising sun headband. The few men wore khaki national uniforms, while Kinuko, like the other women, wore a white overall apron over a blouse and baggy monpe pants. The men from the vigilance corps and the neighborhood chiefs, including Hayashi, stood erect facing the citizens in the neighborhood. One of them solemnly announced the beginning of the special program. As the flag lifted into the gray sky, everyone stoically sang the national anthem. Then a representative of the city defense commission stepped onto the podium, and a newspaperman flashed his box camera. Over the ensuing hush, the representative declared that the soul of Japan would never be defeated, no matter how fiercely the enemy tried.

"Seize this moment to rise above the difficulties that face our great nation," he urged. "When we, the citizens of this great nation, resolve to fulfill our noble duty to serve the Emperor, the final victory will be ours."

He ended with a series of cheering banzais and the crowd followed, incessantly repeating, "Long live the Emperor!"

After each received a bamboo spear, the training finally began. Hayashi demonstrated the maneuver from the podium, shouting, "One, two, three, thrust!" The trainees mimicked him, moving in a half-crouched position, advancing from one end of the field to the other, thrusting their weapons as they went. The fresh damp soil caked their shoes, but they plodded on obediently.

Kinuko moved across the muddy field with the others, holding a bamboo spear to the side of her protruding stomach, trying not to fall behind. "One, two, three, thrust! One, two, three, thrust!" The shout came constantly from the podium. Her legs began aching and grew stiff as the mist settled in and soon thickened into cold rain. Still, she kept moving, telling herself this was nothing compared to Giichi's suffering.

She assumed this was Hayashi's way of punishing her for being the wife of a "traitor." The previous evening, Mrs. Chiba had urged her to ask Hayashi to excuse her from the exercises, and Ichiro agreed.

"I will speak with him," Ichiro said. "Pregnant women should not be required to participate."

But Kinuko was adamant. She couldn't bear the thought of bowing to the man who had reported Giichi. Besides, she wanted to do this. Though she no longer believed in the patriotism that surrounded her, she needed to feel at least a portion of Giichi's suffering.

"One, two, three, thrust!" Kinuko moved on. Her headband drooped over her wet hair; she struggled to slide her mud-caked shoes through the motion of the drills. "One, two, three, thrust!" This is my prison, she thought. Soon her mind began to wander and she found her movements driven by anger more than by her conjured sense of sharing Giichi's suffering. Did the Emperor know that his police force tortured men and women who were against the war? If they had to use torture to silence opponents of the war, then something must be seriously wrong with the war itself. So what if Giichi had a connection with a communist? By now, Kinuko no longer doubted the possibility. Why wouldn't he donate to a communist? That man obviously opposed war as well. Then her anger mixed with fear as she remembered the brutal treatment of communists. She shook her head to deny her dark thoughts, gritted her teeth and kept moving. "... thrust!"

That evening, Kinuko pulled stitches to expand the waist of her monpe pants. During the drills, they had felt tight against her stomach. Her legs still ached, and she shifted uncomfortably on the cushion in the dining room as she plucked at the seams. In the kitchen, Ichiro chopped kindling wood in the obscure glow of candlelight. Both of them were too tired to talk; the only sounds were Ichiro's hatchet striking wood and the ticking of the clock. It had been nearly a week since the jailer brought Giichi's note, and the elation they felt then had dissipated like morning mist. Once again, Kinuko took out the telegram from Okayama and gazed at her daughter's name.

"Listen," Ichiro suddenly mumbled from the kitchen. "We can't lose hope. We have to hold onto it. That is the only way we can get through this."

He raised the hatchet and brought it down hard against the slab of wood, his mouth curved downward. With each stroke, his tired face flickered in the candlelight. But to Kinuko he appeared angrier than tired—angry with the police who took his son, with the military about to turn the country into a battleground, and now, she thought, angry with his daughter-in-law who seemed to be losing hope.

Earlier, while she trudged across the muddy training field, Ichiro had left the police station and gone into the countryside in search of food. He took a tram to Osaka, and from there boarded a train to the farmland in Hirakata. He walked in the rain along a country road from one farmhouse to the next until he found enough food to last for several days. It was dark when he came home, wet and exhausted, with a heavy furoshiki bundle on his back. Yet, there he was, still chopping wood, and Kinuko knew he would get up early again the next morning and go to the police station.

"Father," Kinuko finally said. "It's time for you to go to bed."

"Yes, it's about time." He stood laboriously and reached to knead the muscles of his lower back. His shadow moved slowly against the wall.

Suddenly, the telephone shrieked. Kinuko looked at Ichiro, and their eyes met. He brushed the dust from his hands and tried to move nonchalantly. He picked up the receiver and coughed lightly to clear his throat. "Hello," he said, more a question than a greeting.

"Yes...I am the father of Giichi Sekihara."

His voice turned stiff, and Kinuko felt her chest tighten. She threw her sewing to the floor and rushed to his side.

"Are you releasing him then?" asked Ichiro.

He's alive! she thought, and her legs grew weak.

Ichiro's shoulders hunched tensely and then his voice boomed. "Why can't you tell me?" Kinuko began shivering. "Yes, I'll come over right away."

"What did they say?" Kinuko demanded, as soon as he hung up the phone.

"Virtually nothing," Ichiro muttered, hurrying past her. Kinuko followed him to the guestroom where he grabbed his coat. "They just told me to come."

He was already running, throwing his coat over his shoulders.

"Let me go with you," Kinuko begged.

Ichiro turned. "No."

Kinuko followed him to the door and watched him hurry toward the highway. Dark clouds drifted over a fuzzy moon, and his figure disappeared into the darkness. She returned to her half-mended pants, imagining Giichi's body lying beneath a white sheet, Ichiro signing a form to gain possession of his son's body. Or Giichi writhing in agony and Ichiro signing a paper stating that Giichi was not hurt in order to gain his release. She no longer shivered. She remembered the way her mother had sat the night her father died and tried to imitate that posture. She placed her hands on her lap, dipped her head downward, and sat perfectly still.

An hour later, she heard a popping sound like pebbles exploding beneath tires. Kinuko looked up sharply and leaned toward the door. More sounds—an engine whirring, gravel grinding beneath tires, the opening of a car door, then nothing but the engine. She pushed up from the floor, hearing muffled voices and deep inhuman groans of agony—Giichi, it must be Giichi, he *is* alive! She stumbled to the door. Two shadows staggered as one in front of a dark sedan, one leaning heavily on the other. The black sedan began moving away.

"Call a doctor," Ichiro groaned under the weight of Giichi. For a moment, the joy of knowing Giichi was alive clashed with the fear that he might be near death.

"Giichi-san!" Kinuko cried, running barefoot over sharp gravel. She took Giichi's arm, but he only moaned and pulled away from her and leaned more heavily against Ichiro. She smelled blood. Her teeth chattered. Giichi's swollen face glowed in the moonlight. Across the street, Mrs. Chiba's door opened and faint light spilled from it. Mrs. Chiba emerged from the house and came toward them.

"Call a doctor!" Ichiro said again.

Kinuko ran into the house, grabbed the receiver from the phone, and then didn't know what to do. They followed her into the house, Giichi between Mrs. Chiba and Ichiro. She tried to stop the chattering of her teeth. While the three moved toward the bedroom, she began breathing as she had when giving birth to Yuki. Mrs. Chiba hurried past her into the kitchen. Finally, Kinuko faced the phone and gave the operator the doctor's number. Her jaw felt numb and she wondered if she had actually spoken. She heard Giichi's groans and Ichiro hushing his son softly.

By the time the doctor arrived, she had managed to lay out Giichi's robe, clean underwear, a sheet, and towels. Mrs. Chiba had placed a basin of warm water beside Giichi's futon. Ichiro led the doctor into the room and asked her and Mrs. Chiba to stay away while the doctor examined Giichi. Despite Mrs. Chiba's urgings to sit down, Kinuko paced in front of the door, hugging herself tightly. Periodically, she heard the doctor's voice drifting from the room—a cracked rib, a broken nose, cuts and bruises on his face and back, shock.

An hour and a half later, Kinuko was finally summoned to the room. Giichi lay on his back with thick bandages over his forehead and chest. He breathed with shallow fishlike gulps; rasps and groans of air moved through his parted lips. Red lines of iodine traced the swollen gashes across his nose. His bruised face looked like a contorted balloon with slits for swollen eyes. She sat beside him and stretched her hand toward his.

"Don't touch him now," Ichiro warned.

Kinuko flinched and quickly withdrew her hand.

"He is in terrible pain," whispered Ichiro.

The doctor spoke, also in a whisper, "Right now, it's most important to lessen the swelling of his nasal passage. That's why he is breathing through his mouth. Apply a cold compress to his nose until the swelling goes down and be sure to give him fluids. He's severely dehydrated. But be careful, he will easily choke if you give him too much. Every five minutes trickle a few drops onto his tongue."

It was almost three o'clock in the morning when the doctor left. Throughout the rest of the night, Ichiro and Kinuko took turns sleeping and watching over him. The next day they continued that schedule, breaking it only to eat the food that Mrs. Chiba brought to them. They dipped a towel in cold water and placed it gently across Giichi's nose. As soon as the towel grew warm, they pulled it off and repeated the process. Every few minutes, they dripped water through his parted lips with a glass feeder. All the while, they watched him intently to make sure he was breathing. The same schedule continued, and by the third day, Giichi breathed more easily. The swelling around his nose receded into a purple and yellow bruise. Ichiro told Kinuko it was time for Giichi to start eating.

"I'll make another trip to Hirakata for a chicken and some eggs," he said.

After Ichiro left, Kinuko peeled the two apples Mrs. Chiba had given her, and grated and strained them so they would be easier for Giichi to digest. When she returned to the room with the feeder filled with juice, Giichi lay with his eyes open. He turned his gaze to her and smiled a weak, awkward smile. "Kinuko," he rasped, and her heart soared with joy.

"Giichi-san," she said softly before she sat close to him.

With great effort, Giichi stretched his hand toward her.

"Don't move. Stay still."

Slowly, a teardrop trickled out of the edge of his eye.

"I'm sorry," he whispered.

She shook her head, as streams of tears ran over her cheeks.

"Don't be sorry. You don't have to be sorry at all."

She slipped her hand across the futon to grasp his hand and looked at him through blurred vision. "All I wanted was for you to come home."

"I'm—I'm home," Giichi said. His chest heaved and as he tried to speak more, only air came out from his mouth.

"Please don't talk," Kinuko begged. "You need to rest."

But Giichi continued, "Yuki—where is—"

"She's in Okayama...with your mother."

Kinuko quickly pulled the tattered telegram from her pocket and held it close to Giichi's face. Giichi blinked a few times, then fixed his gaze on the paper.

"She's fine," Kinuko told him. "She is doing fine, and as soon as you get better, we'll go there."

Giichi gazed at it for a while longer, before nodding weakly and closing his eyes.

On the fifth day after his return, the pain from his cracked rib had subsided enough so that Kinuko could help Ichiro roll him onto his side and change the dressing on his back. Ichiro gently rubbed ointment on the crisscrossed lines of welts. From then on, they changed the dressing twice a day. Each time, Ichiro asked her to turn away as he peeled the gauze from Giichi's back. She ignored him, wanting to know the full horror of what he had experienced. After changing the dressing, they carefully propped Giichi against a stack of cushions and handed him a newspaper. Giichi held the open paper in front of his face but stared with glassy eyes and never seemed to read it.

Kinuko noted every sign of Giichi's progress. On the seventh day, he managed to get out of bed and go to the lavatory and brush his teeth by himself. Kinuko and Ichiro smiled at each other as they watched him shuffle from the bedroom. Kinuko felt elation welling inside her as on the first warm day of a long-awaited spring. From then on, Giichi no longer needed them during the night. Ichiro withdrew into the guest bedroom, but

Kinuko remained at his side, sleeping on and off through the night.

While Giichi's physical progress allowed Kinuko to grow optimistic, it also gave her the clarity to see that his recovery was far from complete. Now, when she awoke at night from the troubled sounds next to her, it was not raspy breathing, but Giichi twisting from side to side, moaning, "No!" During the day, he accepted her help but smiled nervously and his eyes glanced away from her or stared beyond her. Even at the dining table, where he began to join her and Ichiro for meals, he avoided their eyes. He kept his head down and spoke only when one of them spoke to him.

She knew he was trying hard to step away from the terror he had experienced, and she cried when she knew he wasn't watching. She wanted to reach out to his heart, but understood she could do so only by staying away from whatever it was he wanted to keep to himself.

On the morning of Giichi's ninth day out of jail, Ichiro announced suddenly at breakfast that it was time for him to leave for Okayama. "The women might be needing me there," he mumbled. Later, in the kitchen, after Giichi had returned to bed, Ichiro said to her, "I'm grateful his body is doing fine, but his mind needs more time. If I stay, it will only take longer. He needs to do this on his own."

The next morning, Ichiro finished packing and went into the room where Giichi lay. Kinuko heard them talk, already missing Ichiro's presence.

"I'm leaving now and I'll wait for you in Okayama."

"Thank you for everything." Kinuko heard Giichi say.

"I'm so happy you've come home to us."

"So am I."

"Take care, son," Ichiro said. "Heal yourself."

"I will."

Kinuko watched Ichiro pat his son's shoulder before coming out of the room. She shut her eyes tight to stop the tears. How could she ever have doubted Ichiro's love for Giichi?

Together, Kinuko and Ichiro walked to the Hanshin Highway. Unlike the day they took Yuki to the Osaka station, it was early spring and the sun felt warm and the air soft as gauze. She knew that she and Giichi would soon join Yuki in Okayama. According to the doctor, Giichi might be able to travel in a few days. That was all she wanted for now—to have all of them together. She wouldn't allow herself to think beyond that, though thoughts of the red paper still simmered beneath the surface of her mind. In Okayama, not only would they be with Yuki, but Kinuko hoped it would also be a better place for Giichi. The clean air, green fields, and Yuki's laughter would help him recover from his trauma.

"Don't worry about Giichi too much," said Ichiro as they approached the highway. "He will be fine, believe me. He just needs some time. That's all."

"I'm only grateful that he's home."

"So am I—I am truly grateful. Anyway, don't try to bring too many things. Just come as soon as you can."

"Yes, we will—with just some clothes. That's what I'm planning."

"That'll do. How happy Yuki will be to see her parents."

Ichiro then squinted, turning his face skyward, as if to take in the scent of spring. Kinuko saw the relief etched on his face. Whatever worries he held at this moment, he kept them unspoken. She understood. At a time like this, they could only deal with one thing at a time. And at this moment, they were filled with gratitude.

They stopped at the bottom of the steps leading up to the highway, and Ichiro suggested that she let him go on by himself.

"I hope you have a safe trip, Father."

"I will. Take care." Ichiro started up the concrete steps with his small suitcase.

"Thank you, Father, for staying with me," Kinuko called to him. At the top of the steps, he turned and nodded with a smile. Kinuko bowed and smiled in return.

CHAPTER 16

Left alone for the first time since his return from jail, Giichi rose from his futon and struggled to the veranda. He slumped into a wicker chair and watched Ichiro and Kinuko walk toward the highway. Seeing his father ascend the steps to the tram stop, a lonely fear like that of an unprotected child began to settle over him. When his father reached the top of the steps, he saw him nod to Kinuko. He couldn't see their expressions very well, but they seemed to smile at each other lovingly, and he wondered why it was so difficult for him to share their happiness, to acknowledge their help and love.

As the tram swallowed his father and moved out of view, Giichi picked up the morning paper and read a headline and the first lines of a story, unable to make any sense of it. He knew he must try harder to focus his mind. Kinuko would be back at any moment, and he wanted her to see that he was making progress. She would now face him alone, without the help from his father. He knew he must strive to be as strong as his father so he could help her, but that it wouldn't be easy. It would have to happen in increments.

Days ago, when the pain first lifted, he had felt a great liberation, as if his life would be normal again, but that feeling lasted only a moment. As quickly as his mind grew empty, devoid of its obsession with pain, it filled with another obsession—anger and hatred for Toda. He often woke up in a sweat and stared into the darkness, picturing himself beating Toda with a bamboo stick until his tormenter could no longer beg for mercy. Of course, those thoughts were followed by guilt and confusion at the ease with which he had descended to the level of the war makers. His only relief came with the realization that he had not given Toda the information he wanted. Toda had crushed his nose and broken his ribs but he did not injured his soul. Now he needed to put that experience behind him. But part of him knew it wasn't possible, he didn't want to forget, and as he stared at the black and white blur of the newspaper, he thought his life might never again be the same.

Two days later, Giichi was sitting on the veranda with a book in his hand, when he heard the telephone ring in the kitchen. "It's Mr. Kato," Kinuko said. "Would you like to talk to him?"

"Yes," Giichi said, more to please her than from any real desire to talk with his boss. Yet as he shuffled toward the phone, he thought this was how it must happen. He would have to return to the world and simply start living again and somehow his anger would vanish beneath the new weight of surface conversation and details. That was how his father had done it. When Ichiro returned from detention, he lingered distantly for a while, but eventually plunged back into his world—tending his bonsais, visiting the temple, writing, whatever was needed. Besides, Giichi realized that his anger had already begun to subside. This morning, he had even been able to converse with Kinuko. They had discussed moving to Okayama, perhaps within a few days, if he could clear his resignation earlier than the originally established date. So he actually did need to talk with Mr. Kato.

"Hello," Giichi said meekly into the receiver.

"How are you doing?" Mr. Kato's eager voice ricocheted back.

Giichi apologized for his long absence and said he was planning to come in to see him as soon as he felt well enough. Then he told his boss apologetically that he wanted to resign immediately, though he still had eleven days left.

"My wife is pregnant, and—and I would like to leave for Okayama, as soon as my doctor thinks it's all right."

"I understand," said Mr. Kato. "That won't be a problem. But I'd like to see you before you leave. Can I come to your house? Everyone here has been worrying about you."

The soft forgiving lilt of Mr. Kato's voice eased his worries. "I'm sorry that I've troubled everyone. I'm the one who should come in to say good-bye and clear my office." Giichi paused for a moment, then added, surprising himself, "How about tomorrow? Will you be in the office?"

"I'll be here in the afternoon, but are you sure you'll be feeling well enough by then?"

"Yes, I'm sure."

"It will be great to see you. Why don't you come in around three or four? We can have dinner later, if you are feeling up to it."

After Giichi hung up the phone, he felt something close to elation and wished he had returned Mr. Kato's earlier calls.

"So, you will be going to the office tomorrow?" Kinuko asked. "Are you sure you are ready?"

"I am not sure if I will ever be ready," Giichi said. "But I want to finish with the company as soon as possible, so we can join Yuki."

A tight smile revealed Kinuko's worry, but he could also see appreciation in her eyes, and he felt good about forcing himself to go.

The next morning, as Giichi walked to the lavatory, he inhaled deeply to test the pain. A thick pain stabbed his ribcage, but he decided he wouldn't let it be a problem. He told himself he felt nearly whole. Certainly, when he breathed in sharply, pain seared through his chest, but as long as he modulated his breathing and moved carefully, he would be fine. When he reached the lavatory, though, the sight of his face in the mirror made his mood sink—purple shadows blotted the corners of his eyes and a dark scab marred his nose, surrounded by raw pinkish skin. At best, he looked like an owl with a broken beak. How would he explain this amid the curious stares of Mr. Kato and the others? Again, his mind boiled with hatred for Toda, but he quickly moved away from the mirror and his thoughts shifted to Okayama and their reunion with Yuki.

At four o'clock, Giichi managed to enter his office unnoticed. He placed his bag beside his desk, hung his coat up, touched the scab on his nose, and then went to Mr. Kato's office three doors away. Mr. Kato looked up from his desk and stared for a moment, speechless. Then he sprang up from his chair. "Sekihara! It's you! Welcome back! Sit down. Sit down. What on earth did they do to you?"

Giichi sat, while Mr. Kato shook his head grimly.

"Well, it was a—it was a...." Giichi stammered, trying to start the story he had concocted on the way.

Mr. Kato suddenly waved his hand. "Sorry, I shouldn't have asked you. This should remain your own personal matter."

"Thank you for your concern. My wife said you called several times while—while I was gone. Anyway, I'm sorry I have to quit immediately."

Mr. Kato waved his hand again. "Don't worry, it's all set. You are on your way. You've already done enough for the company. If we were living in a normal time, I wouldn't let you go. But what can I say to a young man like you when nobody knows about tomorrow. How about dinner then, do you feel up to it?"

"Yes, of course."

"I'll be staying here until about six, then I'll stop in your office. We'll eat somewhere, maybe in Minami."

For the next forty-five minutes, Giichi busied himself by going from office to office to say good-bye to his colleagues. They already knew about his resignation and wished him the best. Surprisingly, unlike Mr. Kato they didn't ask about his detention or his battered face, though many of them appeared uncomfortable and didn't look him in eye.

Around five, he went back to his office and began clearing his desk. First, he went through the documents left in his tray and sorted them into two piles, one for immediate attention and the other for matters that could wait. Then he leaned back and looked around the room. Like it or not, this had been his office for eight years, and he realized he might never sit here again. It was here that he had often thought of Kenji Nakayama and his ideals, slipped part of his pay into an envelope, and looked forward to their meetings. Because of that, he had gone to jail and had been tortured. But all of that was over.

Mr. Kato stepped into his office a little after six, just as Giichi jammed the last of his belongings, including the crystal inkwell from Kinuko into his bag, already laden with an ivory letter opener from his mother, the keys to his parents' home, photos from company trips, and personal letters.

By seven, Giichi and Mr. Kato sat at a restaurant in the Minami district of Osaka—twenty minutes by streetcar from Nippon Motors. Though it was still early in the evening, this once prosperous restaurant was emptier than Giichi had ever seen it. A middle-aged couple ate mutely in one corner and four men caroused at a table near the doorway. For many years, this restaurant had been popular among stiff-mustached military officers. Back then, its private rooms had echoed with laughter and loud confidence. When the war was going well, many civilians patronized the place so they could mingle with their nation's heroes. Now, in March 1945, it exhibited remarkable decline—no seasonal flower arrangements in the alcoves, silk cushions flattened from neglect, once fresh tatamis now a discolored yellow. Giichi and Mr. Kato had eaten here often, mostly at the invitation of military personnel.

Looking at his boss across the table, Giichi thought Mr. Kato probably felt pangs of nostalgia, if he felt anything at all. For a moment, it disturbed Giichi that after all these years, Mr. Kato remained an enigma to him. It seemed that whatever he felt was always buried beneath expressions of optimism.

"Well, I hope this place still serves something edible," Mr. Kato joked, picking up a sake bottle.

Giichi smiled. "I'm sure it does," he said, pondering the fact that he had known Mr. Kato about as long as he had known Kinuko. Though he couldn't compare what he felt for his boss with what he felt for his wife, it was unsettling that he could exhibit more friendliness with someone he really didn't know than with someone he deeply loved. He examined Mr. Kato more intently. Unlike most Japanese in the middle of the war, he was a round man with a gentle, pudgy face and dimpled hands. His neck was buried in the collar of his shirt and his stomach protruded above his belt. Yet he didn't move with the slowness usually associated with overweight people. When other executives sat behind their shiny desks, he stormed through the office corridor like a rumbling train, sticking his head into his subordinates' offices to see how they were doing and often cracking a joke before withdrawing from view. Giichi suddenly realized he would miss him. Without Mr. Kato, his job would have been sheer boredom or an endless conflict with the military.

They continued sipping sake, while Mr. Kato told Giichi how smoothly the company's parts transportation project had gone despite his sudden absence. "But," he said, and then turned silent as he refilled Giichi's cup with the quiet artistry and gentleness required by a shared drink. Finally, Mr. Kato set the bottle on the table and continued, "Guess what?"

"What is it, Mr. Kato?"

"I'm not supposed to tell anybody, but since you are leaving, I think I can tell you," Mr. Kato whispered dramatically.

Giichi put down his cup and waited.

"The Allies are definitely going to bomb our plants. While you were gone, our military shot down B-29s and found their target maps. All of our plants were marked. That's why I talked our big boss into letting you go after you asked if you could resign right away. He didn't like the idea, but I told him we shouldn't keep you after what happened."

Giichi stared at Mr. Kato. Mr. Chiba's charred body appeared in his vision, and he imagined himself and his colleagues suffering the same fate. "Thank you. I appreciate what you've done for me—I only hope the Allies will bomb the plants at night when no one is there or won't get the chance to do so at all."

"That's what I'm hoping, too—well, let's change the subject. How many months along is your wife now?"

"Her due date is in May," Giichi replied, still overwhelmed by his luck at getting away from work as it was becoming more dangerous.

"It's coming up soon, isn't it?"

"Yes, just two more months."

"You've made the right decision to leave Hanshin. You are still young. Even if your luck runs out and you are drafted, you can start over again after the war." Mr. Kato tapped his pudgy index finger on the table. "Come back to the company. If I'm still alive, I'll rehire you any time. We'll rebuild the company together. You should remember that. So, let's forget our worries and drink to the future."

Mr. Kato filled Giichi's cup again.

"That's very nice of you," Giichi said, as he took the bottle and filled Mr. Kato's cup. "I hope I can do that. I'll definitely need a job after the war."

Mr. Kato swallowed his full cup in one gulp and grimaced. Then his face turned sad despite his gusto. Instead of the future, he began talking about how difficult the air raid warnings were for his old mother with arthritis and how he was thinking of sending her to his younger brother's place in the country. He lamented the nation's future and said he might have to go back to his village in Mie to farm if the company's plants were bombed. Mr. Kato's optimism always turned morose after a few bottles of sake, and now, Giichi couldn't blame him. He listened, drinking more than usual himself, while his boss rambled on for nearly an hour.

By then they had finished eating and the restaurant was empty, except for the madam, who worked on her books behind the counter, occasionally looking up from her abacus and glancing nervously in their direction. Giichi grew uncomfortable, but Mr. Kato continued talking.

"How long do you think we can keep the Allies from landing?"

"I don't know," Giichi replied, recalling the news of kamikaze attacks in today's newspaper and the photo of a young pilot, wearing goggles and a white scarf, as he prepared to take off from an airfield in Kyushu.

"I don't either. My wife is busy with bamboo spear training, but I can't even imagine the situation if civilians would really have to use them, let alone my old wife in hand-to-hand combat."

The madam brought the bill and stood next to their table, smiling graciously. In normal times she would have been dressed elegantly, but now she wore monpe pants, like nearly every other Japanese woman in the midst of war. "I'm so sorry to interrupt your conversation," she said, "but it is getting late, and I'm afraid our neighborhood chief is going to scold us for using too much electricity. May I—"

"Yes, yes," said Mr. Kato. "We understand, of course. We'll leave."

"I appreciate your understanding," the madam said with a bow.

Mr. Kato grabbed the bill and tried to lift his sake-saturated body off the cushion. "Let's—let's hope things will be fine," he muttered, and with great labor and strain, finally pushed away from the low table to get to his feet. "Oh, I forgot to tell you," he said. "Let me know if you need a truck to move in case railway travel becomes impossible. They've been talking about shutting down the railway service. Call me anytime."

He staggered to the counter, groping inside his pocket for his wallet. While he paid, Giichi stood behind him, feeling a little tipsy but glad that he didn't feel any pain.

They walked to the main street in silence, Mr. Kato burying his neck in the collar of his wrinkled spring coat, and Giichi dangling his bulging bag at his side.

When a streetcar approached from the west, Mr. Kato stretched his hand toward Giichi. "I will miss you," he said.

Giichi took his hand.

"I will miss you, too, Mr. Kato." Giichi felt a lump in his throat, knowing it was not just Mr. Kato he would miss, but all of Japan's innocence. The people like Mr. Kato and Mr. Chiba, good souls, intent on simplicity, yet overwhelmed by a government intent on egotistical self-annihilation.

"Don't forget. Call me if you need a truck. I'll arrange it."

"Thank you. I might have to do that. And thank you for dinner."

The streetcar screeched next to them; its headlights flooded the empty street. Mr. Kato stepped into the car and waved. Giichi bowed again and watched the streetcar move away. In the darkness, sadness settled over him as he thought of leaving Osaka. He would miss the smell of diesel fumes mingling with fragrant flowers in late summer, the harsh light of winter, these streets, the bars where he met Kenji—the city where he had been born, where he had grown up and worked. Most of all, he would miss his parents' house, where he had spent more than half his life, where his father's office served as his refuge from the cold world outside, where the quiet waters of the pond stilled the turmoil of his evolving soul.

Giichi crossed the road to board a streetcar for his return to Kinuko, but once inside the car, he realized that he was only a few stops from his parents' home, and he felt a sudden urge to spend the night there. He might never again see the light glimmering from his mother's tearoom across the pond, or the koi wavering in the water beneath the hovering spring scent of chinchoge. He knew that he should get back to Kinuko. He wanted to be with her—there would likely be bombings again tonight. But the thought of returning to his past overwhelmed him and comforted him as if he were returning to his mother's womb. He lifted his bag to his lap and groped through its contents. When he found the house key, he knew he had to return one last time. He settled back and watched the dark familiar streets gliding by.

Two blocks from where he stepped out of the streetcar, Giichi found the post office from his youth and remembered that it had a public telephone. A male clerk sat with his chin resting in his hand in the dim light of the window. Giichi filled out the required form, slipped into the phone booth in a dark corner, placed a call to Kinuko, and waited for the phone to ring.

"Where are you?" asked Kinuko. "Are you okay?"

"I am doing fine," he said. "But I am near my parents' home, and I have decided that I must go there. I may never see that place again."

"But it will get too late, you will not be able to come home," she protested.

"I know. I will have to spend the night there." He listened for a response but she said nothing. "I'm sorry. I know that I should come home and be with you. But this is something I must do."

More silence, until Kinuko finally said, "Giichi-san, are you sure? How are you feeling? I wish you would come home."

This time Giichi paused before speaking. "I want to come home, but I hope you will understand."

"Okay," she finally said. "But you will come back in the morning?"

"Yes, I will be fine. I'll come back in the morning. And we can leave as soon as possible and be with Yuki again."

Kinuko suddenly sounded practical, though he could hear the disappointment in her voice. "Mother and Ume slept there the night before they left, so I know there are some futons. But I don't know about the lights and water."

"I think Father said the city wouldn't cut them off until the end of the month. I'll come home in the morning."

"Are you sure you feel all right?"

"Yes, I'm fine. Just tired, that's all."

"All right, then," she said. "I hope you can sleep well there."

Giichi paid the fee at the window, and hurried from the building, feeling the curious stare of the clerk. Until then, he had forgotten about his battered face.

As he approached the house, he smelled spring blossoms and quickened his stride. He unlocked the gate and stepped into the front court where white clusters of chinchoge glowed in the darkness. With its scent filling his nostrils, he unlocked the main door, stepped into the entryway, and groped for the light switch. As the front room revealed itself in light, he felt as if he had returned from a long journey of many years. The room stood completely bare, but the smell—a mixture of wood, paper, tatami, and ink—revived his memories. Though a little stale, it was the same aroma that had been there for as long as he could remember. He stepped up to the front room and proceeded to the dark corridor. When he turned on the hall light, he saw the door to his father's study slightly ajar, and immediately understood why his father always left his door open. No matter what his father was doing, writing madly to meet a deadline or reading or even napping, he never closed it entirely. Nobody asked him why, and he never explained. But now Giichi knew. His father couldn't bear the door being closed after having been locked up in a cell. His mother must have known that, too, and probably couldn't bear to close it even when she left.

Giichi went into his father's study and stood dazed, no desk, no books, no stacks of magazines piled in the corner, no father writing at the desk. Strangely though, the familiar rug still lay across the hardwood floor, with its dark blue border and a circle of the same color in the middle surrounding a single motif of plum blossoms. Its original ivory color had faded to gray over the years. His father had bought the rug at an auction he arranged to raise money for a writer crippled by a police beating. That was in 1933, the same year his father was interrogated for an essay criticizing Japan's incursion into China. In February of that year, the League of Nations voted against the presence of Japanese troops in Manchuria, but the following month Japan withdrew from the League of Nations in protest. Giichi remembered how his father had limped across the rug after spreading it over the floor for the first time.

He sat on the rug and rubbed his hands over its surface, imagining his father's feet walking on it and remembering how often those feet, injured by bamboo beatings, continued to support his strong body and mind. Just a few days ago, his father had told him to heal himself, and still he didn't know how. It was a wonder to him how his father had pressed on. He was certain his father had gone through what he was going through now—the dilemma of trying to forget what had been done to him, of dealing with terrible anger, of confronting the dark side of human nature. As far as he remembered, his father had never let his inner turmoil affect his daily life. He always appeared peaceful. Giichi wished he knew where his father had gotten such extraordinary strength, and yet sitting here in this familiar place, a sense of peace filled him. For a long time he sat and gently stroked the coarse wool of the rug.

As the effect of the sake wore off, Giichi finally stood and looked around for a futon. He wandered through the house, turning lights on and off, wondering where his mother and Ume had slept on their last night in this house. He was surprised to find two sets of folded futon in the corner of the reception room. The family had used the room often because of its view of the garden, but it was mainly used as an area where they received visitors. That formality probably hadn't mattered to them on their last night here, with the house already empty. He imagined that Ume and his mother slept side by side to keep each other company, as he and his mother had done long ago when his father was in jail. With her son in jail, his mother must have ached in the same way for the company of someone sleeping next to her. How shocked she must have been when she first heard he had been detained. And how difficult it must have been for her to pack the house alone and leave Osaka without knowing what would happen to him.

Giichi approached the sliding door and parted the blackout curtain to look out into the garden. Light spilled from the house and reflected onto the pond. Beyond it, the north wing of the house, where his mother had taught tea ceremonies, lay in darkness. Peering into the stark glow of the pond, he felt his mother's never-ending sorrow. He remembered the promise he had made as a boy, that he would never do anything to make her worry. His desire to be her faithful son had never changed. He hoped she knew that, even if he hadn't kept his promise. He closed the curtain, hoping that by the time he joined her in Okayama his face would look better and it would not remind her of his imprisonment.

He took off his coat, laid the futon in the middle of the room, and crawled into it. As he closed his eyes, he seemed to hear the many voices of his father's friends, those who gathered often in this room. They arrived in kimono or coat and tie, their hair slicked with pomade. They sat around the table, murmuring, talking, shouting, smoking pipes and sipping green tea or sake, depending on the time of day. They were mostly writers and journalists who covered every topic imaginable, words and meanings, perhaps history and literature, current events and economics, politics and nations.

When the conversation turned to Japan's future, as it always did, especially late at night, and especially during the later years, only a few of them shared his father's view. The others called his ideas "internationalist" and ridiculed them as naïve and unrealistic. Still, they kept coming back.

His father insisted that Japan should stop its foolish emphasis on the supremacy of the Japanese race. "All nations in the world are equal and should be treated equally.

As writers we have an obligation to foster that idea. We need to advocate world peace, using our pens rather than weapons," he would tell them.

"You are dreaming, Mr. Sekihara," one of them would immediately counter. Then a flurry of anxious voices, each stepping on the other, would join the fray. Giichi would sit on the floor behind them, listening as if in an informal and exciting classroom, while historical evidence erupted against his father. His father's intellectual adversaries would cite Japan's numerous efforts to be considered an equal in the world community, cite the litany of wrongs committed against Japan, such as the 1919 Paris Peace Conference, when the racist arrogance of the United States, England, and Australia rejected Japan's proposal to create worldwide understanding, or the persistent arrogance of Christian missionaries. On and on the lessons flowed—that weapons are more powerful than ideas, that the modernization of the Meiji Era saved Japan from Western encroachment: Admiral Perry, Russia, France, Britain, Holland, Prussia, decades of unequal treaties, exploitation of Asia, Asia for Asians.

Facts and ideas swarmed in Giichi's excited mind. Who was right? His father or the others? His father always sat quietly and waited for the frenzy to settle. In the end, they always turned to his father, and Giichi knew that he must be right, if only because they respected his calmness.

"Wrongs have been committed against Japan," Ichiro would say, "and certainly Japan's industrialization and militarization have prevented the country from falling into the same fate as other subjugated Asian nations. But if we use our force to acquire raw materials and markets, or to inflict our will on other nations, we are doing the very same thing we hold against the West. We must assert a higher moral standard."

After the visitors left, his father would go out to the garden. Giichi remembered how lonesome his father looked then, walking slowly past the moss-clad wooden bench on which his bonsais sat, hands deep in his kimono sleeves. He would eventually pick up a pair of scissors and begin snipping the bonsais with the serious eye of a barber, slowly absorbing himself in the task and finding peacefulness again. He would continue snipping in the quiet garden, tilting his head this way and that, until each of the plants satisfied his eyes.

Though exhausted, Giichi lay on the futon and stared into the darkness. He remembered how sometimes he helped his mother or Ume bring trays of tea and snacks to this room while the men argued. His mother had nothing to do with the men's conversations, although she was always cordial. She brought them sake or tea, exchanged pleasantries with a graceful smile, and then left the room. Giichi now realized that he had gained nourishment from those conversations just as he had from food. Even before he understood the big words the grown men used, he knew his father loved peace. What he didn't understand was why loving peace was a crime and why his father had to be punished by the authorities. He grew up wondering, and by the time he was old enough to understand, his father's dedication to peace had been imbedded in his own soul.

The futon grew warm from the heat of his body, and he struggled to keep his eyes open. He knew that sleep would soon overcome him and hoped that his sleep would be filled with dreams of his life in this house, that it would somehow give him further understanding of who he was. His eyes fluttered. Tomorrow he would go out to the garden, feed the koi, and then go home to Kinuko.

Near midnight, Giichi's eyes jerked open as an air-raid siren shrieked through the silence. He poked his head from the futon cover, at first confused, expecting to be taken to Toda. A cold sweat covered his body, and then he realized that he was not in jail, and he thought of Kinuko and scrambled out of the futon. He stumbled toward the door, knowing he should call her, but stopped and clicked his tongue when he remembered that telephone service had been cut off from his parents' home. He stood in the dark for a few moments before parting the curtain to look into the black garden. He thought enough to unlock the door in case he had to go to the bomb shelter. Then he pulled the curtains aside and went to the entryway to get his shoes. By the time he returned to the reception room, he could hear the drone of the B-29s.

Soon an explosion erupted in the direction of Osaka Harbor, a few miles away. He heard the voice of a vigilance corpsman, amplified by a paper megaphone, "A warning has been issued!" Moments later, another voice joined in, "A warning is out!" Then turmoil exploded all around. The heavy hum of B-29s grew to a roar. A staccato thump of anti-aircraft guns vibrated through the air. Giichi put his shoes on. Before he could tie them, the floor trembled beneath him. His hands moved frantically. A bright light flashed like lightning over his shoes and hands, and in that instant he saw the photographic image of a man fleeing the inferno of the Great Kanto Earthquake, running through streets with a wet futon over his head. "That's what you should do to keep yourself from getting burnt," his father had told him long ago, pointing at the photograph in a museum.

Giichi grabbed the futon from the floor and pulled it out to the garden. The western sky glowed orange at the corner of his vision. Without looking up, he stumbled to the pond, tripping over the stepping stones. "Osaka harbor was hit!" a man yelled. "B-29s are coming this way!" Screams of panic were all around him. Giichi felt the vibration of another wave of B-29s. He dipped the futon in the pond and frantically shook it to soak up more water. It bloated like a corpse. He dragged it back toward the house, stunned by its weight. Then, as an afterthought, he ran back to the pond, jumped in to drench himself. Then he ran back to the wet futon. He struggled to drag it onto the tatami floor of the reception room. Suddenly, a deafening crack knocked him down, and from an odd angle he saw a fierce red column of fire shoot up beyond the fence to the west. The garden shone brighter than daylight. Before he could move, the glass doors along the corridor shattered like a violent waterfall. His mother's tearoom erupted in flames across the pond and a hot wind blasted into the room. Giichi crawled on hands and knees, dragging the heavy mattress behind him. When he reached the entryway, he struggled to his feet and stumbled into the forecourt.

Beyond the gate, a blazing fire engulfed the homes across the street. He quickly retreated into the house only to see thick smoke filling the front room. He could no longer see the corridor he had just left; flames danced and licked like a dragon's tongue. Coughing, he backed away from the house and ran sideways to the gate, stumbling out into the blazing street. Immediately, intense heat seared his exposed skin, and he saw horrors he never imagined he would—screaming bodies tumbling over each other, clothes melting into flesh. He smelled his own hair burning. Frantically, he pulled the dripping futon over his head, gripped the wet underside and stumbled forward, advancing toward the screams. Water dripped across his face and blinded him, and for a strange moment he thought of his mother washing his hair when he was a child. In his limited view, people fell to the ground and writhed in the street. Beside him, a tiny girl shrieked and waved the blazing torch of her sleeve. Suddenly his foot hit something soft and he reached out to stop his fall. His hand skidded across something slimy. He turned and saw raw flesh where his hand had peeled back the skin of an old man lying there. Now he screamed, sprang up gagging and ran, surrounded by the smell of burning flesh. His chest tightened, yet his legs propelled him onward, moving in a way that seemed slow and foreign to him, as if they were somehow separate from him. Again, he heard the roar of approaching B-29s. He dropped onto the rough surface of the road strewn with the rubble of crumbled walls and shattered furniture. He curled into a fetal ball beneath the futon and immediately felt crushing weight of people tripping over him. Still, he held his breath and waited until the rumble of the planes faded. When he finally freed himself, he coughed until he thought his throat would bleed. He struggled to his feet once again and began running, fighting to pull air into his lungs.

Eventually, he reached the bank of a river, where he tumbled down the concrete bank and rolled into the water. He kicked until his feet touched the muddy bottom, while others tumbled in beside him and made the water boil with their struggle. As one flailing mass, they pushed toward a bridge sixty meters downstream. Beneath the bridge, a crowd huddled like cattle. In the sky above more aircraft flickered in the firelight, rumbling and swooping down. Then right in front of him, the bridge erupted in a ball of fire. A hot blast of air rushed against his face and he reeled back and dove beneath the muddy water. When his head bobbed to the surface he gasped for air, then he planted his feet in the mud and pushed toward the bank of the river.

Again, he was running through fire, not certain what he was doing or what he should do. After minutes or hours, it was impossible to tell, he collapsed on a concrete sidewalk. He curled on his side gasping, clawing at his tight throat. When he finally regained his breath, he lay flat, his chest heaving. He wished rain would pour down and drench him. Where was the futon? He wished he still had it so he could squeeze it and drink its last drops of water.

At the edge of his consciousness, he noticed a small park to the left, a dark and quiet place. The sky glowed orange above him, and he knew the city was still burning. He took in the dancing colors for a while, strangely enamored by them, and then closed his aching eyes. The little girl with the burning sleeve appeared at the back of his eyes, jumping and screaming.

He didn't know how long he lay there by the park; but then he was walking again in search of water. His feet throbbed in scorched shoes; he struggled to keep his eyes open. After plodding down several smoldering streets, he came upon one of the main thoroughfares of the city where the iron streetcar tracks had been torn from their bed and rose in the air like twisted snakes. Someone unfurled the end of a tangled fire hose, and a man in burnt rags rushed to grab the end of the hose and press his parched lips over it. Giichi hurried to join the crowd rushing toward the water, but a whistle shrilled, and a fireman yelled through a paper megaphone, "Get away from here. We need this water to put out fires. There are emergency shelters at the local temples."

Giichi shuffled north with the others, thinking only of water. When he reached the temple, he started along the path to the main hall, where he saw people squatting on both sides, staring vacantly amid the clutter of their rescued belongings, futons, blankets, pots and pans. Rescue workers carried the injured into the main hall on stretchers and placed them wherever they could find floor space. He saw a ragged mob in one corner of the dark forecourt, frantic to reach the well. Immediately, he squeezed into the fray and pushed forward to where two monks methodically pumped water into pails. Giichi grabbed a ladle, scooped water, and drank and drank while the crowd pressed against him. Water dripped down his chin. It felt so good that he took another ladle full and poured it over his head and feet. Angry voices boiled up around him, and he felt hands tugging at him and pulling him away. He gave up the ladle and walked back through the mob, wiping his chin with his wet sleeve.

Suddenly aware of the pain in his feet, he searched the forecourt for a place to sit, but there was not a single empty mat or spot against the wall. He hobbled across the forecourt, stepping over legs covered by charred and tattered pants, until he reached the far end where a cherry tree loomed in the obscure light from the hall. Only after he had settled under the tree and closed his eyes did he hear the low moans, muffled coughs, and faint sobs. For the first time since leaving his parents' burning house, he thought of Kinuko and wondered if she was alive.

By the time first light washed over the dead city, Giichi found himself limping north through endless ruin. Little remained between the orange sky and the earth except for smoldering buildings and clusters of dazed people. Every few blocks, a pile of stiff blackened corpses covered a street corner. Vaguely, he wondered what his father, the believer in universal brotherhood, would think if he saw this ruined city and its corpses? Or more than his father, for he was only human, what about Buddha? What about the Jesus the Americans believed in? Why were they so silent? Maybe, Giichi thought, there was no such thing as universal brotherhood or world peace. For a moment, he felt like laughing. But he didn't. All he wanted now was to get home to Kinuko.

In the square in front of the half-bombed Osaka railway station, soldiers and rescue workers swarmed amid dozens of army trucks, unloading bodies and reloading medical supplies, food, and water. Giichi staggered up to one of the trucks, and a soldier rolled down the window. "Was Ashiya bombed last night?" asked Giichi.

"It was just Osaka last night," said the soldier. "But it was very bad."

"No bombing in any other cities, then?"

"No," the soldier said, scrutinizing Giichi from head to toe. "Did you get bombed out?"

"I'm going home to Ashiya."

"You can't. The station is closed. Nothing is running."

"I'll walk."

"Twenty-three kilometers? You can't walk that far like that. I would stay in Osaka until something starts running in a few days. Besides, Kobe and Ashiya will be bombed in a few days. That's what everyone's saying."

Giichi heard the soldier, but he didn't care if Ashiya was going to be bombed in a few days or not. By then he would be with Kinuko and they would be gone from Hanshin. He smiled at the thought of her safety. He thanked the soldier and shuffled to the edge of the square and sat on the concrete curb to rest his throbbing feet.

It was light now and for the first time he could clearly see his gray suit and white shirt, smeared with soot and pocked by hundreds of tiny black-rimmed holes. His tie was gone, and he had no idea what he had done with it. The hems of his trousers hung in limp charred shreds. The tips of his brown shoes were burnt black and the top of his right shoe was torn from its sole. He took his shoes off to see why his feet hurt so badly. When he peeled off his damp right sock, the skin on the side of his foot came off with it, exposing raw flesh. Giichi winced when air hit the wound and thought of the man whose skin he had taken off when he fell on him. He didn't want to take the other sock off. He hung his head, wondering if he would be able to walk home.

Ten meters away, the soldier who had told him Ashiya would be bombed, jumped out of his truck. "You can't walk to Ashiya like that," he yelled. "I'll get a nurse." He disappeared among the trucks and soon returned with a young nurse, who carried a square white box. "Do you want me to take you to one of the shelters?" she asked Giichi.

"No, thank you," Giichi answered. "I just came from a shelter. I want to go home."

The soldier and the nurse looked at each other. Then the nurse knelt down in front of Giichi, took out a roll of white bandage and wrapped it around his foot with amazing speed. The soldier went to his truck and brought back a flask of water. "Here," he said. Giichi took the flask and drank with huge gulps. The sound of whistles shrilled nearby and the truck drivers began revving their engines and lurching away. "I have to go," the soldier said as he took the flask from Giichi's hand. "Thank you," Giichi said, watching the nurse hurry to wrap a stretchable bandage over the white bandage. She snapped her box shut and said, "See a doctor if you ever get home." With that, she ran toward the trucks. "Thank you," Giichi called to her, but she didn't look back.

Giichi sat and watched the trucks until they were all gone. He waited a few minutes more, then stood and began walking with only one shoe. He kept one simple thought in his mind—place one foot in front of the other. As long as he did that, he would eventually reach home. Soon he realized that this simple act wasn't going to be easy. He stopped often to sit at the edge of the road, groaning and sweating. After about five minutes of rest, he would stand again. It became a ritual—walking and resting, but the farther he went, the more his feet burned with pain, and eventually he stopped resting and walked trancelike while trucks growled past, dust swirled around him, and the sun lifted higher above.

When he came to what seemed like the middle of Amagasaki, he saw a rundown bicycle repair shop at the side of the road and shuffled toward it. He stood in front of the shop and stared blankly at the dusty shelves covered with rubber shoes, bicycle tires, wheels, tubes of glue, bells and air pumps. An old man came hurrying out, as though fearful Giichi might steal something.

"Look at you," he uttered, with eyes opening wide. "Oh, merciful Buddha. Were you in Osaka last night?"

Giichi nodded.

"Come, come inside." The old man led Giichi into his dusty, cluttered shop. He pointed at a wooden crate and said, "Sit, sit here." As Giichi slumped onto the crate, the old man disappeared into the back of the shop. He returned with water in a chipped porcelain cup. "Drink this," he said. "I'll get you some more if you like. Water is free, you see." With that, he laughed, revealing his rotten teeth.

Giichi gulped down three more cups of water before he began talking.

"Thank you," he gasped, looking for someplace to set the cup until the old man took it from him. "By the way, where am I?"

"This is the west edge of Amagasaki. Where are you going?"

"Home, west edge of Ashiya," Giichi said, disappointed at the distance he still had to cover.

"Ashiya? Merciful Buddha, you still have to go across Nishinomiya! Why don't you wait until something starts running?"

"My wife must be worried. Do you have a telephone?"

"No, we don't have such a luxurious thing. But rest here as long as you want."

"Thank you, but I have to go." Giichi stood and winced.

"Wait, you need a new pair of shoes."

The shopkeeper jumped up, picked up a pair of rubber shoes and dusted them with his hand. Giichi groped in his pockets, but the old man said, "No, no, don't worry. Pay me some other time. You need to get home."

Giichi pulled a new shoe over his bandaged right foot and it fit perfectly. He knew the left one would be too big, but it didn't matter. He thanked the man and limped out of the shop.

"Come back if you can't go any further," the man yelled.

For a while, with quenched thirst and new shoes, Giichi moved faster, but soon he felt dizzy, and when he neared the intersection before the bridge over the Muko River, he collapsed at the side of the road. He pushed up on his elbows and blankly watched the activities at the dusty intersection. Three traffic policemen chased away private trucks, and soon six army trucks loaded with coffins came from the west and sped away toward Osaka. Kinuko probably thought he was dead. He wondered if she prepared for his visitation as Mrs. Chiba had done for her husband after the shipyard bombing in January.

CHAPTER 17

Kinuko was pleased by Giichi's decision to meet with Mr. Kato. Surely, it meant that he was ready to move on with his life, and that soon they would travel to Okayama and be with Yuki. She knew now that nothing could be taken for granted, but the rekindled thought of a reunion with her child filled her with immense hope, and as soon as Giichi left for his meeting with Mr. Kato, Kinuko set off on a flurry of activity. First, she hurried to find paper and pen and quickly wrote a letter to her mother. She didn't tell the whole truth, but worried about that only briefly. There seemed no need to tell her mother about Giichi's detention. Her mother already had enough worries. Why should she give her more?

When she took the letter to the post office, she hoped the message would ease Etsu's fears:

> *"Dear Mother, I'm sorry that I haven't kept you posted. I've been busy with bamboo spear training and other urgent matters that seem to crop up every day. Please don't worry. Giichi's parents already took Yuki to Okayama two weeks ago, and Giichi and I are joining them in a few days. I'm busy getting ready to leave, so I will write to you as soon as we settle in Okayama. The war seems to get worse and worse. Please do take care. Kinuko."*

As she dropped the letter in the post box, she felt a prick of guilt. All of her earlier rationalization didn't sound as convincing to her now that the letter could not be retrieved. Really, her mother didn't need to know what had happened to Giichi. Yet, she knew she had delivered a lie of omission, and as she left the post office and started for the doctor's office to pay their bills, she carried the lie with her like a thorn in her chest.

After the doctor's office, she set out for an old provisions store to buy black market candles and matches. When she returned to her neighborhood, she marched straight to Hayashi's house. "Mr. Hayashi," she called at the door, brimming with resolve. She wanted her ration card back. Now that Giichi was out of jail, there shouldn't be any reason for Hayashi to deny their right to rationed food. She waited, shifting her shopping basket from one hand to the other. She trembled despite her resolve. Hayashi appeared at the door in his national uniform. Kinuko bowed stiffly and Hayashi nodded.

"What can I do for you?"

"I would like to have our ration card back. We are moving."

"Moving? When?"

"It will be in a few days."

"Well, has your husband learned a lesson or two after this incident?"

Kinuko felt a hot rush of blood to her face.

"That card is rightfully ours. There is no law that denies citizens the right to rationed food. I have an uncle who is an army general in Tokyo. If you don't give it back to me now, I will have him investigate you for abusing your power."

"Try, if you wish," Hayashi spat, then disappeared into the house. But when he returned to the door and thrust the card at her, he added, "By the way, if you like, I can excuse you from the defense drills since you are leaving soon."

She bowed silently.

Later, as she neared the Chibas' low brushwood fence, her face was still hot with anger, and bitterness of using her uncle's name to threaten Hayashi settling in her stomach. Mrs. Chiba bent over her small vegetable patch, pulling a radish from the earth. Noticing Kinuko, she let go of the green top of the plant. "Kinuko-san, did you get your ration card back?"

"Yes, I just did."

"Good. Please come inside," said Mrs. Chiba. "I'll join you in just a minute."

Kinuko entered the Chiba house and proceeded, as always, into the small room off the dining room, which Mrs. Chiba now called the room of the little Buddha. She sat in front of the black altar where Mr. Chiba's mortuary tablet stood beside a set of candleholders, an incense burner, a brass bell, and miniature cups containing an offering of cooked rice. As she struck the bell and heard its silvery sound, her heartbeat slowed a little. She put her palms together and prayed. Soon Mr. Chiba's face appeared in her mind—sad but smiling.

"I'm angry at Hayashi," she said. "I hate him with all my heart, Mr. Chiba." She rang the bell once more and continued praying. "Forget it," she heard Mr. Chiba say. "Nothing on this earth is worth one's anger. Hayashi is only a little worm." Kinuko gazed at his mortuary tablet. She heard Mrs. Chiba come in through the back door but remained sitting until her heart calmed.

When Kinuko finally went to the kitchen, Mrs. Chiba stood at the sink washing radishes.

"Please stay for supper," she said.

"I would love to. Thank you."

Kinuko helped Mrs. Chiba prepare the meal, and soon the pungent smell of warm soy sauce rose in the kitchen, and Kinuko eventually forgot about Hayashi. In a few days, she and Giichi would be in Okayama. They would never have to see him again, but at the same time, the sadness of parting with Mrs. Chiba began to sink in.

Mrs. Chiba lifted the lid of the pot to stir the radishes, and with steam rising to her face, suddenly said, "I will miss you."

"And I will miss you." Kinuko watched Mrs. Chiba turn back and continue to stir the pot. Nothing more needed to be said. They understood each other perfectly. Kinuko peeked into the pot. "Looks delicious."

One by one, Mrs. Chiba picked up the slices of radish with chopsticks and piled them on a plate. Behind her, the kitchen window fogged with steam, except for a small clear circle in the middle that held the obscure color of March twilight. There was a calmness about Mrs. Chiba. Even in the midst of war and after the loss of her husband, she exhibited an incredible grace.

Soon they sat and ate the radishes with a steamed mixture of pressed oats and rice. Kinuko asked the question she had asked many times before. "You still don't want to move out of Hanshin?"

"No. If I have to die, this is the place I wish to die, the same place my husband did."

"But—"

"Besides, there must be a home for our son Takushi when he comes home from war. I want to wait for him here."

As always, her calm determination forced Kinuko to drop the subject.

Kinuko stayed another hour. They washed the dishes together and talked over tea. When Kinuko left, Mrs. Chiba followed her to the door, looked at the dark sky and said, "Isn't that strange? We haven't heard the sirens once today."

"It is strange, isn't it? I hope we won't have a warning the rest of the evening. I don't want Giichi to get stranded."

Kinuko thanked Mrs. Chiba for dinner and began crossing the street. Halfway across, the strap of her right clog suddenly snapped. Because the pair was fairly new, the thought of it being a bad omen crossed her mind, but she shrugged it off, picked up the clog by the strap, and limped home.

Giichi called an hour later, saying he was still in Osaka, near his parents' home. He said he was tired, but she knew he wanted to spend one last night there, and she could understand. It might be a long time before he would see the home of his youth again. Besides, staying overnight in Osaka was better than being stranded in a tram during an air raid warning. She was grateful he had called. A few months ago, he would have left her waiting with no word.

She went to bed at eleven and quickly fell asleep. It had been a long day and much had been accomplished—the packing, the ration card, her evening with Mrs. Chiba.

When the air raid siren broke through the veil of her first peaceful sleep in months, she awoke and immediately thought of Giichi. She changed into her day clothes and hurried to the dining room, where she lit a candle and turned on the radio, which emitted a hissing sound like a deep waterfall. She lifted the candle toward the clock on the wall—twelve-thirty. The siren stopped and silence fell again, but soon the street grew noisy with hurrying steps, a clamor of men's voices and banging on doors. She stood puzzled; there was no sound of B-29s, and yet an obvious air of emergency filled the street. She peeked out through the crack of a curtain and saw candlelit paper lanterns bobbing in the darkness. One of them approached her house. She opened the door and saw Mr. Obata, the retired fireman, with the east sky glowing red behind him.

"Mrs. Sekihara, there is severe bombing in Osaka. We are evacuating everybody to Kotokuji Temple just in case. I'm checking to see if there is anyone who needs help. Is your husband home?"

Thoughts of the snapped clog strap entered her mind. "No, he is in Osaka," she said.

His face clouded for a second, but he quickly added, "I'll take you to the shelter. Please hurry."

"Which part of Osaka are they bombing?"

"Twenty minutes ago, the radio said the west part."

Kinuko felt suddenly numb.

"Let's hurry," he prompted. "Get your coat and blanket, we'll go right away."

She didn't want to go. How could she sit in a shelter when Giichi was in the midst of heavy bombing?

"I'll go to the temple later," she whispered. "I can come by myself."

"Are you sure? You'd better hurry. They might come this way any minute."

As Mr. Obata scurried away, Kinuko stepped back into the house and heard an announcer's voice emerge from the crackles of the radio. She rushed to the radio and jiggled the knob. *"At eleven-fifty this evening, approximately three hundred B-29s flew into Japanese territory through the Kii Peninsula and began bombing the west side of Osaka..."*

Three hundred B-29s! In the past, air raids over Hanshin consisted of no more than thirty planes. She frantically jiggled the knob again but no intelligible sound emerged through the static. It didn't matter, because they couldn't tell her what she needed to hear; they wouldn't know about Giichi Sekihara or even care. She turned the radio off, blew out the candle, and ran from the house into the street. While neighbors ran south toward the temple, Kinuko started in the opposite direction toward the highway. "Kinuko-san! Where are you going?" She heard Mrs. Chiba shout. Still, she kept running. When Kinuko reached the bottom of the stairs leading up to the highway, Mrs. Chiba caught up with her and tugged at her arm. "What are you doing?" she panted.

Kinuko's voice cracked, "Giichi is in Osaka!"

"Giichi-san, still in Osaka?" Mrs. Chiba drew a sharp breath but kept pulling her by the arm. "We must go to the temple!"

"Please go ahead, please."

Kinuko struggled out of her grasp and climbed the dark steps on hands and knees, with cries of, "Kinuko-san," rising up behind her.

Once on the highway, Kinuko ran to the east. Across the dark bay it appeared as if all of Osaka was on fire. A mass of orange flames formed an infernal skyline. She stopped for a moment and stared, dazed by the incomprehensible colors before her, and again Mrs. Chiba caught her sleeve. "You can't go to Osaka!"

Kinuko fell to her knees, and wailed uncontrollably until she felt a hand tighten on her shoulder. She looked up to see Mr. Obata.

"Come with me, right now," he demanded. "They might come this way to bomb the highway!"

"You have to live for Yuki-chan and the baby," Mrs. Chiba pleaded.

After returning home from the temple, Kinuko dropped to her knees in the dining room. She remained there through the night, occasionally lapsing into restless sleep, only to awaken again. Dawn came with no news of Giichi. Instead, disturbing sounds rose from the highway. She went to the veranda, where she saw huge green army trucks racing toward Osaka, honking and bouncing, filled with soldiers, boxes of supplies. She had never seen so many trucks before—a sure sign of immense devastation.

At seven, when the radio began reporting news of the bombing, Kinuko rose from the dining room floor and listened intently, hoping to hear anything that would convince her that Giichi was alive. Her last hope died when the radio reported that the Minato Ward was one of the areas most severely hit by incendiary bombs. The west part of the city had been reduced to ashes.

Kinuko returned to numbness and sat inert until eight, when the telephone rang. She took the receiver and heard Ichiro's voice even before she could say hello.

"You two should get out of there right now!"

"We can't," Kinuko said, and then she erupted in tears.

"Why?" Ichiro demanded. "Let me talk to Giichi."

Kinuko pressed her hands against her chest to control her sobs. Finally she responded. "Giichi was in Osaka last night. He slept at your house."

There was silence and then Ichiro's voice exploded. "He survived jail. Nothing can kill him! Don't ever think he is dead!"

She kept crying, and Ichiro spoke again, sounding more reassuring, almost calming. "He will come home. Believe me. I cannot believe he is dead—never. He might be injured, but he is alive and he will come home. I'll call you again in a few hours. If he still isn't home, I will get there somehow."

"The trains aren't running."

"It doesn't matter, I'll get there somehow. I'll call you again. Tell me you'll be all right until then."

"I'm all right. Mrs. Chiba is here with me."

For the rest of the morning, Kinuko made frantic calls to the telephone operator, only to learn the lines were down in Osaka. At noon, Mrs. Chiba urged her to eat some soup. She had no interest in food. Instead, she laid her head on the dining room table, dreaming and daydreaming about Giichi. Ichiro called again, and she heard Mrs. Chiba's anguished voice telling him that Giichi still wasn't home.

In the afternoon, she awakened to Mrs. Chiba screams. Wearily, she lifted her head from the dining table. Then she heard Mrs. Chiba calling Giichi's name, and she lurched up from the floor, and rushed to the front room, uncertain if she was awake or dreaming. From the doorway, she saw someone leaning against Mrs. Chiba. It looked like Giichi, just as he had leaned against Ichiro only two weeks earlier. He's alive, she thought, and a shock of joy rushed through her with more force than the concussion of bombs.

CHAPTER 18

Even after an army truck had brought him home and Kinuko laid him in their futon, Giichi felt driven by the horror of the inferno he had just escaped. For two days he lay with throbbing feet, coughing and spitting up black phlegm, and growing increasingly restless. Telephone lines and the railway system remained dead. Whenever Kinuko left his side to call Mr. Kato, she came back shaking her head. Still, Giichi clung to the hope that his former boss could arrange a truck for them as he had promised. He was certain Mr. Kato had survived the bombing since he lived at the east edge of Osaka.

The next morning, when Kinuko told him the telephone line to Osaka was still down, he knew he could no longer afford to stay in bed. Rumors of additional massive bombings had already driven three families out of the neighborhood, including the Tanakas next door. And this morning, Kinuko watched the Ishiis scurry back and forth from their house next to Mrs. Chiba's, loading a small beat-up truck with clothing, furniture, and kitchen utensils.

Waiting to reach Mr. Kato was like waiting for death. Giichi sat up and dusted talcum powder on his blistered feet, determined to do anything to avoid being trapped in Hanshin. While he cautiously pulled on socks, Kinuko appeared with a bottle of eye drops.

"I can't wait any longer," he declared. "I'm going to look for a truck."

"You can't go anywhere on those feet," she protested. "They say the telephone lines will be up by tomorrow."

"That might be too late," he said, raising his voice.

"But how? You still need rest."

"I'll borrow a bicycle from Mr. Obata."

Kinuko stood silent for a while, then said, "I will go talk to him, but you need this before you go."

Giichi laid his head on Kinuko's lap, cringing at the thought of the drops falling like fire against his burning eyes. Then he lay still, waiting for the searing pain to fade, while Kinuko went out to visit Mr. Obata. She returned with an old bicycle and a can of oil borrowed from Mrs. Chiba. Giichi dressed and hobbled to the entryway, where he pulled the rubber shoes from the Amagasaki merchant over his socks, before leaving the house. After oiling the chain, he pedaled toward Kobe.

At first he moved gingerly, trying to avoid the burning sensation at the bottom of his feet, but after a while, he decided to ignore the pain and pedaled as fast as he could. He stopped at the first truck rental shop he found, more than two miles away at the edge of Kobe. The owner, a stout man with the ruddy face of an alcoholic, told him no trucks were available. Giichi offered him five times more than the going rate. The owner lamented that ten of his trucks were permanently rented out to the military at a rate so low they might as well be free, two others had been stolen, and the remaining two needed repair. "And I have no idea when the parts are coming," he sighed. "I wish I could rent one to a generous man like you. But that's the way it is."

Next, he stopped at a shabby establishment with a broken door patched by old magazine covers. As he opened the door, an emaciated woman stepped out, drying her hands with her apron. Yes, she said, they had a truck, but no driver. She explained that her son used to drive, but he had left for the war a month ago, and her husband could no longer drive because of arthritis. After two more unsuccessful stops, Giichi wearily pedaled home, feeling as if there was no way out of this death trap.

Just as he reached his neighborhood and returned the bicycle, a warning siren blared, and he hurried to the temple with Kinuko, limping on blistered feet. Kinuko shuffled along beside him, leaning back to balance her heavy stomach. In the temple hall, they squatted with Mrs. Chiba and Mr. Obata, while the rest of the neighbors kept a slight distance from them. The men talked about how Tokyo, Nagoya, and Osaka had all been nearly leveled and agreed that Kobe would be next. They continued to discuss the Allies' capability of taking off from air bases in the Marianas with enough bombs for massive air strikes every few days. Once they gained full control of Iwo Jima, Mr. Obata said, they would surely come every day. In the end, they all nodded in somber agreement that the Hanshin Highway was a likely target.

The fourth day after the Osaka bombing, Giichi finally got through to Mr. Kato. When Giichi heard his voice, his heart leapt with wild joy. But Mr. Kato immediately explained that the military had taken control of most of the company trucks. "Don't get discouraged," he quickly added. "There still might be a truck available. I'll see what I can do."

An hour later, Mr. Kato called back. "I talked to the manager of the Itami Plant, Mr. Kojima. He can let you use a truck from midnight tonight till seven in the morning. If you want to take it, call him right away." Mr. Kato wished him good luck. "Drop me a line when you get to Okayama."

Giichi called the Itami Plant immediately. He thanked Mr. Kojima profusely, and made arrangements to pay one-thousand *yen* to a young plant worker who agreed to drive the truck to Okayama and back. Kinuko sent a telegram to Okayama and received a reply at four o'clock in the afternoon. "ELATED. YUKI VERY HAPPY."

By midnight, they had locked all of the windows and the back door. The house was dark except for a single candle on the dining table. Their luggage sat in the front room—two furoshiki bundles of clothes and a trunk containing photo albums, letters, postcards, diaries, some of Kinuko's smaller paintings, and other personal belongings.

The clock ticked on the wall, and Kinuko's face shone pale in the candlelight. Giichi kept his good ear to the street and the other on the radio. Only hours earlier, they had rushed to the temple after a warning and stayed there for nearly an hour. When they returned home, they learned that bombs had dropped on western Amagasaki. Their only hope was to get out before another warning came.

At twelve-fifteen, Giichi began to worry that the truck might have been caught in the bombing of Amagasaki. He went to the door and looked toward the highway. At twelve-thirty, he called the Itami Plant but no one answered. He sat down and began tapping the table irritably, while Kinuko sat gazing at the candle.

The clock struck one and still no truck. Giichi began pacing with a pronounced limp. Tapping his watch with his index finger, he blurted, "There are only six hours left!"

Kinuko lit a new candle, biting her lower lip. At one-fifteen, the siren shrieked and stopped after a few minutes. Giichi turned the radio up. *"The central district of military jurisdiction has observed approximately one hundred and fifty B-29s off the Island of Shikoku and another one hundred off Kii Peninsula. Both groups are heading north—"*

Giichi heard a bang at the door and rushed to answer it, moving with no sense of pain.

"Sorry," the driver began, "there was bombing in Amagasaki and—"

"Kinuko!" Giichi shouted, "The truck is here! We must go, right now!"

While throwing luggage onto the back of the truck, he quickly figured that if they could get through Kobe, they would reach Okayama in time for the driver to return by seven in the morning. Kinuko rushed past him, and he turned to see Mrs. Chiba running toward them.

"Kinuko-san!" Mrs. Chiba shouted. Giichi watched the two embrace for a moment and then hurried back into the house to make sure Kinuko had extinguished the candle. He quickly locked the front door. The driver sat impatiently in the cab of the truck.

"Please, Kinuko." Giichi reached for her as she and Mrs. Chiba released their embrace. He bowed to Mrs. Chiba and said good-bye, and then climbed into the cab next to the driver, pulling Kinuko onto the seat beside him. Mrs. Chiba pushed the door shut. "Write to me!" she shouted, as the truck jerked forward. "I will!" Kinuko shouted back, her voice quivering with grief.

Giichi and the driver exchanged ideas about the fastest route to downtown Kobe and immediately agreed. When Giichi looked back, Mrs. Chiba had already disappeared in darkness.

The truck passed through the tunnel under the Hanshin Highway, bounced north for a few blocks, then turned west onto a narrow street. On both sides, the homes were closed and dark. Rows of water buckets shone in the headlights and formed a silver line as the truck rushed past. After zigzagging through narrow streets and alleys, they reached the east edge of Kobe and jostled along a dark thoroughfare, racing against the approaching B-29s. If the truck passed through Kobe before the bombers reached the city, Giichi thought, their chances were good. As they approached downtown Kobe, he put one arm around Kinuko's shoulders and rested the other in his lap, clenching his fist. He closed his eyes and prayed.

Suddenly the driver clicked his tongue and slammed on the brakes. As the truck screeched to a stop, Giichi pulled Kinuko to his side, and reached out to steady himself against the dashboard. He saw a paper lantern waving from side to side in the middle of the road. A siren began shrieking. A fireman appeared out of the darkness and banged the window, jumping up and down. As the driver rolled down the window, the shrill cry of the siren blasted into the cab. The fireman shouted above the din, "Turn off your lights, you fool!"

The next second, the drone of bombers approached and the sky lit up with shafts of light. While the driver eased the truck to the curb, the sound of anti-aircraft guns crackled around them. Kinuko pressed against Giichi and covered her ears. Giichi pulled her to his lap and leaned over her. The sound of the planes grew louder. Bombs exploded nearby and the truck rattled. Giichi looked up and saw bursts of fire erupting ahead of them.

"Downtown is hit!" the driver gasped.

Sixty meters away, a huge white cloud mushroomed up, then grew red and mixed with dark swirls of upward spiraling smoke. The metal of B-29s reflected in the sky, soaring above the smoke and releasing bombs. The bombs exploded in mid-air like fireworks, and the underside of the planes glowed red.

"They hit a gas tank," the driver shouted.

"Turn around!" Giichi commanded. "Now!"

The driver slipped the gear lever into low and swung the truck in a tight arc before ripping down the road and buffeting them against the inside of the cab. On both sides of the street, doors were thrown open, and women and children ran outside to gaze into the sky. Streets that had been deserted only minutes earlier were now filled with milling crowds. Everyone stood paralyzed, uncertain which way to run. Then they ran frantically colliding with each other, amid a clanging of fire bells. The driver pressed his hand against the horn and honked his way through the crowd. Kinuko bounced on Giichi's lap like a rag doll. When they drew closer to their neighborhood, retracing their path, Kinuko struggled up. "Let's go to Sasayama, to my mother's house," she whispered hoarsely. "We have no choice."

Giichi remained silent, thinking of Yuki, while she continued, "This might be our last chance for a truck."

"Where to?" the driver yelled above the groan of the engine.

"Sasayama!" Giichi shouted. "Do you know how to get there?"

"Yes! I have relatives there."

Soon, the truck rumbled through the area north of their neighborhood and continued north toward the mountains. After a few kilometers, the truck started up a mountain road, leaving the danger behind. Still, none of them spoke. Every time the truck edged around a curve, they saw fire raging below in Kobe, but eventually, thickets of trees obscured the view, except for the orange glow in the sky.

Giichi felt numb, yet heavy with the burden of knowing they were moving farther from Yuki. He could only imagine her disappointment. Kinuko had been right all along. They should have gotten out of Hanshin months ago. Now it was too late. They would be stuck in the isolated region of Sasayama. It might be days or even weeks before they could reach Okayama. And deep within, he thought he deserved this agony. He shouldn't have been so stubborn. There were so many things he could have done differently—wearing the national uniform, resigning earlier, not going to his parents' house. One little concession and they would be in Okayama with Yuki, none of this would be happening. As usual, Kinuko and Yuki would have to suffer the consequences of his decisions.

They descended into a dark valley and left the vision of war behind. Overwhelmed with guilt, Giichi also felt the ache of nostalgia. The eight years of their life in Hanshin had ended; all that remained of it now was a crimson glow in the sky.

CHAPTER 19

Sasayama was a small castle town nestled at the bottom of a foggy mountain basin called Tanba. Though only sixty kilometers north of Hanshin, the town had avoided Allied bombing because of its absence of war-related industries. For centuries, the basin's unspoiled natural beauty had charmed visitors, mostly travelers to and from Kyoto, the old capital of Japan.

As a child, Kinuko, too, had been charmed by the poetic pace of life within the basin. She had fond memories of family gatherings there. Though she had grown up in Kobe, she felt a firm attachment to Sasayama as an ancestral home. However, her feelings for that region changed after her grandmother died in 1938, and her Uncle Hirobumi inherited the old samurai house. By then she was married to Giichi, and Hirobumi, a general in the Japanese Imperial Army, made no effort to maintain the family home. He lived comfortably in an exclusive Tokyo compound and had no need for the old house, so it stood empty.

In the late summer of 1944, shortly after Saipan and Guam fell to the Allies, Hirobumi wrote to Etsu, Kinuko's mother, and urged her to move into the empty house on Samurai Mansion Street rather than stay alone in Kobe, amid the growing danger of bombing in the Hanshin region. Though he had called Etsu a fool when she allowed Kinuko to marry a man he opposed, more than eight years had passed and the relationship between brother and sister seemed to have softened. Etsu accepted his offer to live in the house.

At the beginning of that fall, Kinuko and Giichi helped Etsu close her house in Kobe and move to Sasayama. It was then that Etsu showed Kinuko Hirobumi's letter.

"Aerial bombardment is imminent," it said. "Our industrial regions such as Kobe will be the Allies' first targets. I know that the Sasayama house is old and will be in dire need of repair, but living in an old house is better than dying. I will help you with the expense as much as I can."

The letter had sparked fear in Kinuko, making her aware once again that Hanshin would face intense bombing. Still, she knew that she would not consider moving away without Giichi.

So she stayed in her home, receiving a steady flow of letters from her mother, each reporting the progress of house repairs and expressing hope that the place would be livable when winter came. Despite the house's deterioration, one of her letters said, the property still held the charm of the long-ago samurai era, and throughout the fall, cosmos bloomed in profusion, with red dragonflies swarming above. Persimmons ripened and turned vividly orange against the blue sky.

The flow of Etsu's letters never stopped. They explained to Kinuko how she had started a vegetable patch in the garden, how she had preserved persimmons, how she had rediscovered the beauty of snow falling in the basin, and how, despite the chill, she enjoyed quiet afternoons reading or darning. But in January after the usual New Year's greeting card, her letters suddenly stopped. Although Kinuko occasionally wondered why, she was too preoccupied with Giichi's decision about the red paper and the death of Mr. Chiba to write a letter of inquiry. January passed with no word from Etsu, and when her letters started up again in February, they offered scant news. Instead, they urged Kinuko to get out of Hanshin, and with each letter her pleas became more desperate, until she finally warned Kinuko, "As you know, it's becoming a matter of life or death. You and Yuki should get out of Hanshin immediately, even if Giichi-san doesn't agree to move..." Those words came in a letter Kinuko received the day Giichi was detained.

Only hours after arriving in Sasayama, Kinuko sat in the old samurai house, stunned by her mother's condition. Beside her, Etsu lay deathly ill, her face glowing red and hot, her thin chest heaving rapidly. Her eyes and cheeks were sunken, her lips parched.

As Kinuko gazed over her, her mother suddenly spoke.

"Kinuko," she whispered with great effort. "I am—so glad—you are—out of danger—I can die—with no—"

"Mother." Kinuko leaned over her and took her brittle hand. "You are not going to die. I'm here, go back to sleep."

A weak smile spread over Etsu's feverish face, before she turned limp again.

The doctor, retrieved by Giichi, had left a half hour earlier, after pronouncing that Etsu suffered from pneumonia.

"I can't guarantee her recovery, this time," he whispered grimly.

"This time?" Kinuko asked.

"Didn't you know? She had it in January, too."

Kinuko couldn't respond. Guilt clouded her mind as the doctor continued. "I don't know how she recovered then. It must have been her samurai spirit, but I'm afraid her spirit might not help her this time."

Kinuko felt dizzy and vaguely heard Giichi say he would pay any amount of money for good medicine, the black market price or whatever was needed.

"There is no good medicine," Dr. Okawa replied. "The military has all the medicine and they are running out of it, too."

The only hope Dr. Okawa offered was for them to pound Etsu's back to loosen the mucus in her lungs. He demonstrated by rolling her to her side and slapping her back with the palm of his hand. Delirious, Etsu only moaned.

"Give her chicken broth," he added. "That might give her enough energy to cough up the mucus."

Kinuko looked at her watch, as she had done a dozen times since the doctor left, taking Giichi with him to the town's main street on his bicycle. Giichi was supposed to contact the rice merchant Mr. Nakano, a longtime family friend, who would know where to find a chicken, then send a telegram to Okayama and return with ice. Fighting her own fatigue, Kinuko worried that Giichi must be exhausted. He had not slept during their bumpy ride from Hanshin, and now he was running through unfamiliar streets on unhealed feet.

Kinuko lifted the moist towel and felt Etsu's frighteningly hot forehead with the palm of her hand. She dipped the towel in a water-filled basin, wringing it out, refolding it, and placing it back on her mother's forehead. She looked at her watch again, anxious for Giichi to return with a block of ice. She left Etsu alone and went into the kitchen to look for an ice bag. Standing in the kitchen, on the verge of tears, she heard footsteps, and Giichi appeared with a block of ice, two ice bags, a hammer and a gimlet.

"Mr. Nakano told me to bring all of this," he said, panting.

Over the kitchen sink, he chipped the ice with the hammer and gimlet, while Kinuko stood beside him, holding one of the bags. She was reminded of a night more than a year earlier when Yuki had developed a high fever and they stood together like this in the kitchen of their Ashiya home. Suddenly missing Yuki, it struck her as utterly strange how the last several hours had changed everything.

"Did you send a telegram to Okayama?" she asked.

He nodded, the rims of his eyes red from lack of sleep, and kept chipping the ice. Kinuko pushed shards of ice into the second bag. When both were filled, they each carried one to Etsu's room. Kinuko lifted Etsu's head and placed the bag shaped like a small pillow beneath it. Giichi suspended the round one over her forehead. Etsu's face pinched amid the commotion, but her eyes didn't open. Kinuko and Giichi sat beside her and watched her expression relax as the ice began to cool her feverish skin. They looked at each other and sighed with temporary relief. Then they slumped to the floor and fell asleep in the same clothes they had worn when they left their home in Hanshin.

Sometime later, Kinuko awoke to the sound of knocking at the front door and a distantly familiar voice from her childhood. "Mr. Nakano," she uttered, quickly straightening her hair. She hurried to the entryway with Giichi following.

"Mr. Nakano!" Kinuko said, seeing him standing at the door with a chicken dangling from his hand. "It's been a while—"

"Since you came to your grandmother's funeral. How have you been, Kinuko-san?"

Kinuko sat at the edge of the front room and explained how she and Giichi had arrived at dawn.

"Mother came to the gate, then she collapsed..." Kinuko's voice grew tearful from the relief she felt at seeing Mr. Nakano. As Mr. Nakano patted her shoulder, Giichi took the chicken from him and asked how much it cost.

Mr. Nakano waved his hand in dismissal. "We have been friends for so many years, since the time my father and Kinuko-san's grandfather used to play Go, a board game. Town folks used to wonder why a judge and a rice merchant played go together, but the two had a secret. They thought they were the best players in town and refused to play with anyone else. Silly, weren't they?" He laughed and continued, "Anyway, your mother must be so happy to have you here, and I'm sure she will get better with both of you taking care of her."

Despite Giichi's insistence, Mr. Nakano refused to take any money for the chicken and left in a hurry, saying he would come back after they had rested. "We have a lot to talk about," he said, turning at the door, "but it should be at some other time; after your mother has recovered."

For the next several days, Kinuko stayed beside Etsu, religiously following the doctor's directions, while Giichi made runs to the ice shop three times a day and cooked meals in an unfamiliar kitchen. Each time Kinuko heard Giichi come home, she hurried to the kitchen to refresh the ice bags. She pounded her mother's back, massaged her chest with mentholated salve, fed her chicken broth from a glass feeder, and kept her bedpan clean.

Between those tasks, Kinuko sometimes dozed at Etsu's bedside and drifted in clouds of anguish that haunted her even when she slept. She often dreamed of Yuki standing at the gate of Ichiro's country house in Okayama, waiting for her parents. She also dreamed of Mrs. Chiba, running to the neighborhood shelter and fretting about Hayashi, who tormented her because she had associated with the wife of a "traitor." Once, she dreamed that Giichi received the red paper and tore it to shreds. Two military policemen arrived immediately and began beating him with wooden clubs. She woke up screaming, and as she gasped with relief at the realization that it was only a dream, she saw Etsu's lips open and close. "What's the—matter—Kinuko?"

"Nothing," Kinuko said. "You must have been dreaming, Mother."

Etsu nodded without opening her eyes, but for the first time since their arrival in Sasayama, Kinuko remembered how much she feared her mother's reaction when she learned the truth about Giichi. From early childhood, her mother tried to instill in her the loyalty to the Emperor that Etsu's father, Hajime, had instilled in Etsu and Hirobumi. Kinuko often heard her grandfather Hajime's maxim, "Excel in learning and work hard for the country, as those are the very best ways to serve the Emperor." According to Etsu, Hajime lived those ideals. He worked hard to overcome the adversity of being a samurai living in the first generation of the post samurai era. Some of his class, stripped of their privileges by the modernization of the Meiji Era, turned resentful and unproductive. But Hajime was optimistic by nature—a trait Etsu had inherited, in Kinuko's opinion—and made the best of any situation.

At seventeen, he left Sasayama and set out for Tokyo, where he first found work as a lowly gardener and eventually graduated from law school by working during the day and studying at night. Ten years after his arrival in Tokyo, he returned to Sasayama to become one of the town's most respected judges. His success restored to his family the honor they had known before the samurai system toppled. He stood as an example to locals of what could be accomplished when loyalty was transferred from samurai lords to the Emperor.

Etsu often related a story from 1905, after Japan fought against Russia and won. She was a schoolgirl then, and she attended the triumphant parade with her classmates to observe the returning soldiers. Springtime cherry blossom petals showered over the excited students who hurried to the town's main street with flags in hand. There, Etsu observed the hard-faced soldiers on horses and the ecstatic spectators waving rising sun flags. That evening, Hajime, euphoric from Japan's victory and a little sake, lectured Etsu and Hirobumi about the fact that Japan, after centuries of isolation, had finally emerged into the world as a powerful nation, and this was the ultimate fruit of the nation's hard-working people and their unflagging loyalty to the Emperor. "Keep in mind," he continued with a rise in his voice, "you will have to make many sacrifices in your lifetime for the Emperor and your country."

Looking at her mother's emaciated body, Kinuko wondered if she still felt the same loyalty to the Emperor, after having suffered deathly illness because of the hardships of war—lack of medicine, food, and fuel. Until the morning of their arrival, Etsu must have lain deathly sick and alone, without heat, without care. As Kinuko continued to gaze at her mother, pity spread in her chest—the same feeling she experienced every time she heard the stories of dying soldiers who shouted, "Long live the Emperor!" Millions of men had already died, and more died each day with those words on their lips. Did the words truly come from their hearts? She knew that she could never die for someone she didn't love. If her mother was dying now, who would she be thinking of, the Emperor or her daughter?

Her mother's life had been a long practice of obeying others—first her parents, then her husband, and then her brother. Yet at times she had shown that when it came to something important to her, she held to her own beliefs. Kinuko thought specifically of Etsu standing up to Hirobumi, who had opposed her marriage to Giichi, for which she was eternally grateful. Suddenly overwhelmed by love, Kinuko wailed, "Please don't die, Mother, please. Live, live for me!" Kinuko no longer cared what her mother would think of Giichi's decision, as long as she recovered.

Etsu's condition remained the same for five days, though her temperature lowered slightly. Like a sick bird, she managed only tiny sips of chicken broth from the glass feeder that Kinuko held above her lips. Then she sent a weak smile in Kinuko's direction with unfocused eyes. Her wheezing often turned into fits of violent coughing that convulsed her twig-like body. After the coughs subsided, she drifted into unconsciousness, occasionally whispering incoherently. One day drifted into another, and the lack of improvement in her mother's condition drove Kinuko into despair.

Then, on the sixth day, Etsu's temperature dropped. Kinuko couldn't believe the sight of the mercury holding at 37.6 degrees centigrade. She was so elated that she ran to show Giichi the thermometer.

"Finally," he uttered with a sigh. "She made it!"

Kinuko saw him smile for the first time since their arrival. "Thank you," she said tenderly. "You have been very kind."

"She is your mother," he replied. "How could I turn away?" Then, returning her tenderness, he held her in his arms.

She felt tears in her eyes and her chest burned with longing for them to grow old together and to watch their children grow old, as well. She hoped she could seal this moment and never let it slip from her grasp, and yet she suddenly realized that beneath his warm chest, his heart probably longed for ideals that had nothing to do with her and the children. She gently pulled away from him. "I need to get back to my mother," she said and hurried away to hide her loneliness.

That day, Etsu took deeper sips of chicken broth, and in the afternoon, she stayed awake for several hours. Despite Kinuko's joy at the sight of her mother's improvement, she suddenly ached for Yuki and realized how far away her daughter was. She wondered if she would ever see Yuki again. She felt completely drained. She also worried that she might have offended Giichi by slipping from his embrace. She wanted to apologize but felt too tired to even look for him.

That evening, while she and Giichi ate dinner, Kinuko noticed he was avoiding her eyes. When they finished eating they carried the dishes to the sink in silence. He washed the dishes, while she dried them. She wished that he would say something and hoped his quietness was only a sign of weariness. Giichi finished the last dish and dried his hands deliberately. After hanging the towel over the edge of the sink, he finally faced Kinuko with downcast eyes.

"Do you regret having married me?" he asked.

Kinuko stopped wiping the dish in her hands. "No," she said. "No."

"I—I just wanted to apologize. I think that I made you unhappy by marrying you."

"No, you don't have to apologize. If you are talking about this morning, I'm sorry."

"It's just that you didn't say anything, and I thought that you were still angry with me, and I started thinking that maybe a man like me shouldn't have married you."

"You are tired. Maybe we should talk about this tomorrow."

"No, I want to talk now. I want to tell you that you made me want to marry—I had never thought that I would ever be married until I met you."

"Please don't feel that way," she said. "If my life was ruined, it would be me who ruined it, not you."

She looked away from him and then felt his hands on her shoulders. She felt his fatigue as deeply as her own and wondered if, deep in her heart, she still hoped that he would do anything for her, even betray his beliefs to be with her. But what if she could convince him to change his mind? Would that make her happy? That no longer seemed possible. All she knew was that she should cherish this moment of her mother's recovery and Giichi's tenderness and wait until tomorrow to think about anything else. Yet her loneliness remained.

CHAPTER 20

As Etsu's health improved and his walks downtown became less urgent, Giichi began to spend more time exploring the town, which eased the burning pain from the failure to join Yuki in Okayama. The town gradually revealed itself to him, and he began to realize that even Sasayama's natural beauty could not conceal the reality of war. The streets were devoid of healthy young men. Those he saw hobbled on crutches or hid in dark corners with faces blasted beyond recognition. Others returned to Sasayama in urns or filled its small hospital with the sounds of coughing, spitting, and weeping.

Giichi happened upon the hospital one day on his way to buy ice, and he felt an inexplicable force drawing him into it. He had already seen enough of war's devastation; yet something urged him inside. The scene was worse than he expected—crowded rooms, malaria-infested men twisting and moaning on dirty sheets. In a dimly lit corridor, the smell of blood and pus permeated the air. Shattered men sat on benches or squatted on the floor and gazed vacantly at the grimy walls. Others hobbled through the halls on crutches. Some waited days for attention, he was told, as most of the region's doctors and nurses had been taken by the war.

The town's main street told a similar story. According to Mr. Nakano, before the war the downtown shops had bustled with town folks and villagers, but Giichi could hardly picture that now. Inside the dilapidated stores, most shelves sat empty and gathered dust. Mr. Nakano also reported that three of the town's five temples housed more than two hundred elementary school children who had been evacuated from Hanshin along with their teachers the previous summer.

"The poor children are starving," Mr. Nakano said. "Their rations are hardly enough for growing children, and they don't have access to black market food. It's no wonder many of them steal vegetables from farmers. I've heard they even have to resort to eating weeds."

The town also housed an inordinate number of elderly, who had fled the cities to avoid the bombings and to live with relatives or friends, hoping to go back after the war. Giichi figured they must wonder if their homes in the cities still stood, just as he did.

As days passed, Giichi struggled to find the inner peace to write to his parents. Though he had promised to write soon in the telegram he sent the day they arrived in Sasayama, he needed to regain his bearings and reflect upon what had happened. The longer he put it off, the guiltier he felt, but he excused his procrastination, telling himself he needed to help Kinuko with Etsu. The morning he watched his mother-in-law finally sit up in her futon and feed herself a breakfast of watery rice porridge, he knew he could no longer cling to that excuse.

That afternoon, he lay on the tatami in the guest bedroom with his feet beneath a desk. With eyes closed, he sought silence in his mind and attempted to reflect on the tumultuous weeks before their escape from Hanshin. Immediately, Toda's face began flashing at the back of his eyes, followed by a flood of horrifying images from the night of the bombing in Osaka. Suddenly, he stood and wandered toward Etsu's room. As he approached, he heard muffled conversation within. When he opened the sliding door, the voices stopped, and Etsu and Kinuko looked up. The room smelled of sickness, and Etsu still looked sickly pale. Kinuko sat beside her with the weight of her stomach on her legs and dark shadows beneath her eyes. As usual, the sight of her pricked him with guilt.

"If—if there isn't anything you want me to do right now, I think I'll go for a walk."

"Yes, please do," said Etsu. "I was just telling Kinuko how well I've been feeling since this morning."

"I'm glad to hear that, Mother," answered Giichi. "It's nice to see you sitting up."

"Enjoy your walk," Kinuko said.

She sounded terse, which made him think of their argument from the night before. "I won't be gone too long," he mumbled.

Closing the door, he momentarily felt sorry for Kinuko; she hadn't had time to rest since the night they arrived. But he hurried from the house, feeling as if he might suffocate from guilt and worry. Instead of walking out to Samurai Mansion Street, he crossed the back garden and walked into the bamboo grove, a shorter route he had discovered one day while returning with ice. The walk through the dark grove elicited in him a mixture of feelings—the quiet calm of being away from humanity mingled with homesickness for the ruckus of Hanshin.

Emerging onto the street that ran beside an ancient moat, he stopped for a moment and blinked at the brightness of the day, admiring the moss-covered stone walls of the ruined castle—a remnant of the Shogun Era. He began walking with the moat to his right, where a brown scum of dead lotus leaves floated on the surface and a few freshly sprouted ones poked through the sludge. To his left the bamboo grove soon ended, replaced by decrepit homes, with roofs rotting and walls crumbling in great chunks. These homes, he had learned, had belonged to the footmen who served samurais during the Shogun Era.

According to Mr. Nakano—so far the only person in Sasayama with whom Giichi felt a connection—the houses were still occupied. But the street was deserted today, which intensified Giichi's sense of loneliness, a loneliness that went deeper than being in an unfamiliar town. It had gnawed at him all of his life. He thought of his friend Kenji and of his father, who he remembered wandering among his bonsais after arguing with his friends.

Hurrying past the crumbling homes, he turned at the next corner onto the street north of the moat. After several minutes, he arrived at the base of the castle and studied its front wall, more dilapidated than he had expected. A portion of the wall had tumbled down, leaving massive heaps of stone and rubble directly in front of him. Just as at the hospital, he felt strangely drawn to this place, as if it contained some lesson he could not yet understand. The gate, lichen-covered and spongy to the touch, still evoked the glorious past and its robust design. He edged through the gate, opening and closing it tenderly lest it crumble from its rusting hinges, and ascended the mossy path winding upward inside the walls.

As he reached the top of the first level of the structure, he was startled by a vast open view. The higher level of the castle obscured a portion of the circumference; otherwise, everywhere he turned there were mountains and more mountains, an endless chain that formed the rim of the basin. With his heart leaping, he waded through the weeds at the center of the deserted grounds to climb even higher. He reached a huge stone and stood atop it, looking all around with his hand shielding the sun from his eyes.

Driven by curiosity, he climbed the stone steps at the far corner that led to the highest level of the castle grounds. There he found a secluded area with a thick cluster of tall Japanese cedars shading a tiny Shinto shrine. He strolled aimlessly among the silent trees. The air was clear and still, the only sound the occasional flapping of wings by the birds hidden among the interwoven branches. In such a tranquil place, Giichi found it almost impossible to grasp that the world was immersed in war. Yet only sixty kilometers away firebombs incinerated innocents—babies, children, women, and the elderly. The enormous tragedy of that realization grabbed hold of his core, and in an instant cemented who he was and what he believed. Smelling the wet earth and lush grass of this old fortress, his heart throbbed with tension. To the depth of his soul he hated the stupidity of war. He knew now that he had been wavering, and that was why he had been drawn into the hospital and to this place, the ancient fortress. For centuries, men had gone to war. What did they have to show for it? Crumbled walls and crumbled lives. Mrs. Chiba, left to mourn her husband the rest of her life. No, he would not participate in war. Nor would he hide here in Sasayama. He needed to do more than that, to sacrifice himself if necessary, to stand against war. He scanned the serene vista of the Tanba Basin and wondered what must have been in the minds of the warriors who stood here centuries ago. Did they see the beauty of life? Or did they think only of war, the prospects of killing and dying?

He stood at the base of a cedar tree and looked up, awed by its beauty, its straight trunk stretching skyward. He scratched the hard bark and its sharp fragrance filled his nostrils. The rough texture and the fragrance stirred his soul and steadily awoke in him an enormous gratitude for being alive, not only for himself but for everyone he loved—Kinuko, Yuki, his parents, Etsu. Giichi stood there for a while, thinking not only of his family but of all the people who lived under the same sky.

He finally walked to the edge of the castle and looked in the direction he thought led to Okayama. Below lay another moat, and beyond it, rows of tiled roofs leading to the end of town, and then empty fields spread out toward the base of the mountains, dotted with the thatched roofs of farmhouses nestled in a sleepy haze. Beyond the rim of the basin, layers of mountain ridges gradually disappeared into a purple haze. How strange it felt to be standing here when his child lived far beyond that haze. He sat down in a bed of weeds, his eyes fixed above the mountains, hoping Yuki would someday understand why her parents had suddenly disappeared from her life. He also hoped Kinuko would someday forgive him for placing his principles before her. He sat there nearly an hour, yearning for forgiveness from the two people he most loved. When the sun had swung to the west and bathed the basin in bronze light, he stood slowly, brushed away the flakes of dead weeds from his backside, and strolled back to the shrine. He took a few coins from his pocket and dropped them into the thin slot of the wooden offering box. He prayed and felt comforted.

Before returning home, he went to the town office to register their arrival in Sasayama and to activate their ration card. He knew that by marking the forms, he sealed his fate; he could no longer hide in Sasayama. His hand shook as he scratched the pen across the paper, and again he thought of Yuki. Would he ever see her again?

Silence greeted him at Etsu's house. He opened the door to her room slightly and found both of them sleeping, Etsu in her futon, Kinuko leaning against the edge of it with an arm draped over her round stomach. Etsu opened her eyes, and with a smile, pointed at her daughter with her index finger and then pressed it softly to her lips. Giichi nodded and closed the door. Then, thinking Kinuko might need a blanket, he took one from their bedroom and tiptoed into Etsu's room. Gently, he placed the blanket over Kinuko. Etsu smiled at him again.

As he walked out of the room, it occurred to him that someday Yuki might be taking care of her sick mother as Kinuko now cared for Etsu. He pictured Yuki as a grown woman sitting beside Kinuko's futon and speaking tenderly to her old mother. It was, he realized, not just a thought but a hope that Yuki would be with Kinuko in her old age, even if he had to leave this world before them. He felt a grip of sadness, but the thought of Yuki taking care of Kinuko gave him comfort. For some inscrutable reason, the truck had been late that night, and all of their lives had hinged on those few minutes in time. Perhaps that was the way it was meant to happen.

That evening, in the dim light of the family room, haltingly, he composed a letter to his parents. As he wrote, word by word, the distance that stood between them gradually faded, and he began to feel their presence close to him. Writing this letter, he also understood, would help him accept the fate that had planted him in this town.

Dear Father and Mother,

I apologize for not having written sooner, but since our arrival in Sasayama, Kinuko and I have been tending to her gravely ill mother. I am happy to tell you that she is finally getting better, and we hope she will continue to recover from her illness.

I still don't know exactly how to describe the terrible things that happened during the last couple of weeks in Hanshin, and perhaps it is better to leave that for when we are together again. You know that your house was destroyed in the bombing, and I am grateful that you were not there that night. Even though the house is gone, I will always hold it in my memories. Especially, I will think of it as the place where you both raised me with such love.

Father, I am grateful that you stayed with Kinuko while I was in jail, and that you came to the Ashiya Police Station every day. There are no words to describe my gratitude for everything you have done for Kinuko and me. Because of you, and by thinking of you, I survived that dreadful place.

Mother, I am very sorry that I have caused you such terrible heartache. On the night I was in your empty house for the last time, I thought about the promise I made when I was a child, that I would never do anything that would trouble you. I have always known that you didn't want me to go through the same suffering Father underwent. But I couldn't keep that promise because I am my father's son. I only wish to be a faithful son to you and hope that someday you will feel as proud of me as you are of my father.

After the Osaka bombing, my boss Mr. Kato arranged a truck for us to leave for Okayama, but by the time the truck arrived, bombers descended on Kobe and the route to Okayama was closed. It still pains me to think that we were so close to making it to Okayama, but we had no choice but to turn back and come to Sasayama.

This isn't what we wanted to happen. When we think about Yuki, our regret is immeasurable. But Kinuko and I are grateful that she is in your care, and that at least all of us are now out of danger, even if we have to live apart. Kinuko is almost eight months pregnant, and I think now, given the present chaotic railway situation, it won't be possible for her to travel by rail. Which means, sadly, that our separation seems indefinite. Kinuko and I are trying to accept the way things are now and are hopeful for what the future may bring.

Several years ago, Father, you said to me that war or no war, life must go on, and I think about that often to remind myself that I must try my best to live each day to the fullest. I am getting accustomed to this new town, although at the beginning, it was strange not to hear the wail of a siren or the groans of B-29s, or to have lights on without drawing black curtains. I hope you can visit this town someday. It's very interesting and quite charming.

Again, thank you so much for taking care of Yuki, and please tell her that Kinuko and I love her very much. Please take care of yourselves.

Your loving son, Giichi

The next morning, Giichi walked slowly through the grove with the letter in his hand. The sharp morning sun filtered through the bamboo leaves in thin slivers of light. Admiring it, he wondered when his letter would reach Okayama. He knew the mail took much longer these days because of the poor railway service. Nevertheless, he felt calm.

But that didn't last long. As he emerged from the grove, he saw a flurry of unsettling activity on the usually quiet street. The crooked doors of several homes stood ajar, and a crowd ran along the moat, moving away from him. A knot of people stood at the end of the street. Several men waded chest-deep in the murky waters, pushing aside the tangle of fresh and rotting lotus leaves. Two uniformed policemen pulled on a rope, while the men in the water struggled to pull something to the surface.

As he drew closer, Giichi saw a lotus-covered body emerge from the water. His chest tightened and his legs turned stiff. He still didn't have the stomach for this sort of thing. He veered to the other side of the street with his face down. As he neared the scene, he heard a woman draw a sharp breath and gasp, "The widow of Yaogen." He stopped and watched as two stiff bodies were dragged onto the bank, those of a young woman and a little girl strapped to the woman's back by a black velvet rope. His heart jolted. He stood motionless, though he wanted to walk away, and without knowing exactly what he was doing, he put his palms together in prayer.

He remembered buying apples from the woman at "Yaogen," a vegetable store near the ice shop. Apples were very rare these days, so they had caught his eye. He went in and bought all four of them. While the woman wrapped them in old newspaper, a little girl about Yuki's age came out from the back of the shop. Her haircut looked exactly like that of Yuki—short black locks bobbed just below her ears, the straight line of her bangs cut across her forehead just above the brows. As he stared at her, the little girl picked up one of the apples. The woman immediately snatched it from her and slapped her hand without a word. The girl put her hands behind her back and looked shyly at Giichi.

"Is she your daughter?" Giichi asked the woman.

"Yes," she said and nodded without looking at him.

"How old are you?" Giichi asked the girl. She twisted her body against the wooden shelf, then clumsily erected three fingers. "Three," she said in a sweet but barely audible voice.

Giichi told her he had a daughter who was a little older. He said his daughter had hair just like hers. As he spoke, he felt immense sorrow, thinking of Yuki. Neither the girl nor the woman spoke after that, but the girl kept staring at him with a half-smile. In the days since, he had stopped at the shop, hoping to get a glimpse of the girl. She was usually there, playing near the wooden stand piled with wilted leafy vegetables or squatting at the front of the shop in patched clothing, playing with sticks. The woman began to recognize him, which caused a slight alteration in her expression, but still she made no effort to be friendly. Only once did she smile, when he said to her that she had a sweet little girl, but it was the saddest smile he had ever seen.

Giichi hurried from the moat, and after a long walk, approached Mr. Nakano's rice shop, tormented by the image of the dead girl—her face stiff and placid, hair pasted to her cheeks, nostrils filled with mud.

Mr. Nakano's shop stood out from the others along the main street. It was two stories high and marked by a large wooden name plaque, symbolizing the old era when the shop had prospered as the town's only Lord-appointed rice shop. Giichi had noted other distinguishing characteristics, such as the intricate work of its black-tiled roof, and he imagined that the shop must have been quite impressive when it was first built. Today it looked neglected, the white walls cracked, the wooden lattice of the doors darkened by time, the roof tiles crooked.

The front door was wide open. Inside, Mr. Nakano stood alone, swishing a broom over the concrete floor in a stark pool of light from the morning sun, the sleeves of his white shirt rolled up to the middle of his forearms. Though he had sold rice all his life, every time Giichi saw him he thought of a university professor. Mr. Nakano lacked the wringing hands and wheedling voice of a merchant, and though he wasn't tall, he looked tall because he always stood lean and straight, with the intelligent and knowledgeable air of a professor. Yet he smiled humbly and easily. The first time Giichi met Mr. Nakano, he sensed that this simple rice merchant was someone with whom he had much in common. Giichi had only visited with him twice since arriving here, but he knew that now he needed to see him.

When Giichi stepped into the shop, Mr. Nakano stopped sweeping. "Mr. Sekihara," he said, stepping toward the threshold. "How is your mother-in-law?"

Giichi stood momentarily with a dazed expression. "She—she is much better. She's been sitting up and eating by herself since yesterday."

"Is she really? What a relief, what a relief." Mr. Nakano nodded vigorously. "Oh, please come in. Well, it's a bit dusty here, but please."

He waved his hand in the air, as if to settle the dust. The shop had a vacant look with a wide-open central space that at one time had probably contained rows of shelves. Three brown sacks of rice leaned against the wall beside the table. Against the left wall, a large metal measuring container sat unused, covered by a sheet of white cloth. In these times, no one could buy that much rice at one time.

Mr. Nakano gestured in the direction of a table and two chairs. He pulled a chair out for Giichi, then asked, "Is anything wrong, Mr. Sekihara? You look pale."

"I—I saw the dead body of a woman and her child in the west moat—it seemed like a suicide."

"Were they—the widow of the Yaogen store and her little girl?"

"That's what people were saying."

Mr. Nakano sat in the other chair, planted his elbows heavily against the edge of the table, and rubbed his face. "What a tragedy," he groaned. "I heard the rumor that her parents-in-law, the owners of Yaogen, couldn't find them this morning. When they woke up, the widow and her girl were gone. People were saying that was very odd, because rain or shine, she was the one who got up in the morning, cooked breakfast, and opened the shop."

Mr. Nakano shook his head grimly and gazed out at the street. Finally, he turned to Giichi. "Her husband died in Borneo last year. Then a few months ago, his brother, seven years younger than her late husband, came back from Java—his left leg completely blown off. Her parents-in-law told her that she would have to marry her wounded brother-in-law if she wanted to stay; if not, she should leave, and without her girl. This is a small town, everyone knows everyone else's affairs—I don't know about the big city, but in the countryside, many war widows marry their brother-in-law, especially when the brother-in-law is disabled. Parents-in-law force this because they know it will be difficult for their sons to find wives. It's not fair, but that's the way it is. It seems the widow didn't want to marry him and didn't want to leave without her child. It's very sad, but I don't think we should blame her."

Giichi stared at the soft pile of dust Mr. Nakano had swept to the middle of the floor. Tiny particles of dust floated above it in a shaft of sunlight. For a while, the two men sat silently and watched the particles drift through the light.

"Anyway, Mr. Sekihara," said Mr. Nakano. "It's getting warm. It's time to think about planting. Are you familiar with vegetable planting?"

"Not exactly," replied Giichi, relieved by the shift in conversation.

"Well, it isn't anything difficult. All you need is seed, soil, and a bit of land, which you luckily have. It's a huge garden, enough to grow vegetables for hundreds of people, actually. But you might need some good soil. I can introduce you to a man who sells soil and take you to the village to buy seedlings in a few weeks."

"Thank you. That's very nice of you."

"Not at all. We have to be prepared, Mr. Sekihara. We have to do everything we can to put something in our stomachs. This year's rice production is expected to be half of last year's. There are hardly any able-bodied men left in the countryside."

Giichi felt odd, even guilty, having an able body and sitting here idly.

"You are still pale," Mr. Nakano suddenly changed the subject. "I don't blame you after having seen such a tragic sight."

As Giichi stood to leave, a man who looked to be in his fifties came into the shop. Mr. Nakano introduced Giichi to the man, president of the Main Street Shop Association.

"Have you heard about the widow of Yaogen?" the man asked Mr. Nakano immediately.

"I just heard from Mr. Sekihara. What a tragedy."

For a second, the man seemed disappointed that he wasn't the first to tell Mr. Nakano. "Oh, so I don't have to explain what happened. But did you know Yaogen is so mad at their daughter-in-law they refused her body and only took the body of their granddaughter? So it has to sit in the basement of the police station until her father comes to get it. What a disgrace to both families! Anyway, there is a visitation tonight at the house and we have to talk about the amount of the offering that will be given from the association. What a disgrace --"

Giichi excused himself, bowed to the two men, and moved toward the door. Mr. Nakano followed him and placed his hand gently on his shoulder. "I'll come over in a few days and we can talk about the planting. Try not to think about this too much."

Giichi bowed and stepped out of the shop, feeling glad that he had at least Mr. Nakano to talk to in this new town. He turned and bowed again before walking away.

Giichi wandered toward home and then remembered the letter to his parents. He backtracked to the post office, and then decided to take the longer route along Samurai Mansion Street in order to avoid the street along the moat. He walked with his eyes on the road, filled with pity for the little girl who had done nothing to deserve death. She happened to be the daughter of a soldier who had died in Borneo. Because of this, her mother had chosen death for both of them. A disgrace, the man had said, and new anguish slowed his steps. His rejection of the red paper would surely disgrace Etsu. News of someone refusing to go to war would be a scandal even in a big city, let alone in a small town like this, where it would be even worse than for the Yaogen widow, especially since Etsu's father had been a revered judge, one of her cousins had been a legendary mayor, and her brother was one of the country's leading generals. He thought of standing on the hill of the ancient castle and the strength of his resolve in that moment, and realized again, how complicated and isolating it was to stand against war. He loved Etsu. The thought of her disgrace bore down on him like a heavy weight.

As if to rescue him from all the disturbing thoughts, an old building on the north end of Samurai Mansion Street caught Giichi's eye. Surrounded by a tall cedar hedge, it appeared at first glance to be a private home. But a large faded wooden plaque hung from the gate. Giichi stopped and tried to make out the illegible characters. Sasayama Town Library, it seemed to read. Suddenly reminded of his quest for new knowledge, he walked up the steps and drifted between the shelves. When he came across the section that contained books about vegetable gardening, it occurred to him that what he should be thinking about now was food, as Mr. Nakano had suggested. He needed to do what he could to ensure the survival of his family. After he left, Kinuko, Etsu, and the baby could all starve. After leafing through several books, he selected a few. This was what he could do for them, he thought, after the red paper came and he was no longer there to care for them.

Walking home with the books, he felt as if he had found a small island of satisfaction in a huge ocean of sadness.

CHAPTER 21

Ichiro took the mail from the box and immediately noticed his son's handwriting on the envelope. Songbirds warbled in the trees behind him, but he ignored their comforting call. He ripped open the envelope without moving from the gate.

Dear Father and Mother,

I apologize for not having written sooner....

Ichiro slumped onto his haunches at the threshold of the gate, holding the letter in one hand and his glasses in the other. He rubbed his eyes with his thumbs. He needed a moment to prepare himself. Since the arrival of Giichi's telegram from Sasayama, he often imagined Giichi and Kinuko arriving at the gate out of the blue, laughing and crying as they hugged Yuki. It was pure fantasy, and he knew from experience that reality seldom resembled his fantasies. More and more, he realized that Giichi and Kinuko might never be reunited with Yuki. So much could happen in times like these. Yet he held in his hands sheets of paper covered with black markings made by his son, words, the unfailing mainstay of his existence. He could not yet read them. They meant too much. They meant more than anything he had ever written. Ichiro gazed blankly at the empty rice field spread below his property. He thought about the world beyond the rice fields. A few days earlier, on April 1, Allied forces had landed on Okinawa, and Ichiro had no idea what would come next except that the military would not give up, they were too stubborn. They would need more soldiers than ever. Unless the Emperor experienced some sudden enlightened vision and gained power over the military, they would not surrender. His son would receive the red paper. Ichiro felt pain throbbing behind his eyes. He wondered if he would ever see his son again.

But, at least, he held something of his son in his hands. He rubbed the moisture from his eyes, put on his glasses, and read the letter slowly, taking in each word as if it were a gift. When he reached the end, he read the closing over and over again, "your loving son...your loving son...your loving son." Finally, he folded the letter and put it back in the envelope as neatly as he could, so that Sumiko might experience the pleasure of opening it as if for the first time.

That afternoon, after he and Sumiko had finished writing their reply, Ichiro looked for Yuki in the house and found her in the back garden. He stood in front of the window and watched her peer into the chicken pen with a basket in her hand, while Ume shooed the chickens away. When the chickens scattered noisily and eventually settled in a corner, Ume crawled halfway into the pen and gathered eggs. "Be careful," Yuki warned her. "They might peck your hand."

Ume backed from the pen and placed the eggs one by one in Yuki's basket. "One," Yuki shouted, stomping with joy, "two, three, four, and five! Five of them, Ume-san."

Ichiro smiled. "Yuki, come into the house please, I want you to do something."

"What, Grandpa?" she said, her eyes searching for him.

"What a busy girl you are!" exclaimed Ume. "Grandma asked you to get eggs, and now Grandpa asks you to do something else."

Ume tried to take the basket from Yuki's hand, but she refused to let go and told Ume that she should be the one to give the basket to her grandmother.

"Yes, that's right. You give them to Grandma," Ichiro said. "Then wash your hands and come to Grandpa."

While Ichiro waited for his granddaughter, he placed a sheet of grid-lined writing paper on the desk and a crayon on top of it. Soon Yuki came running into his study. "I washed my hands," she said. "What do you want me to do?"

"What a good girl," he exclaimed and sat her down on his lap, facing the desk. "Now," said Ichiro, tapping the paper with the crayon. "I want you to draw something for your father and mother. Then we'll mail it to them, because they are now in a town called Sasayama with Grandma Nakamura. Later we'll go to the post office together."

Though Yuki normally loved to draw, she resisted his request. Instead of picking up the crayon, she turned back to him and asked, her eyes seriously searching his face, "When are they coming, Grandpa?"

"Whenever the trains begin running," said Ichiro, pushing a crayon into her hand. "Now, do you want to draw a chicken?"

Yuki still wouldn't hold the crayon. "When will the trains begin running?"

"When the war is over."

"When will the war be over?"

Ichiro felt his resolve breaking. How could he explain war to a girl who wasn't yet four years old?

"I don't know," he said weakly. "I wish I did."

"Why? I want you to know, Grandpa."

Ichiro put down the crayon and gently rocked her. Her pouting cheeks puffed out and her lips pursed tightly.

"There are many things big people don't know. Grandpa doesn't know when the war will be over, but I do know that your mother and father love you very much. They asked me to tell you that in their letter. They are sad because they can't see you. But I'm sure they would like to see how well you can draw now."

Yuki's eyelashes dropped for a moment, as if she were thinking. Then she looked up at him, her eyes dark and shiny like black coral.

"Do you think Mama and Papa like chickens?"

"Of course they do. They would love anything you draw, but a chicken sounds like a good idea to me, because they might want to see what ours look like."

Though she seemed more puzzled than thrilled, unable to understand why her parents remained missing from her life. Still, Ichiro found it amazing that she had adjusted so well after being uprooted from the only world she had ever known. Watching her small hand move on the paper, he recalled what Sumiko had told him about their arrival in Okayama.

The first night, Yuki sobbed inconsolably in Sumiko's arms until she fell asleep, exhausted, her lashes wet and her face smeared with tears. The next morning at breakfast, she first appeared contemplative, then suddenly looked up from her bowl of rice and declared, "I'm not going to cry any more, Grandma." Sumiko said she had turned away to hide her own tears, and now, only thinking of it, Ichiro felt his eyes sting.

Looking at his little granddaughter, he sometimes felt ashamed of himself, still wallowing in sorrow over the lost house and his books that had never arrived. Most likely, all of their possessions had been bombed while waiting to be loaded from the warehouse, or perhaps they were still in the warehouse. As of April 1st, the railway had been designated only for military-related travel. Civilian travel was banned except for work and emergencies such as the death of relatives. Even then civilians had to apply for a pass. Ichiro didn't care so much about their furniture, but without his books, he felt as if his limbs had been severed.

Yuki's hand kept moving, clumsily, but with youthful diligence.

"It's very nice," Ichiro uttered. "I like it very much. It looks just like a chicken."

Yuki smiled for the first time and asked excitedly, her eyes shining, "Do you think they'll like my drawing?"

"Of course, they will love it. Write your name, too, so they can see how well you write these days. Then we'll put this in the envelope with my letter and Grandma's letter and mail them all together. How is that?"

Yuki wrote her name in hirakana in the upper right corner, quite large and clear. "There," said Ichiro. "Show it to Grandma before we put it in the envelope."

With the paper fluttering in her hand, Yuki ran to the kitchen where Sumiko chatted with the wife of Genkichi, the longtime family servant, who had brought them a bundle of mustard greens. The high octave of the two women's voices rose and traveled to the room where Ichiro wrote his son's new address on the envelope.

"Very good, Yuki," Sumiko proclaimed.

"You can even write your name?" exclaimed Genkichi's wife.

"This is for Mama and Papa," Yuki told them, her voice sounding proud. "Grandpa told me to draw."

"That is a very good idea. I'm sure they'll love it."

Ichiro felt uplifted, hearing the women praise Yuki. When she came back, Ichiro folded her drawing carefully and slipped it into the envelope together with his and Sumiko's letters. Yuki looked on seriously while he sealed it.

"Now," said Ichiro, standing up with creaking knees, "we shall go to the post office. Come along."

Under the warm April sun, they walked along the village path hand in hand, Yuki holding the letter as she insisted. But when wildflowers along the path caught her eye, she soon forgot her insistence and handed the letter to Ichiro. She ran ahead of him, squatted at the verge of the path to pick flowers, and came running back with a handful of them. "These are for Papa and Mama," she said breathlessly, thrusting them toward him.

"How nice of you," said Ichiro, taking them into his hand. "I'm sure they love these kinds."

Yuki ran away again, and Ichiro observed the flowers in his hand—endearing yellow clusters of dandelions, tiny purple forget-me-nots, and other flowers whose names he didn't even know. He suddenly felt tears gather in his eyes and pressed the flowers against his nose. More tears came, and he quickly wiped them with the back of his fist, as he saw Yuki returning with yet another handful of flowers. "These are for Grandpa, Grandma and Ume-san!" she said excitedly.

"Thank you, thank you, Yuki."

"I want the letter now!" she said and took it with her green, sticky hand. Holding it, she ran off again, her hair flapping and shining black in the sunlight.

"Don't fall!" Ichiro yelled to her. But she kept going, her little body bouncing along the path.

Watching her, he remembered Giichi's letter. *"A couple of years ago, Father, you said that war or no war, life should go on, and I think about it often to remind me that I should try my best to live each day to the fullest, hoping the war will end soon...."*

By now, Yuki had gone almost to the bend. The sky was wide there, and beneath it her figure was tiny. But to him she seemed to hold the whole universe. "Wait for me!" Ichiro yelled across the empty rice field. Yuki turned and ran back to him. "Hurry, Grandpa!" she said, the white envelope fluttering in her hand, smiling wide as if she couldn't be any happier. He began running, and as he stretched his legs to keep up with hers, he felt as if he had been taken back almost thirty years in time when he used to run with Giichi. He struggled to keep up with her and felt his heart pounding. He might not be able to run as fast as he used to, he thought, but he still had something to live for.

CHAPTER 22

April rain settled over Sasayama like the cloud hovering over Kinuko's soul. It drizzled frustratingly, on and off all day, always hiding the sun. She blamed the rain for her wretched state of mind, though she was grateful that Etsu's health continued to improve.

As rain pattered over the roof, she finally sat to write a letter to Mrs. Chiba, thinking how strange it was that she now lived many mountains away from the woman she held so dear in her heart. Though it had been only ten days since their arrival in Sasayama, she felt as if she hadn't seen her friend for years and said so in the letter. She explained in detail how they had ended up here instead of Okayama, about her mother's frightening illness, and how much she missed Yuki.

"Although I don't know how long we will have to live apart, I believe that we will be together someday as we have always been. It's been raining for several days, and my mother tells me that the moisture brings great benefit to the cherry blossoms, which are expected to open any day. With each wet day, she says, the buds of the cherry trees soften a bit more and when they finally blossom, their color will be richer than in dry years. Just as we now anticipate the cherry blossoms, I anticipate being with you. I am sure the pain we now feel for being apart will make the joy of our reunion even greater."

There was much more Kinuko wanted to tell Mrs. Chiba. She wanted to pour out everything to the friend who had always listened with a kind heart. But she refrained from doing so, afraid her letter might fall into someone else's hands. She couldn't really talk about her state of mind without talking about Giichi's decision, and she couldn't put Giichi in danger simply to seek her own comfort.

After sealing the letter, she again watched the dripping eaves. Though she couldn't see him from where she sat, she knew Giichi worked somewhere out in the garden. "You might get a cold," she had told him that morning, but he answered, "It's the best time to till the ground, the soil is softer now." Kinuko had never seen him so absorbed in physical labor. The last few days, he had spent nearly every waking hour working outside. First, he constructed a chicken pen. He measured and cut wooden planks and nailed them into a skeletal structure, then attached wire mesh around it and covered the top with tarpaper. After completing the chicken coop, he began preparing the garden for vegetable planting. In the morning, wearing the black rubber raincoat, he pried stubborn weeds from the ground with a hoe and shook the dirt from the root wads before dropping them into a bamboo basket. He worked without stopping, his eyes set hard and mouth shut tight. He came in for lunch with water dripping from his raincoat, ate quickly, and hurried back to his tasks. In the evening, he read the books about vegetables he had brought home from the library and scribbled notes at the table in the family room while listening to radio accounts of the war.

Since the night he had asked her if she regretted marrying him, he had acted as if he had never spoken those words. Still, Kinuko could tell that he was trying to hide the pain he felt. Now, seeing him work with such diligence, she regretted even more having behaved the way she did. Without a single word of complaint, he had limped on unhealed burnt feet during his numerous trips for a doctor and ice. He had cooked and washed dishes. He had made every effort to ease her burden. She couldn't imagine why she had pulled away from his embrace amid their mutual joy for Etsu's recovery. Yet she knew that what she had felt in pulling away from him was part of her true feelings. Even though she had come to accept and believe in his decision, there remained something about him she could not truly understand. How was it possible for him to exhibit such love for her and Yuki, and yet exhibit even greater love for something beyond them? Those thoughts made her uncertain about what constituted true love between husband and wife. The only certainty, which by now had settled at the bottom of her heart, was loneliness and pity for Yuki.

Still, the Yaogen widow's suicide forced her to realize that her suffering was abstract in comparison with the real pain the war had inflicted on others. She didn't learn about the suicide until Mr. Nakano stopped in to see them after attending the widow's funeral. With sagging shoulders he told Giichi that it was the saddest funeral he had ever attended. Giichi glanced nervously at Kinuko and mumbled, "It was too terrible to tell you. The girl was Yuki's age." Haltingly, Giichi told the whole story. Kinuko shuddered, imagining a woman her age wading into the moat in the predawn chill with her child strapped to her back. That day Kinuko decided to stop indulging in self-pity for having to live apart from Yuki.

The Allied invasion of Okinawa eventually overshadowed the town's obsession with the widow's suicide. The *Sasayama Shinbun News*, a two-page weekly, was filled with photos of Kamikaze pilots taking off to dive into the advancing Allied fleet and praised their heroic acts. "Folks!" the editorial said, "think about those island people bravely fighting an intense battle day in and day out. It's not only the problem of Okinawa but of the whole country. It's time for us to renew our stagnant spirit and show our firm resolve to fight to the end! Let's learn once again from the burning patriotism of those young Kamikaze pilots. Prepare yourself, folks, Okinawa's problem today becomes our problem tomorrow. Attend the bamboo spear drills to protect our sacred land from the hands of the barbarians!"

Kinuko put down the paper and sighed. She had escaped the bombing in Hanshin, but it seemed she couldn't escape the bamboo training that made her think of Hayashi, someone she wished to erase from her memory. She hoped her new neighborhood chief wouldn't be as ignorant, and decided to further forestall the protocol of meeting him to introduce themselves, at least for now. Etsu was still too sick in any case, and Giichi certainly wouldn't bring the matter up. Still, the general sense of her misery remained. She could avoid spear training for the time being, but not forever, and the same held for the red paper—for all she knew, it could arrive tomorrow.

With Giichi spending most of his time in the garden, Kinuko began making daily errand runs into town, hoping that might lift her spirits. Besides, it gave her a chance to stop at Mr. Nakano's shop, and when he wasn't too busy, they shared memories from her childhood.

One day, she and Mr. Nakano laughed about the time when she learned to ride a bicycle, nearly twenty years earlier. She was ten then and the desire to ride a bicycle had suddenly grabbed hold of her. With that new skill, she would be able to cruise around town and go to the river to swim on her own. She knew her mother couldn't afford a new bicycle, so she asked her grandmother, who immediately objected.

"A girl shouldn't ride a bicycle," she told Kinuko sternly. "It's not lady-like."

Mr. Nakano was there to hear her grandmother's admonition, and a few days later, when he brought Kinuko back from the river on his bicycle after her daily chaperoned swim, he stopped at an empty school ground and told her to get off the back.

"Now," he said, "come around and hold the handle bars. I'll teach you how to ride, but it must be a secret between you and me."

A few days later, she was already pedaling around the school yard by herself with ease. It was so exhilarating that one day she left the grounds. Behind her, Mr. Nakano shouted, "Be careful! Don't go too far!" But she kept pedaling and finally sailed onto Samurai Mansion Street. Alas, her grandmother, who hardly ever stepped out of the house, stood in front of the gate talking to a neighbor. Afraid Mr. Nakano might get into trouble, she lied that the bicycle was her friend's, but the words "Nakano Rice Shop" stood out on the back fender in white paint. Later, Mr. Nakano confessed to Etsu but didn't apologize. "It's a good thing to be able to do what one wants to do," he told Kinuko's mother, matter of factly.

Now standing in Mr. Nakano's shop, Kinuko laughed, remembering the astonished look on her grandmother's face. Then a customer came into the shop, and she turned serious, picked up her basket, bowed and excused herself.

"Tell Mrs. Nakamura and Giichi-san I'll visit soon," Mr. Nakano said, bowing.

Outside, Kinuko opened her mother's black umbrella and started down the street. A few blocks later, she still grinned at the memory of her grandmother's face and the thought of Mr. Nakano's kindness, when a loud shout startled her. She stopped and saw a boy of about ten rush out of a provisions store with the storeowner chasing after him.

"Stop, thief!" he shouted. In a few seconds, the man caught the boy, grabbed his hand, twisted it, and pulled a sweet potato out of his grip. Then he pushed the boy to the ground. Kinuko turned pale, watching the boy's thin body land face down on the rough pavement. The storeowner began kicking the boy, still shouting, "You are not the only one who's hungry. You dirty little bastard!" Kinuko screamed and ran to the boy's side. "Please, he is only a child!" she protested. She knelt beside the boy, and the man stomped away, grumbling loudly, "I have three children who are starving, too!"

"Are you all right?" Kinuko asked, but the boy didn't answer. Blood trailed from his cheekbone and nose. Kinuko took out her kerchief and tried to wipe the blood, but he stood and began limping away. "Wait, please!" When she caught up with the boy, she took a sack of flour out of her basket and handed it to him. "Take this home. Have someone make dumplings."

The boy's black eyes shone like those of an animal from his otherwise boyish face. His shoes were worn, and his body and clothes were smeared with dirt. "Go home," she said. The boy turned and limped away with the sack of flour. The sight of him made her heart throb with pity. She turned away quickly and began walking, now with anger so great it made her shake. When she came to the school grounds where long ago she had learned to ride a bicycle, she saw piles of bamboo spears, ready for the commencement of town-wide defense drills. The familiar stacks of useless weapons refueled her anger. She wanted to scream, "Why don't they stop this war?"

When she reached home, Giichi was sitting on the veranda under the eaves, watching the rain fall over the muddy garden, with a glass of water in his hand. He looked serene and noble, gazing over his project in ordinary work clothes.

He stood when he saw her. "What happened?" he asked, moving toward her. "You look so sad."

"I—I saw a boy." The tear dropped from her eyes.

"Tell me about the boy," Giichi said, guiding her to sit on the veranda. Kinuko haltingly told him about the shop owner, how hungry the boy looked, how cruel the man was, and how badly the boy was hurt. "I just cannot stand to see a child suffer," she said.

"I can't, either," Giichi said quietly. "This war should end soon. Really soon."

Kinuko nodded and felt enormous comfort sitting beside Giichi, knowing how much he wished for peace and justice for everybody. After a while, Giichi stood and patted Kinuko's shoulder lightly, before reaching for his tools to start working again.

Kinuko remained sitting and watched him raise a pickax and bring it down hard. Whenever it struck a rock, he bent to pick up the rock and throw it into a sturdy bamboo basket. He worked at a steady pace, not too fast, not too slow. His arms and legs were long and lean, and his muscles flexed prominently each time he raised and swung the pickax. Rain drizzled over him, but he didn't seem to mind. She was accustomed to seeing him in suits, his white shirt crisp and tie knotted neatly. When he would leave for work dressed that way, she felt her body tense, thinking she should work hard at home as well, and she had loved that feeling. Now watching him in a rain-soaked, round-neck shirt and blue work pants, she felt as if she had found a part of him she hadn't known before. It seemed he possessed something more than other men, the ability to work in two entirely different worlds. This new discovery made her want to be at his side, planting vegetables with him. She surely would, she thought, if she weren't eight months pregnant. She felt a connection with him she hadn't felt for months. She kept watching him, feeling her wounded soul heal.

A few days later, Kinuko became aware of the baby kicking in her womb and felt the sudden inspired joy of carrying a baby she had long ignored. Etsu, who still spent part of each day in bed, dug into her closet in search of old clothes suitable for diapers. Even that minor task exhausted her, and after lunch she went back to bed, muttering in disbelief over the bad turn of her health—until the previous year she had never experienced this much sickness. Kinuko blamed her mother's lingering illness on the weather and assured her that she would feel better once the rains stopped.

After Etsu settled in bed, Kinuko sat in the next room examining the faded *yukatas* her mother had found, thinking about what it had been like when Yuki was born. Then, in 1941, she could still buy a bolt of white diaper cloth and make the seams on her sewing machine. Now those luxuries didn't exist. Kinuko examined the *yukatas* carefully, attempting to figure out how to get as many diapers as possible from them.

When she finished cutting, she counted the pieces of cloth and worried that she might not have enough for weather such as this; the diapers wouldn't dry fast enough. She regretted that she had completely forgotten to pack Yuki's old diapers, in her hurry to get out of Hanshin. In fact, she acknowledged now, she hadn't given this baby a fraction of the attention she had given Yuki during her pregnancy. Moreover, she recalled with remorse that she had even hoped for a miscarriage. Feeling another kick in her abdomen, she vowed to dedicate herself to this long-neglected child, who against all odds kept growing in her womb.

She threaded a needle and began stitching by hand. The work proved tedious, only requiring the movement of her fingers, yet she soon found it soothing, sitting alone on a rainy afternoon with no worries about warning sirens. It occurred to her that getting out of Hanshin was the only good thing she had done for the baby. At least here she could give birth without B-29s flying overhead. In the cities babies were born in cramped bomb shelters beneath the roar of bombers. Many suffered from a lack of milk after birth; the stress and fear of their nursing mothers hampered the proper flow of breast milk.

With Etsu in bed and Giichi gone to a village with Mr. Nakano to buy chickens, she noticed the stillness and thought more about war in the city and here in the country. In the city, tragedy descended instantly and obviously, while in the countryside, it surfaced in a more hidden and complicated way—the starving boy, the Yaogen widow. Wherever you were, the horror of war could not be avoided. She realized she could no longer find reason to oppose Giichi if he chose to refuse the red paper. It no longer seemed foolish to die in opposition to the war. People died anyway, in battles, in bombings, in prisons, or simply from misery, like the widow and her daughter. The boy could die, if left with no food. Why not die for what you believed in? Aware that she was being drawn closer to Giichi's beliefs, Kinuko felt a moment of grim satisfaction, but she soon descended into a loneliness that went deeper than any she had ever known, realizing again where those beliefs would take him.

When the clock struck three, Kinuko heard her mother clear her throat. "Kinuko," Etsu called from behind the sliding door, her voice hoarse. "It's time for you to rest for a while."

"I'm all right," replied Kinuko. "How are you feeling?"

"I'm better. Your eyes must be tired looking at those small stitches. I'll get a cup of tea for you."

"I'll get it. Stay in bed. Do you want one, too?"

"I will do it," said Etsu, as if to herself.

Soon Kinuko heard her mother shuffle into the kitchen. After a while, Etsu called to her, "Tea is ready, Kinuko. Come to my room and look out the window to rest your eyes. It's dark in there."

Kinuko put down the diaper and went to Etsu's room. While she stretched and massaged her stiff shoulders, her mother placed the tray near the sliding glass door that faced the garden, then sat down and smoothed her kimono with the palms of her hands. Her hair was in place; she must have fixed it while waiting for the water to boil. A small woman to begin with, Etsu looked even smaller now, but still she bore herself with dignity.

"The rain seems to have stopped," Etsu said.

"It looks like it has."

Kinuko opened the door a little and inhaled the smell of damp soil. The wet bamboo trees shone with a vivid color that felt pleasant to her strained eyes. She watched sparrows rustle against the leaves, splashing rainwater and chirping sharply.

"Sit down and have some tea," Etsu prompted her. "Don't worry, if those *yukatas* are not enough, I can always ask my cousins for more."

"Thank you," Kinuko replied as she sat down.

"I'm sorry, I have been a burden to you ever since you came. I hope I am fully recovered by the time the baby comes."

"Mother, you are not a burden at all. You are my mother."

"That's very nice of you to say, Kinuko."

"I'm thankful that you are letting us stay with you."

"Well, I didn't have a choice, did I?" Etsu said jokingly.

They laughed, and Kinuko recalled how sick Etsu had been the night she and Giichi arrived at her gate.

"You've made progress," said Kinuko, still laughing, "though slowly."

"Indeed, slowly," Etsu sighed. But in a second her eyes lit up mischievously. "But watch out," she said. "You'll see how young I still am, once I get completely well."

As they laughed together, Kinuko remembered how young and lively her mother had been when they traveled as a family to spend summers at this house. In those days, when they prepared for their trips to Sasayama, Etsu would get up at dawn to make rolled *sushi* for the train ride. Then the three of them, Kinuko, her father and Etsu, would board a commuter train from Kobe to Osaka, and from there take a steam engine north. The train chugged through the mountains and along the rivers, passing through tunnel after tunnel. When they finally arrived, they received a joyful welcome from Kinuko's grandparents, then napped immediately in the south room with the sliding doors open to the side court. In the evening, after her bath, Kinuko put on a *yukata* and lit fire sparklers in the dark garden beneath the stars, while the adults sat on the wooden benches and chatted as they gently fanned their faces. At night they all slept inside a huge sheer, green mosquito net that rustled in the soft breeze.

"Yes, you are still young," Kinuko assured her mother. "But I can't believe how fast time flies, when I look back on those days when we used to come here together."

"It seems like yesterday, doesn't it? And I can't believe how things have changed."

Etsu looked over at the once moss-covered garden, now black with bare dirt. "Those were good days," she said. "But I shouldn't be complaining. Your uncle lets me live here, Giichi-san has been working hard to grow vegetables for us, and you have been taking good care of me. How lucky I am, while you and Giichi-san have to live apart from Yuki. That must be so hard for her and for the two of you."

"We miss her—but we know she is well cared for. Giichi's parents love her so much. And I believe when there is much love, a child does all right, even when away from the parents."

Rain pattered quietly outside, and they watched drops fall endlessly beyond the glass door.

"Kinuko," said Etsu after a while, her eyes still fixed on the rain. "Ever since you married, I have been praying that Giichi-san would never have to go to war. And luckily, it seems that my prayers have been heard so far, for which I am grateful."

Kinuko's chest tightened.

"But," Etsu continued, "with the war getting as it is, I don't know how long my prayers will be heard." She turned to Kinuko. "Anyway, what I wanted to tell you is that I would feel honored to send him off from my house if...if the red paper comes, and that I will be always with you, as you are with me now."

Kinuko looked down for a few moments, but when she looked up, she was surprised by what she said. "What is so honorable about going to war to kill or to be killed?"

Etsu stared at her. Then she gasped, "Kinuko, think about the situation of our country now."

"I know the exact situation of the country. This war has been wrong from the beginning."

"What else can we do? Just sit and wait until we are all killed? It is honorable for a man to try to save the country when he is called."

"The only person who can still save the country is the Emperor. If he truly thinks of his subjects, as we were told at school and as you always told me, he should order his military to surrender before the Allies land all over us. No ordinary men can save the country anymore."

Etsu's face turned pale. "Kinuko, you can be arrested for saying that!" Then her voice floundered, "Is—is that what Giichi-san thinks, too?"

"I—" Kinuko stuttered, "I—think most people feel the way I do. But they don't say that because they know what would happen if they did."

"The country is at stake, Kinuko. If a man loves his country, he should hide his personal opinions or feelings about the war and try his best to save his country. To me, it is a man's highest honor."

Kinuko no longer felt she should hide her opinion.

"Going to war isn't the only way to save the country. Some men are against war because they love their country as passionately as those Kamikaze pilots."

"So, Giichi-san doesn't think it's an honor to go to war?"

"I cannot speak for him, Mother. I'm just telling you what I think. You should ask him directly if you want."

Kinuko glowered at Etsu as if she suddenly faced an enemy, while Etsu stared at her speechless. Then she saw Etsu cover her forehead and breathe through her mouth. "I—I don't feel well," Etsu whispered, slumping toward her futon. Kinuko jumped up to help, and after her mother crawled into bed, she covered her.

"Thank you," Etsu said weakly, pinching her eyes shut. Kinuko regretted having spoken with such straightforwardness. But it was too late; she couldn't withdraw what had already been said. Moreover, she had meant it.

"You should stay in bed the rest of the day," she told Etsu somberly, "I'll bring you supper."

Etsu nodded without opening her eyes. Kinuko sat beside her for a moment, feeling sad and tired. Then she took the tray to the kitchen, washed the cups, and sat on the edge of the landing between the kitchen and the family room, wrapping her arms around herself. While she sat pondering their conversation, she heard the sputtering engine of Mr. Nakano's truck. She stood and started toward the gate to thank Mr. Nakano for taking Giichi along, but by the time she reached the middle of the forecourt, his truck had already moved away, and Giichi came in through the gate with four chickens in a wet bamboo cage.

He stopped and looked into her sad eyes. "What's the matter?"

Kinuko looked down. "I said some things that shocked my mother."

"What did you say? Did you tell her I was beaten?"

"No—I don't know how to explain it to you."

"Go inside, you're getting wet. I'll come in after I put the chickens in the pen."

Kinuko went into the entryway and returned with an umbrella. She approached the corner of the garden and held the umbrella over him while he took the chickens out of the cage and released them into the pen, one by one.

"We went to the farmer Mr. Nakano always goes to. I paid six hundred yen for four chickens, but it's worth it when you think about having eggs every day."

"Did Mr. Nakano buy some, too?"

"He bought another one to go with the one he has, because there are only two in his family."

"Why did you buy four?"

"I want you to eat two eggs because you are pregnant."

Released into the spacious pen, the chickens calmed and began walking about, inspecting their new dwelling. Giichi watched them for a while with satisfaction. Then he latched the door securely, brushed his hands against his pants, and stepped under the umbrella with Kinuko. He smelled of rain and chickens.

"Now, tell me what you've done to your sick mother."

"She said she would be honored to send you off to war. So I asked her what she thought was so honorable about going to war."

"Hmm."

"I have to ask you one last time. Are you definitely going to refuse the red paper? I don't want to argue, I just need to know for sure."

Giichi looked down, pressed his hands against the small of his back to hold himself erect, and shifted his feet nervously.

"Yes...it's definite. I will reject the red paper."

"My mother will think it's a disgrace."

"I'm well aware of that. In fact, I've been thinking about whether I should move out of this house. I could live in the upstairs of Mr. Nakano's shop, if necessary. I don't want you to suffer because of me."

"Have you discussed this with Mr. Nakano?"

"No, I just asked him if he knew of any rental rooms or houses in town. Without asking me why, he said I could live there free if I wanted to. I can still come here and finish the garden."

"Then I will go with you."

Giichi looked at her intensely for a few moments, his wet face only inches from hers. "Please don't do that. You shouldn't abandon your mother. She needs you, and you'll need her after I'm gone. I want you to stay here."

"Then I want you to stay here with me."

"Whatever you want me to do, I will do," Giichi said and then held her. Kinuko felt his breath warm against her ear. "Do you think it's a disgrace, too?"

Kinuko shook her head, and felt his arms tighten around her. She began crying, feeling the warmth of his body through his wet clothes. The rain kept falling around them, as if her tears weren't enough for the depth of her sorrow.

"Let's go inside," Giichi said finally.

He let go of her and took the umbrella from her hand, steering her toward the house.

CHAPTER 23

A week into April, the rain finally stopped. Early in the morning, Etsu received a visit from Mrs. Harada, wife of the neighborhood chief. Etsu introduced Giichi, and he knew he had lost the anonymity he had hoped would never end. He and Kinuko sat next to Etsu and bowed, as Etsu apologized for not having introduced her son-in-law sooner.

"Please forgive my impertinence," she said. "I have been sick, and it just slipped my mind. I'm very sorry."

Giichi listened to the woman's superficial offer of sympathy, saw her broad smile and thought she had the curious eyes of a gossip. The sun shone brightly, and he was anxious to get to the garden, but he knew this formality must be endured.

"I'm glad I finally met you," Mrs. Harada said to him. "I saw a young man walking through the gate the other day and I wondered who it was. I'm sure my husband will be glad to have a young man like you in our neighborhood. So please, be sure to come to the meeting this evening at our house. It will be about the upcoming defense drills."

Giichi had been dreading this moment. The thought of attending a neighborhood meeting filled him with a loathing similar to what he had felt about wearing a national uniform. Still, for Etsu's sake, he felt obliged to stay on friendly terms with the neighbors.

That evening, he crossed Samurai Mansion Street on behalf of Etsu and Kinuko, with a fist-like knot in his stomach. He worried that he should be wearing a uniform, even though Kinuko had thrown away his blood-stained one when he came home from the Ashiya Police Station. At the same time, he detested himself for letting such a trivial matter bother him. He walked through the Haradas' gate—just across from Etsu's—with an icy feeling, but Mr. Harada welcomed him courteously enough, and his feelings warmed a little. Mr. Harada didn't seem overly friendly by nature, but at least he wasn't rude and arrogant like Hayashi.

According to Etsu, Mr. Harada was in his sixties. Before retiring, he worked at the Sasayama town office as a clerk, a position he had held his entire adult life. Giichi noted that his appearance reflected the type of man who could endure a seemingly boring job for such a long time—prudent and tedious, his national uniform buttoned from top to bottom, thin strands of hair carefully combed across his head.

Giichi soon understood why he was the neighborhood chief; he was the youngest of the men gathered for the meeting. The others were in their seventies or eighties—one leaned on a cane. Despite their age, the group had an air of aristocracy, silver hair neatly combed, clothes old, yet worn in a dignified manner, freckled skin well-scrubbed. To his surprise, none wore a national uniform. The older men wore kimonos, while those who looked like they had only recently retired were dressed in shirts and trousers.

The circle of seated men moved to make room for him, and Giichi thought they looked at him with something akin to admiration, as if amazed that a man of his youth and health still existed. Their eyes burned into him as if hoping to prompt Mr. Harada to proceed with introductions. Then, without waiting for Mr. Harada, a man introduced himself as the retired principal of the local high school, and that started the circle on a cordial round of introductions. All bowed respectfully, in spite of his youth, and Giichi grew uncomfortable, thinking these men surely had sons and grandsons his age or younger in the war or who were already lost to it.

As quickly as the introductions ended, the group fell into a somber mood and began mourning yesterday's sinking of the battleship *Yamato*. The news was received like a severe jolt, not only because the beloved state-of-the-art sea warrior had been a source of much national pride, but because the ship was sunk on its way to Okinawa. The last hope of rescuing Okinawa from the Allies now seemed lost.

While the women began to pass teacups, the first to speak was Mr. Ishibashi, owner of the town's only fabric manufacturing factory, in fact, the town's only factory.

"It is hard to believe such a thing has happened," Mr. Ishibashi said.

"Until this day, I believed the *Yamato* was invincible," added Mr. Inagawa, the middle school principal.

"It's a great loss to our combined fleet," rasped Mr. Machida, former superintendent of the basin's education board, his voice hoarse and cracking from age.

Giichi wished the meeting would start and soon be over with, but Mr. Harada seemed in no hurry to convene, and the men continued talking about the Yamato and eventually the imminence of a ground war.

"The intention of the military is to draw the enemy to our shores, and then destroy them with our ground forces," one of them said.

"It seems that you are right." Mr. Harada finally spoke. "The other day at the meeting of the neighborhood chiefs' association, the others were talking about the number of recruits from their neighborhoods. They were saying even the ones who had come back are going out to rejoin the fight again. But of course, we don't have any young ones left in our neighborhood." Then he turned dramatically to Giichi. "Except our new neighbor, Mr. Sekihara."

Giichi looked down and felt his cheeks burn hot, but that wasn't the end of it. He heard Mr. Inagawa say, "Why doesn't the military call a man with such a fine constitution like Mr. Sekihara?"

Everyone looked at Giichi, then Mr. Machida said, "Well, some men are—just lucky, I guess."

"Yes, but the luck of those young men can't last much longer," countered Mr. Ishibashi. "Look what happened to my cousin's son in Osaka. He's a healthy thirty-year-old and he had never been called all these years. Then two weeks ago, the red paper finally arrived. I just got a letter from my cousin."

The conversation continued, and eventually Giichi grew weary. He had heard similar exchanges thousands of times before. He tried to remain attentive, but he nearly dozed off until he heard his name again.

"Mr. Sekihara," Mr. Harada said.

While everyone turned to Giichi, Mr. Harada continued. "It seems you are one of the few who are capable of the defense drills. Most of us already have one leg in the coffin." Everyone laughed, and when the laughter subsided, he outlined the schedule that would include Mondays, Wednesdays, and Fridays from nine to ten at the town's elementary school grounds. Giichi was given three rising sun headbands, though Mr. Harada made clear that Etsu and Kinuko were excused from the drills until they were physically able.

That night Giichi went to bed dreading the bamboo spear drill. He imagined himself thrusting a spear into the air with apron-clad women and felt sick with humiliation, but he knew he would have to do it in order to keep the peace between Etsu and Kinuko.

The next morning, after returning from the drill, Giichi immediately plunged into the garden work with renewed concentration. Initially, he had planned to grow only enough for his family, but he kept tilling the soil, not caring how large the garden became. Perhaps he could feed the whole town. Mainly, he needed to stay outside, where he found solace—in the smell of the earth and his own sweat. The rest of the world, the war and its worries, evaporated into the heat of the day as the soil responded to his labor, its appearance and texture transformed as he worked. He churned in the compost he had bought from the farmer he met through Mr. Nakano. The day the farmer brought the mound of compost in a horse-drawn cart and dumped it in a huge pile near the gate, Giichi began the endless trips back and forth between the gate and the garden. By the end of the day, his body ached and reeked of powerful field sweat, but it gave him pleasure—it came from an earnest desire to get the planting done before the red paper came.

Four days after the meeting at the Haradas', Kinuko stepped through the back door carrying a tray of tea and a rolled mat. "A letter from your father," she said with a smile. "Take a break and read it."

She strode past him and unrolled the mat in the shade of the bamboo grove, placed the tray and the letter on top of it, and sat down to wait for him. "Come here and open it, please," she prompted him. "You open it," said Giichi, lowering the pole and bamboo baskets to the ground. He approached the mat and sat down beside her with a groan. "Open it," he said again.

While he wiped a cloth across his forehead, Kinuko slit open the envelope, pulled out the folded sheets of paper, and opened them one by one. When she came to the last, she dropped the others onto her lap and covered her mouth. "Look at this," she said, her eyes brimming with tears. "Yuki drew this."

Giichi leaned forward for a better look. "It's a chicken," he said. "It looks just like a chicken." He laughed. "She's talented like her father."

Kinuko laughed and cried. "Oh, Yuki," she uttered, pressing the drawing against her chest. Then she dried her eyes with her apron and gazed at the drawing dreamily. After a while, she handed the bundle to Giichi.

"Are you ready for Father's letter?" Giichi asked, and Kinuko nodded.

Giichi smoothed the paper. Light filtered through the bamboo leaves above and fell across his father's flowing script. He cleared his throat and began reading, with Kinuko leaning slightly on his shoulder.

Dear Giichi,

> *How wonderful it was to hear from you. Mother and I are elated to learn that you and Kinuko are now in the safety of the countryside, though of course we were terribly disappointed when you didn't arrive. But considering Kinuko's mother's illness, we should say that it was a blessing that you two got there when you did. We do hope she is well by now.*
>
> *You don't have to worry about Yuki at all. It is our great pleasure to take care of her. Although she misses you greatly, she has adjusted very well, actually better than any of us adults. She loves collecting eggs with Ume and often plays with Genkichi's grandson, which she enjoys enormously. It seems so long since she has had playmates. She also enjoys learning how to write and has mastered almost all of katakana and hirakana since she arrived here. You and Kinuko should be proud of what she has accomplished despite your forced separation.*
>
> *Speaking of being proud, that's how Mother and I have been feeling about you, Giichi. You are such a brave son, and our hearts go out to you when we think about how difficult it was for you to be in such a disagreeable place for so many days. But you made it through and came back to us. Words cannot describe our gratitude. We are very sorry you had to go through the terrible bombing even before getting over the trauma you experienced during your imprisonment. We hope by now you have recovered from the injuries.*
>
> *Our house is a great loss to all of us, and I have to admit that Mother and I have been depressed ever since. We've cried many times remembering how you grew up there and the many years we lived together as a family. Alas, it is*

time to move on and we have concluded that we should be thankful you've escaped, and that we still have this place to live in.

Now the Allies are in Okinawa, and our defeat seems unavoidable. It seems that our country is going to experience an enormous devastation such as we have never seen in our history. I wish the military would come to its senses and put an end to this reckless war immediately to minimize the suffering of the people who have already suffered enough. But unfortunately, it seems that they won't easily give up what they started, and that they will drag this war on no matter the cost in human lives.

Now, I must say the most difficult thing a father ever has to say to his son. Although I still hope that the conscription will never come to you, it seems that the time is coming for us to prepare ourselves. What I would like to tell you now is that you should only do what truly makes sense to you. Looking back, I have to admit that I raised you according to my beliefs. And it might be possible that because you are my son, you have felt obliged to follow my path. My son, you must follow your own heart. I will be with you whatever you decide. If you decide that you must reject the conscription when it comes, don't worry about the family you leave behind. As I have promised you, I will take care of them the best way I know how. If you change your mind and decide to go to war, I will take care of them just the same. Either way, I'll be with you always.

Lastly, Mother and I are looking forward to the arrival of our second grandchild. Please tell Kinuko to take care. Our hearts are with her, however far apart we are now. Best regards to Kinuko and her mother.

P.S. Yuki still sleeps with the wounded doll.

Father

For a while, Giichi and Kinuko sat still. Soon Kinuko began smoothing her monpe pants, and Giichi plucked a tiny weed from the ground next to him, tore it into bits, and tossed them aside.

"How is your mother doing now?" he asked at last.

"She is up. She was cleaning her room when I came out."

"Is she well enough for that?"

"I told her I would do it, but she said it was time for her to be doing something."

They fell silent again.

"I understand that living here makes you feel uncomfortable," she said, "living in her house and not being able to tell her that you will not go to war."

"I feel as if I am betraying her. But what can I do? I don't want to put you in the middle."

"You don't have to worry about me," said Kinuko. "Besides, she is a reasonable person. She won't like it, but she will try to understand. The only thing that worries me is how it will affect her health."

Giichi lay down on the mat. Above, he saw light dancing slowly amid the leaves. Knowing that Kinuko was near, he felt happy, even though he worried about Etsu and about the red paper. For a while, he let the feeling of happiness soak into his heart, as he focused on the light, the leaves, and the sky.

"You have to come home," he heard Kinuko say. "You have to come home just like you did from jail, just like you did the night Osaka was bombed."

"I will try," Giichi answered. "I can't promise, but I will try my best."

CHAPTER 24

On April thirteenth, the day Etsu had predicted the cherry blossoms would be in full bloom, Kinuko arose early to prepare breakfast for Giichi. He ate quickly and dressed in an old white shirt, khaki work pants, and his jikatabi shoes. Before stepping outside, he showed Kinuko the list of seeds he would buy today and explained his master plan—which vegetables should be planted in which area of the garden based on the amount of sunlight each vegetable needed.

Through the window, Kinuko watched him walk away toward the furrows he had finished only the day before. It had been a long time since she had seen him so obviously full of excitement and satisfaction, and some of that feeling crept into her. When Mr. Nakano arrived, Kinuko went to the garden to tell Giichi.

"Will you be home before lunch?" she asked, drying her hands with her apron.

"I should think so," replied Giichi. "It's only three kilometers from town. But you never know, considering Mr. Nakano's truck."

Kinuko laughed, and they walked to the gate together.

"How kind of you to take him to the village," Kinuko said to Mr. Nakano.

"No problem at all," he said. "Buying seeds in town is easier, but I have been going to this farmer for years. His prices are more reasonable." Mr. Nakano smiled brightly. "Besides, it's a nice day to drive out to the village and see the cherry blossoms."

Giichi climbed into Mr. Nakano's rickety truck, and Kinuko bowed as the engine started.

An hour and a half later, the mailman's red bicycle stopped in front of the house. Kinuko was brushing old spider webs from the eaves of the gate, holding the broom upside down. When she heard the rattle of the old bicycle, she lowered the broom and brushed the dust from her apron. The mailman, in a faded blue uniform, stepped around his handlebars and peeked into his black bag. He pulled out a white envelope, then removed his cap, tucked it under his arm, and announced that he had an express registered letter for Giichi Sekihara. He said he needed the recipient's chop as proof of delivery.

When she saw the sender's name on the back of the envelope, a numbing chill rushed through her body. It came from the Minato Ward Office.

"Are you Mrs. Sekihara?" asked the mailman, darting a glance at the bulging stomach that pushed against her apron. Kinuko meant to say yes, but couldn't force the word out of her mouth. Instead, she stared at the mailman's face. "I need your chop, Mrs. Sekihara," he repeated.

She nodded, dropped the broom to the ground, and went into the house with wobbly knees. She reached the trunk she had brought from Hanshin and sat in front of it for a while to compose herself. But the tips of her fingers were numb and her hands wouldn't stop shaking. With great effort, she reached into the trunk and took out the small leather case that contained the Sekiharas' ivory signature chop and a tiny red ink pad. When she came back to the gate, the mailman glanced at her stomach again and pointed his gloved finger at the place on the paper where she was to press the chop.

"Thank you," he said tersely. Then he handed the express mail to Kinuko, slipped the paper into his bag, and briskly walked back to his bicycle.

By now, the numbness had spread through every fiber of her body, and as she walked back to the house with the envelope, she felt as if her feet weren't touching the ground. Although the letter was addressed to Giichi, she opened it and didn't care if he would be offended. She found exactly what she had expected—the red paper, though it was pink now instead of red because of the shortage of red dye. Without reading the whole page, she pushed it back into the envelope and covered her face. With her eyes closed, she saw Giichi sitting upright in a dark prison cell. He seemed to be meditating. A sharp, thin light came from a barred high window and crossed over his upper torso. His face was in shadow, yet Kinuko could tell his expression was as serene as that of the Buddha statue she had seen in Nara. Then she saw a torturer emerge from a corner of the cell with a wooden stick raised high, and she emitted a high piercing wail.

"What's the matter?"

Kinuko heard her mother come into the front room.

"Finally," Etsu whispered, kneeling next to her.

Kinuko felt her mother's hand on her shoulder. "I hate this war," she said in a low moan. "I hate it!"

"Kinuko, listen." Etsu stood and with her frail arms, tried to lift Kinuko. "Listen," repeated Etsu. "Please, someone might be coming through the gate. You shouldn't be saying that here."

Hearing her mother's trembling voice, Kinuko got to her feet and followed her into the altar room, where she threw herself onto the floor and began pounding the tatami with her fist.

"Kinuko, listen now," she heard Etsu's voice again and felt her hand on her back.

"Let's pray to your father," Etsu whispered. "That's all we can do."

Kinuko stopped hitting the floor, but she couldn't stop crying. Etsu placed the registered mail in front of her husband's mortuary tablet and struck a match. After several failed attempts, she finally managed to light the candles and incense. As the scent of incense spread in the room, she rang the brass bell and began praying. After a while, Etsu brought her hands down to her lap and turned to Kinuko. "I think you should pray, too," she said, "for Giichi-san's safe return."

"I don't believe in praying," Kinuko said defiantly. "I think everyone in this country has prayed enough already and look what happened to us. Soon all of us will be dead from bombing or fighting or starvation or—"

"Listen," Etsu interrupted. "You don't have to pray if you don't want to. But where is your dignity?"

"Dignity?" asked Kinuko, facing Etsu straight on. "That's what you always preached. Die for the Emperor. Endure hardship. That's dignity. What a convenient word for them to use, when they deprive us of everything, food, medicine, clothes. Still, people say nothing and let the military and the government do whatever they want in the name of the Emperor."

"Kinuko," Etsu's voice cracked. "Dignity isn't something someone gives you. It doesn't have anything to do with the Emperor or the government or the military. You don't have to have faith in any of them if that is your choice, but you do have to have faith in yourself, because that's where one's dignity comes from."

"I do have faith in myself, but I also have feelings I cannot hide. I'm angry at this war, because it's wrong."

"There is no point in arguing whether this war is right or wrong. A war is going on and your husband is called whether you like it or not. Your duty now is to send him off without displaying your selfish feelings, so he can serve the country without worrying about you."

"That is exactly what the government wants us to do," Kinuko cried. "So they can carry on with this war. Don't you understand? They force women to send off their sons and husbands with smiles and they don't even let them cry when their men come back dead. They mold you to their convenience so they can do what they want."

"What is the point in talking about what they do to you? The point is how we conduct ourselves. Please, don't let your feelings take over. It only makes you feel bitter and in the end—"

"Yes, I am feeling bitter right now and I can't help it. But please don't tell me to pray, because it doesn't help."

Etsu stared at Kinuko with sadness in her eyes. "There is nothing else I can say to you," she said, then rose from the floor and blew out the candles. She stopped just before the door and placed her hand across her forehead as if gathering herself. After a while, she turned around to look at Kinuko. "We seem to look at things differently," she said, "but that doesn't keep me from loving you. We'll make it together, while Giichi-san is gone."

"I'm sorry," whispered Kinuko. "I didn't mean to speak to you this way."

"That's all right," Etsu said with a slight tremor in her voice.

For a moment, Kinuko thought about telling her Giichi's decision, but Etsu walked away.

Alone in the altar room, Kinuko stared vacantly at the dark altar. The tip of the incense stick glowed red in the darkness; a twisting line of smoke rose from it. Gazing at the smoke, Kinuko remembered a night when she was eight years old, one week after her father's sudden death. She was seated in the altar room of her childhood home in Kobe, listening earnestly to her mother, amid a smell of incense and feelings of devastation. All of the funeral visitors had gone, and a real awareness of her father's absence was settling into the house. "Kinuko," her mother began quietly. "You are a smart girl. I am sure you will understand what I'm going to say to you. By now your father has taken up residence in heaven and he will watch over us from there. Both of us are terribly sad right now, but his death should bring us strength. What is most important is that we should live a life we won't regret later." And then, as if to reinforce her point, her mother moved right on to the mundane. "Well, it's getting late now. Tomorrow you have to go back to school, so brush your teeth and go to bed."

Kinuko sat up straight. She regretted having vented her anger on her mother, who only days earlier had difficulty getting out of her sickbed. She realized that she was now the same age her mother had been when her father died, and now she might have to walk the same path Etsu had been forced to take. She had no choice in this matter; she had only this life to live. She realized she didn't want any other life. Even if Giichi didn't return, being married to him for eight years was far greater than being married to a man for a lifetime without love or respect.

She stood. Giichi would soon be home and her mother's anguish would only get worse. Giichi would tell her mother that he wasn't going to war, and this would all happen in the house that belonged to her uncle, who had opposed her marriage to the son of Ichiro Sekihara, perhaps foreseeing this event years ago. Kinuko finally went to her room. She needed to compose herself so Giichi would feel her strength and not feel guilty about leaving her behind.

CHAPTER 25

As soon as Mr. Nakano brought his truck to a lurching halt, Giichi jumped out and thanked him. "I can't wait to start planting," he said, imagining how the careful design of the garden would look once green plants covered the black furrows.

"I'm sure you'll have a wonderful garden," Mr. Nakano replied, helping Giichi unload the bamboo flats covered with plants. "I have no doubt you're going to have plenty of vegetables this summer."

Filled with excitement, Giichi stepped through the gate with one of the flats. Immediately, he sensed an unnatural stillness. He saw a broom lying haphazardly across the path and tried to ignore the bad omen of a broom left in front of a house. He and Mr. Nakano unloaded the rest of the woven bamboo flats and the sacks of seed potatoes and carried them to the garden, savoring each step. After Mr. Nakano left, he stood outside the house, knowing he could no longer delay the truth. He felt certain the red paper had come.

He walked into the house, through the back door, into deep silence, and saw Etsu's and Kinuko's wooden clogs neatly placed on the step stone. He stopped at the kitchen sink and scrubbed his hands more meticulously than necessary, hearing his heart drumming in his ears. Then he sat at the edge of the landing and slowly unclasped the hooks of his jikatabi shoes, grasping at the thin hope that Kinuko or Etsu would suddenly appear and apologize for having been so busy making diapers that they didn't hear him.

Finally, he stood and heard Kinuko's hesitant footsteps coming through the family room, then to the landing. She was pale, and there was redness in her eyes.

"The red paper came, didn't it?" said Giichi.

Kinuko nodded with a slight contortion of her face as if she was going to cry, but she didn't. "It's in there," she said with deliberate calmness, and Giichi followed her to the altar room.

She lifted the envelope from the altar, handed it to him, and sat down with rigid grace. Giichi sat beside her and pulled the pink sheet of paper from the envelope. He breathed in deeply and read:

Date: April 17, the twentieth of Showa (1945)

Time: 10:00AM

Place: The Osaka 34th Division, 10th Regiment

"Four days," he groaned, gazing down at the paper. "Actually only three and a half." He wondered if that would be enough time to finish the planting. He wanted to prepare stakes for some vegetables as well. Then he gazed into space, scratching his chin. The moment he had dreaded for so long had finally come, and strangely it didn't seem so bad. He would just have to carry this out as methodically as making a garden, one step at a time, just do the best he could. He folded the paper and put it back in the envelope.

"Where is your mother now?"

"In the south room," Kinuko replied with her face down. Then she looked up at him. "I thought about telling her but decided I should leave that to you."

"Of course," Giichi answered. He had noticed recently that her eyebrows had grown thinner like a pale crescent moon. And a hardness—not exactly a coldness—had settled on her face. Etsu claimed that the baby was a boy and that a boy made his mother's face take on the harshness of his gender. Though Giichi wasn't sure if that was true, he did believe the hardness on Kinuko's face reflected her inner life. He had seen the same thing on his mother's face every time his father was taken away to jail. Then eventually, the hardness fixed itself permanently, blending with her natural grace until it became part of her visage. Looking at Kinuko now, even as she attempted to hide her sorrow, he found her strikingly beautiful, like the kannon statue that used to sit on the chest in the reception room of his parents' bombed house.

Giichi stood. "I'll talk to her right now."

When he slid open the door to the south room and asked if he could come in, he saw Etsu sealing an envelope with paste. "Yes," she said, quickly wiping the paste from her finger with a scrap of paper, "in a moment." She seemed in a hurry, quickly glancing at the clock before turning to Giichi.

Giichi sat rigidly and she glanced at the clock again. Then she finally spoke. "I'm sure you have heard from Kinuko."

"Yes, I have," Giichi answered. "That's what I wanted to talk to you about."

He looked straight into her eyes and saw her shift her posture a little. "I hope that what I have to tell you will not shock you. The last thing I want is for you to fall ill again."

Fear flickered in Etsu's eyes, while she waited for Giichi to continue.

"I am going to refuse the red paper. Though that might seem unpatriotic from your point of view, I want you to know that I love my country as much as those who are fighting in the war."

Etsu turned so pale that he wondered if he should continue. She looked as if she might faint, or at best, that she couldn't believe what she had just heard. But he decided that he must plow on, do the best he could.

"As you might have imagined, I have been strongly against the war from the beginning. I didn't want to have anything to do with it and hoped all these years that I would never be called. But my hope has finally ended and now I have to act according to my beliefs."

Giichi stopped and wondered again if she had heard him. She stared at him with a rigid face and unblinking eyes, her lips colorless.

"I am truly sorry that I am going to disgrace your name. I'm not asking you to understand or forgive me."

Giichi bowed, his hands planted firmly on his lap, and looked down waiting for her to speak.

"Does—does Kinuko know this?" Her voice came with barely controlled anger.

"Yes."

"Did you tell her just now?"

"I told her in January."

"In January?" Now her voice came out like a whistle, through lips pinched with undisguised anger. "How—how can you do this to my daughter?"

"I'm very sorry. I can't tell you how sorry I am."

"Sorry? Do you think sorry is enough? I let her marry you despite my brother's objections because I wanted Kinuko to be happy. I entrusted you with her happiness. Do you know what is going to happen to you? Oh, no—no." Etsu shook her head and covered her face. "Why? Why do you—"

"I have no words to adequately explain. I have asked myself the same question over and over again, but in the end I realized I have to do what I feel in my heart."

"You are telling me that how you feel is more important than your wife and children?"

"It's not a matter of which is more important, Mother."

"But I can't think otherwise from what you are doing."

"Then maybe, yes. There is no more honest way to answer your question."

Etsu looked as if she might lose her balance. He started to rise to help her, but she held her hand up, palm toward him, as if to say, "Don't touch me." She turned to the desk and picked up the letter she had been sealing when he came into the room.

"Giichi-san, I've written to my brother. You said you hoped you wouldn't have to go to war. It's not too late. Please take it to the post office right now—so it will go out with the twelve o'clock mail."

Giichi looked at the letter, then at her. "Is this to ask him for draft exemption?"

Etsu nodded.

"I appreciate that, Mother. And I know Kinuko would be very grateful. But it's too dangerous. I've heard that the military has begun quite a thorough investigation regarding any irregularities. Just the other day there was a report of an official in Kyoto who was court-marshaled for accepting bribes from people to avoid conscription."

"I'm not bribing him," said Etsu. "I'm just asking him."

"Still, I don't want Kinuko's uncle to get into trouble because of me."

Etsu sighed and kneaded her temples.

"I thank you again," said Giichi, "but it's not a good idea."

Etsu gazed at the letter. "Well, then," she said finally. "I shall have to go to the post office myself."

"Mother," said Giichi. But Etsu rose and hurried out of the room. When Giichi followed her, she shook her head hard and raised her hand to stop him. She struggled into her clogs and stumbled out of the house. Giichi stood for a moment, shaking his head sadly, and then went out to the garden to start planting the seedlings he had brought home. He stooped between furrows with a shovel in hand and moved steadily from one end of a furrow to the other, all the while worrying about Etsu. Though she had been out of bed the last couple of days, she had yet to leave the house. He wondered if she was capable of walking to and from the post office. But he kept working and thinking about their conversation.

Etsu was right. He had clearly failed as a husband. As Kinuko had pointed out, if he died fighting a war, his death wouldn't be his choice. On the other hand, if he died in prison, his death was his own choice. This was what Etsu was talking about, and from her perspective, no matter how sincerely he professed his love for his family, it was evident that he had chosen his beliefs over that love. If he could make amends, he would, but it was too late, and nothing seemed worthy of the love Kinuko had given him. Then it suddenly occurred to him that she should remarry if he didn't come home. He shuddered at the thought, imagining Kinuko in the arms of a stranger and his children calling another man father. But he had to understand, he told himself, that it would be his own making, and that he should want her happiness instead of hoping that she remained faithful the rest of her life as many widows did. Still, he longed for Kinuko's forgiveness. He hoped that someday she would understand why he had to do this.

Close to one o'clock, Kinuko stepped out of the house with a tray of lunch and placed it on the veranda. "Lunch is ready," she called. Giichi stood up slowly, wiped the sweat from his forehead with the back of his dirt-crusted glove, and hobbled stiffly to the veranda. Kinuko filled his teacup with both hands, holding one steady with the other.

"Have you eaten?" he asked.

Kinuko shook her head. "I'm not hungry."

Giichi sat, the tray between them, then asked, "Did Mother come home?"

"Yes."

"Is she all right?"

"She is resting."

"Good."

Kinuko sat with her head down. She wasn't shaking visibly, but he sensed that she was still shaking inside. He picked up a rice ball, took a bite, and chewed slowly.

"You can take Yuki's drawing with you," she said, without looking at him.

"You should keep it—I don't deserve that."

Kinuko looked at him. "Yes, you do. She loves you very much. I can ask your parents to send me more."

"I'll take it with me then. Thank you."

Giichi could eat no more. "I'll eat the rest later," he said. "You can leave it here."

"All right," replied Kinuko.

Giichi stood and took an unsure step toward the garden. "Kinuko, you should remarry if something happens to me. There is no sense staying alone like your mother."

"Why? Why must you say such a thing?"

Her voice was so sharp that Giichi turned around and found her face red with rage, her eyes brimming with tears. She began pounding his chest.

"I said." Giichi tried to fend off her fists. "I said if—"

"Don't ever say that!"

Giichi gripped her wrists and took her into his arms. Her head slumped to his shoulder and shook with sobs.

"All right. I won't say that again. Please, your mother might hear you."

"I don't care!"

"All right."

Giichi sat her down on the veranda, where she covered her face. "I'm trying to believe you will come home."

"I understand—I'm sorry I said that."

Giichi went back to planting and his uneaten lunch dried on the veranda. Later, when Kinuko came out to tell him supper was ready, she tossed the remains of his lunch to the chickens. He went into the house for a supper of dumplings in miso soup. Etsu sat next to him at the table but did not speak to him, and he could think of nothing to say to her. As soon as he finished, he returned to the garden and worked until it was too dark to see.

In the evening, he sat at the desk in the south room and wrote down detailed instructions for Kinuko regarding the care of the vegetables—which ones should be thinned and when, which ones needed stakes and how high they would grow. He drew a meticulous map of the sections to show the location of each vegetable so she would know what they were. After that, he put all of his cash, his bond certificates and a bankbook into a manila envelope and wrote Kinuko's name on it. He gazed at her name—"silk child"—for a moment or two longer and placed the envelope in the drawer, deciding to give it to her the night before he left.

Early the next morning, he was already at work, on his knees spreading seed potatoes on a rice stalk mat to air them out, when Mr. Nakano came around the corner of the house with a grim expression. "I just heard," he said, stopping beside the mat. "The ladies told me."

Giichi stood and brushed the dirt from his hands. "It came yesterday," Giichi said, pulling up his work pants, "while I was in the village with you."

"I had a feeling. I don't know why, but—I felt something. That's why I came."

Giichi had already decided to tell him the truth. He would find out eventually and Giichi wanted to be the one to tell him, though he had no idea how he would react.

"Mr. Nakano, I have to tell you something."

Giichi began moving slowly toward the bamboo grove. Mr. Nakano followed him, tilting his head slightly as if asking what it was Giichi had to say.

"I am refusing the red paper. Did they tell you?"

Mr. Nakano stopped and looked at Giichi, unblinking, his face turning pale.

"No, they didn't. Are you serious?"

"Yes, I am."

Giichi started walking again.

"I—" Mr. Nakano mumbled, "I had an inkling of something like that, but—

They entered the grove. A flock of sparrows stirred among the leaves above and fluttered wildly, almost colliding and chirping sharply. Some flew away in a hurry, others eventually settled.

"How are you going to do that?" Mr. Nakano asked as soon as the commotion of the birds stopped.

"That's what I'm wondering. If I send it back where it came from, the Military Police will come here eventually, and that's what I don't want."

"Don't go to Osaka," Mr. Nakano advised him. "They are tough, those big city police. Don't go there. Refusing the red paper can be done anywhere. I know the police superintendent here. I went to school with him. He is a reasonable man. I can ask him to keep you here and try you here. The sentence might be the same, but the prison conditions would be better."

"Thank you, but that would embarrass my mother-in-law. It's going to be a big scandal in town."

"Listen, wherever you are tried, people will eventually know. I understand how you feel, but the important thing is to survive, even if you embarrass your family along the way. I don't even know if the superintendent has the authority to keep you here but think about this—half of Osaka is gone, that means half of Osaka's jails are gone. So it's possible that they might decide to keep you here. Of course, I'm not sure, but just talking to him can't do any harm."

"Maybe you're right, but I'm not going anywhere until April seventeenth. First I have to finish the planting."

"Of course, but be sure to go to the police station before the time you should be at the regiment in Osaka, otherwise failure to report could be added to the charge of draft evasion. Once you tell the police here that you aren't accepting the red paper, it will be their responsibility to inform the Osaka regiment."

"How do you know these things?"

"Well," Mr. Nakano said, scratching his head, "I pay attention. When I was young, I wanted to become a judge like Kinuko-san's grandfather. He even offered to help with my education. But my father told me to know my place. 'You are the son of a rice merchant,' he said. But anyway, I'm glad I didn't become a judge. I would have hated to be a judge in times like these."

Mr. Nakano suddenly grabbed a bamboo tree with both hands and shook it hard. Sparrows fluttered and squeaked and fled. Looking up at them, he said, "I admire you." Then he looked at Giichi. "I really do, Mr. Sekihara. Not many men can do something like this."

Giichi didn't know what to say; he had never thought he was doing anything even vaguely heroic. Even so, he was flattered and felt a warm lump in his throat. Mr. Nakano patted his shoulder. "Anyway, I have to go back and open the shop. I'll be in touch."

After he left, Giichi went back to work, ignoring the fact that he was supposed to be at the bamboo spear training. He planted tomatoes, cucumbers, eggplant, endo, pumpkins, cabbage, and onions. After that he split bamboo stalks for stakes. And when the sun swung down beyond the roof of the house, he prepared to scatter morning glory seeds in the corner along the south garden fence—Kinuko's favorite flower. Each summer their delicate bell-shaped flowers had bloomed on the east side of their house back in Ashiya. The first spring after they married, Kinuko planted the seeds Mrs. Chiba had given her. Mr. Chiba came over on a Sunday afternoon with split bamboo and built a trellis. At the end of each summer, Kinuko picked some dry pods, shook the seeds out, and stored them in an old tin that once held Darjeeling tea imported from England. She kept some seeds for the next year and gave the rest to her friends and neighbors. Remembering all this, Giichi couldn't resist buying some of the tiny black seeds when he saw them at the farmhouse the day before. He also thought of planting morning glories as a way of honoring his father.

As he churned the soil with a spade, scattered the black seeds, and sprinkled soil over them, he thought about his father's anguish when *"Morning Glories"* and another of his novels had been banned. He hoped that someday his father's books would reappear on shelves and continue to touch people's hearts. He imagined the flowers blooming in his absence, and suddenly longed for his previous life—waking up to see morning glories on summer mornings, getting ready for work while Yuki looked on, and coming home in the evening where Kinuko and Yuki waited. This sudden yearning brought him stronger resolve to survive in prison. Kenji Nakayama had once told him that among all prisoners, communists were treated most severely. Still, Giichi knew that some of them survived. If they could do it, why couldn't he? He had already experienced jail life. That thought gave him confidence; yet he felt tremendous fear and knew that he must truly believe in his will to survive.

CHAPTER 26

After the arrival of the red paper, Kinuko spent an entire day preparing for the baby, determined to carry on with her life, no matter how much she dreaded Giichi's departure. She decided that was the only way to send him off with dignity. She sewed baby clothes, using old furoshikis and some of the yukatas, all the while knowing that her activity was directed by avoidance more than dignity. Periodically, she stepped to the veranda and watched Giichi working frantically in the garden.

Almost as much as the red paper, she dreaded the soon-to-come evening meal. Not only would it be one of their last meals together, it would be a time when they were joined again by her mother. As dusk fell, she looked at the clock and, with a small sigh, noticed that it was already past their usual suppertime. Yet there was no sign of Giichi coming into the house, and no sound from Etsu's room.

Since Etsu's return from the post office the day before, Kinuko had only seen her mother in the evening, when the three of them ate in silence with their eyes downcast. The rest of the time, Etsu stayed in her room, claiming a lingering headache, though Kinuko knew more than a headache kept her mother from joining her.

Kinuko laid the half-done baby clothes on the floor and reluctantly went into the kitchen to prepare supper. She thought of going to Etsu's room to see how she was doing but decided against it. Through the open back door, she saw Giichi in the twilight, squatting at the south end of the garden, sprinkling some seeds over the soil. Even in the fading light, she could see how much he had done. Green seedlings already covered most of the plots.

She felt dizzy momentarily, realizing he would be gone in only two days. She sat down on the landing, feeling her resolve breaking. After a while she stood, thinking he must be hungry. As she stepped down to the kitchen floor, she heard a quiet rustle behind her. Turning, she saw Etsu at the doorway of the unlit family room, dressed in a going-out kimono and holding a furoshiki bundle.

"I'm sorry, Kinuko," she said, "I'm going to the Furukawas for a few days. Please don't misunderstand. I'm not doing this to make you feel bad. I just need to be alone for a while."

"I'm sorry," Kinuko whispered.

"I have to say goodbye to Giichi-san." Her voice cracked slightly, and she stepped into her clogs in a way that made Kinuko fear she might lose her balance. But she quickly straightened herself once her feet settled into them. As Kinuko watched her mother's frail figure approach Giichi in the twilight, she felt warm tears forming in her eyes. She knew how much her mother loved Giichi, despite the gulf of their political differences. Kinuko hid behind the door and listened.

"Giichi-san," she heard Etsu say. "I have to say goodbye."

"Where are you going?"

"To the Furukawas for a few days."

"Mother, I'm the one who should leave. Not—"

"No. You should stay with Kinuko."

"I'm sorry—"

"Let's not talk about it anymore."

"Please, Mother, take care of Kinuko for me, please," he said.

"And you, please come home. Come home for her. That's all I ask."

Unable to suppress a sob, Kinuko ran to her room and wailed without regard for who might hear her. Later, when she went back to the kitchen, the garden was already dark, and her mother was gone.

Neither Kinuko nor Giichi mentioned Etsu's name after that, though both moved in and around the house reverently, feeling the depth of her love and resentment.

On the afternoon of April 16, Kinuko sat in the bedroom and mended Giichi's clothes, preparing for his stay in jail. She didn't know exactly what he would need but decided to pack his bag as if he were going on a short trip—three sets of clothes, an extra pair of shoes, toiletries, nail clippers, and Yuki's chicken drawing. She kept her eyes on the needle and thread, remaining constantly mindful of his bag resting at her side and his real presence within her reach. Today, he was in the garden. She could still go to the veranda to see him or run to him and speak to him or touch him. Tomorrow, he would be gone, and she wouldn't be able to touch him or see him or talk to him, no matter how much she longed for him. The thought was unbearable, yet, as she ran her fingers over his shirt, a feeling steadily rose in her heart, and she thought that she was the most fortunate woman on earth to have spent part of her life with such a noble man. What he was going to do, she understood now, was for everyone, regardless of race or nationality. At that moment, having been part of his life seemed more precious than anything she had done or ever would do. She couldn't imagine why she had been so foolish as to think he didn't love her enough. She suddenly understood that the love he felt for her and Yuki was greater than the love a husband would feel for his wife and daughter; it was a love of all humanity.

Kinuko's thoughts were suddenly disrupted by a voice calling from the entryway. She recognized the voice and frowned. She had no interest in visitors or in talking with anyone, especially Mrs. Harada, who repeated gossip like a senile old woman, though she wasn't any older than Etsu. Nevertheless, Kinuko stepped into the front room, where she saw Mrs. Harada grinning broadly from the entryway.

"Sekihara-san," she said with a neighborly twang—part of her technique of extracting news from one family and passing it on to the next. "A few days ago, didn't you get some registered mail?"

"Yes," said Kinuko, with a tone that implied, "So?"

"Was that the red paper for your husband?"

"Yes," answered Kinuko, feeling sickness spreading through her stomach.

"Congratulations," said Mrs. Harada. "My guess was right. I've been away for a few days, and when I came home just now, my husband told me to ask you if it was really the red paper, because he wants to arrange a send-off party, even if your husband isn't a local recruit. My husband says no man should go off to fight without a send-off party, local or not."

"Mrs. Harada," said Kinuko firmly. "Please tell your husband not to bother. We've been here less than a month. We don't deserve such an honor. But please tell him we appreciate his kind consideration."

To her surprise, Mrs. Harada didn't press harder.

"Well, my husband will be disappointed, but I will tell him that. I'm sure our neighbors want to at least congratulate him. When is he leaving?"

"Very early tomorrow morning," Kinuko promptly answered. "So please don't bother to tell anybody. He still has many things to do this evening."

Kinuko bowed as deeply as her stomach allowed, hoping Mrs. Harada would understand that this was the end of the conversation. But Mrs. Harada stayed on to offer any help that Kinuko and Etsu might need after Giichi left. And then before Kinuko knew it, the visitor sat down at the edge of the front room and began reciting the tragic stories of the sons and husbands from Samurai Mansion Street.

"The Sasakis' oldest son died in Guadalcanal three years ago, and Mrs. Sakurai and Mrs. Kobayashi both lost their husbands, and their official death reports came on the same day. Ever since, they've become inseparable. They do everything..."

Kinuko shifted nervously, wanting her to leave. She didn't doubt that by this time tomorrow, Mrs. Harada would be darting through the neighborhood talking about Giichi's crime and how his wife declined the offer of a send-off party without a hint of shame. She felt a peculiar urge to tell Mrs. Harada that Giichi was going to refuse conscription; that he was going to risk his life for peace rather than for the war that caused the numerous tragedies she continued to drone on about.

"Mrs. Harada," Kinuko finally said. "I don't mean to be rude, but I have to start cooking for my husband. He has been planting vegetables all day, so he must be hungry by now. I'm sorry."

The smile left Mrs. Harada's face, but Kinuko didn't care. She hurried to the kitchen and hastily cooked a meal, her mind racing with the thousands of words she wanted to say to Giichi. Yet when she finally sat down at the table with him, she hardly spoke. Afterward, Giichi went out to the garden again and didn't come back into the house until it was completely dark. By then, Kinuko had prepared a bath with more water than usual.

While Giichi soaked in the bath, Kinuko laid a futon mattress in their bedroom and spread a clean sheet over it. She had washed the sheet earlier in the morning, and it smelled of the sun as she smoothed it with her palms. She smoothed it until her palms grew warm, then neatly tucked its sides under the mattress, before placing two pillows side by side and finally the top futon over them. When the bed was prepared, she sat in front of the small mirror on the desk, let her hair fall loose, and began combing it.

Giichi came into the room, wearing the clean *yukata* she had washed that morning. His black sash was crisply tied around his waist. His hair was wet and neatly combed. "That was a nice bath," he said with a pleasant sigh. He approached Kinuko and stopped behind her. He lowered himself to kneel and wrapped his arms around her shoulders. Their eyes met in the mirror, and Kinuko lowered her gaze. "I'll take a bath now," she said, feeling again the finality of his departure. Giichi stroked her hair for a while and silently helped her to her feet.

When she came back from her bath, Giichi lay in the futon with his eyes closed and his hands clasped under his head. Kinuko went to the mirror quietly and found an envelope next to it. On the envelope he had written her name. She touched it but did not open it, and began combing her wet hair.

"You smell good," Giichi said. Kinuko turned and smiled, trying to hide the sadness that grew deeper by the minute.

While she stood and turned off the light, Giichi held the top futon open for her, stretched out his arm, and placed it under her neck as she lay beside him. He stroked her shoulder. She felt her body stiffen and her heart pound fretfully as if for the first time. They lay beside each other silently in the darkness, smelling the scent of each other's skin. Kinuko felt a tautness in her throat. Then Giichi turned toward her and breathed deeply with his nose pressed against her hair. With his right hand, he untied her sash and began stroking her stomach. "Is the baby moving?" he whispered. Kinuko guided his hand to the side of her abdomen where the baby usually kicked. "You have to stay still," Kinuko told him. They waited quietly for a few minutes until the baby began kicking. "It's moving," Kinuko said. "Can you feel it?"

"Yes—yes, I can." Giichi whispered. "Yes, it's moving—Akira, his name will be Akira. Is that all right with you?"

"Of course," Kinuko nodded, "but what if it's a girl?"

"Akiko—light. It's time for light. I was thinking that out in the dark garden. The world has been too dark. So I want to name the baby Akira or Akiko."

"Akira, Akiko," Kinuko whispered, looking into the dark. "I like the names."

They waited a few more minutes with their hands clasped together on Kinuko's stomach. When the baby didn't move again, Giichi's hand left her stomach and began untying his sash. Kinuko shifted toward him and helped him separate the front of his *yukata.* For a while, all she heard was the quiet rustle of their *yukatas* slipping aside to bring their bodies closer together. Giichi pushed the soft pile of her *yukata* across her back and pressed his lips against hers, his hand stroking her bare skin. Kinuko arched her back, and grasped his neck. Then she ran her hand down his body, along his hip, felt him and guided him into her. Giichi moved gently, though his heart felt like a drum pounding against her. Despite her wish to forget about tomorrow, the familiar feel of his skin and the connection of him inside her brought a sorrow deeper than she could remember. Tears began streaming down to her pillow. As her sorrow intensified, so did her desire for Giichi. She immersed herself in the deepest unity of soul and flesh as they moved together, and in the end, she didn't know which part was her soul and which part was body. All she knew was that she kept repeating, "You must come home, promise me, you'll come home."

"I will," Giichi groaned. "I will try."

CHAPTER 27

On the morning of April 17, Giichi arose at dawn and sat down to meditate on the floor of the room at the southwest corner of the old samurai house. That room remained unused most of the time and smelled slightly of mildew in the chilly early morning air. Through the shoji doors, he could see the simple rock garden. Though neglected now, it had been built by Kinuko's grandfather during the Meiji Era as a place of meditation. Feeling it appropriate to be in this room on the morning of his departure, Giichi adjusted his posture. His back was straight and his hands lay relaxed on his knees. He began breathing deeply to empty his mind of fear and sorrow, of desire and attraction to this world, of the many scenes of his life that drifted through the vision behind his eyes. He sat for about an hour, unmoving, unthinking, until he could feel the first light through his closed eyes. He opened his eyes slowly and saw that the light had turned white on the screen doors. He lingered there for several more minutes, thinking of the brief segment of his life that had taken place in this house. He then slipped out to the garden one last time.

Beyond the bamboo grove, the sun rose, brightening the hazy fog that hung among the leaves. It was so tranquil that even the sparrows were scarcely awake. He began walking along the rows, carefully observing each plant. He watered those that appeared too dry and pulled the weeds that had already begun growing here and there. When he came to the bare end of one row in which he had planted the radish seeds, he was surprised. They were already coming up, barely above the soil. According to the book he had read, the germination time of radishes was three to twelve days. He hadn't expected to see them before he left. They were so tiny and fragile that they could be mistaken for specks of weeds. Giichi squatted down for a closer look and found them amazing. It seemed as if they were proclaiming their lives by breaking through the soil determined to grow. Gazing at the tiny specks of life gave him the same exhilaration as when he placed his hand on Kinuko's stomach and felt the baby move. It warmed him; he considered it a good omen to see them on the morning of his departure. He felt it symbolic—this combination of the seeds, the baby, the light, which would be the meaning of the baby's name. He walked around some more, picking up rocks and adjusting the trellis for the morning glories.

Then at seven, he went into the house, took a bath, and dressed in a white shirt and dark blue trousers. On the table was the meal Kinuko had prepared for him: a bowl of rice, steaming miso soup, eggs, slices of pickled radish, all on fine porcelain dishes. Kinuko busied herself, placing food on Giichi's serving dish and filling his teacup often, all the while avoiding his eyes. Giichi tried his best to eat, until he absolutely couldn't. He apologized, putting down his chopsticks. "It was very good," he said.

After helping her carry the dishes to the sink, he sat again and read the morning paper. Kinuko had made him promise to carry on as normally as any other morning. The night before, after their lovemaking, she told him she didn't want him to say or do anything special or different, and that when he had to leave, he should walk out the door without saying good-bye, as if he were going on an errand and would be coming home a few hours later.

At nine, he put down the paper and walked to the entryway. While he was lacing his shoes, Kinuko came to the front room. Feeling her eyes on his back, he began trembling. Once again, he tried hard to remember the things she had asked him not to do—no good-bye, no hugs. He stood and picked up the bag she had packed the day before, including Yuki's drawing.

"I'm going," he said.

Kinuko bit the inside of her lip. "I want you to know," she said, tears now streaming down her face, "that I'm very proud of you."

Giichi moved forward, forgetting his promise. He let go of his bag and hugged her. "Thank you," he whispered, burying his nose in her hair. "I'm proud of you, too—I will be back. I promise."

"Go now," said Kinuko, gently struggling out of his arms.

Giichi picked up his bag, and quickly wiped his tears with the back of his fist. He stepped through the gate and walked out onto Samurai Mansion Street.

CHAPTER 28

The instant Giichi disappeared from view beyond the gate, Kinuko ran into the south room, gasping for air. She rolled the shoji door open to the side court, sat down on the floor and breathed deeply. Her whole body throbbed with fear for the torture that might be inflicted on Giichi's flesh, the warmth of which still remained on her own. She didn't know how long she sat there, but when her struggle for breath eased slightly, she began to realize how badly she had misjudged the severity of this moment.

For months she had maintained hope that this time might never come, yet she could not avoid moments of imagining what it would be like. And as she had imagined, she now clung to a thin blade of hope that Giichi would survive, but the pain that had gripped her chest surpassed anything she had ever experienced before. She had not foreseen the chastising effect of that pain, the way in which it so clearly revealed the gap that stood between her and Giichi. Like an artist who studies a technique and understands it and then discovers she cannot execute it, Kinuko felt that all of her newfound understanding and agreement with Giichi's decision had come to nothing. What had separated them all along was not his coldness or her frustration, but the quality of their souls. While Giichi accepted his decision with quiet resolve, she showed her agreement with it through anger and pride—shouting at her mother, desiring to throw Giichi's decision in Mrs. Harada's face, feeling joy at her ability to make Mr. Hayashi cringe, even hoping her baby would die. She recalled that once she had accused Giichi of not taking this matter seriously, and now she knew that it was she who had not taken it seriously. If anyone could survive the ordeal ahead, Giichi could; that should never have been questioned. What she questioned now was whether she had the strength of spirit to survive. Giichi had spent years, perhaps his entire life, preparing for this moment, and she had foolishly thought she could reach such a level of understanding in only months.

Kinuko finally stood, suddenly longing for Mrs. Chiba. She tottered through the house as if an invalid, looking for paper and pen, before remembering they were in the drawer of the desk in the south room. She arranged them on the desk, hoping that writing to Mrs. Chiba might summon her friend's tranquil and comforting presence. But she could not move her hand to write and didn't know what to write anyway. She sat inert, barely aware of the passage of time. At one point, she heard the back door open and close, and some part of her mind thought it must be her mother returning, but she could not respond.

Only later, when Mr. Harada's voice boomed from the entryway, was she able to lift herself from the painful mist of self-loathing and grief.

"Mrs. Sekihara! Mrs. Sekihara!"

Kinuko rose from the desk, shuffled into the front room and found Mr. Harada pacing angrily in the entryway. As soon as he saw her, he began wagging his finger. "That hu—husband of yours," he stammered, "is such a—such a disgrace to our neighborhood. People are already laughing at me. Oh, he is from—he is from Harada's neighborhood. That's what they are saying. And you, you are Judge Higashino's granddaughter. Who would think of investigating your husband? This is a disgrace. You know what they are saying, the other neighborhood chiefs? They are saying that I was negligent!"

Harada stomped on the entryway floor, while Kinuko sat expressionless in the front room.

"No wonder you declined my offer of a send-off party. Shame on you!"

"That was very nice of you, Mr. Harada," Kinuko managed to say. "I thank you on behalf of my husband."

"Thank you!? That's all you have to say? You and your husband betrayed me. Why, you betrayed the whole neighborhood. Actually, the whole country."

"I'm sorry, but we didn't mean to betray anyone."

"Sorry? You can say that a hundred times. But what about my reputation? I'm the one who suggested a background check for all newcomers. Outsiders like you and your husband have flooded Sasayama. Now they're all laughing at me. How can I—"

"Mr. Harada." Kinuko heard her mother's determined voice. "Excuse me for interrupting," Etsu continued as she entered the front room and sat erect next to Kinuko. "But I must mention that what my son-in-law has done is neither your fault nor my daughter's—"

"Mother," Kinuko interrupted. "This has nothing to do with you, please let me—"

"I understand your anger, Mr. Harada," Etsu continued, "but would you please leave my daughter alone? She is already devastated by this, as you can imagine. If my son-in-law has done wrong, the courts will punish him. That's why he is in jail right now. So please—"

"As for you, Mrs. Nakamura," Mr. Harada sneered. "I have been very generous excusing you from the bamboo spear training. But it's about time for you to resume your duties as a citizen. You should be at the school grounds at nine o'clock sharp tomorrow morning."

Harada clicked his heels together, pivoted abruptly and left.

"That would be my pleasure," Etsu answered, then bowed, even though he had already stepped through the door.

Kinuko remained sitting, unable to fully grasp the meaning of the incident. She heard her mother say, "I'll take you back where you were." Kinuko stood like a sleepwalker and shuffled along, supported by her mother.

"I'll be in my room," Etsu said, "if you need anything."

Kinuko nodded and knelt on the floor, slowly realizing that the unstoppable aftermath of Giichi's decision had already been unleashed. There would be much disgrace; it had already started with Harada, and the worst of it would fall upon her mother. She hoped she might find even a fraction of her mother's strength. She lifted a pen, willing herself to carry on with her life, but all she could write was "Mrs. Chiba." The image of Giichi stepping through the gate flickered behind her eyes. She put the pen down and curled up on the floor in a fetal position, wondering how many days or months or years she would have to endure this pain. She wished she could die and after a while realized she could at least sleep.

Suddenly, Kinuko heard a thud above her head, and then another. As she pushed herself up from the floor and looked toward the ceiling, she heard yet another thump against the roof and a sound like a rock tumbling down along the roof's incline. Then silence. In a few moments, she heard the opening of a door and the sound of Etsu's footsteps hurrying to the main door. Harada, Kinuko thought, it must be him.

She stood, unable to bear the hostility against her mother, and stepped out to the corridor. Then a sharp pain gripped her lower abdomen, and she dropped to the floor, holding her womb.

"Kinuko!" Etsu rushed to her side. "What's the matter?"

A deep protracted moan rushed from her lips, and Etsu held her shoulders. "Oh, Kinuko," she uttered.

"It was Harada, wasn't it?" Kinuko said through gritted teeth.

"Don't worry about that. I'll go get the midwife right away."

Etsu helped her back into the room and placed a cushion beneath her head. Another rock hit the roof. Etsu held Kinuko's hand. "I already locked the main door," Etsu said. "Don't go near the window. I'll go out the back door."

"I'm sorry, Mother."

"Don't worry. I'll have Mr. Nakano come over. Everything will be fine."

Left alone, Kinuko settled into the rhythm of her new pain and, in between, thought of Giichi, feeling it strangely apt to suffer the pain of giving birth to his child on the day he had to go away.

Sometime later, Etsu returned, and in the early evening, Mrs. Makita, the midwife, and Mr. Nakano arrived. For the next ten hours those three voices and the occasional thumping of rocks drifted at the periphery of her pain...

"It has to be Mr. Harada."

"Don't worry, I'll stay here tonight, said Mr. Nakano. "Tomorrow I'll talk with the police superintendent."

"How can he do that at a time like this?"

"Just relax and breathe deeply."

At the end of that tunnel of voices and pain emerged the light—Akira, the name suggested by Giichi. Kinuko heard the baby's cry, followed by Etsu's excited voice. "It's a boy, Kinuko, it's a boy."

Kinuko smiled weakly, watching the midwife bathe and dress the baby, barely able to stay awake after two sleepless nights. Nevertheless, she noted his long fingers with their tiny pink nails and toes curled tightly at the ends of his angular feet. He was small—only 2.3 kilograms, almost a kilo less than Yuki weighed at birth. But perfectly formed, Mrs. Makita announced, and Etsu agreed vigorously. Kinuko closed her eyes and drifted into clouds of fatigue.

When she awoke, the room was bright, and she found Akira next to her. The midwife was gone, but Etsu was still sitting beside her, staring at the baby with relief and fascination. Kinuko wrapped her arms around Akira and gazed into his face. She saw how much he looked like his father—the broad forehead, deep-set eyes, and high cheekbones. Etsu stroked the baby's head with the tips of her fingers and then brushed a strand of Kinuko's hair from her brow.

"His name is Akira," Kinuko whispered. "That's what Giichi wanted to name a boy. He said we needed light, as the world has been too dark—I want Giichi to know Akira is born."

"I was just thinking that," Etsu said. "I'll go to the police station this morning and ask them to inform him. There shouldn't be any reason they can't tell him about the birth of his son."

Bathed by the light seeping in through the shoji doors, her mother's face glowed with hope, so different from the illness and disappointment that had etched her face until now.

Kinuko reached out her hand. "Thank you, Mother," she said. "I couldn't have done this without you."

"You are my daughter," Etsu said, taking her hand. "I just did what mothers do for their daughters. I'm very happy you have such a beautiful baby. Now sleep."

Two weeks later, May arrived with clear bright skies and bursting foliage that only increased Kinuko's longing for Giichi. All she knew of him was that he awaited transfer to Osaka from a basement cell in the Sasayama Police Station. He was allowed no contact with the outside world. Her mother and Mr. Nakano had pleaded with the police superintendent, their childhood friend, to keep Giichi in Sasayama and at least allow him letters from his wife. But according to Etsu, some foolish charges about a communist complicated Giichi's case, and for that reason the superintendent couldn't make any concessions; though he did agree to convey the news of Akira's birth. Kinuko hoped thoughts of his son would give Giichi more strength to survive, while she herself couldn't seem to rise above misery, even in Akira's presence.

Each morning, as his hungry cries awakened her, she felt the day looming ahead like a mountain too high to climb. She lingered, floating in thoughts, first of Giichi and then Yuki, until finally Akira's persistent cries forced her out of bed. She often heard her mother pacing nervously outside the door, obviously worrying about her new grandson. Yet Etsu never accused Kinuko of neglecting Akira or complained about the disgrace that had fallen upon her because of Giichi. Nor did Etsu comment on the editorial in the *Sasayama Shinbun News* that condemned Giichi's crime and called for his execution. When Etsu had to go out on errands, she held her head high. She also seemed unbothered by the rocks still occasionally thrown against her roof, even after the police superintendent, at Mr. Nakano's request, arranged a patrol three times a day on Samurai Mansion Street.

Eventually, her mother's stoic demeanor and unspoken understanding helped Kinuko develop a growing sense of perseverance. She began by writing to Mrs. Chiba to report Giichi's arrest and Akira's birth. Mrs. Chiba would likely be shocked, but writing helped release the long-held burden of keeping a secret from her best friend. Then she wrote to Ichiro and Sumiko, who only knew what Etsu had told them in a telegram sent on her behalf. She also wrote to Yuki, knowing her grandparents would read the letter to her.

Yuki,

Thank you so much for your lovely drawing of the chicken. How happy Papa and Mama felt when we saw it! We love it so much that we wish you could draw some more. We are very proud that you can write your name now. Grandpa and Grandma told us that you have been a very good girl in Okayama. That made Papa and Mama very happy, although we miss you and wish we were there with you. Mama is very well, though I'm a bit tired from having a baby. Remember that Mama had a big tummy? Now the baby is out of my tummy, and his name is Akira. Isn't that a beautiful name? Right now, he is still very small, and all he does is drink Mama's milk just as you did after you were born. But by the time the war is over, and you, Papa, Mama, and Akira are together, he will be old enough to play with you, and I'm sure you will be a kind sister to him, and he will love you so much, just as Papa and Mama do. Grandma Nakamura was very sick, but she is well now and sends you her love. Papa and Mama hope you continue to be a good girl. Please say hello to Ume and your new friend. Will you send us another drawing, maybe of some flowers in Okayama?

Love, Mama and Papa

When she thought of her daughter, probably doing well in the safety of rural Okayama, Kinuko knew she could no longer dwell on her sorrow. She felt ashamed that she had allowed weeds to cover many of the plots Giichi had tended so diligently. Though even looking at the garden still gave her great pain, she knew she must continue the work he had started with such love.

The day after writing letters, Kinuko awoke early to feed and bathe Akira. Then she left him with Etsu and ventured out to the garden in monpe pants and a wide-brimmed straw hat. Along the north fence, the persimmon trees bore soft leaves, and the fragrance of the succulent greens of the tomato, eggplant, and green bean plants filled the air. She first walked between the rows, admiring Giichi's work. She saw him everywhere and felt his hidden touch beside every plant, some of which had already grown knee high.

When she pulled Giichi's gloves over her hands, she found them molded into his shape. They reminded her of his hands, the same hands that stroked her body the night before he left, and tears began falling from her face and dotting the caked soil. Though the gloves were too big, she decided to wear them anyway; it felt like Giichi's hands were covering her own. She wiped her tears, stooped down, and began pulling weeds. Sensing the soft yielding tug of the earth, she felt as though he were with her. She worked for several hours, and from that day on, work in the garden became part of her daily schedule.

Each morning more weeds seemed to have poked from the ground than the day before, but she immersed herself in the task, moving slowly along the rows with a bamboo flat beside her. When the flat was heaped with weeds, she carried it to the corner of the garden and emptied it onto a growing mound of compost. Then she stood for a moment in the cool shade of the grove and stretched from side to side before returning to pull weeds once again. Mid-morning, when Etsu brought Akira, she sat on the veranda and nursed him. Always she returned to the garden. It became her sanctuary, a place to sweat and remember and think and hope. At night she slipped into her futon and willed herself to sleep before the sorrow of Giichi's absence could invade her.

In mid-May, before Kinuko's letters could have reached Okayama, a parcel came from Sumiko. It contained a set of red and black carp streamers—symbols in honor of Akira's first Boy's Day, though it was already past May 5, the day for that celebration. Nevertheless, Mr. Nakano, who stopped in the evening, cut a bamboo tree in the grove and erected it at the edge of the garden after Kinuko tied the streamers to the top of the pole. At ten o'clock the next morning, Kinuko watched the streamers swim in the breeze, while Akira nuzzled at her breast. Again, she thought of Sumiko's letter. She had already read it three times and remembered it by heart.

Dear Kinuko,

Father and I are elated to hear that you have a healthy baby boy. And we know Giichi is as well. My heart breaks when I think about how much he must want to see his son. Enclosed are the streamers I found in our storage house. They are a bit tattered as they were bought for Father when he was born! We also used them when Giichi was a boy and we wished for him to be healthy and to grow into manhood and to be able to swim like the streamers in the unlimited sky, unbeaten by the wind and weather. So, I thought Akira deserved the same celebration of Boy's Day, even though the times are bleak, and his father is gone. I hope you get the package in time, but these days, nothing seems to work as it used to. It must be difficult for you with Giichi gone, but you are a strong woman, Kinuko, and Father and I believe that you will make it through his absence. In fact, all of us need every bit of our strength to get through these difficult times. Let us hope all will be well in the end, and in the meantime, we all must believe that Giichi will come home once the war is over.

Yuki is well and excited about her little brother. She asks me many questions about him, such as how big he is, what he looks like, how many times he eats, if he can play yet and so forth. She sends her love to all of you.

By the way, Father applied for a travel pass to come to Sasayama giving the reason of a family emergency, but we still don't know whether it will be approved. Recently, as you might know, railway authorities began issuing passes for civilians who need to travel in an emergency. But nobody seems to know exactly what the definition of an emergency is, since someone who needed to travel for a relative's funeral was rejected while another who wanted to visit his healthy daughter somehow received a pass. According to Genkichi, some give food to officials as a bribe for passes. But even if you have a pass there is no guarantee that you will be able to board the train you choose. Often it never arrives, and when it does arrive, it's too full to board. Needless to say, the railway situation is a mess, and so is everything else. So don't keep your hopes high. We will keep you posted. Best regards to your mother.

Love, Mother

Kinuko kept watching the carp streamers swaying in the soft breeze. She understood Sumiko's hopes and sorrows because they were her own. She wondered what it would be like when Akira was an adult, twenty or thirty years from now. She couldn't imagine what the world would be like then but hoped it would be a peaceful place. Feeling Akira at her breast, she shuddered at the thought of him following the same path as his grandfather and his father. But she didn't want Akira to go to war, either. This little baby of hers was born amid such pain, and yet he filled her with so much love. She couldn't bear the thought of anything taking him away from her. The Sekihara men before him had suffered enough. She felt certain she could endure no more.

She began to think of Ichiro's visit. The last she had heard from him was his reply to the telegram sent the day after Akira was born. He said he would come as soon as possible. At the time, she doubted he would be able to leave Okayama, but now it seemed there was hope. How wonderful it would be to show Ichiro his grandson thriving despite his father's absence. She knew Ichiro would love to see Akira even though he would not be able to see his own son. She remembered how Ichiro demonstrated his strength during Giichi's previous incarceration, and how his presence helped her stay strong. She needed to feel that again—to be with someone who loved Giichi as much as she did and who understood and accepted his decision without question.

A few days after the streamers came from Okayama, Akira turned one month old. Etsu, planning a traditional celebration, took all of her rationed sugar to a cake maker and asked him to make celebration cakes. She had been saving the sugar for months, ever since Kinuko told her of her pregnancy. Kinuko was apprehensive about following the custom. She thought it unlikely the neighbors would show respect for the birth of a draft-resister's son, but Etsu insisted on a proper celebration for Akira's one month birthday.

The first thing in the morning, Etsu went to the cake maker to pick up the cakes, and marched onto Samurai Mansion Street carrying Akira in the formal baby kimono she had sewn months in advance. Kinuko admired her mother's fortitude, but as she followed along with the boxes of cakes, she feared the reaction they would elicit from the neighbors. One by one they stopped at the doors of the five nearest neighbors, where Kinuko handed a pink cake and a white cake to whoever came to the door to greet them. To her surprise, every family except the Haradas invited the three of them into their entryway and fussed over Akira, who slept through the whole affair. Deprived of anything sweet for many months, they didn't hide their elation over the cakes and thanked Etsu and Kinuko profusely when they left. At the Harada home, only Mrs. Harada came to the door. She acted cordial and seemed elated to have cakes, but she didn't bother to call her husband and only nodded acknowledgement of Akira.

When they returned home, Etsu bounded through the house with more energy than Kinuko had seen since coming to Sasayama. "You see," she said to Kinuko, "the war hasn't destroyed our humanity. All it takes is a baby, new life, to bring it out."

Kinuko wanted to believe her mother was right but she couldn't shed the worry that had hung over her since the cold reception at the Haradas', and a few days later, her apprehension proved warranted. She was in the garden, when she heard her mother's frantic footsteps coming out through the back door.

"Kinuko," Etsu called in a strange blend of whisper and shout. "Akira is crying for food and Mr. Harada is at the door with a policeman."

Kinuko looked up and frowned. "A policeman?"

"Mr. Harada is talking about the sugar," Etsu said. "Please, Akira is crying."

Etsu hurried back to the house, and Kinuko followed her, peeling her hat from her head. In the kitchen, she quickly washed her hands and rushed to the room where by now

Akira was screaming. She opened her blouse and lifted him to her breast, and listened intently to the conversation in the entryway, her heart pounding with anger.

"You have been saving sugar since last October?" Harada said. "How can I believe such a preposterous story?"

"Yes, since I learned of my daughter's pregnancy. I value tradition and customs. I had planned to ship it to her, but luckily, we both ended up in Sasayama."

"I don't believe such nonsense, sugar rations are less than two kilograms per year."

"I don't have a sweet tooth, Mr. Harada."

"Just tell me where you got the black market sugar."

"Nowhere. As I told you, I've been saving it for months."

"Anyway, it is my duty to have the police search your house. If we find anything suspicious, sugar or anything else, I'll have to turn you and your daughter in. Both of you!"

"As you wish," replied Etsu. "We have nothing to hide." Her voice was dignified, with no hint of panic or dread, but Kinuko seethed with anger for neighborhood chiefs and the war that allowed them to abuse their authority. She could barely control herself and felt her heart pounding against Akira's little body.

She heard Etsu lead Harada and the police officer through the corridor and into the kitchen. Her mother's footsteps sounded unruffled as if walking into a tearoom. Soon a clatter of kettles and pots and pans erupted from the kitchen, accompanied by the rough opening and slamming of drawers and hutch doors. Kinuko abruptly pulled Akira from her nipple, and Akira immediately screamed, but Kinuko ignored him. She laid him on the bed, buttoned the front of her blouse and stood.

Etsu suddenly appeared at the door. "What is the matter with Akira?"

"Why are you allowing this to happen?" Kinuko hissed.

"Calm down," said Etsu. She stepped into the room and knelt down beside Akira. "Your milk doesn't flow well when you are upset." She gently lifted Akira, and Kinuko stepped toward the kitchen.

"Don't go," said Etsu, with a voice so firm Kinuko sat down like a reproached child.

"It's not fair," Kinuko blurted.

"Nothing is fair," said Etsu, rocking Akira. "There is no use arguing with them."

"But they don't have to tear up our kitchen."

"They don't have to, but they will."

Akira quieted in Etsu's arms, and she cooed at him, "When all around is darkness, the only way to live is to keep ourselves free from darkness. Don't you think so, Akira?"

The clatter continued for several minutes then suddenly stopped, replaced by Harada's stomping in the corridor. Etsu quickly handed Akira back to Kinuko and hurried out of the room. Akira yelped again, and Kinuko quickly pressed him against her breast so she could hear what Harada said.

From now on, I'll have to keep a very close eye on you. After all, your son-in-law is a draft evader, the most unpatriotic criminal! How can I trust you and your daughter, even if you are the daughter of the Higashinos and a cousin of Furukawa?"

Harada's angry footsteps and those of the policeman faded toward the front room, then out into the entryway.

"Good day," Kinuko heard Etsu say from the front room.

Trying to release her anger, Kinuko sat as patiently as she could while Akira worked at her breast. When he was finally satisfied, she changed his diaper, and carried him into the kitchen, where Etsu calmly lifted a pot from the floor, slid it into the cupboard, and then bent to lift another. She thought of Toda and Konno tearing her house apart and of her anger toward Giichi then—all the wasted anger; she had much to learn. More than ever, she hoped Ichiro would visit, and she began to picture him holding Akira, telling her of Yuki, walking in the garden.

CHAPTER 29

Immersed in darkness, Giichi lay on a futon in a windowless cell in the basement of the Sasayama Police Station. After eighteen days of solitary confinement, these few minutes after he awakened and before he reached full consciousness had become his most pleasant. He could almost believe that he was anywhere—in his parents' Osaka home as a child or lying next to Kinuko in Ashiya or Sasayama. At seven o'clock the naked forty-watt bulb blinked on, revealing the unevenly patched, white clay walls that encased him. He rubbed his eyes, then rolled from the dingy futon and crawled to the wall to scratch his nineteenth mark. He found his previous eighteen fingernail scratches surrounded by scores of others, along with scuff marks from fists and feet, and long stripes of four parallel lines, the lashing out of fingernail marks from frustrated hands.

He lifted his hand to make the mark but lowered it, wondering how many more scratches he would have to make. What if he had to make hundreds more? Already the monotony was pushing him toward insanity. Every day here was the same. The light came on at seven in the morning and went out at ten in the evening. In between, the jailer brought three identical meals—a gluey mass of barley porridge and a stale cup of tea. He even urinated and defecated at the same time each day, when the jailer led him to the lavatory at the end of the hall after breakfast and supper.

Prisoners came and prisoners went. In the beginning, he had leaned against the metal grate of his cell door to watch the comings and goings and listen intently to the conversations shouted into the hallway, only because he needed to hear human voices. Eventually he lost interest in their conversations, and their voices became a nuisance. Hanging from the metal bars like monkeys, they either laughed at disgusting jokes or retold the desperate or proud acts that led to their incarceration—the theft of chickens or vegetables or shoes or a bicycle. Now, Giichi kept his grate closed and sat against the wall in his gray uniform or paced in his cell—five steps forward and five steps back or twelve full steps around his futon.

Only once had he been given reading material, a copy of the *Sasayama Shinbun*, the town's weekly newspaper that had dwindled to two pages due to the shortage of paper and ink. As he scanned the top page, Giichi immediately noticed the article announcing his arrest. It mentioned that he was the town's first known draft evader, and specifically mentioned that he was linked by marriage to two of its most revered former leaders—Etsu's father, Judge Higashino, and her first cousin, Shozo Furukawa, one of the town's legendary mayors. Trembling with agony at the thought of Etsu and Kinuko facing constant shame, Giichi moved on to the editorial below the article.

"Sasayama has long been known as a town loyal to the Emperor and as a town that welcomes visitors with open arms. Now both of those qualities have been disgraced by a visitor who refuses to stand in defense of his country. We cannot tolerate such an unpatriotic act. He should be severely punished. In fact, this man should be sentenced to death. Our country faces a crucial moment in its history. Its fate wavers in the balance. If this man is let off with a mere prison term, where would the justice be for those brave men who have died for our country?"

Giichi wadded the paper into a tight ball and threw it into the corner. He slumped on the futon and, glaring at the ceiling, wondered if the police superintendent had ordered that the paper be delivered to him so he might reconsider his decision to refuse induction. It made sense. After all, on the morning of his second day in jail, when the superintendent came to his cell to report his son's birth, he also raised the issue of his decision.

"The baby was named Akira, as you wished," the superintendent said.

Giichi stood quietly, stunned by the news. Kinuko's due date was weeks away. Only two nights before, he had felt the baby moving inside her. Now Akira lived among them as a separate being. "Are they both well?" he finally managed to ask.

"Yes, that's what your mother-in-law said. Congratulations," the superintendent replied before quickly changing the subject. "The Osaka Police want to investigate your case there, and I cannot argue over jurisdiction with them." Then he paused. "I have known your mother-in-law since we were children and I sympathize with her greatly. I wonder if you might reconsider your decision in light of your son's birth and the great pain this will cause your mother-in-law. I would be willing to write a letter of excuse for your tardiness, so you could still report to the regiment in Osaka without repercussions."

He paused again before adding, "You now have a son. Do you still refuse to go to war?"

"I appreciate your consideration for my mother-in-law," said Giichi, still absorbing the news. "But—yes, my decision will not change."

The superintendent sighed. "All right—then I'm sorry to say that you'll have to wait here until the Military Police come from Osaka—I'm sorry to say."

"When are they coming?"

"I'm not certain. It could be a week, maybe less."

With that, he turned and walked away. As the sound of his footsteps moved toward the stairway, Giichi suddenly called to him. "Please. Would you ask Mr. Nakano to tell my wife that I am very happy about the birth of our son? And—and that I'm doing fine?"

"I shall do that," Giichi heard him say.

Giichi never saw the superintendent again, but for days afterward, he continued to hear the diminishing echo of his footsteps and grieve over the lost opportunity. If he had agreed to go to war, he could have gone home to see Akira before leaving for Osaka to join the regiment. But it was too late. Though Akira was less than two kilometers away, he might as well be on the other side of the earth.

As each day melted into the next, his worries about the missed opportunity and about how Etsu and Kinuko were being treated gradually settled at the back of his mind. He established a routine of meditating after breakfast and daydreaming in the afternoon, when he allowed images to rise from the past, most often fixating on the last moments of his time with loved ones—Yuki waving to him from the doorway as he left for the tram station where Toda detained him, Ichiro touching his shoulder and telling him he would see him in Okayama, and, the most vivid memory of all, Kinuko telling him she was proud of him the morning of his departure. That was the image he held the dearest, and yet whichever scene he played in his mind like a motion picture, it always ended with the same question: will I ever see them again? That question wrenched his gut and shredded his heart.

The morning of the nineteenth day, as he squatted with his hand poised, debating whether he wanted to make another mark on the wall, he heard the jailer unlock his cell door.

"You're going to Osaka," the jailer announced. "An officer of the Special Higher Police is waiting upstairs." He placed the food tray on the floor, and beside it some fresh clothes and toiletries from the bag Kinuko had packed for him. "You'd better hurry."

A sudden, peculiar excitement rushed through Giichi's body. He quickly ate the porridge and gulped the tea, and then peeled off the stale jail uniform. He splashed water over his body, shaved and brushed his teeth. When he finally slipped into his own clothes, he felt human again, and his excitement grew wilder. At that moment, he didn't care where he was going, so long as he could get out of this place—this boredom and darkness—even for a few hours. Trembling inside, he let the jailer handcuff and shackle him.

On the main floor of the police station, the officer from Osaka waited in front of the counter—mid-forties, tall, with mustache and hard eyes. A tough, seasoned Special Higher Police officer. He scrutinized Giichi with a glance and then looked down at the release paper that lay on the counter.

"We need your thumbprint here," the officer said. "It's just a formality. We have to get going- the train's coming."

Giichi squinted at the paper, blinded by the light from the windows after the darkness of the basement. Finally, he made out the words, and realized he was being sent to the Minato Ward Police Station, which he thought had been destroyed by the Osaka bombings in March.

"Is this where I'm going?" he asked.

"Technically, yes," answered the officer. "Hurry up, will you?"

The officer lifted Giichi's cuffed hands, pressed his right thumb against the red ink pad, and then against the paper below Giichi's name.

Minutes later, Giichi sat in the back seat of a black car parked outside the building, dizzy from the natural light. On the floor in front of him rested the bag of belongings he hadn't seen since his arrest. He thought of Yuki's drawing, but ignored the bag, knowing he wouldn't be able to look at it without crying. The car moved from the curb and began threading through the morning pedestrians. When they passed the post office, Giichi looked intently through the window to find Mr. Nakano's rice shop. To his surprise, he saw Mr. Nakano in his shop, facing the street, and his heart began to pound. Mr. Nakano stepped from the shop and waved to him. But the car passed his shop so quickly, he had no time to wave back. He turned to see Mr. Nakano run out to the middle of the street and nodded through the back window. Mr. Nakano nodded many times in return. Giichi kept looking through the back window until the car turned from the familiar main street.

Giichi settled back in the seat, his heart pounding with fresh guilt. How could he have forgotten Mr. Nakano and all the others who meant so much to him? How could he have allowed himself to be so selfish?

Giichi turned to the officer. "Where am I really going?"

"Abeno Prison," the officer replied, looking straight ahead, his elbow resting at the base of the window he had rolled down.

"Abeno Prison?" Giichi repeated.

"The jail was bombed," the officer said. "You should know better than to ask questions."

Giichi sat with his mouth shut, squinting at the shops grazing past the window. Soon the car left town and sped over dusty country roads. He noticed a carp streamer swimming high in the air above the back yard of a farmhouse and thought of Akira—his first Boy's Day. His son would be eighteen days old today. Giichi averted his eyes and looked straight ahead. After twenty minutes, the car stopped in front of the Sasayama Railway Station—an old one-room building at the base of a mountain. The officer stepped from the car, walked around to Giichi's side and helped him onto the street.

"Don't forget your bag."

Giichi leaned back into the car and grabbed his bag with his cuffed hands.

The officer led Giichi into the station, where a train waited along the platform. All of the passengers pushed into one car; off limits signs were tacked next to the doors of all the other cars. Giichi's shackles clanked on the concrete platform, and the passengers turned to watch him shuffle along. A departure bell began shrieking and echoed through the covered platform. The officer tugged harder at Giichi's chains, causing Giichi to move with short quick steps like a Kyoto woman hurrying through an alley on a cold winter day. He felt humiliated.

When the train edged away from the station, Giichi suddenly panicked. He realized that while he had escaped the stifling basement cell and now felt the warmth of the sun, he was moving farther from his family. He might never see Kinuko or Yuki or his parents again; he might never see Akira. With cuffed hands, he grasped the window ledge and pressed his nose to the glass pane, staring intently at the platform as if Kinuko might actually be standing there with Akira in her arms.

"Get away from the window," the officer ordered. Then he checked to see if Giichi's handcuffs were securely locked and squatted at his feet to tighten the shackles. Giichi continued to search the platform. The officer stood and clapped his hands together. "First class," he announced, glancing around the cubicle and frowning at his apparent joke.

Soon the train reached full speed, and Sasayama's low wooden station disappeared from Giichi's view. His heart was still pounding, but now more from bitter resignation than from anticipation. As the train moved farther from Sasayama, Giichi wearily scanned the compartment. It struck him as a place for train engineers in need of rest. A few tattered magazines and an old newspaper drooped from an overhead shelf, and a gray smock and dented aluminum flask hung from a hook on the wall. A metal ashtray, attached to the wall below the window, overflowed with cigarette butts and reeked of stale tar. Overriding the smell was the oppressive odor of coal smoke seeping through the closed window. He peered across the hall, where a faded curtain hid the opposite cubicle.

The officer took a startlingly shiny cigarette case from his back pocket and thrust it at Giichi. "Want one?"

Out of politeness, Giichi accepted. The officer struck a match and lit Giichi's cigarette then his own in cupped hands. He inhaled the first puff deeply and released the smoke in one protracted exhalation, glancing at Giichi through the veil of smoke. The disdainful burst of smoke reminded him of Toda, and he quickly looked down from the officer's stare. Giichi took in a shallow puff and coughed, immediately regretting having accepted the cigarette. It was humiliating to smoke with his hands cuffed together, and his head began spinning from the sudden intake of nicotine.

"Listen," said the officer, suddenly leaning forward. "I'll tell you what."

Giichi coughed again, shook his head, and looked at him with watery eyes.

"It's not too late. You can still save yourself and your family. I'll take you straight to the Tenth Regiment. No questions asked. Everything will be fine. I've already checked with the chief regiment officer. He said they wouldn't hand you over to the military police." He took another puff from his cigarette. "How does that sound?"

Giichi looked out the window, recalling the dull insanity of the cell he had just left. The officer leaned closer. "Think about it. With your education, you'll be a unit commander right away. On the other hand, Abeno Prison is one of the worst, a very tough place. Besides, the war is nearing its end. Perhaps you'll come back alive. Go to war instead of ruining your life. If I were you, I would go to war, with a wife and two children, one just born."

"How did you know?" As he asked the question, Giichi wondered what impelled all of these officials to attempt to change his mind. Was it a hopeful sign of spiritual resurgence? Were elected officials and even military personnel beginning to see the error of the nation's path? Or was it something more practical and still just as hopeful? Men who saw the war coming to an end and exhibiting kindness because they could not predict who they might be taking orders from in the future?

"I know everything about you," the officer said, dispelling Giichi's hope with typical arrogance.

Giichi stared at him.

"Well, think about it, your family, your wife and mother-in-law. They are already in trouble—terribly disgraced. The neighbors are even throwing stones at them."

"Is that true?" Giichi gasped.

"Of course, what did you expect?"

"Who told you that? The superintendent?"

"Listen. It's my job to gather information. It's not your business to know where it comes from."

Ashes fell from Giichi's cigarette, and awkwardly he tried to stub it out in the ashtray. The officer grabbed the cigarette from Giichi's hands and snuffed it out for him. Giichi stared out the window, his hands dangling between his thighs.

"Have you been listening?"

Giichi turned to him again and was surprised to see a flicker of sincerity in the officer's cold eyes. "Why?" Giichi said, "why do you care if I go to war or not?"

Now the officer turned to look out the window. He remained silent for a moment, his cigarette burning between his fingers. He began slowly, still looking out the window, "You know, I've been doing this for more than twenty years—but recently I've begun to wonder about what I've done in my life, chasing after 'thought' criminals, day after day and—oh, forget it."

He abruptly crushed his cigarette in the ashtray and stood up. "Think it over," he said. "You have two hours, the Tenth Regiment or Abeno Prison."

A few minutes later, the officer returned from the lavatory, buttoning his fly. "I need some sleep," he said, holding onto the doorframe of the cubicle to keep his balance against the swaying of the train. "Couldn't sleep at the inn. People were having a send-off party. The boy was only seventeen years old, a volunteer for the Navy. Even a boy that young is willing to serve and die for the country."

He shook his head, then stepped into the compartment to check Giichi's handcuffs and shackles before moving across the aisle and settling on the bench in the opposite compartment.

Giichi's head began spinning with anguish. He had known that Kinuko and Etsu would face dishonor but never considered that they might be in physical danger. Even while he was in the Ashiya Jail nothing like that had happened, and the neighbors on

Samurai Mansion Street didn't seem capable of throwing rocks at women for a crime they didn't commit. Then he remembered the newspaper editorial, and he imagined Kinuko and Etsu huddled together in the house, holding Akira between them, unable to get onto Samurai Mansion Street, unable to run errands or go for food. Suddenly, anger flared up inside him, and he threw a sharp glance across the aisle. He wanted to ask what the Sasayama Police were doing to help Kinuko and Etsu and Akira, but the officer appeared to be sleeping—his head drooped over arms, his body bouncing limply with the motion of the train. Below the officer's right elbow, Giichi noticed a pistol strapped in a leather case. He wondered if the officer was really sleeping. His mind began racing. Escape seemed possible. He could grab the pistol, order the officer to remove his handcuffs and shackles, jump from the train, and run back to Sasayama to protect them. It was all so bizarre, unlike anything he had ever thought, but now it seemed real and possible. His heart pounded with anticipation, as if he actually waited for the moment to pounce. They weren't that far from Sasayama, they had left only half an hour ago. Then, more logical thoughts sifted into his mind. He could run, he could make it to Sasayama, then what? Sooner or later, he would be arrested again and thrown right back into jail. The punishment would be even harsher, most likely death by hanging. He settled back into his seat; still, he couldn't keep from staring at the pistol. Without thinking, Giichi suddenly stood up, his heart beating crazily. Immediately he found his shackles were so tight he could barely move. After a few shuffling steps, he stumbled and reached out with both hands to keep from falling. The officer jumped from his seat, his hand flying to his pistol. "What now?" he bellowed.

"I—I have to go to the lavatory," Giichi stammered, leaning against the wall for support.

He grabbed Giichi's arm roughly, led him down the corridor, pushed him into the lavatory, and remained there, holding the door open. Giichi's shackled hands shook and he wet his trousers, feeling as if hundreds of bees were buzzing in his head. Back in the compartment, the officer demanded, "Where did you get the idea of going to the lavatory without telling me?"

"You were sleeping."

"Don't talk back. You've got a lot to learn, wherever you end up going, the military or Abeno Prison. You talk back once and you're in big trouble. You try something like that again and I'll shoot you. Do you hear me?"

For the next hour, the train passed through a series of tunnels. They rushed into darkness and emerged just as quickly into light, over and over again, while Giichi's mind wavered just as dramatically. One moment he saw a stone striking Kinuko's head and a gaping bloody wound, and he thought he should go to war to spare her the pain. He would be a unit commander, Etsu would be proud of him. The war would end soon. He would come back alive. Then the next moment he was convinced that the officer was lying, it was only a trick. Why would a Special Higher Police officer, who had spent his life torturing thought criminals, suddenly have a change of heart and help a draft evader? None of the neighbors would throw stones, not Mr. Machida or Mr. Sakata or Mr. Ishibashi or Mr. Harada.

Then his mind would reverse itself again. Maybe Mr. Harada. He could see that skinny man, with his shirt buttoned from neck to belt, throwing rocks. There was something dark about him. But no, even he would not. It had to be a lie. And even if it were true, Kinuko and Etsu were proud, strong women. Defeat wasn't in their blood. Together, they would carry on. And Mr. Nakano would be there with them, always. Mr. Nakano had verified his support by going into the street and nodding to him as he passed in the police car. Mr. Nakano wouldn't let anyone throw rocks at Etsu's family. He knew the superintendent of the Sasayama Police—his friend, a reasonable man, a classmate. A reasonable man would never turn his back on innocent women.

The wavering would not end. Just as his resolve settled on Abeno Prison, his thoughts went back to the beginning. He saw Kinuko running away from a mob, blood streaking her face. What about Akira? She might have to take him to a doctor, and a stone might hit him, even if Kinuko protected him. Giichi gasped. Yes, he should go to war, if that would stop the stone throwing. He had to think about his family, he had to be a father. He couldn't ignore his son's suffering after having given him life—his own flesh and blood. The officer was right. Go to war, come back alive, and watch his son grow.

When the train slipped from the last tunnel, Giichi saw the Sanda Plain sprawled in the sunlight. He closed his eyes and thought of the vast distance that now separated him from Sasayama. This was the moment. For years, he had been in anguish over the war; for months, he had avoided Kinuko, tormented by this decision; and now he must finally decide. He had one last chance. After a few minutes, he began to feel as if his soul were rotting. His father had taught him many things, but above all, he taught him to follow his heart, and what his heart told him now, as it had always told him, was that he couldn't be part of this war, of any war. Giichi remembered the smell of the Japanese cedars in the ruined castle in Sasayama, their uninterrupted, straight trunks and their hard bark that reminded him of an inviolability he couldn't resist or deny. That was where his soul belonged. Even if he died in Abeno Prison, he would feel satisfied when he breathed his last breath, smelling the cedars. Someday, Kinuko would understand. If a stone killed their son, she would hate him forever. Yet she would understand while lying in her deathbed, breathing her last breath, because she was the woman he loved.

The last remnants of doubt vanished. Giichi turned away from the window. He would stay in Abeno Prison and learn to accept life there—he would play out his destiny. No. He would not go to war. Definitely. Absolutely.

When the train stopped at Amagasaki, the last station before Osaka, the officer awoke, went to the lavatory, and returned to sit across from Giichi, as the train began to move again. They chugged through the ruined city—charred trees and electric poles, chunks of darkened concrete and rusty metal littering the streets, burned out shells of homes and factories. Both of them gazed through the window in silence.

"What did you decide?" the officer suddenly asked.

"I'm not going to war."

"Hmm," he sighed. "Be prepared. You should know you're going to one of the toughest prisons in the country."

Soon the train rumbled over the Yodo River and into Osaka. The landscape looked no different than Amagasaki, another dead metropolis, like the surface of some barren world. But it was the home of Abeno Prison and the newest site of Giichi's destiny. He thought of Kinuko and then of his father, and hoped for the strength to survive.

CHAPTER 30

By the beginning of June, Kinuko realized she wasn't producing enough milk for Akira. At each feeding, he suckled contentedly for a few minutes, and then no matter how hard he struggled and whined at her breast, the milk wouldn't flow. After two days of Akira's frantic wails, she took him to Dr. Okawa, who told her she needed to switch to bottle feeding.

"But baby formula hasn't been available for months," he said. "You'll need to use goat's milk."

As a prescription, he wrote a note to a local shopkeeper who sold goat's milk brought in by village farmers. Kinuko hurried to the shop with Akira in her arms, realizing she would have to pass the Sasayama Police Station, which she had avoided since Giichi's arrest. But today she had no choice; her baby was hungry. She kept her gaze straight ahead and hurried past the station without looking at it.

On the way home, though, she walked more slowly, relieved by the supply of goat's milk she carried. When she approached the police station, her heart beat faster at the thought of being close to Giichi. She stopped and looked at the station's open door. Compared to the Ashiya Police Station, Sasayama's wooden building was much smaller and less intimidating. No one moved in or out of the doorway. Only a single bicycle leaned against the wall near the door. Suddenly, she thought of meeting the superintendent her mother and Mr. Nakano had talked about—their childhood friend, a decent man. A decent man, she decided, wouldn't refuse to tell her how Giichi was doing and that was all she wanted to know. She looked at Akira in her arms. He might start screaming at any moment, but at least for now he was sound asleep.

Kinuko stepped toward the door with trembling legs. At the reception desk, she gave her name and asked for a meeting with the superintendent. She waited with her heart beating wildly at the thought of being in the same building with Giichi. Soon, the receptionist returned and pointed to the door he had just come through.

As Kinuko stepped into the room, a man Mr. Nakano's age stood up, with a hint of sympathy behind his broad smile. "You are the granddaughter of Judge Higashino," he said.

"I'm Kinuko Sekihara, the wife of Giichi Sekihara," Kinuko said and bowed.

"Oh, yes, yes, please have a seat."

With another bow, Kinuko sat on the chair in front of his desk and settled Akira on her lap. The superintendent leaned forward. "Oh, so this is the baby you had recently. Congratulations."

"Thank you. I appreciated that you conveyed the news of his birth to my husband."

"No problem at all. He seemed elated with the news."

"I'm glad to hear that."

"And how is your mother doing?" the superintendent asked.

"She is doing very well, thank you. She told me that you went to school together."

"Yes, Mr. Nakano and I were in the same grade, and your mother was a year behind us. I'm sure she has told you I was a rascal."

"No, not at all."

"Anyway, I'm glad your mother is well."

Then he clasped his hands on his desk, looked down, and shook his head. "I'm sorry I still haven't heard from Osaka. I don't blame you for wanting to know where your husband is. It's been almost a month, hasn't it?"

Kinuko blinked. "Osaka?" she said. "Is my husband already in Osaka? I thought—I thought he was still here."

"I'm sorry, I thought you knew. Didn't Mr. Nakano tell you your husband was no longer under my custody?"

She felt suddenly cold, recalling how harshly the urban police had treated Giichi only a few months ago. She understood why Mr. Nakano had chosen not to tell her. She tightened her arms around Akira and tried to compose herself before finally asking, "What day exactly was he transferred?"

"On May fifth," the superintendent answered. "I remember that day because it was All Boy's Day. Of course, we have the official record, as well."

"And you still don't know where he is?"

"I'm afraid not. The officer from the Osaka Special Higher Police is supposed to send us the information, but he hasn't yet. He didn't even know where he was taking your husband at the time of his release."

"Why? Why didn't he know?"

"I wish I could tell you, but according to the officer, one thing that's complicating your husband's case is his alleged connection with a communist, and the other is the shortage of prison facilities after the March bombing of Osaka. All I know at this moment is that he is under the custody of the Osaka Special Higher Police. Officially, he is being detained by the Minato Ward Police, but I know that station no longer exists. By now they should know where he is. I'll write a letter of inquiry."

Akira stirred, and Kinuko stood up. She could think of nothing more to ask. The superintendent stood up, repeating, "I'll write a letter of inquiry. And I'll let you know as soon as I hear."

"May I ask how he was when he left?"

"I didn't see him when he left, but later I received a report saying he was in good health."

Kinuko hastily thanked the superintendent for his time and left his room with a bow.

By the time she stepped out of the police station, Akira was screaming. She stopped and gently rocked him before she began walking again. Despite his continued cries, she felt strangely calm. She doubted the Osaka Special Higher Police would bother to tell a small town police superintendent where Giichi was actually detained. Even if they did, they wouldn't allow her to visit or write. Giichi was already beyond her reach. For the first time, it occurred to her that she must prepare for life without him. She would still wait for his return, she would still hope, and she would keep worrying about him and agonizing over his future. But in this moment it seemed possible for her to live her own life, just as Giichi had chosen to live his own, no matter how difficult it was for him to leave his family behind. As she told the superintendent, she had her own name. She wasn't only Judge Higashino's granddaughter, or Etsu's daughter, or Giichi Sekihara's wife. There must be a part of her that belonged to herself only. Akira screamed again, and she stepped up her pace, feeling as if she were in a hurry to find that unique part of herself.

When Kinuko arrived at home, Etsu immediately took Akira from her, grabbed the bottle of goat milk from Kinuko's bag, and then announced the arrival of a telegram from Okayama. "It's in the south room," Etsu said.

Kinuko hurried to the south room, picked up the small tri-fold paper from the desk and opened it to see the familiar *katakana* teletype. "TRAVEL PASS CAME THROUGH WILL ARRIVE 0612 5 PM FATHER" Kinuko ran to the kitchen, where Etsu bustled around, starting a fire to pasteurize the milk and cajoling Akira, who lay in a bassinet on the floor. He was furious by now, his face contorted and red, mouth open as wide as it could stretch. Kinuko picked him up and cuddled him. "Listen! Your Grandpa is coming!"

"Is he really?" Etsu turned, pouring the milk into a pan. "That's wonderful!"

"He's coming June Twelfth." Kinuko paced, bouncing Akira on her shoulder. Her mind danced with excitement.

"We will have to start cleaning the house," Etsu said.

"Maybe we should have him stay in Grandfather's room. He loves to meditate."

Kinuko realized it had been a long while since she had felt this happy. Actually, she had rarely smiled since the January night when Giichi told her of his decision, and even for several months before that. And now, five months later, Giichi had followed through on his decision, and she didn't even know where he was. So why was she feeling this way?

She wondered which Giichi would prefer—to imagine his family well and maintaining a normal life or miserable because of his absence. If she were in his position, she would want to believe her family was happy instead of grieving every minute of her absence. Faith in the happiness of their family was probably the greatest gift anyone could hold during the darkest time of their life.

"Akira," Kinuko said again. "Grandpa is coming. We'll have a good time, won't we? Yes, we will."

"Kinuko," Etsu called, washing the pan she had used to heat the milk. "We will have to start thinking about how to get food for his visit."

Etsu sounded nearly as excited as she felt, which dispelled a worry Kinuko had carried during the weeks since they first became aware Ichiro had applied for a travel pass—her mother obviously held no animosity toward Ichiro for Giichi's decision. Kinuko wondered how her mother could accept everything so easily. Probably because of Akira, she thought, recalling Etsu's words on Akira's first month birthday: the war hasn't destroyed our humanity. All it takes is a baby, new life, to bring it out. For the next ten days, Kinuko and Etsu kept happily busy. Each morning, Etsu got up early to fetch milk for her grandson. Kinuko made another trip into town in the early evening. Three mornings a week they attended the bamboo spear training, with Akira tied to Kinuko's back, but even that didn't bother them. Meanwhile, they cleaned the house from corner to corner, looked for farmers who could sell them vegetables, and contacted amateur fishermen who might have some extra fish.

Mr. Nakano reacted to the news of Ichiro's arrival with pure joy, almost like a child anticipating an approaching holiday. He said he would bring a plump chicken and offered to pick up Ichiro at the train station.

"I never dreamed of meeting Ichiro Sekihara in my life," he said. "It would be a great honor to meet such a famous author."

Finally, the day arrived, and Kinuko began worrying about Ichiro's safety. Bombing in Hanshin had become an everyday occurrence, and according to the radio, the last two days' bombings had been especially intense. All day, amid the flurry of last minute preparations, the image of bombs falling on the shipyard repeated itself at the back of her eyes like a newsreel. The grief she felt for Mr. Chiba simmered to the surface of her mind, and triggered her longing and concern for Mrs. Chiba. Though she had written to her friend three times, she had yet to hear from her during the three months since they left Ashiya. It wasn't like Mrs. Chiba not to write. Kinuko began to imagine the worst and puzzled Etsu with her sudden somber mood.

Suddenly, Kinuko heard the clatter of Mr. Nakano's truck approaching and forgot all of her worries. She ran to the front room and heard the voices of Ichiro and Mr. Nakano near the gate.

"The same truck Giichi-san rode in," said Mr. Nakano, "when we went to the village to buy chickens and seedlings together. It's getting too old but it still runs."

"Yes, it does run, and it was a great treat to have you meet me after that crowded train ride," Ichiro said. "I thought I would have to take a bus from the station."

Kinuko ran to greet them. "Father!" she cried.

"Kinuko!" Ichiro said and took her hands.

"Father!" she repeated. Then she choked.

"All right, all right." Ichiro tried to calm her, though tears welled in his eyes. "You look very well. I'm glad. I'm so glad—by the way, where is Akira?—well, I have to say hello to your mother first, don't I?"

Just as he said that, Etsu called from the front room, "Welcome, Mr. Sekihara." Kinuko led Ichiro into the entryway, and Mr. Nakano followed.

"How nice to see you again," Etsu said with a bow and a smile.

"It's very nice to see you, Mrs. Nakamura."

"It's been a while since we last saw each other."

"Indeed. It was at Yuki's second birthday, if my memory is correct."

After a few minutes of cheerful greetings, Etsu urged him into the house and led the two men to the family room, while Kinuko carried Ichiro's luggage to his room.

Kinuko returned, carrying Akira in a bassinet, just as Etsu seated Ichiro and Mr. Nakano for tea.

Ichiro immediately jumped up. "Oh," he said. "That must be my new grandson."

Etsu said, "Your grandpa has come all the way from Okayama."

Ichiro quickly picked him up and smiled at him.

"You haven't met me yet, but I'm your Grandpa," he said. Akira looked up at Ichiro and blinked. "I'm your Grandpa," Ichiro repeated. Akira smiled.

Kinuko started laughing. "He normally cries for food the minute he wakes up, but today he seems to know how to welcome his grandfather properly."

"He does, indeed," Ichiro exclaimed, before gurgling at his new grandson. Akira gurgled back, and everyone burst into laughter.

Ichiro paced through the room, rocking Akira at his chest. "He looks just like Giichi at that age. It's amazing. I feel as if I've been thrown back thirty years and I'm holding Giichi."

Kinuko's heart momentarily ached at the thought of Ichiro lovingly holding his son thirty years earlier, and now none of them knew where Giichi was or how he was doing. Nevertheless, she joined the fuss and soon took Akira from Ichiro. While she held Akira and fed him, Etsu served tea, and eventually their conversation moved from Akira to Ichiro's treacherous railway journey—a carriage packed with people hanging from doorposts and even windowsills.

"It's was a mess," Ichiro said, sadly shaking his head. "But I got here in one piece. That's all that matters."

Kinuko and Etsu and Mr. Nakano nodded eagerly. When the teacups were empty, Etsu suggested that Ichiro take a bath.

"You must be exhausted after such an awful trip."

"That sounds like a good idea, Mr. Sekihara," Mr. Nakano said. "I must take this opportunity to go back to my shop. Otherwise, I'm afraid I will never leave." "No, Mr. Nakano," Etsu protested, "You must stay for dinner."

"I'll come back some other time," Mr. Nakano said. "You have much to talk about."

As Mr. Nakano backed toward the door, Ichiro thanked him several times for the ride and said he hoped they would see each other soon.

"Certainly," Mr. Nakano replied. "I'll come even if you don't invite me."

They all burst into laughter again.

Later in the evening, over dinner and more tea with the dried persimmons Etsu had preserved the previous fall, their conversation continued. They talked about everything and everyone—Yuki, Sumiko, Giichi's escape from the bombing in Osaka, Ichiro and Sumiko's lost house, the bombing in Kobe that changed the course of Kinuko and Giichi's travel, Etsu's illness, Akira's birth. For Kinuko, the evening seemed too short, after so many lonely ones.

Kinuko rose early the next morning and saw Ichiro standing in the middle of the garden. The house was quiet as Etsu and Akira still slept. As she stood at the shoji door and watched, Ichiro walked slowly between the rows, stopping here and there to study the vegetables, his hands clasped behind his back. Unlike the night before, he carried an aura of sadness. When he came to the end of a row, he stopped and gazed into the bamboo grove, as if searching for his son.

Kinuko put on her shoes and stepped out into the garden. As she approached him, Ichiro turned around. "This is quite an undertaking," he said.

"Yes, I never suspected Giichi would be good at this kind of work, but he certainly taught me. You can't imagine how hard he worked to prepare the ground and plant all these vegetables."

"Well, he doesn't do anything halfway. Once he decides on something, he does it all the way. That's him. Don't you think?"

"Yes," Kinuko answered. "Just like you, Father."

"I suppose," Ichiro replied, and though she had meant that as a compliment, she sensed that somehow he seemed troubled by the thought. As they began walking through the garden and its rich earthy aroma, Kinuko couldn't help herself from pointing out each plant and explaining what it was.

After they completed the circuit, Ichiro stopped and turned to her. "Tell me, if you don't mind, how Giichi looked when he left."

"Very calm—just as he had been every day. He left as if he was going out for an errand."

Those words brought back the image of Giichi walking out the door so vividly that she felt momentarily dizzy. As she lowered herself beside the tomato plants, she felt Ichiro's hand on her shoulder. "Thank you, Kinuko," he said. "That's all I wanted to know. And I feel very proud of you. I know how difficult this must be for you, but—"

"I'd been wanting to see you so much—and you finally came."

"How could I not come?"

Kinuko stood and began walking slowly, and Ichiro followed.

"Father, Giichi is already in Osaka. He left Sasayama on May Fifth."

Ichiro was silent for a moment. "That doesn't surprise me, but where in Osaka is he?"

Kinuko turned and shook her head weakly. "Even the officer who took him from Sasayama didn't know where they were taking him."

"I'll stop in Osaka to see the officer. At the very least, I want to know where he is. Don't you?"

"Of course I do, but please don't. It's getting more and more dangerous. Even your passing through Osaka worries me. I just don't know what I would do if something happened to you. Let's just wait to hear from the superintendent."

Ichiro was silent again before he finally said, "All right, I'll write to the Osaka Special Higher Police after I get back to Okayama, though I doubt they'll reply. But I want to try, at least."

During breakfast, Ichiro suggested that some plants needed to be staked, and offered his help. "The rainy season is coming soon, and after it's over, it will be too hot for you to do it alone, Kinuko."

Kinuko was elated and explained that Giichi had already split bamboo trees to make enough stakes. After ten o'clock tea, despite Etsu's protests that she would feel uncomfortable having her daughter's father-in-law work in the garden, the two ventured out, Ichiro wearing Giichi's work clothes. Kinuko, as usual, wore a white cotton blouse and baggy monpe pants. Together, they staked the fifteen-meter rows of tomatoes, eggplants, and green beans. Ichiro pushed a bamboo split into the soil, and then while Kinuko held the split and the stem of each plant, Ichiro tied them together with reeds of straw. The taller plants required two or three supports. The task was much harder than Kinuko had expected, but Ichiro surprised her. Despite his inexperience with farming, he worked with vigor, yet handled each plant gently, taking time to avoid crushing leaves to the stake and making sure each plant stood straight. His careful work reminded her of what Giichi had once told her about his father. Though a novelist by trade, he had a deep respect for the land and what it produced. After all, he was a son of the land, born into a village family that had thrived in the countryside for centuries. If his father hadn't become a writer, Giichi said, he was certain that he would have become a farmer. As if to prove the truth of his son's words, Ichiro worked for hours, telling Kinuko to rest whenever she felt tired. But the weather was perfect and the fragrance of the young vegetable plants pleasant, and they kept working side by side. She moved with him from one plant to the next, feeling a quiet glow of appreciation, not only because he helped her, but because of who he was, the father of Giichi, the grandfather of Yuki and Akira, and her father-in-law, and even more, a great human being she respected and loved.

When they finally stopped, she noticed the sun going down behind the roof. She stood watching the pink hue blending into the pale blue sky. Ichiro stood beside her, also watching the sky and rubbing his back. "How beautiful," he said. "I've never seen the sky so beautiful."

The next day, they tackled the weeds that had cropped up while Kinuko was busy with preparations for Ichiro's arrival. Keeping the same pace, they worked along a row, Kinuko on one side and Ichiro on the other, the fragrance of soil cool and deep between them. Compared with the staking of the previous day, the work was less laborious, just stooping and pulling. The simplicity of the task allowed them to talk more than they had while staking. Ichiro talked about his childhood, which Kinuko knew little about, and explained that he had yearned to leave his village and see the world, but the world he discovered wasn't a very kind place. As an aspiring writer, he lived a very poor existence, he said and then laughed. "To this day, I still don't like *udon* because I ate it every day in those times."

Kinuko told him of her childhood, too, about the times when her family visited Sasayama in the summer, about the death of her father, and her mother's suffering as a widow. "That was why I vaguely sought an independent life rather than marriage, before I met Giichi."

Kinuko suddenly fell silent, enormously missing her life with Giichi, yet realizing she had completely lost the portion of her mind that sought independence, buried beneath everyday life—child rearing, household chores, and the war. "But," she continued, "I recently realized that I hadn't known what being independent really meant. I married Giichi, then foolishly thought he was responsible for my happiness. I suppose that was one reason I was devastated when he first told me of his decision."

Ichiro listened quietly, nodding, his hands steadily pulling weeds, while she continued.

"I also didn't realize there is love beyond ordinary love, beyond the love between husband and wife, or parents and children. I thought he didn't love us enough, but now I know he has an enormous capacity for love. He loves not only me and Yuki and Akira but all of mankind. Compared with what I've thought of love, his love is much larger, immeasurable—I learned a lot after Giichi left."

Ichiro still remained silent. Kinuko looked up and saw tears falling from his eyes, while his hands still pulled weeds. She had never seen him cry like this. Kinuko squeezed between the tomato plants. Ichiro stumbled up and they embraced.

"Oh, I miss him so much, Father—"

"I know, I understand—I miss him so much I almost lost the strength to keep living."

"Father—"

"But you gave me the strength—you and Akira."

They stood as they were, their mutual love and longing for Giichi melting together with the scent of the damp earth all around them.

Mr. Nakano came that afternoon, which delighted Ichiro. Kinuko and Etsu sat with the two men, sipping tea while Mr. Nakano related the history of Sasayama to Ichiro. For centuries, Mr. Nakano explained, the town had thrived as an important crossroad to Kyoto. Before the Shogun Era, Sasayama often became a victim of the warfare fought between warlords of larger territories. At such times, whoever ruled the basin fiercely defended the region against attacks from the outside. Still, Mr. Nakano continued, the samurai code did not ignore the possibility of surrender. If enemy warriors surrounded the basin, the highest-ranking samurai was obliged to dispatch a mission on horseback to the enemy camp to surrender. Members of the mission expected to be taken hostage and knew that they, and even their families, would be killed if their master betrayed the terms of surrender. "But that was the samurai code of conduct, the spirit of samurais," Mr. Nakano added.

"I wish our military followed that code," Ichiro said.

"I do too," Mr. Nakano answered. "What is happening now is akin to being trapped in the basin surrounded by warriors, our weapons and able bodies and food and medicine running out—just waiting to die."

"That is a very good example of our nation's situation, unfortunately," Ichiro responded.

There was a short silence, before Mr. Nakano abruptly changed the subject with a joyful tone.

"How would you like to drive around the basin on Sunday? I can show you some historic landmarks, if you don't mind my clattering truck."

"How wonderful," Kinuko said to Ichiro, "that's what you need instead of working in the garden every day."

"I like working in the garden," Ichiro said, but Kinuko saw the glee in Ichiro's face as he accepted Mr. Nakano's invitation. It warmed her to see him so happy.

Two days later, when Kinuko and Ichiro walked out to the garden for their usual weeding session, they discovered that some of their carrots and *natsudaikons* had been stolen from the ridges closest to the bamboo grove. Footsteps were visible in the upturned soil where the thief had pulled the vegetables—some that would have been no larger than Kinuko's thumb.

"This is very common in town now," said Kinuko, looking at the bare part of the ridge with sadness. "It happened a few days before you came, too. They took snow peas and *endo* last time. Mr. Nakano offered to fence off the grove with wire, but my mother doesn't like the idea very much. She's afraid it would ruin the view of the grove, which I more or less understand."

"I don't blame her," Ichiro said. "I myself have grown fond of the view."

"But I want to keep some vegetable for us and take the rest to the temples."

"Temples?"

"Some local temples keep elementary school children from the city. They arrived with their teachers last summer and are starving so badly they can't even learn."

"That's a very good idea, Kinuko. But I suppose you have to go along with what your mother thinks for now. If more vegetables are stolen, your mother might change her mind."

"I know everybody is starving, but I would rather give vegetables to those children."

"I understand. I would do the same, if I were you."

At ten o'clock, they went to the veranda to drink tea with Etsu as they had done each morning since Ichiro's arrival. Ichiro held Akira clumsily and fed him from a bottle, and the three talked idly as if the war did not exist, about the weather and the garden and Akira, his steady weight gain and the way he slept so soundly when he was full. Kinuko cherished these moments. She felt the bond between Ichiro and Akira with great satisfaction and admired the green hues of the garden and the bamboo grove beyond and the scent of the green perfume. She credited Ichiro for bringing her this peace and didn't want to think about the fact that he would soon leave.

The night before Ichiro was scheduled to go on a tour with Mr. Nakano, Kinuko finished sewing a shirt for Akira in the family room and stood up, thinking about going to bed. A clock struck ten somewhere in the house, and then she heard something land hard against the roof. Not Mr. Harada again, she thought with a frown. It had been weeks since he had harassed them and she hoped there would be no incidents while Ichiro visited. As she feared, she heard Ichiro stomping to the entryway. She followed his footsteps and when she reached the front room she saw him rushing out the main door. "Father," she called, but Ichiro didn't seem to hear and disappeared into the dark frontcourt. She stepped down to the entryway and strained her ear at the door. Soon she heard the side door of the gate close and Ichiro's hurried footsteps coming back.

"Kinuko," he said. "Did you hear anything?"

"Yes," she said. "It's Mr. Harada, the neighborhood chief, throwing rocks onto our roof. It has been going on since Giichi was arrested. But it's nothing to worry about; you should be getting to bed."

Then another stone rattled on the roof and tumbled slowly down to settle in the soft soil at the base of the house.

"That is not acceptable," Ichiro said.

"You're right, it isn't, but it hasn't happened much lately. We thought he might have stopped."

"Have the police been notified?"

"Yes, both Mother and Mr. Nakano spoke to the superintendent."

"And nothing was done to stop him?" demanded Ichiro.

"Policemen patrol the street, but it's a long story," said Kinuko wearily. "We just don't care anymore."

"I do care," Ichiro insisted, "when someone throws rocks at your mother's house and you and Akira are inside. Tell me."

Kinuko nodded, and then led Ichiro into the family room, where she explained the whole story. She described Mr. Harada and how he had lost face, adding that according to Mr. Nakano, he was a small-minded man who wouldn't harm anyone directly but was capable of doing something petty such as throwing rocks at their house.

"Is he short and skinny, bald with little strands of hair across his head?" Ichiro asked.

"Yes, have you met him?"

"I saw him the other day when I went out for a walk. He came out through his side door and glared at me. Then he asked me who I was, so I just said I was a visitor to Mrs. Nakamura. I thought he was odd, but just bowed and walked away."

"Yes, that's like him. It's nothing to worry about. Mr. Nakano offered to fix the roof before the rainy season."

"I can do that while I'm here. But I still don't like this."

"Mother and I don't like it either, but there isn't much we can do except be careful going in and out through the gate. That's another reason my mother doesn't want to fence off the bamboo grove, so we can still go out that way."

Ichiro rubbed his face, deeply troubled. "But it's happening less and less?"

Kinuko nodded. "You have to get up early tomorrow, you should get to bed."

The next morning, Kinuko got up earlier than usual to pack lunch for Ichiro and Mr. Nakano. She padded to the lavatory and noticed that the window at the end of corridor had been opened a crack. Wondering why, she peered through it and held her breath. In the faint dawn light, she saw someone leaning over the garden. The next second, the chickens began squawking and she saw Ichiro jumping over the rows, heading toward the man who now ran from the garden into the bamboo grove. Bamboo leaves rustled and shouts rose from the grove.

Kinuko watched and listened intently. Etsu came out of her room and asked, "What is it?"

"Shh—Father might have caught someone stealing vegetables."

They hurried to the back door. As Kinuko opened it, shouts rang from the grove. "Stop throwing rocks! Promise me...you are a neighborhood chief."

Kinuko and Etsu looked at each other with disbelief.

They heard Ichiro's bellowing voice. "Yes or no? You promise? Otherwise, I'll tell the police."

They stood speechless, huddling together. Eventually, Ichiro's dark form emerged from the grove. He stumbled toward them, his night clothes askew. "Are you all right? What happened?" Kinuko called. He nodded but didn't speak. As he drew nearer, Kinuko saw that he was breathing heavily, a sack dangling from his hand. When he reached the back door, he dropped the cloth sack on the landing between the kitchen and family room and slumped down. Inside the sack, Kinuko could see snow peas and soil-covered carrots.

"It was Harada," he gasped. "I told him to keep the vegetables, but he ran away."

"Why on earth would he have to steal vegetables?" Kinuko asked.

"The Haradas only have a tiny garden," said Etsu. "The creek runs right behind all of the homes on the other side of the street, and beyond that is a rice field."

"Still—" Kinuko protested.

"People don't have enough food, Kinuko," said Etsu. "People on Samurai Mansion Street don't want to tell anyone, but it's true. We're lucky because of Giichi-san."

Ichiro struggled to stand and Kinuko helped him to his feet.

"Your mother is right," Ichiro said, rubbing his back. "He must need food badly."

They stood in silence a moment longer and then Ichiro finally gathered his breath and added, "But it worries me. He promised he would leave you alone if I let him go. I had him by the collar, we wrestled for a while but I made him promise. I just hope he'll keep his promise."

When Mr. Nakano arrived later, Ichiro explained the events and said it would probably be better if he stayed home.

"I understand," Mr. Nakano agreed. "We should keep our eyes on him today."

Instead of a tour of the basin, the two men decided to fix the roof. Kinuko watched them climb up the ladder to survey the damage.

"Not so bad," said Mr. Nakano. "Tiles are chipped and loosened, but none are completely broken. We can fix them easily."

At ten o'clock, Kinuko called them down for tea. As soon as they settled on the veranda, Ichiro asked Mr. Nakano, "Do you think Harada will keep his promise?"

"I think so," Mr. Nakano replied. "He would kill himself rather than go to jail. He's probably pretty frightened right now. But I'll still talk to the police superintendent tomorrow. He doesn't have to arrest him, but he should know about this, just in case."

From that day on, Ichiro went to the gate every morning to survey the Harada house and then walked around Etsu's house and back to the grove. He did the same in the afternoon and again before going to bed. On the fourth day after the incident, the day before Ichiro's scheduled departure, he came back into the house with a crumpled newspaper in his hand and said he would stay an extra day.

"What is it?" Etsu asked.

"The *Sasayama Shinbun,*" Ichiro said.

"What does it say?" Etsu added.

Ichiro lifted the paper. The word "traitor" was scrawled across the front in Chinese ink.

"It must be Harada again," Kinuko said.

"Yes," Etsu agreed, "but let's ignore it. That's best. We can't react to such trifling matters."

"I agree with you in a way," said Ichiro, "but I am thinking about taking this to the police."

"I understand," Etsu said, "but I don't think they can do anything about it."

"Just as evidence," said Ichiro. "Even if they can't do anything about it, there is no reason you should keep quiet. I want them to know what he's been doing."

"I agree, Father," said Kinuko.

"You are probably right," said Etsu. "We'll have Mr. Nakano talk to the superintendent."

"I'll take this to Mr. Nakano then," said Ichiro, folding the paper. "I wanted to see his rice shop before I leave anyway, so this is a good chance."

When Ichiro returned from Mr. Nakano's shop, he told Kinuko he had sent a telegram to Okayama, explaining to Sumiko he would arrive home the day before Yuki's birthday, instead of two days before.

"I think it's best to keep an eye on Harada for another day," he said.

Luckily, Ichiro's last day passed peacefully. He went for a walk with Mr. Nakano early in the morning and after breakfast weeded in the garden. Kinuko protested, saying he should relax on his last day, but realized that working in the garden was his way of feeling a connection to his son. The rest of the day, he periodically went to the gate to check on the Haradas, but mostly played with Akira and packed.

Finally, on a soft mid-June morning, Ichiro stood at the gate, carrying in his suitcase Kinuko's letter to Yuki, a paper doll, and pressed flowers Etsu had prepared as a birthday gift. "I wish I could stay longer," he said, "but I promised Yuki I would buy her a windmill for her birthday."

Kinuko nodded. "She will be so happy to have you back. And if she is happy, I'm happy."

"I wish you and Akira could come with me, so you could be with Yuki again. Let's hope that day will be soon."

Ichiro put down his luggage and hugged his grandson one last time and held him against his cheek. "Be a good boy," he said. "Next time I see you, you'll be a big boy, won't you?"

Then Mr. Nakano's truck wouldn't start, and there was a flurry of discussion about what to do. In the end, Kinuko walked with Ichiro and Mr. Nakano to the bus stop, and then rode with them on the bus to the train station, while Etsu and Akira stayed behind. At the station, Ichiro pushed into the crowded train, and Kinuko waved to him, unable to believe how quickly the last ten days had passed. As the train began moving, Mr. Nakano yelled. "Please come again! We have to do the tour of the basin!"

"I will," Ichiro shouted back.

The train grew small in the distance and disappeared in Kinuko's tear-blurred vision.

CHAPTER 31

At six o'clock each morning, a whistle blasted from the speaker atop a guard tower at the Abeno Prison. Within seconds, the iron door to the solitary cell block was thrown open with a sound that reverberated through the concrete corridor, and Giichi awoke with familiar dread. Inside cell number twelve, he lunged from his grimy futon and frantically raced through his routine as the cold footsteps of the guard approached for morning inspection. In less than fifteen seconds, he folded his futon three times, shoved it into a corner, straightened his gray prison uniform, and opened the grate of his door. At Abeno Prison, Giichi had quickly learned that promptness was crucial to his survival.

The very first morning, even before he awakened enough to realize where he was, a guard unlocked his cell door, burst inside, and kicked him—first in the legs, then in the groin, then in the stomach. The pain came so unexpectedly, he simply tightened himself into a ball and writhed on the cold floor without uttering a cry. "At the whistle, open the grate and stand at attention!" the guard roared. Giichi wasn't allowed breakfast that morning, though his stomach ached so much he wouldn't have been able to eat it anyway. At lunchtime, another guard placed Giichi's tray at the opening in his door and then pulled it away as he reached for it, saying he had opened the grate too late. Before leaving, the guard whispered, "Watch out for Bowleg," and Giichi thought he might have found an ally, like the old guard at the Ashiya jail, but he discovered later that this guard was no ally. He, too, kicked and slapped inmates, only less severely.

Another part of survival, Giichi quickly learned, was a keen sense of hearing. He would press his good ear to the grate and listen carefully to the footsteps of each guard. Slight variations in the sounds of the footsteps told him which guard was approaching. When he recognized the staccato clack of Yamada the Bowleg's heels against the floor, his stomach muscles tightened, and he stood in a stiff military position, while the Bowleg's piercing eyes appeared through the grate and penetrated his cell. When his grate slammed shut and he heard Yamada clacking toward the next cell, Giichi deflated like a balloon as relief rushed through him.

On the third day, Giichi learned his survival would require not only promptness and keen hearing but constant attentiveness. After the bell announced morning free time and his cell door was unlocked, he hurried through the corridor, anticipating sunlight and fresh air. Out of the corner of his vision, he noticed an approaching guard, but paid little attention to him, until a fist smashed against his face, knocking him to the concrete floor. Stunned, he attempted to sort through what he had done wrong, as the guard reached down, grabbed the collar of his shirt, lifted him a few inches, and slammed his fist into Giichi's face again. A shower of red sparks exploded behind his eyes and warm liquid spurted from his nostrils.

"Salute when you walk past a guard!" he screamed.

Giichi clawed his fingernails into the floor, attempting to find his way back to his cell. Two inmates grabbed his arms and dragged him along the corridor, while blood dripped from his nose and soaked into the front of his shirt. Eventually, the blood crusted, leaving a dark stain, but he wore the same uniform for three more weeks until the first of June, when fresh uniforms were issued. During those weeks, the stain served as a reminder that he must always heed the ways of Abeno Prison, if he was to survive.

Only when the lights went out in the evening did Giichi feel he could cautiously relax his attentiveness, but that soon changed the night he huddled in a ball and listened to the brutal beating of the inmate in cell fourteen. He heard the clang of the door opening and then the shuffling steps of two guards entering the cell, and then groans and shrieks, muffled by the concrete wall that separated them. Giichi cringed with each piercing cry, and pressed his hands to his ears, thinking of his own torture at the hands of Toda. He had no idea why number fourteen had been selected for a beating. Maybe for no reason. When the cellblock finally returned to silence, he felt the wretched mass of supper push against his throat. He swallowed hard to keep it down, afraid that soiling the floor might be reason enough for a beating. The next morning, standing in the lavatory line, Giichi glanced back and forth, searching for the inmate from cell fourteen. When he didn't see him, he assumed the worst.

Still, for all its violence, most days Giichi oddly preferred Abeno Prison to the dull monotony of the Sasayama jail. The pain was mainly physical; there was little time to languish in mental torment. By the end of each day, after he had sat for more than thirteen hours on the concrete floor, attempting to complete a daily quota of sewing one-hundred-sixty buttons on twenty army uniforms, Giichi's mind grew numb and his back felt as stiff as a plank of wood. Forcing the needle through the military fabric, rigid as a thin board, required great force, and the needle often pierced the tattered leather thimble and punctured his thumb. In a matter of days, his swollen thumb throbbed with pain like a rotten tooth.

Like the other inmates, he was required to do all his work in the solitude of his cell. Still, he could leave his cell four times a day, though three of those were supervised trips to the lavatory at the end of the hall. Only during the morning free time, did he experience any sense of release, when he went out to the prison yard and strolled freely among other inmates, though he rarely spoke to any of them. He especially avoided the red-uniformed communists, attempting to emphasize that he had no link with them. On sunny mornings, he sat alone on a bench and listened to chirping birds, amazed they still existed in the ruined city, while only muted conversation drifted through the yard. Laughter, loud talk, and gathering in groups of more than three resulted in immediate beatings.

Giichi focused every thought and action on avoiding the savagery of the guards. Only at night, when he lay awake in relative tranquility on his smelly futon, did he think of his family and remind himself that Kinuko was proud of him and that she waited for him to return. Eventually, even those thoughts died away. Kinuko began to shimmer in his mind like someone he had known only in a previous life. For a time, that worried him. He thought he must cling to the memories of his loved ones as he had done in the Sasayama jail. But instinctively, he knew his chances for survival here depended on something harsher, a hardened soul. If he hoped to leave this place alive, he could not afford to be distracted by thoughts of those who made him want to live. It was a cruel irony; yet he must succumb to the cold shell forming around his emotions and become a machine—blind to injustice, devoid of feelings.

On rare nights, when Giichi completed his sewing quota before the 22:00 lights out, he leafed through "The Record of Ancient Matters" and "Nihongi," books that had been handed to him after his initial and only interrogation upon arrival at the prison. The simple sight of printed words gave him pleasure, but he couldn't help but laugh at the notion of basing a war on myths from books taught in elementary school. He remembered his teacher telling the class that the Sun Goddess, Amaterasu no Okami born to Izanagi and Izanami, gave birth to the Japanese race and was the ancestor of the Japanese imperial lineage. He also remembered being taught that the first Emperor of Japan, the legendary Jimmu Tenno, prophesized that because Japan was created by the Sun Goddess, the country was destined to bring all corners of the world under her roof. To Giichi, this was ridiculous, and even more ridiculous was the country's late 19th Century use of this prophecy to justify territorial expansion. Throughout the wars in China and the Pacific, the myths had been used as metaphors to mislead people and lend credence to the concept of a "Greater East Asia Co-Prosperity Sphere." Eventually, the pleasure of seeing printed words could not outweigh his disgust for such propaganda, and he shoved the books into a corner of his cell, where dust settled over them.

While Giichi focused on survival, he couldn't help but wonder about the lack of investigation into his case. There had been no interrogations, no Toda-like beatings.

He was often tempted to ask other prisoners about the reasons for their incarceration and how their cases were proceeding. One morning, while mingling with the others in the prison yard, he edged toward two men in the blue prison uniforms that signified former communists who had disavowed their beliefs, usually after severe torture. In return for recanting, they received shorter prison terms than the red-uniformed, hard-core communists. Giichi approached them in his gray uniform, the color worn by most inmates. He nodded to them cautiously, and they nodded back and smiled slightly, as if inviting him to join them. To his surprise, they knew the nature of his crime, even though he had told none of the other prisoners why he was there. The older one explained, "I can tell the difference between thought-criminals and the others."

Giichi felt an instant bond, though deep down he questioned the convictions of the men, knowing they had disavowed their beliefs. Nevertheless, he told them of his concern about the delay in his case, to which the younger one immediately replied, "Forget it, why would you want to be interrogated and tortured on top of all this shit?"

Then the older one glanced toward the guard in the middle of the yard and began to murmur his story—three days of unspeakable torture, four months of solitary confinement, a miraculous recovery from his injuries, then the trial, during which he rejected communism and received a ten-year sentence. "It's possible the war will end before you're tried," he added. "They may not even care anymore if you go to war."

"Why?"

"I overheard a conversation between some of the red-uniforms the other day. They hardly speak to us, but I know they communicate with the outside, and they said the end of the war isn't far off."

"Why do they think that?" Giichi asked, feeling his whole body lighten.

"Did you know that in February, Stalin secretly promised America to enter the war against Japan after the defeat of Germany?"

"No, I thought Japan had a neutrality pact with Russia."

"They don't care about pacts with Japan. With Germany out of the way, Russia will certainly not stay quiet. There is no way Japan can withstand the combined forces of America, England, and Russia. The end will be soon."

Giichi felt a strange, mixed sensation of euphoria and sadness. The end of the war might mean his release, yet a corner of his heart throbbed with sadness for Japan. The military had made a serious mistake in attacking Pearl Harbor, but Japan was still his country and the people did not deserve the subjugation that would naturally ensue.

"Japan should negotiate a surrender right now before it's too late," he blurted out, and then looked toward the guard, fearing he might have spoken loudly enough to invite a beating.

The younger one muffled a laugh. "Who cares? All I want is to get out of this place. I'll take whichever comes first."

The bell shrieked, announcing the end of free time. Immediately, Giichi turned from the two blue uniforms without formal words of departure. Only two days ago a prisoner had been beaten for loitering beyond break time. He walked quickly toward the solitary cell block. Now he had real reason for hope. By the time he was locked in his cell, the undercurrent of sadness had evaporated. Like the young former communist, he no longer cared how the war ended, as long as it did. Then he could get out of this place. The rest of the day, that hopeful notion repeated itself in his mind—he might make it, he might survive, get out of this place alive; as long as the prison escaped Allied bombs.

A few days later, his hopes were crushed. The day began with the usual morning inspection and breakfast—a bowl of gluey barley porridge and a cup of water. Giichi sat on the hard floor and ate in a hurry, knowing he needed to push his empty tray through the opening in his door before a guard came to pick it up. He emptied the bowl and scraped his finger along its surface to get the last strands of food, then picked up his cup and rinsed his mouth before swallowing all of the water. He stood and placed his tray on the ledge of the door grate. Soon, he heard the wheels of a cart clattering against the floor and stopping outside his door. The tray vanished from the ledge. Moments later a metal key rattled in the lock and his door swung open. A bag of army uniforms sailed through the door and landed at his feet.

"Lavatory," the guard yelled, giving Giichi permission to leave his cell.

When he stepped into the corridor, Giichi saw a dozen or so inmates lined up at the far end of the dark hall, a dismal collection of murderers, rapists, thieves, arsonists, and dissidents of one sort or another. The line was shorter than usual, and Giichi was relieved that he wouldn't have to wait long. Apparently the guards had found fewer infractions among the thieves and rapists, who were sometimes brought here as a scare tactic and then returned to their cells in the mixed-residence block across the prison yard.

Still, something about the scene unsettled him. There were more guards than usual; in particular, both Yamada the Bowleg, and Kobayashi, as savage as Bowleg, stood near the lavatory line. The two seldom shared the same shift, but when they did, the entire cell block stood as quiet as a temple. The inmates, even the murderers, tiptoed to the line and remained nearly motionless, moving forward in a barely perceptible shuffle, and uttering not a word. Giichi walked quietly to the end of the line. It moved slowly, but not too slowly because all the inmates knew Yamada or Kobayashi or both would descend in a fury on any inmates who stayed too long in the lavatory.

Giichi reached the door after ten minutes in the line and wasted no time inside. On his way back to his cell, he shuffled quietly and kept his head slightly bowed. As he approached cell eighteen, its door suddenly swung open to block his path. He quickly swerved to the left and glanced inside. Two guards emerged from the cell, dragging a limp red-uniformed body by its armpits. The head drooped down to the chest; the feet scraped lifelessly across the floor. The familiar shape of the man's body and the top of his head paralyzed Giichi. He knew for certain. It was Kenji Nakayama. He told himself to keep moving but didn't know if he moved at all.

"Number twelve, get to your cell right now!" Yamada bellowed.

Giichi felt as if in a dream, wanting to run from a savage beast but unable to make his legs move. He wanted to take Kenji in his arms and comfort him, but his instinct for survival urged him to look away. He willed the rubbery muscles of his legs to move, then felt Yamada's angry hands shove him and give him the impetus he needed. He veered back to the right, stumbled through the doorway of his cell, and slumped onto the floor beside the bag of army uniforms. At last the door slammed shut, and he gasped for air, fighting back the image of Kenji's lifeless body. Slowly, terrifying possibilities sifted into his thoughts. No wonder they had never interrogated him. They had only been waiting for this moment, for him to become complacent. They intended to bring Kenji into the prison and beat him to death and drag him into the hallway just as Giichi returned from the lavatory, and then witness the guilt of recognition in his face. Now the torture would begin. He had survived all of this madness for nothing—now they had him. It had all been planned, even the two blue uniforms in the prison yard, all a set up to make him complacent, to increase his shock at seeing Kenji.

Giichi inhaled deeply and held the air in his lungs, attempting to stop the racing of his mind. He focused on a fleck of concrete on the wall next to his futon and exhaled slowly. He could not allow himself to fall into their plot. No matter what, he could not afford to display any hint of recognition of Kenji Nakayama. Perhaps Kenji was not dead, perhaps they had only beaten him unconscious and in a few days they would release him into the prison yard, and again they would observe his reaction. Even if Kenji approached him in the prison yard during free time, he would have to ignore his friend completely.

Giichi finally reached into the bag of military uniforms and pulled out a jacket. He began sewing, pushing the needle and thread into the stiff cloth as if that might allow him to hide from what he had seen. But in the dim light of the cell, the haunting image of Kenji's swollen face constantly replaced the jacket, and he felt as though he poked the needle into his friend's face and added to his pain. Then his own face replaced that of Kenji, battered and swollen as it would surely be, sooner or later, when he had no choice but admit his connection with Kenji. His hands shook, and he inhaled deeply again and clenched his fists to regain control.

After the evening meal, Giichi grew frantic. Even though he had worked through the morning free time, he was well below quota. As the evening hours wore on, his despair deepened; he would definitely not finish on time.

As he had feared, before lights out, the familiar clanking of Yamada's boots approached, and the door creaked open. When Yamada found Giichi four jackets short of his quota, the guard began kicking him. "You draft evader!" The tip of his leather boot landed on Giichi's right hipbone. Still, Giichi didn't let go of the uniform, until Yamada's second kick to his tailbone sent an electrifying pain through his spine. He jerked and the uniform fell out of his hands. Instinctively, he leaned over to protect his groin. After that, the kicks came randomly, the side of his stomach, arms, back, head, and shoulders. "A traitor like you deserves to die!" Yamada screamed, so loudly that another guard burst into the cell and joined in the kicking. Giichi could no longer tell which part of his body hurt. He suddenly felt a peculiar detachment, as if there were two Giichi Sekiharas, one feeling horrific pain, the other indifferent to pain.

Later, Giichi tipped over onto the futon, wincing and moaning. For a long moment, he didn't know if he was awake or asleep. In one segment of his blurred consciousness, he thought about Kenji. He vaguely wondered if Kenji was still alive in cell eighteen. He recalled how they had talked late into the night at his boarding house in Kyoto, how passionately they felt about fighting fascism, and how noble Kenji looked in the moonlight that flooded into the room. Now, these years later, this filthy prison was where they both ended up. It occurred to Giichi that this might be the place where they would both die, amid military uniforms and brutality, without seeing their shared dream materialize. So be it, he thought. If it was their destiny to live and die on this earth with ideas that did not conform, so be it. He wept softly, thinking of Kinuko, and then drifted into sleep.

Three days after witnessing Kenji being dragged from cell eighteen, Giichi shuffled his aching body into the prison yard, desperate for information. It was a clear blustery day in early June. The wind, peculiar for Osaka at this time of year, ballooned his baggy uniform and made it flap against his emaciated body. Swirling dust showered grit onto his unwashed hair and into his eyes, as he approached the man from cell twenty for news about Kenji.

The tough-looking inmate—said to be serving time for murder—whispered to Giichi, "They beat the shit out of him for two nights straight. But that poor guy was something. He never cried out once. All I heard was thump, thump, thump, you know? It's been awfully quiet since. They probably killed him. Those murdering bastards." The inmate spat on the ground and walked away.

Giichi shuffled to a corner bench on wobbly knees and collapsed onto it. He leaned forward heavily, elbows on knees, and hands pushing through hair that blew wildly in the wind. Dusty poplar leaves rattled overhead. He didn't notice the inmate from cell seventeen approaching until he sat on the bench next to him. The man began whispering, "The murderer said you wanted to know about cell eighteen."

Giichi lifted his head.

"They removed his body last night, about three hours after lights out, probably didn't want the rest of us to know."

Giichi opened his mouth to say, "Thank you," but no words came out. Instead, he nodded with an odd smile, then buried his face in his hands. The inmate stood and drifted away in the swirling dust. Through his grief, Giichi realized the guards might be watching him. He sat up mechanically and draped his bruised arm over the back of the bench, attempting to appear as relaxed as if sitting at a lakeside café.

When he scanned the yard for guards, he saw the red-uniformed communists gathering in a far corner. In the shadow of the concrete wall, they formed two circles—four in one and three in the other, apparently attempting to comply with the prohibition against large group gatherings. With faces down and eyes closed, they stood unmoving, their hair and uniforms fluttering crazily.

Seeing them, Giichi sensed the finality of Kenji Nakayama's death and felt a strange comfort; at least Kenji would suffer no more. Yet, he felt numbingly alone and jealous of the communists who could openly grieve the death of his friend. He looked away, but his eyes kept drifting back to the two reverent circles.

CHAPTER 32

As his train rattled toward Osaka, Ichiro already missed Kinuko, Akira, Etsu, and Mr. Nakano. Yet he felt satisfied with his visit to Sasayama, where he had found his daughter-in-law and grandson doing well despite his son's absence. He still worried about further harassment by Harada but felt certain that Kinuko would be able to handle the matter with the help of her mother and Mr. Nakano. She was a strong woman like her mother, he thought, picturing her hands that had once played the piano and painted pictures, now stained green, fingernails black with dirt.

Squeezed into a train car mostly filled with men, he missed the real closeness of working in the garden with her. He had seen the way the garden connected her to Giichi, and had felt that connection himself, along with pride in his son for having started the garden. The work tested him physically, made his back ache, but in its simplicity it now seemed far more important than his intellectual life, full of books. He had attempted to change the world with words, and now he saw that the world could be changed through simple acts.

As his train slipped into the Osaka station, Ichiro's heart began fretting, thinking of his son imprisoned somewhere in this city. He felt an urge to find Giichi, yet thought of the promise he had made to Kinuko. Fighting against the urge to at least know where his son was, he carried his luggage from the train and started down a set of concrete steps. When he stopped to rest for a moment, he noticed a boy of nine or ten playing alone near the bottom of the stairs. The boy slid down the handrail, then bounced up several steps and slid down again. His soiled clothes and bare feet, black with embedded dirt, made it obvious he was a war orphan, abandoned to the streets.

"Hello, old man," the boy said. "Is your luggage too heavy for you?"

"Yes, it is," Ichiro replied.

"I can carry them for you."

"No thank you," replied Ichiro, afraid the boy might walk off with his bags. "I'm just going to the next platform."

When Ichiro started moving again, the boy reached out and grabbed the handle of his trunk, lifting it enough to lighten its load, as they descended the steps together.

At the bottom, Ichiro stopped and asked, "What are you doing here alone?"

"Nothing."

"Nothing? Where is your family?"

"Dead."

Ichiro looked at him sadly.

"In the bombs," the boy continued.

He eased Ichiro's trunk from his hand and struggled toward the stairs leading to the next platform. Ichiro followed, tears moistening his eyes, as he watched the orphan's scrawny body tilt to one side to balance the weight of the trunk. Ichiro slowly climbed the stairs, while the boy waited for him at the top.

"Where do you want to sit, old man?"

Ichiro scanned the platform, gasping for air. "Anywhere is fine."

The train hadn't arrived yet, but passengers who had been waiting hours or even days milled around boxes of luggage at the edge of the platform. The boy walked about twenty meters to an empty spot and placed the trunk against the wall.

"Thank you," said Ichiro as he sat on the trunk. "Listen, tell me how you live alone, if you don't mind. Do you have sisters or brothers?"

"Nope." The boy shook his head and squatted on the concrete floor beside Ichiro, rubbing his chin against his bony knees. "I came here with my neighbors."

"Oh, you live in one of those shacks outside the station?"

The boy nodded. "They said I could stay until the war is over. Then the city is going to look for my uncle in Kyushu. If my uncle doesn't want me, they'll put me in an orphanage."

Ichiro suddenly reached out and hugged the boy. Tears formed in the boy's eyes. Ichiro let go and leaned back to grope in his pants pocket for his handkerchief, while the boy wiped his eyes with his dirty fists, smearing his face with black streaks of dirt. A soldier approached them and shooed the boy away with a wave of his hand.

"Get out of the station. You aren't supposed to be here."

"Please," Ichiro said to the soldier. "He isn't doing anything wrong. We're just talking. He'll leave soon."

The soldier studied Ichiro suspiciously and then walked away with his rifle slung over his shoulder.

"Do you have food?" Ichiro asked.

"Yeah, we get food from the city. I ate canned beef for lunch."

"That's good. I'm glad to hear that."

"Where are you going, old man?"

"I'm going home. I live in Okayama now. I used to live here in Osaka, but my house was bombed too, in March."

"But you didn't die, like my father and mother."

"No, I wasn't there when it happened. I'm lucky."

"So why do you look so sad?"

"Do I look sad?"

"Yeah, why?"

"Well, my son is in jail."

"Jail?"

The boy's voice rang out so loudly that several heads turned in their direction, but Ichiro didn't care. He thought it must look strange to them to see him leaning down and talking to this disheveled boy, but it felt comforting to talk with someone about his sorrow. The boy looked at him seriously.

"What did he do wrong to go to jail?"

"My son didn't do anything wrong. Actually, he did the right thing. He refused to go to war, so they put him in jail somewhere in Osaka. I don't even know where he is. That's why I look so sad."

The boy stared into Ichiro's eyes, as if trying to understand what he had said.

"Don't be sad," the boy said finally.

"Okay, I'll try not to look sad, but tell me, why don't *you* look sad?" Ichiro asked.

"I don't know," said the boy, shrugging his shoulders. "I guess because I'm not supposed to. My neighbors told me they wouldn't keep me in their shack if I cried. So when I go to sleep at night, I tell myself, don't cry, don't cry, don't cry, and after a while I don't cry and I'm not sad anymore."

The soldier swept back across the platform. When the boy saw him, he sprang to his feet.

"Wait," Ichiro said. He quickly took his billfold from his pocket and handed the boy a ten-*yen* bill. Then he opened his trunk and pulled out a book of poems by Takuboku Ishikawa. "Take this, too," Ichiro said, "and read it. Someday you will be old enough to understand."

"Thank you." A smile spread over the boy's dirty face. He opened the book, placed the ten-*yen* note inside, and closed it. Then he hugged the book against his thin chest. Behind him, the soldier was only a few meters away.

"Hey, boy!" yelled the soldier. "Get out now!"

The boy turned around and stuck his tongue out at the soldier. Then he started running toward the stairs. "Hurry!" Ichiro called to him, but the soldier didn't pursue him. He only clicked his tongue and proceeded along the platform.

Just before the stairway, the boy tossed the book into the air and the bill came flying out. He stood and waited for the book to come down, caught it, and then scrambled to pick up the bill before running down the stairs. As the boy's small head disappeared from view, a warmth spread in Ichiro's chest. He compared their losses. The boy had lost his parents and his home and somehow still found happiness; while he had only lost his home and time with his son and his family, and still he could find no happiness. He hoped the boy would one day have a chance to grieve for what he had lost and still be able to go on.

It suddenly occurred to him that a new generation would emerge from the rubble. Despite the war's devastation, some of them would survive, and perhaps because of it, they would have the sense to form a new world of peace. There had been many wars, he thought, but none of them lasted forever. This one, too, would surely come to an end. Like a river flowing in a vast plain, history would move on, hopefully for the better. The orphan boy, and others of his generation, Akira and Yuki, and all the boys and girls who managed to survive would make sure of that. And then at last, all the world would recognize the suffering of his son and others like him, and know that it had not been in vain.

CHAPTER 33

The evening after Ichiro left Sasayama, Kinuko and Etsu sat in a house suddenly gone empty. They idly leafed through books in the family room, as if lost without his company. Kinuko often glanced at the clock on the wall. Ichiro's train from Osaka was supposed to arrive in Okayama City at four in the afternoon. From there he would have to take a bus to his village, which would add, at most, another half-hour. It was now nine-thirty. He must have arrived home several hours ago. Kinuko regretted that she hadn't asked him to send a telegram when he arrived home, but figured he would anyway since that was what he had done after staying with her during Giichi's incarceration. He'll notify us eventually, she thought, there must have been some kind of delay.

When the clock struck ten, she wondered if Ichiro had decided to stay in Osaka overnight despite his assurance that he would not. As the clock kept ticking, she grew angry, imagining him struggling with his luggage through the streets of Osaka in search of Giichi. Then her anger turned to worry.

Etsu closed *Kokinwakashu*, the book of classical Japanese poetry she had been reading and glanced at the clock. "Ten-thirty already," she mumbled with a small yawn. "Let's go to bed, shall we?"

"I'll stay up for a while," Kinuko said.

"Would you turn off the light at the gate then?"

"I will."

"You'll hear from your father-in-law tomorrow," Etsu said, rising from the floor. "He must be exhausted."

As Etsu slid the family room door open, they heard loud knocks at the gate. "Telegram!" a man shouted. With all worries suddenly melting away, Kinuko sprang to her feet and ran outside.

"Telegram!" the mailman shouted again.

"Coming!"

Kinuko unbolted the gate. "Telegram for Mrs. Sekihara," the mailman said, waving his hand impatiently to chase away the insects flying around his face. Kinuko thanked him, and he scurried back to his bicycle. She opened the tri-fold quickly and held it under the light. "IS FATHER STILL THERE? MOTHER."

Now she was angry at Ichiro for making Sumiko worry. She went back to the house, feeling new anguish for Sumiko.

Etsu was standing in the front room. "Is it from Okayama?"

"Father hasn't come home yet."

"Isn't that strange?"

"He must have stopped in Osaka. I have to go to the post office to let Mother know."

Kinuko walked past Etsu and went into her room to fix her hair. "I'll go with you," Etsu said, following her.

"I can go alone," Kinuko said, but Etsu wrapped Akira in a blanket.

Kinuko quickly tied her loosened hair at the back of her neck, and they headed out through the dark grove, Etsu carrying Akira, Kinuko holding a lantern.

At the dimly lit post office counter, Kinuko wrote on the form, "LEFT BY TEN O'CLOCK TRAIN THIS MORNING. MUST BE IN OSAKA. LET US KNOW WHEN HE ARRIVES. KINUKO."

That night Kinuko slept fitfully, her mind filled with endless possibilities—Ichiro in Osaka looking for Giichi, or visiting Mrs. Chiba or his friends, or going to the bombed site where his house once stood, or a delay or cancellation of the train, or of the bus in Okayama City. But as she traveled down the route of each possibility she always returned to the conclusion that it wasn't like Ichiro to change his schedule without letting his wife know, especially on the day before Yuki's birthday. Although in the past he had caused his family great anguish because of his writing, he always kept them informed of his whereabouts, at least when he could. It wasn't like Ichiro to break his word either. Those thoughts forced her to consider even worse possibilities—what would prevent him from contacting Sumiko; falling ill or being in an accident or....

Her anguish continued through the morning and part of the afternoon, until she finally heard banging at the gate and the shouts of the mailman again. She inhaled deeply and slowly opened the telegram, hoping it was from Ichiro, but even before she read it, one word leaped out as if typed in bold ink, "DEAD." "FATHER DEAD. TRAIN BOMBED. NO NEED TO COME. TOO DANGEROUS. MOTHER."

Kinuko reached out for the gate to hold herself up. Denial swirled in her head; this is untrue, this is a lie, this is a mistake. She didn't know how she got into the house, but when she saw Etsu feeding Akira from a bottle, she collapsed onto the floor beside them and wailed. The fragile strength she had discovered after Giichi left suddenly vanished, leaving her with nothing but deeper grief and terrible guilt. She was aware of little else until several hours later when she told her mother she must go to Okayama.

"Have you lost your mind?" Etsu said. "Even your mother-in-law is telling you not to come."

"But I have to go. I can't leave Mother alone, and Yuki. Today is her birthday."

"What about Akira? You are the mother of Akira, too."

"This is all my fault. If I didn't make him promise not to stop in Osaka, he wouldn't have died. I have to go and apologize."

"It is not your fault, Kinuko, but if you feel that way, you can write."

"Write? His train was bombed and he is dead! I have to go! A letter wouldn't do anything!"

"It is not safe. That's what I'm trying to tell you. You have to think about your own safety."

"I can't stay in Sasayama when all I can think about is the sorrow I've caused Mother."

Etsu begged, "Kinuko, please don't blame yourself. How can anyone blame you? No one knew such a horrible thing would happen. It's not your fault. Please don't risk your life."

Neither of them had noticed Mr. Nakano at the back door, until they heard his quiet but firm voice. "Kinuko-san," he said, "I will go with you. But first you must sit down and calm yourself."

His voice quieted her, and she sat as told. Mr. Nakano stepped into the family room—for the first time ever without being invited—and sat next to her. Etsu sat down, too. Mr. Nakano put his hand on Kinuko's shoulder. "Are you sure that you want to go?"

"I must."

"Your mother is right, it is very dangerous to travel."

"I must," she said again.

"It can be done. Not by the normal way. We will have to go through the countryside. It will be a long, difficult trip. There are local trains and buses not affected by the military restrictions, but they do not run very regularly, so we will probably have to wait many hours. And there will be times when we will have to walk for many kilometers over mountain roads. It will take days, and the rainy season may start while we're in route." Mr. Nakano took his hand from her shoulder and looked at her intensely. "Are you sure that you still want to go? You don't have to answer right now. Think about it tonight and let me know tomorrow."

"I don't have to think about it, Mr. Nakano. I have to go."

"Then we will leave tomorrow."

"Where—where are you going to stay at night?" Etsu asked fearfully.

"Each village must have at least one inn. We'll make sure we sleep well at night."

Etsu bowed to Mr. Nakano. "Thank you," she said with fresh tears. "I can't thank you enough, Mr. Nakano."

The next morning, Etsu boiled water for them to take in flasks, and packed rice balls, crackers, mentholated salve, a first aid kit, and the raincoat Giichi had used in the garden. While Kinuko got ready, a second telegram came from Sumiko saying she would have a proper funeral after the war. She repeated that Kinuko shouldn't come, but that still didn't change Kinuko's mind. After Mr. Nakano arrived and Kinuko was ready, clad in a clean blouse and monpe pants, Etsu saw them off at the gate.

"Don't worry about Akira; he will be fine with me," she said.

They left Sasayama on a local train, and the trip went as Mr. Nakano had predicted. For the next five days, they worked their way westward on short-distance trains and buses, learning the best routes from villagers. Often they walked for hours to make a connection, and once waded across a river. They rationed their food and supplemented it with fruits they sometimes found in village markets. On the third day, the rainy season set in and soon their clothes were soaked and never completely dried for the remainder of the trip. Sometimes the physical suffering seemed worse to Kinuko than the pain of childbirth, and yet she welcomed it, feeling as if it might earn her forgiveness. Even more than the physical pain, she felt unlimited remorse, something she thought would be with her as long as she lived.

As they finally reached the bend that led to the bottom of the Sekihara property, they were beyond exhaustion, and drenched by rain that now came in heavy sheets. Huddled together, Kinuko and Mr. Nakano stumbled up the steps toward the gate. When Kinuko thought she couldn't take one more step, she heard Sumiko's shrieks.

"Kinuko, Kinuko!"

She stopped and saw Sumiko running down the steps without an umbrella.

"It's you! Oh, Kinuko!"

Sumiko took her arm and started up the steps, but Kinuko stood motionless, her face contorted with pain. "Mother, it's my fault," she wailed, and burst into tears.

Sumiko tugged at her arm. "Let's get into the house quickly. Oh, how exhausted you must be!"

"I'm sorry, it's all my fault," Kinuko sobbed.

"What is your fault? Oh, how glad I am! I've been so worried."

"I—I—"

"All right, Kinuko-san," Mr. Nakano pulled her arm gently. "We are almost there."

As soon as they stumbled into the entryway, Sumiko screamed, "Ume! Ume! Would you bring towels? They are here! You were right!"

Kinuko collapsed at the edge of the front room, while Mr. Nakano stood in the entryway, rain dripping from his clothes.

"Ume, hurry please!" Sumiko shouted again.

Ume ran into the entryway with towels, and Yuki followed.

"Yuki!" Kinuko whispered. She stretched her arms toward her daughter, but Yuki hid behind Ume.

"Yuki, it's your mama!" Sumiko said.

Kinuko edged closer to her daughter, but Yuki now hid behind Sumiko.

"Don't you remember me?" Kinuko said.

"Yuki, Mama is here, she is your mama." Sumiko pushed Yuki toward Kinuko, but she wouldn't budge and clung to her grandmother's wet monpe pants.

"She is just frightened," said Sumiko, now holding Yuki to her side. "Please dry yourself and change first."

"Young Mistress," Ume said with tears glistening on her face. She began patting Kinuko with towels.

"Ume, oh Ume," Kinuko whispered.

With a start, Sumiko remembered Mr. Nakano. She urged him to come into the room and helped him pat his clothes with towels. She apologized for her impertinence and thanked him over and over again for bringing Kinuko. He could only mumble a response.

When water no longer dripped from Kinuko's clothes and hair, Ume led her to a room where a futon was laid with fresh sheets. Ume placed a dry *yukata* and towels beside the mirror stand and left the room. Kinuko changed into dry clothes, fighting the drowsiness that suddenly crept over her. By the time she sat in front of the mirror, she couldn't even lift a comb to her hair. All she wanted was to crawl into the dry futon and sleep.

Sometime later, Kinuko heard voices, Yuki's and Sumiko's. Yuki's was sweet, and Sumiko's soft and suppressed. Their voices sounded more pleasant than music drifting through the curtain of sleep. They seemed both far and near.

"Mama, wake up."

"Shh...she is still sleeping."

"I want to eat dinner with Mama."

"We'll wait. We'll eat after Mama wakes up. Let's go."

"No, I want to stay here. I want to ask Mama why Papa didn't come."

"Papa is on his trip. It's a very important trip."

"Grandpa said they all will come after the war is over. Is the war over yet?"

"No, not yet, but it will be soon. Let's go back to help Ume."

"Then Grandpa will come home, too?"

There was silence for a moment.

"No. Grandpa—Grandpa is on his way to paradise. Come here."

"Where is that?"

"It's—it's in the sky. It's far away, but he'll be watching us, always."

Kinuko felt tears filling her closed eyes and knew she must awaken. She forced her eyes open, and at the end of the tunnel of her blurred vision, Yuki crouched on the floor, holding a windmill and facing Sumiko who stood at the doorway.

"Yuki," Kinuko called.

"Mama is awake, Grandma!"

"See? You woke her," Sumiko said to Yuki, but her voice sounded happy.

Soon Kinuko saw two faces looking into her eyes.

"You didn't look like my Mama," Yuki said. "Why were you so wet?"

Kinuko sat up and hugged her. "I walked a long, long way in the rain because I wanted to see you."

Yuki wiggled out of her embrace and thrust out her windmill. "Look at my windmill," she said. "Grandpa didn't come home for my birthday so Grandma bought this for me."

"How nice." Kinuko again hugged her. "I'm glad you had a nice birthday—I hope you've been a good girl for Grandma and Grandpa."

"Grandpa went to paradise. Grandma said it's in the sky."

Sumiko lifted her fingers to the corners of her eyes. "Let's let your mama get ready for dinner," she said. "Yuki, would you go tell Ume we are eating soon?"

Yuki ran from the room, but Kinuko could hear her calling, "Ume! Grandma said we are eating soon!"

Sumiko smiled toward the corridor and then turned to Kinuko, her eyelashes wet.

"I hope you slept well," she said.

"I'm sorry I fell asleep—without even thanking you for taking care of Yuki."

"Kinuko, you don't know how much Yuki has helped. Without her, I wouldn't even know where I am—how is Akira?"

"He's fine. Father was so happy to see him—and how much I enjoyed—"

"I'm glad. That was the purpose of his visit. He must have been happy to have seen you and Akira."

They cried quietly for a while. Then Sumiko looked up. "Kinuko, don't blame yourself. I heard from Mr. Nakano how you've been feeling about Father's death. It's not your fault. If we have to find someone to blame, it's those who fight. Not you, Kinuko. That's what Father said all along, and Giichi still believes that."

"Mother," Kinuko threw herself into Sumiko's arms, "but I miss him—I miss him. I miss Giichi, too."

"Oh, how I miss them, too, Kinuko."

"Grandma!" Yuki scurried back into the room, and Kinuko and Sumiko quickly wiped their tears.

"Ume said Mr. Nakano is ready for dinner. Please come, she said."

The two women stood slowly and followed Yuki to the reception room where Ume had already seated Mr. Nakano and was placing dishes in front of him, apologizing on behalf of Sumiko for the poor meal and for leaving him unattended.

After dinner, Sumiko said she planned to go to Kobe to collect Ichiro's ashes the next day. She explained that Genkichi's brother, who because of the war had lost his job as a driver for an Okayama City shipping agency, was asked to replace a sick driver and deliver goods to Kobe Harbor tomorrow, rain or shine.

"Genkichi came only hours before your arrival to see if I wanted to ride along, and I jumped at the opportunity, not knowing when such a chance might come again."

Kinuko held on to Yuki, who had clung to her throughout the meal, while Sumiko continued to explain that Ichiro's ashes, along with those of the other victims, were kept at a temple called Eifukuji, "the temple of eternal happiness, an appropriate name for Father."

"Will there be enough room for another person in the truck?" Kinuko asked. "I would like to go with you, Mother."

"I'm sure it's quite a big truck, but I think it would be better if you stay home. There's no need for you to go into Hanshin."

"But I don't want you to go alone."

"It's nice of you to offer, but it's not safe, Kinuko."

"I know that, Mother, but if there is a god, he won't take us away from Yuki and Akira after taking their grandfather."

Sumiko fell silent, and Kinuko watched her intently.

"I still think you should stay here and keep Mr. Nakano company. Actually, I don't like to be away myself when I have a guest."

Yuki held her windmill up to Mr. Nakano and asked him to blow on it and make it spin. Mr. Nakano smiled and huffed at it, and then quickly turned to Sumiko.

"Please don't treat me as a guest," he said. "I'm perfectly fine here. Yuki-chan will keep me company."

"Please Mother," Kinuko said. "Please allow me to go."

Sumiko didn't reply. Instead she looked down for a few moments, then looked up and finally said, "All right. Let us believe that god is kind. I'll ask Genkichi if the truck is big enough for both of us."

The next morning, while Yuki repeatedly asked Kinuko if she was coming back "really soon," the two women boarded the truck at the bottom of the steps below the gate. Rain fell like strands of thread, and Yuki stood between Mr. Nakano and Ume beneath the eaves of the gate with her arms bent upward, one hand held by Mr. Nakano and the other by Ume. As the truck began moving, they released her hands and all waved. Just before they turned out of sight, Kinuko saw Yuki cry and Ume scoop her up into her arms.

Sumiko slipped her hand toward Kinuko's, and Kinuko took it into hers. Through her palm, she felt the depth of Sumiko's sorrow. It amazed Kinuko that her mother-in-law had maintained her composure so well. Now her hand felt thin and vulnerable, as if seeking protection, as they headed to the place where her husband's life had ended. Once again, guilt pierced Kinuko's heart like a gimlet, and she felt no words or acts could convey her remorse to Sumiko or to Ichiro.

During their bumpy three-hour ride, the two rarely spoke, except out of politeness to Genkichi's brother who didn't seem to know how to speak to grieving women and sporadically quipped about the weather and the road conditions. As they passed through Himeji and Akashi, he silently moved the truck through several detours around bombed areas.

When the truck finally bounced into the west side of Kobe, the clouds miraculously split and the sun appeared. Though the region was disguised by rubble, Kinuko could see that they had unmistakably returned to Hanshin. The familiar green contour of the Rokko Mountain Range came into view, and she choked back a tightness in her throat. They were only a short distance from Suma, Kobe, where she had grown up and where Etsu had lived alone until the previous summer. Fifteen kilometers to the east lay the old neighborhood where she lived with Giichi until three months ago. When the truck passed just north of Ashiya, she felt an overwhelming longing to see Mrs. Chiba, but said nothing. The truck made several turns and finally stopped at the base of the mountain. Genkichi's brother jumped out and helped them to the ground, promising to come back as soon as he finished unloading at Kobe Harbor.

After his truck bounced away, Kinuko and Sumiko stood together and looked up at the steep incline of stone steps that led through the foothills to the gate of the temple. Sumiko swayed dizzily for a moment and Kinuko took her arm to support her. She wondered momentarily if either of them could make it to the top. Her own legs and feet ached from her recent journey, but it occurred to her that these steps had been placed here by some godly design to test her strength.

"I must do this," Sumiko said as if to herself.

Kinuko nodded, wondering if similar thoughts were going through her mother-in-law's mind. Together they slowly began the steep ascent, one step at a time. Kinuko kept her grip on Sumiko's elbow, tightening her jaws and feeling sweat gathering against her clothes. Halfway up the steps, she heard a drone of B-29s approaching from the east, but Sumiko kept moving, her eyes focused on her feet. They continued climbing in a journey that began to seem eternal. By the time they finally reached the temple gate, the planes had flown past to the west.

Both gasped for air. Kinuko felt oddly elated, until she looked across the small forecourt of the temple, where a ring of mourners stood around a metal tub, scooping ashes from the tub into urns. She had expected to find some semblance of Ichiro's personal remains, but remembered that after the bombing at the shipyard, the unclaimed or unrecognizable bodies were eventually mounded in a pile, doused with gasoline, and ignited in a mass cremation. Now she understood that Ichiro's remains had been handled the same way. It would be impossible to find anything of him scattered among all the others.

The distant rumble of the B-29s faded away, and Kinuko heard the shrill chirp of cicadas rising from the trees behind the temple and the crunch of pebbles beneath their slow footsteps. As they reached the tub, a man looked up with eyes full of mournful sympathy and moved aside to make room for them. He went to the outer corridor of the temple hall, brought back an urn, and handed it to Sumiko. She thanked him and then gazed bewildered at the tub in which bits of white bones protruded from the powdery gray ashes. The man handed her the pair of chopsticks he had been using to pick up bones.

"It was my wife," he murmured. "She went to help our daughter have a baby and never came back."

"I'm sorry to hear that," Sumiko said. "My husband went to see our newborn grandson and..

Kinuko bit her lip to keep from crying.

"So, I might have your husband's bone," the man said, "and you might have my wife's."

The man bowed sadly and walked away, clutching his urn. Kinuko watched Sumiko pick up a few fragments of bone and gently drop them into the urn. Then she turned to Kinuko. "I want you to gather Father's ashes on behalf of Giichi." She handed the urn and chopsticks to Kinuko, who took them with shaking hands. She lifted two scoops of ashes from the bucket and gently poured them into the urn. Sumiko pulled a white cloth from the fold of her kimono, and Kinuko handed the urn to her. Sumiko crouched and wrapped the cloth around the urn. She took her time, wrapping it gently and trying to tie a neat bow on the top. When it was neat enough to satisfy her, she lifted it to her cheek and briefly closed her eyes. Two more mourners approached, an old man and a young woman, huddled together with eyes sadly fixed on the tub. Kinuko bowed to them and helped Sumiko to her feet. At the top of the steps they stopped, and Kinuko held Sumiko's elbow. "Are you all right?"

They began their descent, Sumiko holding the urn to her chest, taking one step at a time just as they had done in coming up, though this time more carefully. Halfway down the stone stairs, Sumiko seemed unable to go on. She squatted down at the edge of a step, and Kinuko sat next to her.

"Until now," Sumiko began, "I've kept thinking Father might come home again and scratch behind his ear like he always did. Silly isn't it?"

"Scratch behind his ear?"

Sumiko nodded, smiling shyly through tears. "That's what he used to do when he did something wrong or made me worry—he would sneak into his room after coming home from a police investigation—his expression apologetic and sort of embarrassed. And then no matter how much I'd been worried or even angry at him for making me worry, I'd see him scratch behind his ear and I'd forget everything and life went on again—but I've just realized I'll never see that again."

Sumiko shook the urn gently beside her ear, as if listening to his voice. "He was a big man," she said, "but he is so light now—oh, how I will miss that—Father scratching his ear."

They continued to sit on the stone step, gazing down at the ruined city of Kobe. Beyond it spread the Inland Sea of Seto, shimmering beneath the sun. The blue contours of small islands blended with the sea. To the far left, the shoreline of Osaka Bay stretched in a hazy white line above the blue water. Not so far from that shoreline a house once stood where Ichiro and Sumiko had lived together with Giichi.

"This is Father's last glimpse of Hanshin," Sumiko said, "the Hanshin he so loved." With that, she turned her face toward Osaka and gently shifted the urn on her knee, like a mother on a park bench moving the child on her lap for a better view. "Look, Father, look," she whispered. Kinuko felt certain Sumiko was telling her husband that Giichi was down there somewhere, still carrying his father's hope.

When they returned home, they found a swarm of villagers pouring in to offer condolences. Ume explained that many rumors had spread, though Sumiko had only told close relatives of Ichiro's death. Ume said some had seen the Young Mistress of the Sekiharas coming into the village in the rain with a stranger. Others saw Big Mistress leaving the village in a truck driven by Genkichi's brother with Young Mistress who had only arrived the day before. Everything seemed out of place, and they asked Genkichi what was happening. Genkichi broke into tears, admitting that he had been unable to keep the sad news in his chest.

Most brought fresh vegetables instead of the customary cooked food, due to the shortage of fuel. Bright orange bunches of carrots, dozens of eggs, and baskets of *endo*, *chisha*, and *daikon* covered the kitchen floor, and Mr. Nakano cleaned chickens in the back yard—more food than all of them could eat in weeks. Genkichi's wife bustled through the kitchen, preparing food and tea for the arriving visitors. Ume moved constantly through the corridor, delivering trays of fresh tea and returning with trays of empty cups.

After placing the urn in the altar room, Sumiko went to the reception room to greet visitors, while Kinuko received more visitors in the front room and led them to the reception room for food and tea.

In the evening, Kinuko helped Sumiko sort the telegrams that had poured in from all corners of the country—old friends, writers, poets, journalists, publishers, faraway relatives, and people whose names even Sumiko didn't recognize.

That night, Sumiko changed her mind and decided to have a funeral while Kinuko and Mr. Nakano were in Okayama. She set the date for two days later, so Kinuko and Mr. Nakano could get back to Sasayama before the local trains stopped running, as rumors indicated they might.

On the morning of the funeral, Kinuko held Yuki's hand and together they trudged up the hill to the village temple, Yuki still holding her windmill, as she had once held the broken doll. The temple sat nestled in a cleft of hills overlooking rice fields, with soft rain drizzling down. Though it was perfect weather for planting rice, Kinuko noted that most of the local farmers were dressed in their finest clothes, slogging up the hill to attend the funeral.

By nine forty-five, mourners, moving in half-crouched and speaking in low tones, packed the temple hall and spilled out into the outer corridors. At ten o'clock, when three yellow-robed monks entered the hall and sat facing the altar, the whispers and coughs ebbed away. A rustle was heard momentarily as the mourners shifted to sit erect. Soon the monks began reading a sutra amid the ringing of bells.

In the front row, the center seat reserved for the first son stood vacant. Sumiko, in black mourning silk with the Sekihara family crest, sat next to the empty seat. Kinuko was at her other side, also in black silk, with Yuki on her lap. Mr. Nakano, though he had insisted on sitting in the back, was seated next to Kinuko at Sumiko's urging. Across the aisle, Ichiro's relatives occupied the first row and Sumiko's the second.

From the altar, a black-framed photo of Ichiro smiled at the mourners through blue swirls of burning incense, his eyes slightly sad and embarrassed. Ichiro rarely allowed his photo to be taken, and the previous night Kinuko had helped Sumiko dig through boxes and drawers to find this one. It had been taken fifteen years earlier for an article in a literary magazine announcing his award-winning novel, *The song of Villagers.* Occasionally, a soft, moist breeze drifted in through the open doors of the temple, setting Yuki's windmill in slow motion, making the candles flicker and wafting the incense smoke over the monks. But the photo remained still, Ichiro's expression fixed forever in the same embarrassed smile, yet appearing to Kinuko as if he could slip out of it at any moment and scratch behind his ear.

The sutra continued, the deep, ringing voices of the monks filling the packed hall and echoing down the rainy hills. Sumiko sat immobile, her face down and her eyes closed. Next to her, Kinuko also sat immobile, her chin touching the top of Yuki's head, remembering something Ichiro had told her when Giichi was in jail and they were together in Ashiya. Everything in this human world is transient and temporary: humans are like migrating birds pausing briefly. "The difference is that the birds know exactly where they are going, while we humans don't really know where we came from or where we are going. Perhaps that's why we seek and search while on earth, even if what we seek might not be eternal." His words seeped into her like water into sand.

When the sutra reading ended, everyone rose and made a long queue toward the altar for individual prayer. Sumiko and Kinuko stepped to the altar first in keeping with custom. Then they moved to the entrance of the hall to personally thank each of the mourners for sharing their grief as they filed from the temple. Ume hurried from the back of the hall to take Yuki from Kuniko so she could thank the mourners without hindrance, but Yuki refused to leave Kinuko's side and clung to her kimono. Nevertheless, Ume scooped her up, blew at the windmill she held, and hurried toward the back room behind the hall.

Kinuko stood beside Sumiko and watched the mourners standing back to wait for Tamekichi Hotta, the oldest among them, so he could be the first to leave. Although she hadn't met him before, she had heard Ichiro and Sumiko talk about the Hotta family often. Tamekichi's family had farmed part of the Sekiharas' land for many generations—his father before him, his son after him, and now his grandson. But his grandson, Eikichi, was in the war and his sixty-three year old son, Eisaku, farmed in his absence. Supported by Eisaku and his wife, Tamekichi tottered to the hall entrance where Sumiko and Kinuko stood awaiting him. He could barely walk. His back bent like the branch of an ancient tree, and his mouth sank deep and settled at the end of many wrinkles. Finally, the old man reached the end of the long hallway and faced Sumiko. He stretched his back as straight as he could.

"I wish to say," Tamekichi began haltingly, "that we are saddened by the death of Big Master. He was a very compassionate man. Ten years ago, my son here fell from a ladder and broke his hip—terrible pain and all. That year we didn't have enough rice. Couldn't pay the rent. So Genkichi wrote a letter to Big Master on behalf of us, and we got a letter back right away. It said, 'Don't worry about rent. Hope Eisaku's hip is getting better. Take care.' Every summer he came to see us, and about three weeks ago, he visited me because Genkichi told him I was sick. I told Big Master I wanted to die because I don't have any use for living. Can't do a thing, just a nuisance to the younger ones here. But Big Master took my hand like this," Tamekichi held Sumiko's hand. "And he told me I would live many more years because I've worked hard all my life."

Tears rolled from his murky eyes and worked their way along the wrinkled terrain of his face. "I think god took the wrong person. I got well just as Big Master said I would, and he passed away."

His hands looked as brittle as dry twigs resting on Sumiko's. Tears formed in Sumiko's eyes. "Please Tamekichi-san," she said, "I want you to live many more years as my husband wanted you to. I'm sure he is very happy that you got well."

Now many mourners crowded behind him, and Eisaku and his wife tried to steer Tamekichi toward the steps. But he wouldn't let go of Sumiko's hands. "I wish to say one more thing," he said. "I can't read but I always knew Big Master wrote things the *okami* didn't like. He was never afraid of the powerful ones. He was not only a kind man but a courageous one, and such a man will live in paradise peacefully. Take care of yourself, Big Mistress. And you, too, Young Mistress."

"Thank you, Tamekichi-san," Sumiko said.

Kinuko watched the old man finally wobble down the steps into the wet forecourt. She recalled the day in the garden in Sasayama when Ichiro talked about his childhood, how he fished and climbed trees, how during his adolescence he read books incessantly and dreamed of the world beyond these hills and rice paddies, and how finally he left this place to seek and search for the real meaning of his life. Now, only two weeks later, he had returned permanently to the village he once left, and in his return she could clearly see the meaning of his life, the way he touched his fellow villagers, just as he had touched millions with his writings.

An hour later, Sumiko and Kinuko, just the two of them, buried Ichiro's ashes beside the new tombstone added to the Sekiharas' lot behind the temple. After another short sutra reading by a monk, they stood in the rain and gazed at Ichiro's freshly inscribed name. Soft drops of rain fell from the overhanging branches of a Japanese maple and dripped onto the tombstone and their umbrellas. Resignation and loneliness began to settle over Kinuko more deeply than she had ever felt them. First Mr. Chiba, then Ichiro, and what would happen to Giichi? And she must soon leave Yuki. Tomorrow, she and Mr. Nakano would begin their long journey back to Sasayama.

"I'm glad you came," Sumiko said, her eyes still on the fresh soil. "I couldn't have done this without you."

"So am I—I wish I could stay longer."

"I wish you could, too, but after the war, you can come back again with Akira—and hopefully with Giichi. Until then, I think Yuki should stay with me. The travel is too treacherous for a small child, and—I think I will need her."

"Of course, mother," said Kinuko, looking down. "There is no way I can take her with me."

"Thank you," Sumiko said. "Thank you."

They stood in silence until Sumiko chose to speak. "I know it is difficult for you to part with Yuki again, but someday all of you will be together. Let's believe that day will come."

"When that time comes, I want you to live with us, Mother," Kinuko said.

"Thank you, Kinuko. But I think I should stay here with Father."

Kinuko didn't know how Sumiko could stand the loneliness, recalling her own after Giichi had left. "You are a strong woman, Mother," she said.

"Well," Sumiko said shyly, "I'm not so certain if I was born strong, but I learned to be strong, I suppose, being the wife of Father—and being the mother of Giichi. And probably being the grandmother of Yuki and Akira will make me even stronger. Actually, I didn't know what I was getting into when I married Father. He was a very progressive man with new thinking, but when it came to marriage, he went with tradition and married a woman who didn't know much about anything. I didn't know him, either, except that he was a poor writer who lived in Osaka."

Sumiko's eyes remained on the tombstone but she appeared to be picturing those years when she was the young wife of Ichiro.

"Well, shall we go?" she said abruptly. "Yuki must be waiting for you."

They bowed to Ichiro's burial site before they began walking down the hill. In the rain-soaked fields below, farmers in straw hats stooped in the water, planting rice seedlings one by one. A red cord circled the brim of every hat, and another one was tucked high up on the sleeve—red tokens representing their hopes for a rich harvest. With many young men gone, most of the farmers in the fields were women, old men and children.

"Look, Kinuko," Sumiko said. "They're already back in the field—those who came to the funeral. Some of them grew up with Father and went to school with him. Others are their sons and their sons' wives. Father was gone from here for a long time, but he never forgot his roots were here."

Sumiko stopped for a moment and gazed at the village spread below the hill. Kinuko stopped as well, filling her lungs with the smell of the rain and the rich fields. She felt the soul of Ichiro everywhere around her, in the fields, along the village paths, over the farmhouses, over the mountains and hills, and even in the hearts of the farmers. Ichiro had come home to rest. He had gone out into the world, but this was where he belonged. Kinuko could understand why Sumiko would not want to leave this place.

CHAPTER 34

Despite Giichi's constant fear, three weeks passed after Kenji's death with no investigation into his case. Instead, the rainy season arrived in mid-June, adding more misery to his life at Abeno Prison. Rain fell steadily from dark clouds that hung above the guard tower, and dampness settled in his cell as oppressively as his grief. Everything smelled of mildew—the walls, the floor, his grimy futon. He developed a deep, barking cough that kept him awake through much of the night and invited angry threats from the inmates in neighboring cells.

"Just die, you draft resister, or I'll kill you myself."

He went to bed exhausted and woke up exhausted, and still, each morning, the guards delivered fresh piles of army uniforms with relentless regularity. He often stayed in his cell and worked through the morning free time and well into the night, jabbing furiously with his needle to meet his quota in order to avoid a beating. Some mornings, he could no longer bear the oppressive stench of his confining cell, and, with the others, he shuffled through the corridor of the solitary cellblock. While inmates paced along the covered pathway leading to the yard or mingled in small groups, he leaned against the entry wall and stared blankly at the beads of water dripping from rusty gutters.

As the rain continued, day after day, frustration mounted and a weary edge of anger swelled among the inmates. It seemed that every morning some trivial matter resulted in a scuffle, either in the pathway or in the corridor between the cells of Giichi's block. Inmates sneered and jostled each other when a toe was stepped on or when someone skipped ahead in the lavatory line. Most of the skirmishes ended as quickly as they started, but some lasted long enough to draw attention from the guards. Then the offending inmates were hauled back to their cells, and their painful screams soon pierced the closed doors and echoed down the musty concrete corridor. If Giichi was outside his cell when trouble started, he always hurried back and resumed his stitching, thinking vaguely that the inmates should have controlled themselves, yet feeling anger toward the guards welling up in his chest.

One morning, Giichi stood in his usual spot at the cellblock entrance when a shoving match broke out in front of him. Within seconds, a dozen inmates were tangled in a clump of flailing fists. Some tumbled out into the muddy yard and continued to swing and kick. Before Giichi could move, three guards rushed into the melee, bashing anyone in their way with swinging clubs. Inmates pressed into the entryway and wedged Giichi against the wall. The warning bell began shrieking, and more guards quickly appeared, kicking and bashing, as they waded into the crowd. Giichi struggled to turn. Amid the swishing sound of the clubs, eyeglasses flew through the air and blood spurted from noses. Finally, the tight cluster began to move back into the cellblock. Giichi stumbled along with them, gripped by nausea.

In the safety of his cell, he pulled the door shut, picked up the uniform he had been working on, and tried to sew. The needle shook in his hands as the corridor exploded with noise—clubs thumping against flesh, screams of pain, cell doors slamming, shouts of guards, "Free time is over!" "Get back to your cell!" "Keep moving!" followed by locks clamping shut, including his own. Soon, the scuffling footsteps of guards faded from the hallway, and Giichi shivered in the cold, fearing greater reprisals.

Lunchtime came with eerie ordinariness. The food felt like sand in his mouth, and all afternoon he felt queasy. Tonight would be brutal, but he was determined to stay out of it. He couldn't let the horrifying sounds affect his emotions or the pace of his work. He just wanted to survive this craziness and go back to Kinuko. She was waiting for him. She had his baby. Yuki was waiting, and, of course, his father and mother. Despite everything, he had done well so far. He had endured beatings; he had seen his dear friend beaten to death, and still he had kept himself relatively sound, physically and mentally. The war would end soon; it had to. There was still hope, as long as he could avoid the beatings.

Contrary to his tough thoughts, the queasiness in his stomach persisted and his hands continued to shake. He fell hopelessly behind in making his quota. By the end of supper and the lavatory break, he still had almost eighty buttons to sew on before lights out. Frantically, he jabbed the needle though the unforgiving fabric, and then, two hours into the evening, the iron door to the solitary cellblock slammed open, reverberating through the corridor and settling in his gut. Panicked, he took a breath and held it deep in his lungs, listening to the violence he had expected all day, praying they would not open his door. The guards rampaged through the corridor, dragging one inmate after another from his cell. Giichi tried to focus on his fingers, on moving the needle and thread. The quota must be completed. He repeated those words in his mind like a mantra. Yet with each new scream, a sharp jolt seized his body and sweat crawled over his cold skin. His fingers jerked, causing the needle to miss the uniform and poke his finger. When the violence finally stopped, he collapsed onto his futon, limp as a punctured balloon. Soon the light in his cell blinked out, and in the dark he softly chanted a sutra, feeling the pain of the beaten inmates, wishing his chanting could ease their agony.

The next morning, everything seemed out of the ordinary; the guards didn't check on his uniforms or deliver any new ones, and breakfast was only tea. Giichi was so relieved that they hadn't noticed his unfinished work that he didn't care about the lack of food. At ten o'clock, when the bell rang for free time, he didn't know what to do. By then he had finished yesterday's quota, but it didn't seem wise to leave his cell. Still, he felt a curious urge to go outside and talk to someone, anyone, and find out what was happening. Why hadn't they been given food? Why was it so quiet?

By the time he reached the pathway to the yard, it was already filled with an agitated crowd. Guards walked through, thumping their clubs lightly against the sides of their trousers. Giichi kept to his spot, listening to the hushed conversations that rose from inmates as soon as a guard stepped past them.

"With no food, how can we work on those stupid uniforms?"

"Shit, they're as hard as wood, like sticking needles in boards."

"What do they think we are, cattle?"

"I'll kill the next one who lays a hand on me!"

Their eyes glinted with hatred. The stubble on their pale skin trembled as they spoke. Only the red-uniformed communists seemed to be floating above the misery of prison life. They cruised slowly back and forth with hands clasped behind their backs. Though thin as sticks—according to rumor, they received even less food than the others—their backs were straight, and they greeted each other with crisp nods. They always reminded him of Kenji, and now he wondered what Kenji would do in this situation. Would he act like the rest of the red-uniformed communists, drifting among the other prisoners as if they hadn't heard anything the previous night? Or would he try to stop the violence? Giichi grunted bitterly. If Kenji could have stopped the violence, he would still be alive.

Suddenly, Yamada rushed into the pathway. At the sight of him, Giichi stepped quickly aside. "Get out of my way!" Yamada barked, kicking the legs of the man standing next to Giichi. The inmate crumpled against the one in front of him, and together they sprawled to the concrete floor. As they tried to get up, Yamada continued to kick them. To Giichi's surprise and horror, the two pushed up from the floor and retaliated, swinging as fiercely as starving dogs fighting for food. They wrestled Yamada to the floor, and the crowd pressed over them. Others joined in kicking Yamada, now helpless against the onslaught. Cheers of fervent joy erupted, as first one man, and then another, stomped on Yamada's chest.

"Kick the bastard!" "Kill him!" "Kill him!" Their shouts rose above the din of the shrieking bell. Some howled with glee and ran dancing out into the rain. Yamada gurgled like a dying animal, and more cheers rose up.

Feeling the blood drain from his face, Giichi ran back to his cell and collapsed onto his rolled-up futon. Out in the corridor, footsteps hurried past his door and then an eerie silence settled over the cellblock. His heart thumped, as he continued to lie still with his arm over his eyes. If he hadn't stepped out of Yamada's way, surely he would have been the one kicked to the ground. What would he have done then? He felt cold as he wondered.

At noon, the prison resumed its usual schedule. The guards moved quietly but with frightening purpose. Doors were opened; the stacks of uniforms that should have been delivered in the morning were thrown into cells, and the ones that should have been inspected yesterday were collected. After the doors were closed, lunch arrived. Giichi ravenously emptied the bowl of oat gruel, though it didn't settle well in his stomach. For the rest of the afternoon, he kept wondering if Yamada was dead. Part of him wanted Yamada dead and another part of him wished otherwise, not because he felt sympathy for a beast like Yamada, but because those who retaliated couldn't possibly get a fair trial. If anything, they would be killed tonight.

That evening, supper was delivered as well, and Giichi thought grimly that he and the other prisoners were being prepared for slaughter. During the lavatory break, news of Yamada's death filtered through the cellblock, passing in hushed tones. Some raised their fists defiantly when they heard the news, though they were careful to do so when the guards were not looking. The inmate behind Giichi in line whispered, "It's too early to be celebrating." And another added, "Exactly, just wait until tonight." The guards stood by silently, but Giichi saw the murderous anger seething in their eyes.

He returned to his cell more agitated than ever. Tonight would be worse than the previous one. The guards would retaliate randomly, without mercy. Giichi tried to resume work on the uniforms. He had barely started when he heard the guards bring the inmates responsible for Yamada's death back to their cells. Giichi tore a piece of dirty cotton from the batting protruding from his futon, compressed it into two balls and stuffed them into his ears. When the screaming began, he realized how little the cotton balls helped. His stomach knotted with pain, yet he kept his shaking hands moving, all the while anticipating the opening of his door.

Yamada was dead, but Kobayashi or any of the others could beat him just as brutally. The evening gruel pushed up to his throat. He crawled to a corner of his cell and vomited. After a while, he crawled back to the futon and ripped more cotton from the batting to brush the saliva from his mouth. He used the same cotton to wipe the floor and soak up his vomit. He looked around the cell for a place to hide the soggy cotton, then simply left it on the floor. After wiping his hands on the sides of his prison uniform, he picked up the needle. Cries of torment echoed all around. With trembling hands, Giichi wanted to scream out for the madness to cease.

When the beatings finally stopped, he sagged back on his futon. Every muscle in his body relaxed. Then the light went out, and he realized the guards had neglected to check his quota again tonight, but he feared they would remember in the morning, so he fumbled in the darkness to find the uniform he had been working on. He felt the button and probed at it with the needle. Suddenly Giichi threw the uniform into the air and leaned back with laughter surging from his belly in hysterical strings. He pressed his face into the smelly, mildewed futon so the guard wouldn't hear him. That made him laugh even more, and he ended up rolling on the floor, with airy emptiness expanding in his chest. In the end he wasn't certain if he was laughing or crying.

When he finally calmed, he felt completely empty. The entire world seemed meaningless, one huge folly. He felt sick of being alive. What was life, anyway? Or being human? Just a pile of flesh and bones that would eventually die and rot away, one way or another. He settled on his futon with the sluggishness of a sick old man and closed his eyes, vaguely thinking tomorrow could easily be his last day on earth, and it really didn't matter. The guards had only begun their work tonight. Tomorrow, they would still be full of rage. They might kill him for not completing his quota or for soiling a floor so filthy it couldn't be soiled. So what? He didn't care anymore. He was tired of living.

During a fitful sleep, his father appeared in a dream. Giichi wanted to reach out and touch him, but his arms wouldn't move. His father smiled sadly, yet beamed with love that melted his heart. Giichi felt his father's hand on his shoulder just as it had felt the day his father left for Okayama. His chest filled with longing. He wanted to speak, but no words came out of his mouth. Still, his father listened quietly, nodding and smiling. Giichi kept mumbling, he and his father standing so close, hoping this moment would go on forever, but morning came again.

During breakfast, an announcement came through the speaker that ten o'clock free time was canceled and the inmates in the solitary cellblock were to remain in their cells for the next seven days.

Shit!" someone shouted.

"Murderers!" cried another.

Soon a roar of furious voices blended inside the cellblock, followed by guards banging on doors, shouting above the din, "Be quiet!" "Shut up now!" "Shut up!"

"You shut up," an inmate screamed back.

Then the commanding voice of the superintendent came through the speakers. "Until everyone is quiet, the doors will remain locked. This is an order. Those who don't obey will be severely punished."

"Then I'll shit right here and you'd better clean it up, bastard!"

More angry shouts followed, but eventually the cellblock settled into silence, and the guards began unlocking the doors for lavatory use, opening only four cells at a time. Giichi picked up the needle and began sewing again. It would be impossible for him to complete his quota, but he didn't know what else to do.

After about twenty minutes, his cell door was unlocked, and he shuffled into the corridor, where a guard immediately grabbed his upper arm. He saw another guard shouting at the middle-aged arsonist in cell eleven. "Hurry up!" The guard's voice echoed through the musty, dark corridor. As soon as the prisoner emerged from his cell, the guard kicked him in the leg and he stumbled into the corridor.

For the first time since his arrival at Abeno, Giichi forgot where he was and lurched toward the prisoner to catch him before he fell. Immediately, the guard swung his wooden club so hard against Giichi's left shin that he heard his bone crack. A burning sensation rushed from his shin deep into his gut, and he gasped for air. Still struggling to breathe, he tried to scream but only wheezed, "Stop the violence." By then the arsonist was clawing at the guard who hit Giichi, and Giichi plunged between them, ignoring the pain, as he pushed the arsonist to the wall. "Stop it!" This time he actually screamed, then slumped to the floor and twisted around to see four guards surrounding them, gripping their clubs, ready to strike.

"Kill me if you want!" he shouted. "Go ahead, if you must see more blood! This is not a prison. This is a slaughterhouse!"

One of the guards, his face contorted with anger, raised his club above his head. As he swung it toward Giichi's skull, two others grabbed at his arm and the blow grazed Giichi's shoulder. The two pulled the angry guard away from Giichi, one of them bellowing, "Just take him to the lavatory, then lock him up!"

Giichi was lifted by his arms and dragged down the hall. He groaned as his leg crumpled beneath him and collapsed onto the floor. The guards lifted him again and continued toward the lavatory. Cheers and clapping erupted from the cells, echoing faintly in Giichi's ears.

Sometime later, Giichi awoke on his futon. Even without moving, pain throbbed in his shin, and with the slightest movement, it shot through his leg like an electric shock. At noon, he heard his meal being slipped through the door but could not bear to move. By evening, a languid fever wrapped his body, and he thought vaguely that he would slowly starve to death. Certainly his injury was not as severe as the ones that had killed Kenji Nakayama, but he would die just as surely without food or water. And it would be nothing out of the ordinary at Abeno Prison; he would not be the last to die here. Yet he had no fear of dying. If anything, the thought of death was sweet as he floated in a feverish delirium that eventually pulled him into sleep.

He awoke to the sound of a voice next to him. Giichi opened his eyes slowly and saw the arsonist kneeling beside him with anxious eyes looking into his own.

"What are you doing here?" Giichi sat up, but sharp pain knocked him down again.

"It's free time. They decided to let us out for fifteen minutes today. All the guards are outside, so I came to see how you're doing."

"Get out of here," Giichi mumbled. "You'll be killed if a guard finds you in here."

"Who cares? You saved my life. It's time for me to save yours."

"Don't, they'll just kill us both."

"Right, so what's the difference? I'll bring your stinking lunch later."

"No. I don't want food."

The arsonist moved to the end of Giichi's futon and slowly rolled up his bloodstained pant leg. "Shit!" he sputtered. "This is bad, really bad."

"Get out of here," Giichi said through clenched teeth.

Left alone, Giichi lifted his head with great effort and saw his left leg grotesquely swollen to twice the size of his right, its skin purple and tight and covered with dried blood. He fell back and drifted to sleep. When he awoke again, he heard squabbling voices outside his cell.

"What are you doing there?" came a guard's commanding voice.

"Unlock this cell," replied the arsonist. "The guy's in pain. Can't even get up to eat!

"Stay away from there!"

Giichi listened intently, momentarily forgetting his pain.

"Look, all I want to do is feed the poor guy. Would you leave a friend to starve to death? Maybe you would, but I won't. Just unlock the door!"

Giichi heard a kick against his door, and another inmate yell, "Unlock the door!" He flinched, expecting to hear a club pulverizing the arsonist, but to his surprise, the lock clicked and the door swung open. His insistent caretaker scuttled in with a meal tray in one hand and a bedpan in the other.

In the background, the guard commanded, "That's all you can do in there, feed him and come right out."

"What else do you expect me to do? I'm going to feed him and take care of his piss and shit."

The tone of the arsonist's voice frightened Giichi. He couldn't believe the guard didn't strike him. Instead, he only stood in the doorway and glared, feet spread wide and arms folded across his chest.

The man sat next to Giichi and picked up the chopsticks. "Now, you'd better eat," he ordered.

Giichi shook his head. "I'm not hungry." He wanted to be left alone; free from everyone—guards, inmates, anyone.

"Open your mouth" he said, thrusting the chopsticks at Giichi's mouth.

Giichi ate a few bites and shook his head again. "Sorry, that's all I can eat."

"You're worse than a rotten kid," he said, putting down the chopsticks. "At least drink some water." He lifted Giichi's head a little and pressed a tin cup to his mouth.

Giichi took a few sips and tipped his head back.

"Do you want to piss?" he asked, as he lifted the edge of the futon and wiped the water that trickled onto Giichi's throat.

Giichi shook his head.

"All right, but use this later when you have to," he added, moving the bedpan next to the futon. "I got it from the custodian."

"Out, now," ordered the guard, jiggling his key chain. "Get back to your cell, now!"

From then on, the arsonist showed up every day during meal breaks, while the others were in the lavatory line. Giichi was astonished that the guards allowed it. They eventually stopped harassing his helper and unlocked his door without a fuss. They even agreed to suspend Giichi's uniform quota until he was able to work again. He felt like an injured bird that had found its way into the cellblock and had been adopted as a hopeless project. After a few days, his fever subsided and he felt stronger. When he propped up on his elbows, he saw that his leg had turned black, but the swelling had gone down and wrinkled skin covered it. Still, it was impossible for him to stand. The pain throbbed constantly. Even the slightest movement felt like a fire had been ignited on his leg.

Giichi began to look forward to his caretaker's visits and ate more with each passing day. He admired the arsonist's diligence and was astounded by the way with which he carried out his assumed responsibility. With each visit, the arsonist rushed from his cell with the bedpan, washed it in the lavatory, then returned to sit cross-legged and feed him patiently with the square, callused hands of a laborer. Giichi asked him how in the world he was able to take care of both of them in the mere thirty minutes allowed, but the arsonist only replied, "Shut up and stop worrying."

Giichi observed the man's heavily tattooed arms and back, the intricate patterns of flowers and dragons, the scar that creased the side of his face, and thought that he was probably the type of person who had gotten himself into trouble by running up huge debts after years of reckless gambling. But despite his rough appearance and language, his kindness seemed genuine.

They seldom conversed, aside from exclamations of disgust with prison life, but one day Giichi said to him, "I can't believe how the guards are acting these days."

"Yes. It's strange. Everything changed after we killed the Bowleg. They had one last night of beating and then it seemed like they finally got sick of it. Or maybe they suddenly knew we could kill them, too. You know? Anyway, things are better. That's all that matters."

As the arsonist stood to leave, Giichi said, "Thank you for your help."

"Shut up," he said. "If you start that, you're on your own."

Giichi grinned. "I never asked, but...I don't know your name."

"It's Shuzou," he said, "What's it matter? A name is a name, just more shit that follows us through life." Then he stepped from the cell.

Giichi slumped back, his chest filling with joy and pain. Somehow the man's gruff kindness had softened his hardened heart, and thoughts of his family poured into his mind. He had been wrong to no longer care about life, to give up hope.

Five days later, Shuzou came into Giichi's cell with his lunch tray, smiling slyly. He set the tray next to Giichi, and said, "I got something for you."

Giichi watched him return to the door, reach outside and pull his hand back into the cell, holding a battered pair of crutches.

"I'm sick of taking care of you," Shuzou said. "It's time for you to get up."

"Where did you get those?" Giichi sat up, but as he tried to bend his leg, he yelped with pain.

"The custodian. He found them at a bombed out doctor's office."

When the rainy season ended in mid-July, life at Abeno changed even more drastically. Of the prison's one-hundred-and-twenty inmates, eighty, the youngest and healthiest, were selected to clear the city's bombsites, though none of them seemed healthy enough for such heavy labor. At eight-thirty each morning, they left in shackles and were brought back in time for the evening meal. Giichi no longer saw Shuzou, who was not only among those selected for work detail but had been moved out of the solitary cellblock. Giichi thought of him often, as he hobbled down the hall and into the yard on his crutches, and hoped there might be some way he could repay him after the war. He would have been helpless without the crutches. The pain in his leg persisted and became unbearable when he put weight on it. He thought it was possible he would walk with a limp for the rest of his life, but that didn't matter, as long as he lived.

During the day, the prison was nearly deserted, and the few left behind faced changes as well. In order to provide more food for the inmates working outside, their allotments were cut in half. At the same time, the number of uniforms coming into the prison continued to diminish. Giichi relished the smaller quotas and the slower pace of work but grew weak from the diminished rations. He shrunk as thin as a stick until his rib cage pressed against his sunken chest. During the Sunday wash hour, he staggered dizzily on crutches from his cell into the washroom. Standing in front of the mirror with a toothbrush, he stared at his sunken eyes and cheeks, feeling as if the man in the mirror were a stranger.

One morning, the inmates raided the small garden at the far end of the prison yard that had been started by a live-in custodian. They broke through the wire cages and picked everything—tomatoes, cucumbers, eggplants and *endo,* even the tiniest unripe vegetables. Giichi struggled along behind the others, extending his crutches as far as he could with each step. By the time he reached the patch, nothing remained—even the shells of *endo* had been eaten. One of the prisoners charged with the murder of Yamada handed him a cucumber smaller than his thumb. He gobbled it down, but within an hour his bowels erupted with diarrhea and for days afterward, he felt even dizzier.

The guards didn't react to the raids on the garden. Giichi could see that Shuzou had been right; they no longer seemed to care about anything other than their own survival. Perhaps they were as hungry and weak as the prisoners

Soon another big change came, making Giichi sense that the end of the war was near. The supply of military uniforms dried up entirely. The remaining inmates were assembled in a room in the non-solitary block to learn the skills they would need for their new tasks. Most were assigned sandal weaving, but Giichi drew the fortunate assignment of working in the prison library.

The initial excitement he felt for being among books was soon overwhelmed by the realization that he had little strength for even that type of work. Propping his crutches against the wall, he hopped around on one leg, sweeping and mopping the floor. After completing his cleaning duties, he placed checkout cards into the sleeves inside the tattered book covers and returned books to their shelves. By the time he finished, he slumped onto a chair, too exhausted to read, yet heartened by the thought that he just needed to hang on a little longer.

A few days later, his anticipation of the war's end grew even stronger, when one of the red-uniformed communists approached him in the prison yard and whispered, "The government is thinking about surrendering."

"Are you sure of that?" he asked, unable to conceal his elation.

"Absolutely," the communist replied. "The end is soon, finally."

Back in the library, skepticism rose in Giichi's mind. He doubted the military would readily agree to surrender, even if the government wanted to. But he buried his doubts and pictured the day of his release, walking out of the prison on crutches, and finally riding the train back to an awaiting Kinuko. Akira would be more than three months old now, so how old would he be when he reached home? Four months? Five months? Swishing the mop across the library floor, he immersed himself in endless imaginings of Kinuko's smile, Akira's milky smell, the three of them traveling together to Okayama to join Yuki. He was sure he would cry at the sight of his mother. And his father would pat his shoulder and nod. Occasionally though, Giichi tried to restrain the excitement of anticipation, anything could happen between now and then, but it served as an antidote to the endless pangs of hunger gnawing at his stomach and the throbbing in his leg, and he let his daydreams continue.

Toward the end of July, the heat grew oppressive in the cramped cells at Abeno. Combined with the lingering moisture from the rainy season, the heat and filth created perfect conditions for lice to breed in their futons, in the seams of their uniforms, and in their hair. During free time, Giichi sat at the edge of the concrete pathway with the other inmates, where he picked lice and pinched them between his thumbnails, one by one. Looking at the emaciated naked chests of the other inmates, sitting side by side, preoccupied with picking nits, Giichi recalled the monkeys he once saw at a zoo, except that those monkeys were fatter than these prisoners.

In the evening, he squinted at a worn copy of poems he had taken from the library. Holding the pages close to his eyes, he was able to read slowly, as the words drifted in and out of focus. It was a collection by Ishikawa Takuboku, a tragic, destitute poet from the Meiji Era who died at twenty-six. His poems invariably expressed sorrow for perpetual poverty and yet at the same time a beautiful hopefulness. Lying in the dim light of the cell, Giichi remembered finding the same edition in his father's bookcase, and how reading Takuboku's poems had inspired to do something good for the world like his father. Eventually, a little before being drawn into sleep, he placed himself in the mind of the poet and imagined himself wandering in grief along a remote beach, yet eternally hoping for something better...an end to the war.

Death permeated the prison all through July. By the beginning of August, eight of the forty inmates who stayed behind had been dragged from their cells, dead from heat stroke or malnutrition or dysentery or all three. When the skeletal bodies were carried from their cells, the other inmates stood silently and watched with glassy eyes. Sometimes, death came even more quietly. Inmates did not return from work. Their cells simply remained empty, and the others eventually learned that the missing had collapsed or been injured at some bombsite and died. The news was conveyed as casually as if describing a leak in the lavatory faucet.

While those around him died, Giichi clung to his desire to live, though he had grown so weak that it was often difficult to get out of bed and push himself up onto his crutches. The pain in his leg, which he had learned to accept as a persistent ache, had suddenly become intense again. On the morning of August 2, he awoke only dimly, feeling cold and nauseous. He hadn't the strength to get up. Eventually, he stirred enough to notice his pant leg clinging moistly to his flesh. With great effort, he pulled up the cloth and found a huge, oozing sore where the club had struck his leg. He settled back on the futon and drifted in and out of consciousness.

This time, no one brought him food or water. When he was conscious, he faintly noted the smell of rotting flesh, and placed his hand on his chest, where he thought his loved ones lived—Kinuko, Yuki, Akira, his father, his mother, Etsu, Mr. and Mrs. Chiba, Kenji, Mr. Nakano, Shuzou, and all the others who had touched his heart. At the center of his chest, Kinuko always smiled. He remembered her many tears, but no matter how vividly he saw each teardrop, her expression turned to a smile in the end—the beautiful, radiant smile he loved. Sometimes he thought of the morning glories he had planted in Etsu's garden and wondered if they were blooming by now.

Eventually, Giichi knew he would die, but it didn't feel so bad. He had had a good life, loving parents, a beautiful wife—a talented, strong woman named Kinuko, healthy children. He had done what he felt was right. There were no regrets. Yet he was lonely. He wanted to see them one more time. He wanted to hold Akira in his arms just once.

In Giichi's final moment of consciousness, Kinuko appeared to him. He was floating in the gentle swell of Lake Biwa, where his parents had taken him when he was a boy, and where he later went with Kinuko. That was...that was shortly after he married her. Kinuko was smiling, so beautiful in her peach-colored kimono. Her stomach wasn't big as he remembered her when he last saw her. He wanted to be near her, but his body drifted from the shore where she stood. He called to her across the water, glinting in the sunlight.

"Sorry Kinuko, I tried my best to survive...I don't think I can any more...forgive me for not being able to come home...take care of the children...and go on...find someone nice and forget me...that's the best...yes, it is." Kinuko's tiny figure disappeared. He heard her voice call to him, "Giichi-san!" The water felt pleasantly warm as he floated in it. He wanted to float like that forever, but a bright light appeared over his shoulder, and when he turned to it, he was absorbed into the peaceful warmth of nothingness.

CHAPTER 35

The day after Kinuko and Mr. Nakano arrived home from Okayama, Mr. Nakano fell ill with a fever. He was diagnosed with dysentery and quarantined with scores of other male dysentery patients in a one-story building annexed to the town's hospital. Aware of a popular saying at the time—city people die in bombings, while country people die of dysentery—Kinuko feared for his life.

The next day, she came down with the same symptoms. Dr. Okawa concluded the two had encountered contaminated food or water somewhere during their return from Okayama. Nonetheless, he immediately arranged for complete sterilization of Etsu's house. While Etsu took Akira to the Furukawas, an ambulance transported Kinuko to a quarantine site where nineteen other women lay sick with the same illness, as brittle and thin as dry twigs. The room smelled of powerful disinfectant, and white walls hovered around the lined iron cots. Kinuko lost weight rapidly. Between frequent humiliating trips to the lavatory, she lay exhausted, with no hope of visitors.

On her second morning, as she sipped watery porridge, the woman next to her was declared dead by a doctor. Kinuko dropped her bowl and averted her eyes from the corpse as it was wheeled away. Its horrifying image, pale as wax, beleaguered her all day. She understood that she could easily suffer the same fate. From then on, someone died each day. As quickly as a body was removed, fresh sheets were spread and a new patient arrived to occupy the cot.

Outside the window, rain pattered endlessly, reminding her of the hill in Okayama where she was forced to part with Ichiro eternally. It seemed to her that dying might not be so bad, if she could join Ichiro and Mr. Chiba, and maybe even Giichi. But when she thought of Yuki screaming in protest when she left Okayama, she shifted her body and pulled the sheet over her head to hide her tears.

Nine days later, Kinuko was released from the hospital to recuperate at home, by then reduced to thirty-nine kilograms. While carried by stretcher to the south room where Etsu had laid a futon for her, she apprehensively asked her mother about Mr. Nakano. Etsu, as if not hearing her, helped Kinuko into the futon and then led the men from the room. After they left, she sat rigidly beside Kinuko and, fighting back tears, said, "His funeral was yesterday."

Kinuko pulled the top futon over her head and cried inconsolably. She wondered why god kept her alive when everything she did caused someone else's death.

The weather remained damp, and the house harbored a smell of disinfectant as thick as her despair. She lay in the south room alone, asking herself how she could possibly tell Giichi, if he ever returned, that his father had died because of her? Or that Mr. Nakano, too, had died because she insisted on going to Okayama? She felt completely desolate. Everyone who made this life worth living had been taken from her. The war would never end, Giichi would not return, Ichiro was gone, Mr. Chiba was gone, she would never see Yuki again. And now Mr. Nakano. Probably, Mrs. Chiba had already died, too. Even if by some small miracle the war did not destroy the world, her world had already been destroyed.

She stayed in bed beyond the ten days suggested by Dr. Okawa, with no desire to recover. Food did not interest her, nor did the thought of caring for Akira. Only when Etsu begged her, did she take a few sips of watery rice porridge or vegetable broth or pick at a poached egg.

While she lay numb, the rainy season gradually gave way to summer. Each day it rained less and the sun shone more. In the garden, the vegetables absorbed the warmth of the sun and grew taller and greener. So, too, did the weeds, Etsu told her. The thought of Giichi's vegetable plants being taken over by weeds barely registered in Kinuko's mind.

One morning, Etsu, clad in work clothes, lowered Akira and a bottle of goat's milk to Kinuko's side and announced that she was going out to the garden. It would be a shame to let the weeds choke out the vegetables Giichi-san had planted, she said. She patted Akira on the head, saying, "Mama will take care of you this morning."

Left with no choice, Kinuko picked up the bottle and began feeding Akira, vaguely regretting that her own milk had dried up completely during the month since she last breast-fed him. Watching him, she felt pity for the child who would never remember the brief time with his grandfather and might never see his father. Still, he ate eagerly, as if none of that mattered, and she noticed that he had grown while she was gone and while she lay sick and grief-stricken. His cheeks were fuller, and there were deep folds around his wrists. When he was full, he smiled at her and gurgled, waving his small arms. He looked at her with absolute trust and love, and she couldn't help but feel pure joy at the sight of such innocence despite death being all around them. She cuddled him, feeling as if the emptiness in her heart were being filled. "Akira," she said, and the sound of her own voice reminded her how much Giichi wanted to see light in the world and how he had bestowed hope in his son. "Akira," she repeated and rubbed her cheek against his. He smelled of milk and nestled softly. That day Kinuko began eating.

A few days later, with the morning sun streaming through the south window, Etsu rushed in from the garden. "Kinuko," she uttered. "Come and look at the morning glories. Giichi-san must have planted them!"

Kinuko scurried out of the house and into the garden, her legs still wobbly. There they were, blooming over the bamboo trellis—purple, white, and pink flowers, the bell-shaped blossoms delicate in the crisp morning air. She approached the trellis, her eyes fixed on their fragile radiance. As she leaned closer and drank in their simple beauty, she remembered Giichi dropping seeds where the flowers now bloomed and she felt resurrected. That twilit evening in the garden, he had probably envisioned this moment, hoping she would one day stand in this very spot and gain the kind of strength Ichiro described in his novel, *Morning Glories.* In that moment, Giichi probably thought she would realize, like the old carpenter in the novel realized, that life must go on.

That morning, full summer fell over Sasayama. The delicate vines of morning glories climbed higher on the bamboo trellis, and each day more flowers bloomed—purple, fuchsia, white, and striped. Kinuko's artist's desire, dormant for years, suddenly came alive. She couldn't resist painting morning glories in watercolor to preserve their beauty on canvas, along with her hope for Giichi's return. Even more than that, she desired to announce to all the world, through the language of her paintings, the love she had learned from Giichi and Ichiro.

She dug into the wicker trunk she and Giichi had brought from Hanshin and found the box filled with dried tubes of paint, brushes and rolled canvases. She broke the tubes open and with a few drops of water, dissolved each color in a small dish. Then she set up a studio on the desk she had placed on the east veranda overlooking the morning glories. Each morning for three days, she painted. She titled the first one, *Chibas' Garden,* in remembrance of a summer morning—the first summer after she and Giichi married, the first time she stood in the Chibas' garden admiring their morning glories, thinking there could be nothing more beautiful than a glimpse of those flowers on a cool summer morning.

"Speaking of morning glories," she remembered Mrs. Chiba saying, "I love Ichiro Sekihara's *Morning Glories.* Have you read it, Kinuko-san?" Kinuko replied, "yes," and for the first time told Mrs. Chiba that the author of that book was her father-in-law. Mrs. Chiba's eyes widened in surprise, and at the end of that summer, she brought Kinuko a small envelope, which Kinuko opened and tipped into her hand, spilling the tiny black seeds into her cupped palm. "You can plant them in the spring," Mrs. Chiba said with a smile. Kinuko remembered her excitement, as she envisioned morning glories growing in her own garden.

While working on that painting, Kinuko wondered what had happened to Mrs. Chiba. She had written to her many times, and each time anxiously awaited her reply, but so far there had been no response.

She titled the next one *Yuki on A Summer Morning.* It portrayed Yuki leaning down and sniffing a yellow tomato flower with morning glories in the distance. Forming Yuki on the canvas with gentle strokes of the brush, she felt certain her daughter would someday feel enormously proud of the grandfather she had lost and hoped she would grow up to be a loving person, even if her father didn't return to her.

The last one was *Sasuke and His Morning Glories.* She took more time with it, trying to capture the flowers' burst of life through the eyes of Sasuke, the old carpenter in Ichiro's *Morning Glories.* As the brush danced on the canvas, she saw him in her mind, sprawled on the tatami floor of his small house in Honjo, Tokyo—his snoring, his breath reeking of *sake*, his widowed daughter-in-law silently taking the empty bottles away, and his old wife wearily clearing the *sake*-stained table. Then the two women carried him to his futon. When they tried to wake him in the morning, he barked at them and went back to sleep. It had been several months since his son died in the war, and still Sasuke didn't know what to do with his sorrow. Then one morning, his grandson found morning glories blooming in their small garden. It was the beginning of summer after the rainy season, and even in a cramped neighborhood like Honjo, the air was fresh and sweet. "Grandpa, Grandpa!"

Kinuko moved the brush across the canvas, now using purple. She could hear the little boy's voice and could see him shake his sleepy grandfather and pull back his futon. She could feel the grandson's love, and the ache of Sasuke as he crawled out of bed, groaning and rubbing the sleep from his eyes. Then the little boy pulled his grandfather to the edge of the room, and between the cracks of the wooden shutters, Sasuke could see three purple flowers bursting on the mildewed bamboo trellis. He sat cross-legged, scratching his messy hair, as the fog of grief and *sake* slowly lifted from his heavy head. "Aren't they pretty, Grandpa?" asked his fatherless grandson. The old man nodded and bought the little boy into the triangle of his crossed legs. He looked at the wrinkled day clothes he slept in, and soon tears began to fall from his eyes and he wiped them with his fist. He stroked his grandson's head as they sat together.

Ichiro's book ended there, but Kinuko kept moving her brush, glancing at the flowers as if she were Sasuke, trying to bring to the canvas his sorrow and astonishment, realizing just how much her own resurrection resembled that of Sasuke, hoping her painting might spread Ichiro's message of hope as effectively as his writing.

When she finished, Kinuko leaned back and felt the warmth of Giichi spread through her. She suddenly understood that when he came home, he would surely carry on with life, however deep his grief. After all, he was the son of Ichiro, who had always written about the sorrow of ordinary people, but also about their hope and love and their ability to endure. In fact, Ichiro's ultimate message was one of hope. Everyone, no matter how unimaginable their suffering, would finally and truly find hope once they found themselves. She realized then, as she viewed the glowing colors splashed on her paintings, what she must do. Whatever happened around her in this world at war, she must find herself and know that she was capable of surviving, no matter what happened to those she loved.

One morning in mid-July, Kinuko went to the mailbox and found a letter from her uncle addressed to Etsu. On the envelope, the word "confidential" was stamped in red. She hurried into the house. "A letter from Uncle Hirobumi," she said, handing it to Etsu, who frowned slightly.

"I wonder what he wants to say after all this time," Etsu mumbled.

"Mother, you wrote to him when Giichi's red paper came, didn't you?"

Etsu didn't answer. She slid her fingernail through the seal, pulled the letter from the envelope, and finally said, "I was desperate that day."

"I saw you leave with a letter, even though you were too sick to go. Mother, I know you did it for me, to save Giichi from the red paper." Kinuko wanted to say more. She knew that writing the letter must have been a great sacrifice for her, a compromise of her principles, especially difficult after she had ignored her brother's objection to their marriage.

"Well," Etsu said. "Let's read it. He might have some news about Giichi-san."

Kinuko felt her body tense as her mother unfolded the letter, but immediately calmed when Etsu began reading. Her quiet tone reminded Kinuko of childhood evenings—storybook readings by her mother after her father had died.

Dear Etsu,

It is getting hot in Tokyo, and I'm sure that it is in Sasayama, too. I hope that you and Kinuko are well. I also hope that Kinuko had a healthy baby. Three months have passed since I received your letter, and I'm certain that you have been wondering why I didn't reply sooner. I apologize for the delay. As you have already guessed, I chose not to change Kinuko's husband's enlistment status, as you requested. However, I made an inquiry upon receiving your letter and found that he was already under the custody of the Sasayama Police. Though I could have erased the record of the conscription issued to him at that time, I chose not to. That may sound cruel to you, and that was the reason I had difficulty writing back, but I hope that in the end you will understand my decision. I would have done the same for my own son or son-in-law.

After a second inquiry, I learned that he has been in Abeno Prison in Osaka since May. Although he has a minor health problem, he is doing fine according to the most recent report I received. I still don't know when he will be tried, but my guess is that he will be sentenced to ten years in prison, provided he didn't have any involvement with communist activities prior to his rejection of the conscription. Prison is a harsh place, but so is the war front. When I think about the millions of our men who died fighting the war, I should say it is only fair that one who rejects conscription should go to jail.

Though I regret the situation deeply, it is time for me to admit that our defeat is now imminent. There is no doubt that the Allies will rule our country after our defeat. Although I don't know exactly how they will rule, it is easy to imagine that they will force us to change the fundamental laws of our country. So Kinuko's husband will probably be released whenever our present conscription law becomes null, at which time, I shall no longer be a general. However, I have no regrets, as I have served my country with all my heart.

I hope that Kinuko's husband will come home safely as much as I hope those who are still fighting will come home to their families, as they are the ones who will ultimately decide our future fate, regardless of who rules our country. When I think about it, we may have been wrong to try to free Asia from Western domination. Until now I have sincerely believed that this war was sacred. Now I am beginning to think that no country can free another, however sincere their intentions. If nations are oppressed by foreign powers, they are the ones who must free themselves. As I have been pondering these thoughts, days have gone by.

Be aware of the more difficult time that is yet to come. I have faith that you will survive because you are the daughter of our father, who taught us that those who endure would always survive. I'm certain that you raised Kinuko in the same philosophy. Tell Kinuko to take care, and you, too, Etsu.

Your brother, Hirobumi

As she neared the end of the letter, Etsu's voice cracked and tears dropped from her eyes. Kinuko took her hands and wept with her. Almost nine years had passed since that autumn day when Hirobumi appeared in Kobe to oppose her marriage to Giichi. Now as they sat in Sasayama, uprooted from their homes, separated from their families and friends by the war Hirobumi pursued, it seemed Giichi's ideals would triumph and Hirobumi's would fail. Yet, for the first time, it seemed to Kinuko her uncle revealed himself as truly human. She thought of the photo of him prominent on a wall of this very house while her grandparents were still alive. He sat high on a horse with shiny medals covering the chest of his stately uniform. Even when Etsu struggled as a poor widow, she continued to view her brother as he appeared in that photo, an icon of Imperial Japan.

"I'm so glad Giichi-san is alive," Etsu finally said, drawing her hands from Kinuko's to dry her tears. She turned her gaze toward the bamboo grove. "We, your uncle and I," Etsu began slowly, "often ran around out there together, when we were little. He was a kind brother, always protecting me from harm. Once, he sat in front of your grandfather and accepted a reprimand for something I had done. I followed him wherever he went. We were carefree, too young to know the complexity of the world. I loved him so much, and even as life changed, I knew that I would always love him as much as I did then."

Etsu looked to Kinuko. "After the war, I will go back to Kobe, and your uncle can come home here and live quietly, maybe tending the garden."

Kinuko thought of Giichi and pictured her uncle tending the garden Giichi had planted.

Despite Hirobumi's prediction, July wore on without a sign of the war ending. August came and brought with it scorching sun that baked and cracked the floor of the Tanba Basin. Still, Giichi's garden provided a bountiful harvest. Early each morning, Kinuko went outside before the heat grew oppressive to pick ripe tomatoes, cucumbers, eggplants, green beans and pumpkins, and load them onto bamboo flats. Then she suspended the flats from both ends of a pole, lifted the pole to her shoulders, and carried the flats to a trailer hitched to a bicycle parked outside Etsu's gate. She had received the bicycle and trailer from Mr. Nakano's estate.

When the trailer could hold no more, she pedaled into town and delivered vegetables to three temples that housed children from the city, who began calling her "Vegetable Aunt." Each morning, when she saw them run to the temple gates with smiles, she wished she could tell Giichi how much they enjoyed the fruits of his hard work. One day, an eleven-year-old girl asked her to stay, and other girls joined in, pulling at her hands.

"Please!" they shouted, and she let them pull her toward the temple hall.

"What do you want me to do here?" she asked, once they were inside the temple.

The girls stopped and looked at one another. "Sing songs with us!" a round-eyed girl said. "Yes, sing with us, please!" said another. Then they settled on the floor, surrounding Kinuko and giggling.

"What do you want to sing?" Kinuko asked.

Finally, one spoke up. "The song you like best."

"What can I sing?" she said, and a moment later remembered Yuki's favorite, *The Home of Sparrows,* and began singing as if Yuki were among the girls around her.

"Sparrow, sparrow, where are you going, flying through such a dark place as a bamboo grove? My home is a happy place, because Grandpa and Grandma, Father and Mother, Brother and Sister, we all live together, merrily....."

The girls started singing along, and when they finished, each sang their favorite song, and Kinuko sang along with them.

From then on, the girls expected her to stay for a singing session every day, and Kinuko began to look forward to her time with them, and eventually with the boys and the teachers.

One day, as she pedaled home with the empty trailer bouncing behind her, it occurred to her that she no longer wondered if she could survive without Giichi; instead she wondered *how* she should survive without him. She hoped she would never have to face that prospect, but for the first time, felt she could if she must.

A few days into August, Kinuko finally received a letter from Mrs. Chiba. When Etsu brought it out to the garden, Kinuko pulled off her straw hat and sat down between the rows of plants. The envelope felt thick between her fingers, and her mind raced with joy while she tore the seal. Mrs. Chiba's familiar handwriting appeared, small and neat, and brought on a flood of memories, afternoons and evenings she had spent in Mrs. Chiba's modest dining room and in her garden. She could smell radishes cooking in soy sauce on her earthenware hibachi, just as she had smelled them a few days before she and Giichi fled Hanshin.

Dear Kinuko-san,

I am very sorry that despite my promise, I haven't written to you for so long, and I don't know what I should begin with. I have gotten all your news and first of all, congratulations on the birth of your baby boy. I am glad to hear both of you are doing well. Akira-chan must be three months old by now. I can easily guess how much Yuki-chan wants to see her new baby brother. I too wish I could see him.

Now, I have to tell you the saddest news. Shortly after you left, my son Takushi died in Mandalay, Burma. Then I fell ill. I couldn't eat or sleep for weeks, and I wished I could die as well. He was only twenty-four. My first thought at the time I received the telegram was that he had died without knowing the joys life usually brings such as having his own family. But now when I think about it, I feel it is a blessing that he didn't have a family to leave behind.

I'm sorry that I've written about myself first, when you have your own sorrow. But Kinuko-san, I agree with you wholeheartedly that Giichi-san did the right thing in his own way, however difficult a time he will have to go through. He is a noble man. I've always felt that there was a part of him that I couldn't get to, even though he was always friendly to me. Now that I think about it, probably it was the depth of his soul that he didn't reveal to anyone, and that no ordinary people could fully understand. And I believe that because of that part of him, you loved him in the first place and will love him forever.

As you might have noticed from the postmark, I now live with my daughter. In May, Katoko and her husband came and brought me here, where I continued to lie sick. About a week ago, I began to feel well enough to take care of my grandchildren, so Katoko can help at their tofu factory. Here too, we have air raid warnings quite often, but compared with Hanshin, this is a paradise and quite a charming city. From the windows upstairs, I can see the Chugoku Mountain Range to the north and the inland sea to the south. There are a few rivers running through the city, and I live close to the one called Motoyasu. When I stroll along the river with my grandchildren, I can't help but feel that one's fate is so strange. I've never thought I would live here, so far from Hanshin and the place of my husband's burial. I often stay awake at night, missing my husband, my son, and you and Giichi-san and Yuki-chan, but during the day I try to keep myself busy with the children, which makes me feel grateful that I still have something to live for.

Someday when the war is over and both of us are still alive, there must be a day we can meet again. Until then, please take good care of yourself, and I will, too. I will also try to write more often. I will be praying that Giichi-san will come home, and that all of you are together again. Wouldn't that be nice if you, Giichi-san, and I can get together once again as we used to do?

Best regards to your mother.

Sanae Chiba

Kinuko read the letter twice. She couldn't believe that Takushi was gone. How could Mrs. Chiba lose her husband in January and then her son so soon afterward? Clutching the letter, Kinuko sat unmoving. She pictured Takushi in his black student uniform on a rainy afternoon in Hanshin. She had been on her way home from grocery shopping, pushing infant Yuki in the buggy with one hand and carrying a basket and holding an umbrella in the other. When she passed through the tunnel beneath the Hanshin Highway, Takushi, who had just gotten off a tram, came trotting down the steps, and immediately took the umbrella and basket from her. They walked home together, Takushi holding the umbrella carefully over her and the buggy. He was a student then and smelled of rain and ink. He was a youth of few words, but looking into the buggy, he said, "She is cute, isn't she? I love babies." Kinuko said, "You can have your own someday, Takushi-san." He blushed under the umbrella and mumbled shyly, "I hope so." Soon after, he went off to war, and now she would never see him again.

Kinuko sat still, picturing Mrs. Chiba walking along a river in a city so far from Hanshin and her life with Mr. Chiba, pushing a buggy that carried the baby born two days after Mr. Chiba's funeral with two other little ones walking beside her. The baby boy would be almost seven months old, and Takushi would have loved him. It was right for Takushi to want a family, as it was right for everyone to want that, but Kinuko now realized that no one could enjoy the simple life of a family if people like Giichi did not stand against war.

She kept imagining Mrs. Chiba walking beside a river, the daughter of a Buddhist priest, carrying with her the calmness of a person who believed in the mercy of Buddha. Kinuko remembered what Mrs. Chiba once told her—whatever one's struggles, sorrows and triumphs, they would eventually float away like lanterns on a river on the August night of the Buddhist All Soul's Day, and that our souls would someday rest in peace in Buddha's paradise.

That afternoon in Sasayama, the sun beat down as usual in the garden and a shimmering haze rose from the drooping vegetable plants. The air was heavy and still.

Though the oppressive heat drained her energy, Kinuko decided to write to Mrs. Chiba. She sat in the south room with a fan in her left hand. First, she expressed her sorrow upon learning of Takushi's death. She had difficulty finding the words. Then the writing proved easier, as she mentioned how happy she was to have finally heard from Mrs. Chiba despite the sad news. She went into the latest news—Ichiro's death, her trip to Okayama, her illness, Mr. Nakano's death, Giichi doing fine in Abeno Prison despite a minor health problem, and finally her desire to study painting more after the war. Through painting, she added, she hoped to spread the love she had learned from Ichiro and Giichi. "My role might be as small as a grain of sand," she continued, "but I can't help but feel the urge to make the world a better place to live. Then my marriage to Giichi will have meaning, even if he doesn't come home. Before he left, I kept wondering what I meant to him; now I realize it is more important to know what he means to me."

When she finished the letter, she decided to enclose her painting, *Chibas' Garden.* On the back of the painting she wrote: *"In our garden, the morning glories bloom each day. Before he turned himself in, Giichi planted the seeds, remembering how they used to bloom in your garden and ours. Do you remember giving me the seeds? Every morning when I look at the flowers, I think of you. Having known you and Mr. Chiba is one of the best things that ever happened to Giichi and me."*

She folded the painting and slid it into a large envelope with her letter. She wrote Mrs. Chiba's new address on the envelope and thought of her words, "Isn't one's fate strange?" Only months ago, who would have thought that she would be living in Sasayama and Mrs. Chiba would be so far away with her daughter in Hiroshima? Kinuko sealed the envelope and smoothed it with the palm of her hand. She walked to the post office under the sizzling sun, hoping the war would end soon so Giichi could come home and they could be a happy family once again—she and Giichi, and Yuki and Akira, the son he had yet to meet. Kinuko wiped her face with a kerchief as she walked and wondered if it was hot like this in Hiroshima.

EPILOGUE

Three days after Hiroshima, Nagasaki became the second city to fall victim to the atomic bomb. Five days later Japan surrendered. Giichi and Kinuko had been waiting long years for the war's end. It came on August 15, 1945, 12 days after Giichi died in Abeno Prison.

Three days after Japan's surrender, Hirobumi committed suicide in Tokyo.

In February of the following year Kinuko received Giichi's ashes, together with the bag he carried to Sasayama Police Station. It had been nine years since their wedding anniversary. Kinuko carried the urn with Giichi's ashes to visit the shrine where she and Giichi were married. She sat on a bench in the fragrance of the plum blossoms they enjoyed together on that day. That spring, Kinuko traveled to Okayama and reunited with Yuki.

In April 1950, almost five years after the war ended, an art museum in Kobe staged an exhibition of Kinuko's paintings. The collection included morning glories in Chiba's garden, Yuki in Okayama, and scenes of inferno in Hiroshima and Nagasaki caused by the atomic bombs. Kinuko framed the chicken Yuki had drawn, which she found in Giichi's bag. The first day of the exhibition was Akira's fifth birthday. From that exhibit until her death 50 years later, Kinuko created works of art to advocate for world peace.

About the Author

Michiko Yoshikawa Johnson was born in Osaka, Japan in 1941. She graduated from college in Japan with a BA in Social Work and later studied psychology in Hawaii. She lived in Hong Kong and Singapore before moving back to the United States.

Michiko wrote *The Red Paper* over a ten-year period while living in Iowa and raising two daughters. She resides in Des Moines, Iowa.

Cover and book format by Kate Milligan

36951192R00180

Made in the USA
San Bernardino, CA
25 May 2019